PRAISE FOR
Pray for Silence

"Another knockout job. I love this series." —Alex Kava

"Castillo excels at detailing gory crime scenes." —*Publishers Weekly*

"[The] unique setting and a very human heroine make this a good recommendation for readers seeking an alternative to the urban whodunit." —*Booklist*

"The second book in Castillo's series is . . . as well crafted, interesting, and unique as the first. The combination of Amish life and the brutal work of a police chief create plenty of tension and excitement." —*RT Book Reviews* (Top Pick, 4½ stars)

"With a serial killer and now a mass murder in tiny Painters Mill, Castillo will need to be inventive to maintain the plausibility in this addictive series. Fortunately, she seems up to the task." —*Akron Beacon Journal*

"Castillo keeps the pace quick, the story compelling, and her manner toward the Amish reverent." —Katherine Osborne, *IndieBound*

PRAISE FOR
Sworn to Silence

"Balancing chilling suspense and a nuanced portrait of the English-Amish divide . . . *Silence* is the opening salvo in what promises to be a gripping series." —*People* magazine

"A teeth-chattering debut thriller . . . This first in a series will delight fans of Chelsea Cain and Thomas Harris . . . compelling characters, excellent plotting, and a hair-raising finale."
—*USA Today*

"Absolutely stunning . . . a perfectly crafted thriller."
—Lisa Scottoline

"Excellent . . . Adept at creating characters with depth and nuance, Castillo smoothly integrates their backstories into a well-paced plot that illuminates the divide between the Amish and 'English' worlds."
—*Publishers Weekly* (starred review)

"[Castillo] makes police procedure anything but tedious."
—Sandra Brown

"Complicated, haunted protagonists, shocking murders, psychological twists, and bizarre crime scenes . . . *Sworn to Silence* is a nail-biting series debut."
—Chelsea Cain

"Very well done. The small-town setting, complicated relationships among the inhabitants, and the strong but battle-scarred protagonist bring Julia Spencer-Fleming's series to mind."
—*Library Journal* (starred review)

"*Sworn to Silence* packs a healthy dose of twists, but it's Kate's memorable voice that will leave you wanting to hear more."
—Alex Kava

"Kate Burkholder is the real deal and *Sworn to Silence* is a vivid, intense, and brutal page-turner of a novel."
—C. J. Box

"Castillo's hardcover debut should come with a warning: Pick up when you have time to finish. Excitement, danger, mystery, a fascinating setting, and a conflicted heroine make this a book you won't put down."
—*RT Book Reviews* (Top Pick, 4½ stars)

"With an utterly compelling protagonist, sharp twists, and a setting so real you feel it, Castillo doesn't just hit the ball out of the park, she knocks the skin off the ball."
—John Hart

"Think Harrison Ford in the movie *Witness* and add just a touch of the Coen brothers' *Fargo* and you have the feel of this brilliant, nail-biting thriller. . . . Very dark, intricate, and packed with twists, it literally chokes the breath from your body. It's that good."
—*Daily Mail* (UK)

"An evocative and often heartfelt look at Amish society . . . chillingly realistic . . . Set during a bitter Ohio winter, *Sworn to Silence* will make you forget about any summer heat wave."
—*South Florida Sun-Sentinel*

"*Sworn to Silence* is filled with blood-chilling storytelling, fair play with clues, and arresting prose. But it's Castillo's fully fleshed characters that will linger in the reader's mind, with feisty, flawed—and ultimately heroic—Kate foremost among them."
—*Richmond Times-Dispatch*

Also by Linda Castillo

Sworn to Silence

Breaking Silence

PRAY FOR
SILENCE

LINDA CASTILLO

MINOTAUR BOOKS ❧ NEW YORK

PRAY FOR SILENCE. Copyright © 2010 by Linda Castillo. All rights reserved. Printed in the United States of America. For more information, address St. Martin's Press, 175 Fifth Avenue, New York, N.Y. 10010.

www.minotaurbooks.com

The Library of Congress has cataloged the hardcover edition as follows:

Castillo, Linda.
    Pray for silence / Linda Castillo.—1st ed.
        p. cm.
    ISBN 978-0-312-37498-3
1. Women police chiefs—Ohio—Fiction.   2. Amish—Ohio—Fiction.
3. Families—Crimes against—Fiction.   4. Family Secrets—Fiction.
5. Amish Country (Ohio)—Fiction.   I. Title.
PS3603.A8758P73 2009
813'.6.—dc22

2009046147

ISBN 978-0-312-54003-6 (trade paperback)

First Minotaur Books Trade Paperback Edition: May 2011

20 19 18 17 16 15 14

For my husband, Ernest.
Always.

ACKNOWLEDGMENTS

The creative side of writing a novel is only part of what it takes to get a book published. I have many publishing professionals to thank for bringing this one to fruition. First and foremost, I wish to thank my agent, Nancy Yost, who has a brilliant creative mind and unparalleled business savvy, not to mention a wicked sense of humor. All are very much appreciated. Thank you to my New York editor, Charles Spicer, whose razor-sharp instincts and editorial genius *always* make the book better. To my UK editor, Julie Crisp, whose insights, sharp eye for all the details I miss, and undying passion for a good, scary, thriller shine through all the way across the pond. To Allison Caplin, for bringing your own editorial expertise to the book and helping to keep me on track (a full-time job in itself!). Thank you to Andy Martin, for the whirlwind trip to four Ohio cities during the pre-launch tour for *Sworn to Silence*. It was great fun, and the wine was fabulous. To Matthew Shear and Jennifer Enderlin, for taking time out of your busy schedules to have a drink with me in Washington, D.C., and chat about the books—thank you.

I'd also like to extend a big thank-you to all the fine folks at Roasters Coffee and Tea Company in Amarillo; you guys have the best COD in the state of Texas and absolutely no idea how much I appreciate it.

To fellow authors and sisters-in-crime Catherine Spangler and Jennifer Miller; thank you for always being there when I need you most.

Last but not least, I'd like to thank my intrepid critique group: Jennifer Archer, April Redmon, Marcy McKay, and Anita Howard, for making Wednesday nights at Jenny's both productive and fun as hell. You gals are the best!

Three may keep a secret,
if two of them are dead.

—Benjamin Franklin

PRAY FOR
SILENCE

CHAPTER 1

Officer Chuck "Skid" Skidmore wished he hadn't indulged in that last cup of coffee. If it wasn't for the new waitress at the diner, he would have stopped at just one. But damn she was cute. So he'd sat at the counter the entirety of his dinner break and sucked down caffeine like a ten-year-old gorging on Kool-Aid. Brandy obliged by keeping his mug full, and entertaining him with her twenty-something chitchat and a full two inches of jiggling cleavage.

He'd been eating at LaDonna's Diner every night for two months now, since the chief assigned him the graveyard shift. He hated working nights. He respected the chief, but he was going to have to have a talk with her about getting back on days.

Skid turned his cruiser onto Hogpath Road, a desolate stretch of asphalt bounded by Miller's Woods to the north and a cornfield on the south side. The cruiser's tires crunched over gravel as he pulled onto the shoulder. He was reaching for the pack of Marlboro Lights in the glove box when his radio crackled.

"Three-two-four. Are you 10-8?"

Mona was the third-shift dispatcher and his sole source of entertainment—after the diner closed, anyway. She'd kept him from dying of boredom many a night. "Roger that, Dispatch."

"So did you talk to her?"

"That's affirm."

"You ask her out?"

Throwing open his door to keep the smell of smoke out of the cruiser, Skid lit the Marlboro. "I don't see how that's any of your business."

"You're the one who's been talking about her for the last two months."

"She's too young for me."

"Since when does that make a difference?"

"You're tying up the radio."

Mona laughed. "You're chicken."

Wishing he'd never told her about his crush on Brandy, he drew on the cigarette. "Whatever."

"Are you *smoking*?"

He mouthed the word *shit*.

"You said you were going to quit."

"I said I was going to either quit drinking or smoking. I sure as hell ain't going to do both in the same week." He sucked in a mouthful of smoke. "Especially when I'm stuck working nights."

"Maybe the chief's still pissed about that old lady you roughed up."

"I didn't rough her up. That old goat was drunk out of her mind."

"She was sixty-two years old—"

"And naked as a jaybird."

Mona giggled. "You get all the good calls."

"Don't remind me. The sight of her wrinkled ass has damaged me for life." He sighed, his bladder reminding him why he'd stopped in the first place. "I gotta take a piss."

"Like I need to know that." She disconnected.

Grinning, Skid got out of the cruiser. The crickets went silent as he walked around to the bar ditch. Dry cornstalks crackled in a light breeze. Beyond, a harvest moon cast yellow light onto the tall grain silo and barn roof of an Amish farm. It was so quiet, he could hear the cacophony of frogs from Wildcat Creek a quarter mile to the south. Skid relieved himself and tried not to think about the long night ahead. Yeah, he was going to have a talk with the chief. Get back on days. He'd had enough of this vampire hours shit.

He was zipping up when a distant sound snagged his attention. At first he thought maybe a calf was bawling for its cow. Or maybe a dog had been hit by a car. But when the sound came again, he realized it wasn't either of those things. It was a man's scream. Looking out across the cornfield, he felt the hairs on his nape stand straight up.

Skid rested his hand on the .38 strapped to his hip. He scanned the field beyond where the corn whispered and sighed. Another scream sent a chill scraping up his spine. "What the hell?"

Yanking open the door of the cruiser, he leaned in and flicked on the strobes, then pulsed the siren a couple of times. He hit his lapel mike. "Mona, I'm out here at the Plank farm. I've got a 10-88." They used the ten-code radio system at the Painters Mill PD; *10-88* was the code for suspicious activity.

"What's going on?"

"Some crazy shit's screaming his head off."

"Well that's strange." She went silent for a moment. "Who is it?"

"I don't know, but I think it's coming from the house. I'm going to check it out."

"Roger that."

Back in his cruiser, Skid turned into the long gravel lane that would take him to the house. The Planks were Amish. Generally, the Amish were quiet and kept to themselves. Most were up before the sun and in bed before most folks finished their suppers. Skid couldn't imagine one of them out this time of night, raising hell. Either some teenager on *rumspringa*—their "running around" time before joining the church—was drunk out of his head, or there'd been an accident.

He was midway down the lane when a figure rushed from the shadows. Skid braked hard. The cruiser slid sideways, missing a man by inches. "Holy shit!"

The man scrambled around the front of the cruiser, hands on the hood, eyes as big as baseballs. Skid didn't recognize him, but the full beard and flat-brimmed hat told him the guy was Amish. Setting his hand on his .38, Skid rammed the shifter into Park and got out of the cruiser. "What the hell are you doing? I almost hit you."

The man was breathing hard, shaking harder. In the moonlight, Skid saw sweat glistening on his cheeks, despite the October chill, and he wondered if the guy was high on drugs. *"Mein Gott!"*

Skid didn't understand Pennsylvania Dutch, the Amish dialect, but he didn't need to be fluent to know the guy was terrified. He didn't know what he'd walked into. The one thing he was certain of was that he wasn't going to let this cagey-looking sumbitch get any closer. As far as he knew, the guy was on crack and armed with a machete. "Stop right there, partner. Keep your hands where I can see them."

The Amish man put his hands up. Even from ten feet away Skid could see his entire body was trembling. His chest heaved. It was tears—not sweat—that glistened on his cheeks. "What's your name?" Skid asked.

"Reuben Zimmerman!" he choked.

The Amish man's eyes met his. Within their depths, Skid saw fear and the sharp edge of panic. The man's mouth worked, but no words came.

"You need to calm down, sir. Tell me what happened."

Zimmerman pointed toward the farmhouse, his hand shaking like a flag in a gale. "Amos Plank. The children. There is blood. They are dead!"

The guy had to be out of his mind. "How many people?"

"I do not know. I saw . . . Amos and the boys. On the floor. Dead. I ran."

"Did you see anyone else?"

"No."

Skid's gaze went to the darkened farmhouse. The place was silent and still. No lantern light in the windows. No movement. He hit his lapel mike. "Mona, I've got a possible 10-16 out here." A *10-16* was the code for a domestic problem. "I'm going to take a look."

"You still out at the Plank place?"

"That's affirm."

"You want me to call the sheriff's office and get a deputy out there?"

"I'm going to check it out first. Will you run Reuben Zimmerman through LEADS for me?" LEADS was the acronym for the Law Enforcement Automated Data System police departments used to check for outstanding warrants.

"Roger that." Computer keys clicked. "Be careful, will you?"

"You got that right."

Anxious to get to the scene, Skid approached the Amish man. "Turn around and put your hands against the car, partner."

Zimmerman looked bewildered. "I did not do anything wrong."

"It's procedure. I'm going to pat you down. The handcuffs are for your protection and mine. All right?"

As if realizing he didn't have a choice, Zimmerman turned and set his hands against the cruiser. Quickly, Skid ran his hands over the man, checking pockets, socks, even his crotch. Then he snapped the cuffs into place. "What are you doing here at this time of night?"

"I help with the milking. Work begins at four A.M."

"And I thought I had bad hours."

The Amish man blinked.

"Never mind." Opening the cruiser door, Skid ushered him into the backseat. "Let's go."

Sliding behind the wheel, he put the cruiser in gear and started toward the house. In the rearview mirror, dust billowed in the red glow of the taillights. Ahead, a massive barn and silo stood in silhouette against the predawn sky. The postcard perfect farm was the last place Skid expected any kind of trouble. He'd lived in Painters Mill for going on four years now. Aside from a few minor infractions—like that time two teenaged boys got caught racing their buggies down Main Street—the Amish were damn near perfect citizens. But Skid had been a cop long enough to know there was always an exception to the rule.

He parked behind a buggy, his headlights reflecting off the slow-moving-vehicle sign mounted at the rear. To his right, the house stood in shadows; it didn't look like anyone was up yet. Turning, he made eye contact with Zimmerman. "How did you get in?"

"The back door is unlocked," the Amish man said.

Grabbing his Maglite, Skid left the cruiser. He slid his .38 from its sheath as he started down the sidewalk. Stepping onto the stoop, he banged on the door with the flashlight. "This is the police," he called out. "Open up."

That was when he noticed the dark smear on the jamb. He shifted the flashlight beam and squinted. It looked like blood. A handprint. Skid shone the light down on the concrete porch. More blood. Black droplets glittering in the moonlight. Bloody footprints led down the steps to the sidewalk that led to the barn.

"Shit." Skid twisted the knob and opened the door. His heart rate kicked as he entered the kitchen. He could feel the burn of adrenaline in his midsection. Nerves running like hot wires beneath his skin. "This is the police," he called out. "Mr. and Mrs. Plank?"

The house was as silent and dark as a 1920s noir film. Skid wished for a light switch and cursed the Amish people's aversion to modern conveniences. Slowly, his eyes adjusted to the semidarkness. Gray light from the moon bled in through the window above the sink, revealing plain wood cabinets, a bench table draped with a blue-and-white checked tablecloth. A lantern sat cold and dark in its center.

"Hello? This is the police. Anyone home?" Midway through the kitchen, he noticed the unpleasant odor. Not spoiled food or garbage or pet smells. It was more like the plumbing in the bathroom had backed up.

Skid entered the living room. The stench grew stronger, pervasive. A chill crept up his spine when his beam illuminated the body. An Amish man wearing a blue work shirt, trousers and suspenders lay facedown in a pool of blood the size of a dinner plate.

"Holy shit."

Skid couldn't look away. The dead man had a horrific wound at the back of his head. Blood oozed from his left ear into his full beard and then trickled down to pool on the floor. His mouth was open and his bloody tongue protruded like a fat slug.

He hoped Zimmerman was wrong about the number of victims. He

hoped the other lumps on the floor were piles of clothing in need of mending or maybe feed bags someone had brought in from the barn. That hope
was dashed when the beam of his flashlight revealed two more bodies. A
teenaged boy wearing dark trousers with suspenders. A little red-haired
boy encircled by more blood than could possibly fit into his small body.
Both boys had gunshot wounds to the head. Both had their hands bound
behind their backs. Skid knew without checking that they were dead.

He'd been a cop for going on ten years, first in Ann Arbor, Michigan,
and now here in Painters Mill. He'd seen death before. Traffic accidents.
Shootings. Stabbings. None of those things prepared him for this.

"Holy Christ." He fumbled for his lapel mike, surprised when his
hand shook. "Mona, I'm 10-23 at the Plank place. Call the chief. Tell her
I've got a major fuckin' crime scene out here. A shooting with multiple
vics. Fatalities." His voice broke. "Shit."

"Do you need an ambulance?"

He looked down at the staring eyes and the ocean of blood, and he
knew he'd be seeing that image for a very long time to come. "Just send
the coroner, Mona. It's too late to save any of these people."

CHAPTER 2

I'm caught in that weird twilight between wakefulness and slumber when the phone on my night table jangles. The last time I looked at the clock, it was just after three A.M. A glance at those glowing red numbers tells me it's now four-thirty. I feel lucky to have gotten a full hour and a half of sleep.

"Burkholder," I rasp.

"Chief, it's Mona. Skid says there's been a shooting out at the Plank farm."

The words jolt me upright. "Anyone hurt?" I envision an accidental shooting; someone putting a bullet in his foot while cleaning his .30-06.

"He said it was a major crime scene with multiple fatalities."

Multiple fatalities.

For an instant I think I've misunderstood. Then my brain clicks into place, and I get to my feet. "He get the shooter?"

"I don't know. Skid sounded pretty shook up."

Four full-time officers comprise my small police force; Skid is one of my most experienced. He's not the sensitive type nor is he easily rattled, so I know it's got to be bad. "Get an ambulance out there, will you?"

"Sure. And I called Doc Coblentz."

"Good." Dr. Ludwig Coblentz is a local pediatrician and acting coroner for Holmes County. "Tell him I'll meet him out there."

My mind spins through possible scenarios as I cross to the closet and yank my uniform off a hanger. The Planks are Amish. I know many Amish families keep rifles on hand for hunting and livestock slaughter. They are a peaceable, pacifistic society; violent crime is rare. I can't get my mind around the fact that there are multiple victims. Maybe because that tells me the shooting was no accident.

Painters Mill is a small town located in the heart of Ohio's farm country. About a third of the 5,300 residents are Amish. I myself was born Amish in this very town just over thirty years ago. Though 80 percent of Amish children join the church at the age of eighteen, I was one of the few who chose not to be baptized. But roots run deep, especially if you're Amish, and it was those roots that brought me back.

I've been the chief of police for nearly three years now. It's a good job. Painters Mill is a good place to live. A wholesome town in which to raise a family. I want to believe major crime doesn't happen here, but experience has taught me even small, idyllic towns are not immune to violence.

I'm acquainted with most of the local families, both Amish and English. I'm fluent in Pennsylvania Dutch, the Amish dialect. Though I no longer live my life according to *Gelassenheit*—the foundation of Amish values—I have great respect for the culture. It's a respect borne of genuine understanding, not only of the people, but the Plain life in general, and the religion so integral to both.

As I drive toward the Plank farm, it strikes me that I don't know much about Bonnie or Amos Plank. I search my memory and recall that they're new to the area, having relocated from Lancaster County about a year ago. They have several children and run a small dairy operation. As I start down the gravel lane, I wonder what problems might have followed them here from Pennsylvania.

I arrive to find Skid's cruiser parked behind a buggy. The emergency strobes cast red and blue light onto the house and outbuildings, giving the farm the appearance of some weird rock video. Grabbing my Maglite, I get out, draw my .38 revolver and start toward the back door. I'm midway there when my beam illuminates a bloody handprint on the jamb. A quiver of unease goes through me when I spot the shiny black droplets on the concrete porch and sidewalk. Shoving open the door, I step into a large kitchen.

Moonlight slants through the window above the sink, but it's not enough to cut through the shadows. "Skid!" I call out.

"In here!"

The stench of blood fills my nostrils as I traverse the kitchen. I go through the doorway into the next room. The first thing I see is the yellow-white slash of Skid's flashlight beam. We're standing in a large room backlit by two tall, narrow windows. I make a 360-degree sweep with my flashlight. "What happened?"

Even as I ask the question, my beam lands on the first body. A middle-aged Amish male lies facedown in the center of the room.

"We got two more over there." Skid's voice seems to come from a great distance.

My hand threatens to shake as I run my beam along the floor, but I hold it steady as the light reveals two more bodies. My vision tunnels when I realize the victims are children. The first is a teenaged boy. Gangly arms and legs. Bad haircut. Lying prone, he wears a faded work shirt, suspenders and trousers that are slightly too short from a recent growth spurt. His hands are bound behind his back. I see the black shimmer of blood at the back of his head.

A few feet away, a younger boy lies on his side in an ocean of blood, some of which has soaked into a homemade rug. I guess him to be nine or ten years old. He's wearing a nightshirt. Like the other boy, his hands are bound. The soles of his feet are dirty, and I know that just scant hours before he'd run barefoot and carefree through this house. From the pale oval of his face, cloudy eyes seem to stare right at me. I see blood on his cheek and realize the bullet exited through his mouth, tearing through his lips, blowing out several teeth.

It's a surreal scene and for the span of several heartbeats, I can't get my mind around it. Shock is like a battering ram, assaulting my brain. *Dead kids,* I think, and a hot bloom of outrage burgeons in my chest. The urge to go to them, perform CPR, try to save them, is powerful. But I know they're gone. The last thing I want to do is contaminate the scene.

I shift my beam back to the adult. A hole the size of my fist mars the back of his head. I see bone fragments, flecks of brain matter and blood in his hair. *Exit wound,* I think, and realize he was shot from the front.

"Did you check for survivors?" I hear myself ask.

Skid's silhouette looms against the window. Even in the near darkness, I see him shake his head. "I checked pulses. They're DOA."

I look around, and it strikes me that the son of a bitch who did this could still be in the house. "You clear the place?"

"Not yet."

I hit my radio. "This is 235. Mona, I'm 10-23."

"What's going on out there, Chief?"

"I need you to call Glock and Pickles at home. Get them out here 10-18."

"Roger that," Mona says.

"Use your cell, in case some insomniac has his scanner on. Tell Glock we need a generator and some work lights, will you?"

"Got it, Chief."

I look at Skid. "Let's clear the rest of the house."

I start toward the hall. I hear Skid behind me, and I know he's got my back. Our feet are silent on the oak floor as we move toward the bedrooms. In the back of my mind, I wonder if there are more victims. If anyone survived. I wonder what kind of a monster could kill innocent children. . . .

I reach the bathroom and shove the door open with my foot. My .38 leading the way, I enter, drop low and sweep the room. I see an old-fashioned claw-foot tub. A single window, closed and locked. A porcelain sink. I check the tub. "Clear."

I turn to see Skid start down the hall. I bring up the rear this time, watching his back. He sidles into the first bedroom. I follow close behind, my every sense honed on our surroundings. I see two twin-size beds. Two windows, closed. A chest of drawers. A pair of ice skates tossed in the corner. Skid shifts his weapon, yanks open the closet door. I move in, but the small space is empty. I go to the bed, drop to my knees and look beneath it.

"No one here," Skid says.

"Let's check the upstairs."

"There a cellar?" he asks.

"I don't know. Probably."

It takes us ten minutes to clear the rest of the house, which includes the basement, the second-level bedrooms and the small attic. I'm comfortable working with Skid; I trust his instincts as a cop, and we work well as a team. In the end, our efforts are in vain. The house is vacant.

We end up in the living room. For a moment, neither of us speaks. We don't look at the bodies, and I get the sense that we're both struggling to comprehend the cold brutality of the crime.

"What do you think happened?" Skid asks after a moment.

"Hard to say." I glance down at the dead boy at my feet. So young and innocent. I look at the father and for the first time it strikes me that his hands aren't bound. As a cop, I know things aren't always as they appear at first glance. Preconceived notions are a dangerous thing when you walk into a crime scene, so I strive to avoid making snap judgments. But as I stare down at the dead man, all I can think is, *Why aren't your hands bound, too?*

"You find a weapon?" I ask.

"Handgun there."

My eyes follow his beam. Sure enough, protruding from beneath the man's right hand is the blue barrel of a semiautomatic handgun. "Looks like a Beretta."

"I didn't know the Amish kept handguns."

"They don't, usually, especially a semiauto," I reply. "Rifles for hunting."

"His hands aren't tied," Skid comments.

"That wound at the back of his head looks like an exit."

Skid's gaze meets mine. "You think he did this?"

I don't want to acknowledge the ugly suspicions knocking at my brain. That this man snapped, murdered his two sons and then turned the gun on himself. The scenario goes against every conviction most Amish hold dear. I know it's a generalization. But murder is extremely rare in Amish society. Suicide is almost as uncommon. *It is the one sin for which there is no redemption.*

"I don't know." I look around. "Any sign of the mother?"

"No."

"I think they have more kids," I say. "Girls." I recall the bloody handprint on the back porch, and I'm disheartened by the possibilities crowding my brain. "Let's check the yard and outbuildings."

Best-case scenario, we'll find Mom and the girls hiding and frightened, but alive. The knot in my gut tells me that hope is optimistic.

Without holstering our weapons, we pass through the kitchen and go out through the back door. We glance briefly at the bloody print.

"Could be a woman's," Skid says.

"Or a teenager's." If my memory serves me, the two girls are in their teens.

His beam illuminates droplets of blood and a single bloody footprint on the concrete. "Looks like someone ran out of the house."

"Toward the barn."

After being inside the house, the moonlight seems inordinately bright. My shadow keeps pace with me as I move down the sidewalk. We've gone about ten yards when I spot the body. A mature female wearing a plain dress, an apron and white *kapp* lies facedown in the grass. But it is the sight of the dead infant in her arms that rocks me.

"Jesus Christ." Skid scrapes a hand over his face. "A fuckin' baby."

The gray skin and glazed eyes tell me both mother and child are deceased. Blood clings to the grass like a spill of motor oil. I see a hole the size of a dime in the fabric between the woman's shoulder blades. "Looks like the bullet went right through her and into the baby."

"Shot her in the back."

"While she was running away."

"Chief, who the hell would do something like this?"

"A monster." Hoping the look I give him doesn't reveal the dark emotions thrashing inside me, I motion toward the barn. "Let's hope he left someone alive to tell us."

The barn is a massive structure with a stone foundation and rusty tin roof. A cupola and weather vane jut two stories into the night sky. Lower, half a dozen small windows watch us like old, sorrowful eyes. Like many of the barns in the area, the building is well over a hundred years old.

Skid and I move down the sidewalk in silence. The chorus of crickets seems unduly loud, but I know it's because my senses are hyperaware. Somewhere in the near distance, I hear cattle bawling. Having spent many a predawn morning pulling teats, I recognize the sound. The animals' udders are full, and they're waiting to be milked.

I reach the barn first and push open the door with my foot. "Try not to touch anything," I whisper.

The hinges creak as the door rolls open. The earthy smells of livestock, hay, and manure waft out on a breeze. The barn is pitch black inside. Holding my Maglite in my left hand, my weapon in my right, I step in and quickly sweep the area. I'm aware of Skid behind me, his beam cutting through the darkness to my left. I can hear his quickened breaths rushing between his teeth.

"This is the police!" I call out. "Put your hands up and come out! *Now!*"

We move deeper into the barn. The rush of blood through my veins is deafening. If someone were to ambush us, I wouldn't hear them coming. I nearly jump out of my skin when I see movement ahead. I straighten my gun arm, snug my finger against the trigger. It takes a second for my brain to process the sight of a dozen or so Jersey cows standing in stanchions, waiting to be fed and milked.

"Glad I didn't plug a cow," I mutter.

"Some goddamn light would be nice."

"There's probably a lantern around here somewhere."

I see the outline of livestock stalls to the left. Straight ahead lies the milking area; from where I stand I discern the curdled-milk stink common to dairy operations. I see the brick and concrete floor upon which stanchions and hay racks were built. Though many Amish have begun using modern milking machines powered by either diesel or gasoline generators, I see no such machinery here, telling me the Planks still milk by hand.

Catching Skid's eye, I motion him left. I go right and enter a wide aisle with a hard-packed dirt floor. Ahead is a large equipment area. I see a steel-wheeled plow with hit-or-miss shares. A buggy missing a wheel sits propped up on a hand jack. A wood-and-steel manure spreader gathers dust beneath a moonlit window. To my right I spot yet another door. It's closed. The proximity to the stalls and equipment area tells me it's probably a tack room, where harnesses for the horses, grooming supplies, halters and veterinary medicines are stored. Seeing no movement in the aisle, I cross to the door, twist the knob and shove it open.

The beam of my flashlight illuminates a large room with rough-hewn walls and a wood plank floor. High ceilings transected by beams as thick as a man's waist. A rush of adrenaline burns through me when I spot the girl. On instinct, I bring up my weapon. At first glance she appears to be standing with her arms stretched over her head. Then I realize her wrists are bound and tied to an overhead beam.

For a second, I'm so shocked I can't speak or move or even think. Then my cop's mind switches on and the horrific details of what I'm seeing slam into my brain. The victim is young and female. Nude except for a *kapp,* she hangs limply from the overhead beam. Her head lolls forward so that her chin rests on her chest. I see dried blood, where it ran between her breasts and down her abdomen. Her knees have buckled, but the rope holds her upright.

"My God," I hear myself say.

I shift my light, scan the rest of the room. I hear myself gasp when my beam illuminates a second victim. A female, slightly older. Also nude, but for her *kapp*. Like the other victim, she hangs suspended from an overhead beam.

In the course of my law enforcement career, I've seen death more times than I care to think about. I've seen terrible traffic accidents. Death from natural causes, heart attacks and strokes. A drowning occurred just two months ago out on Miller's Pond. I've seen murder in all its execrable forms. But I will never get used to it.

My hands tremble as I reach for my lapel mike. "Skid . . . I got two more."

"Where are you?"

"Tack room. Just down the aisle."

"I'm on my way."

I train my flashlight beam on the nearest victim. I can smell the blood now. Dark and metallic with the sickening undertone of methane gas. I'm not unduly squeamish, but my stomach quivers uneasily as I draw close. I can't imagine what happened here. I sure as hell don't want to think about the horrors these girls must have endured.

"Aw, man."

I nearly drop my Maglite at the sound of Skid's voice. I turn to see him standing in the doorway. He holds his revolver in his right hand, his flashlight in his left. His eyes are fastened on the two bodies.

"Jesus Christ, Chief." He steps into the room, his voice little more than a whisper. "What the hell happened?"

Skid is usually pretty laid-back. He's cocky with a dry sense of humor, a quick wit, and has never been overly sensitive to some of the things cops are forced to deal with. As he takes in the carnage before us, his brash façade falls away. His expression relays the same horror and disbelief I feel burgeoning in my chest.

He moves closer to me.

"Watch for footprints," I tell him.

His beam illuminates the plank floor, sweeps left and right. As if of its own accord, my beam paints the nearest body with terrible light. Dozens of bruises, contusions and abrasions mar the dead girl's torso, arms and legs. Small patches of skin are bright red. Other areas are nearly black. At some point, she'd vomited. I can smell the sour stink of it from where I stand.

"I got a footprint," Skid calls out.

"Mark it." I don't take my eyes off the corpse. "Looks like they were tortured."

"Someone tied them up and just went to fuckin' town on them," Skid says after a moment.

He lowers his flashlight and in that instant of light, I notice two small marks on the floor. "Wait," I say. "What's that?"

I squat next to the marks. Upon closer inspection, I can see there are actually three of them. They look like scuff marks in a thin layer of dust. If I were to connect them, they'd form a perfect triangle.

"What the fuck?" Skid whispers in a baffled tone.

"Mark them, will you?"

"Sure thing."

"Keep your eye out for more footprints."

"You bet."

I shine my beam around the room. A few feet from where we stand, a propane torch, a small wooden club, a knife smeared with blood, and a foot-long skewer-like instrument sit neatly atop a workbench. Not the kinds of things you'd find in an Amish barn, and I know that whoever did this left them behind. "We might be able to lift some prints off those . . . tools."

"Yeah." Skid's beam joins mine, and he makes a sound of disgust. "How the hell could someone do this? I mean, for chrissake, a couple of Amish girls?"

I have no answers. I have no words at all. For a moment the only sound comes from the stirring of the cows down the aisle and the muted song of the crickets outside.

"You think the *father* did this?" Skid asks.

I hear doubt in his voice and shake my head because I can't imagine. "I don't know."

He shifts his beam back to the nearest victim. "Were they shot?" he asks. "Stabbed?"

Taking a deep breath, I train my beam on the victim nearest me. I see pale flesh speckled with blood. My beam stops on the black, gaping hole just below her navel.

"What the hell is that?" Skid's voice comes from behind me.

"Knife wounds?" My voice is steady, but my beam quivers as a tremor of revulsion moves through my body.

"It looks like someone cut her open."

I move the beam lower. A lot of blood now. Caked in her pubic hair. Dark rivulets that ran down the insides of both legs. I look for evidence of a bullet wound, but see nothing. In the back of my mind I wonder if she was alive when they did this to her.

The thought makes me sick. The terribleness of it frightens me on a level so deep that for a moment I can't catch my breath. I've never been a crier, but I feel the burn of tears at the backs of my eyes.

"Chief? You okay?"

I choke back a sound I don't recognize. A sound that echoes the barrage of emotions banging around inside me. For a full minute, I don't respond. When I'm finally able to speak, my voice is level. "Call Glock and Pickles again. Tell them we need those lights and generator yesterday."

"Yes, ma'am."

"Tell Mona to notify the sheriff's office. Let them know what's going on and get some patrols out. Tell her to brief T.J., get him out patrolling. Until we figure out what happened here, we've got to assume there's a cold-blooded son of a bitch out there with a gun."

As Skid speaks into his radio, I look at the two dead girls, and I feel the crushing weight of my responsibility to them settle onto my shoulders. I've heard veteran cops talk about life-altering cases. Cases that haunt a cop long after they're closed. I've had cases like that myself. Cases that fundamentally changed me. Changed the way I view people. The way I perceive my job as a cop. The way I see myself.

Standing there with the stench of death filling my nostrils, I know this is going to be one of those cases. It's going to take a toll. Not only on me, but on this town I love and a community that's already seen more than its share of violence.

CHAPTER 3

I'm standing on the back porch one puff into a Marlboro I bummed from Skid when a police cruiser hauling a small trailer barrels down the lane. Light bar and siren blaring, it slides to a halt behind my Explorer, stirring a cloud of dust that alternately glows blue and red, lending yet another layer of surreality to an already surreal scene.

Rupert "Glock" Maddox gets out of the car and goes around to the trailer, opens dual rear doors and pulls down a small ramp. A former Marine, Glock has the dubious honor of being Painters Mill's first African-American police officer. He's built like a young Arnold Schwarzenegger, can shoot the hair off a groundhog, and is one of the best cops I've ever had the pleasure of working with. As I start toward him, I hope his level-headedness will balance out the jagged emotions roiling inside me.

He rolls a portable, diesel-powered generator down the trailer ramp, then watches me approach. Under normal circumstances, he'd probably give me a hard time about smoking. I might have tried to hide the evidence if I hadn't been standing in the midst of a crime scene. I figure both of us are too distracted by what we face in the coming hours to bother with something so mundane.

"Must be bad if you're smoking," he says.

"It's bad." The words feel like an obscene understatement.

"I would have been here faster, but I had to pick up the generator and lights."

"It's okay." A sigh shudders out of me. "None of these people are going anywhere."

"You get the shooter?"

"I'm not exactly sure what we're dealing with yet."

He looks at me a little too closely as I drop the butt on the gravel and crush it out with my boot.

"Could be a murder-suicide," I clarify.

"Shit."

I motion toward the generator. "Get some lights set up, will you?" I start toward Skid's cruiser. "I'm going to talk to the witness."

I've met Reuben Zimmerman several times over the years. He's a quiet, serious man, one of the few Amish I know who does not have children. He and his wife, Martha, own a small house on a couple of acres down the road. Reuben is a retired carpenter and spends most of his time building decorative birdhouses and mailboxes for the Amish tourist shops in town.

I open the back door of the cruiser and bend slightly to make eye contact with him. Zimmerman leans forward and looks at me. "Did you find Bonnie and the other children?" he asks.

Though Skid had only been following departmental procedure, I'm dismayed to see the Amish man's hands cuffed behind his back. I pull the key out of my belt. "Turn around, and I'll take those off for you." I speak to him in Pennsylvania Dutch, hoping it will help break down the barrier of mistrust that exists between the Amish and the English police. This morning, I need his full cooperation.

Turning, he offers his wrists. I insert the key and the handcuffs *snick* open. "What are you doing here at this hour?"

He rubs his wrists. "I help with the milking."

"Why does Amos need you when he has two sons?"

Zimmerman looks perplexed by my question, but only for a moment. "He has twenty-two head of cattle and milks twice a day. I deliver the cans to Gordon Brehm in Coshocton County."

His answer is consistent with the absence of a milking machine and generator in the barn. Without refrigeration, there's no way to keep the milk cold, therefore it cannot be sold as grade A for drinking. Stored temporarily in old-fashioned milk cans, it can only be sold as grade B for cheese-making, which would require a buggy trip to the local cheese-maker in the next county.

I tilt my head and snag his gaze. "Reuben." I say his name firmly, letting him know I want his undivided attention. "I need you to tell me everything you saw when you arrived this morning."

He nods. "I arrived early, so I sat on the back stoop for a few minutes. Usually, there is lantern light inside. Amos and I have coffee. Sometimes Bonnie fries scrapple. This morning the house was dark."

"So you went inside?"

"I knocked, but no one answered." He gives a small smile. "I thought, *Er hot sich wider verschlofe.*" He overslept again. "So I went inside."

"How did you get in?"

"The back door was not locked."

My brain files that away for later. Many Amish don't lock their doors at night. It's not that locks go against the *Ordnung* in any way; most simply don't see the need. And it's not just the Amish who are lax. I'd estimate half the folks in this county don't lock up before going to bed. Having been a cop in a large, metropolitan city for six years, I don't share the mind-set. I snap my dead bolts into place every night with the glee of a paranoid schizophrenic.

"Did you see anyone else inside the house?" I ask.

"Just Amos . . . and the two boys."

"What about outside? In the yard? Or the barn?"

"I saw no one."

"Any vehicles or buggies?"

"No."

"Have you noticed any unusual behavior from Amos? Has he been under any pressure? Or talked to you about any problems?"

"Amos?" The Amish man shakes his head. "No."

"Was there any disharmony within the household?"

"No."

"Were there any problems between Amos and Bonnie? Or between Amos and the children? Problems with outside friends? Money problems, maybe?"

He shakes his head so vehemently, his beard flops from side to side. "Why do you ask these things, Katie?"

"I'm just trying to find out what happened."

Zimmerman stares hard at me. "Amos lived his life in the spirit of *Gelassenheit*. He was a good Amish man. He was modest and yielded to God's will. He worked hard. And he loved his family."

"Did the Planks have any enemies?" I ask. "Were they involved in any kind of dispute?"

Another emphatic shake. "The Planks loved their Amish brethren. They were generous. If you needed something, Amos and Bonnie would give it to you and were happy to go without themselves."

But I know that even decent, God-loving Amish families keep secrets.

For a moment, the only sound comes from the blast of the generator on the back porch and the chorus of crickets all around us. Then Zimmerman whispers, "Are Bonnie and the other children all right?"

I shake my head. "They're gone, too."

"Mein Gott." Bowing his head, he sets his fingertips against his forehead and rubs so hard the skin turns white. "Who would commit this terrible sin?"

"I don't know."

"I do not understand God's will," Reuben says.

I don't think murder is what God had in mind for the Plank family, but since my views aren't popular among my former brethren, I remain silent. "I'm going to have one of my officers drive you to the station so we can take your fingerprints. Can you do that for me?"

"But what about the cows?" he asks. "They must be milked."

Dealing with cattle is the least of my worries this morning. But having grown up on a farm much like this one, I know the animals must be dealt with. "I'll have Bishop Troyer send some men over as soon as possible. They'll take care of the milking."

He nods. "It is the right thing to do."

It's no small sacrifice for Zimmerman to ride in an English police car; it's against the *Ordnung,* the rules set forth by the local church district, but he nods. "I will help any way I can."

I close the car door and cross to my Explorer. Opening the rear hatch, I pull out my crime scene kit. It's not very high tech. Just a box of latex gloves, disposable shoe covers, a sketch pad and notebook, a stack of miniature fluorescent orange cones used for marking evidence, a roll of crime scene tape, a couple of inexpensive field test kits, and the new digital camera I recently had approved for purchase by the town council.

I find Glock on the back porch, marking the bloody handprint for the CSU, a work light in his hand. "Zimmerman any help?" he asks over the drone of the generator.

I shake my head. "He didn't see anything."

"You believe him?"

"For now."

We enter the kitchen. After being outside in the fresh air, the reek of death is suffocating. Setting the kit on the table, I remove a small tube of Vicks and dab it beneath my nose.

I offer it to Glock, but he refuses with his usual, "Can't stand the smell."

It's an ongoing joke that usually garners a laugh. We don't laugh this time around.

Quickly, we don latex gloves and shoe covers. This kind of crime scene is every cop's nightmare. It's spread over a large area, some of which is outdoors, which makes the collection and preservation of evidence extremely difficult. Even though I'm not yet sure exactly what we're dealing with—a mass murder or murder-suicide—I opt to err on the side of caution and preserve as much of the scene as possible.

I hand the camera to Glock. "Photograph everything before you touch it. You know the drill."

Nodding, he takes the camera. Neither of us speaks as we cross through the kitchen to the living room. Stopping in the doorway, I shine my Maglite on Amos Plank.

"Bad fuckin' scene," Glock says.

"It's worse in the barn."

He casts a questioning look at me.

I tell him about the teenaged girls.

"Damn." I see his cop's eyes taking in Plank's unbound hands. The proximity of the handgun to the body. The exit wound at the back of his head. Like any good cop, he's making judgments based on what he sees. "You think he did this?"

"I don't know." It's the most honest answer I can give. By all appearances, Plank went berserk, murdered his family, then put the gun in his mouth and blew his brains out. But the part of me that is Amish, that will always be Amish no matter how far I stray, can't fathom an Amish man—an Amish *father*—inflicting these horrors upon his family. Granted, I didn't know Amos Plank. But I do know the Amish culture. I know violence is not part of it.

While Glock snaps photos, I walk the living room, trying to envision what might have happened. I study the position of the bodies. The wounds. The proximity of the Beretta to Amos Plank.

"What did you do?" I whisper.

It's a keenly unsettling feeling to share such a small space with so many dead, particularly those who've suffered a violent death. In the periphery of my consciousness, I'm aware of Glock moving around, snapping photos. I see the flash of the camera. I hear the *click* and *whir* of the shutter, the high-pitched whine of the battery charging between shots.

"Chief."

I glance at Glock to see him kneeling, looking at something on the floor. I cross to him as he snaps the shot.

"Got a partial print here." He takes a second shot.

I pull one of the evidence markers from my coat. "Plenty of tread."

"Looks like a boot. Men's. Size nine or ten."

I arch a brow. "You're good."

"That's what my wife says."

We exchange small smiles, and I'm glad I have him to help me keep things in perspective. I kneel beside him, study the print. It's a partial, the front half of a shoe or boot. "Where did he pick up that blood?" I wonder aloud.

"Had to have stepped in it somewhere." Glock glances my way. "I didn't see any other prints."

"Gotta be." I rise, look around, heartened by the promise of evidence.

He shoots a final photo, gets to his feet and we look around. He walks slowly toward the small boy on the other side of the room and snaps a shot.

I go to the nearest body and kneel. It's not easy looking at a dead teenaged boy. He's lying facedown, his hands bound behind his back. His head is turned to the side and I see blood in his hair. Bits of brain matter and tiny white bone fragments from his shattered skull spatter the floor. His lips are parted. I see blood between his teeth. The small pink nub of a tongue that's nearly been bitten off. Though I used the mentholated petroleum jelly, the reek of urine and feces repulses me.

Then I notice the binding at the boy's wrists and my petty discomforts are forgotten. It's some type of insulated wire. *Speaker wire,* I realize. Something an Amish man would never have in his home or anywhere else. The double knots are tied off neatly. The wire is tight enough to cut skin.

The fact that the killer used speaker wire niggles at me as I go to the kitchen. Who would have speaker wire on hand? Someone putting a sound system into their home? Their car or RV? Someone who works with audio or sound systems? Computers maybe? I'm working the possibilities over in my head when Glock calls out.

"I think I found where he picked up that blood."

I walk to him and he motions down at the dead little boy. "There's blood on that rug. I'd say the killer stepped on the rug and tracked it."

He's right. Disappointment presses into me. "I was hoping we'd find a better print."

"Never that fuckin' easy." He snaps several shots of the blood-soaked rug.

I go to the kitchen and pull the sketch pad from my kit. Back in the living room, I begin a crude illustration of the scene, concentrating on the location and position of each body. I'm not a very good artist, but combined with the photos, this depiction will be a good record of how we found the scene.

I go to Amos Plank's body. He, too, lies facedown with his head turned to one side. The pool of blood surrounding his head glitters beneath the work light. I kneel next to him. "Glock, did you get photos of the father?"

Lowering the camera, he comes up beside me. "A half dozen or so from different angles."

That gives me the go-ahead to move the body. "Help me roll him over," I say.

Squatting next to me, Glock places his hands on the dead man's left hip. I put my hands on his left shoulder. "Go," I say and in tandem we roll him onto his back.

A cup or so of blood spills from his mouth when his head lolls. Glock and I move quickly back to avoid getting biohazard on our clothes. Plank's face goes beyond macabre beneath the stark light. I see several broken teeth. Gray-black powder burns around his lips. Nostrils filled with coagulated blood. Jaw broken, mouth hanging open. A tongue shredded by a bullet.

Livor mortis has set in; the right side of his face is dark purple. Lividity occurs when the heart stops and blood, no longer being pumped, settles to the lowest part of the body. The bruise-like discoloration begins as early as half an hour after death and becomes more pronounced with time. It's my first clue with regard to his time of death.

"Looks like he's been dead at least an hour," I say.

"If people knew what bullets did to their fuckin' faces, we'd have a hell of a lot less suicides," Glock comments.

The bullet wound appears to be self-inflicted. It entered via his mouth and exited out the back of his head, shattering his skull and taking a good bit of brain with it. Some might think it an apt end for a man who'd just murdered his family in cold blood.

"If he put the gun in his mouth and pulled the trigger," Glock begins, "wouldn't the concussion send him backward? Wouldn't he land face-up?"

"Usually, that's the case," I say. "But if he was leaning forward. Clutching the weapon. Head down." I ward off a chill the image conjures. "There may not have been enough momentum."

"Hell of way to go."

"Why would an Amish man have speaker wire?" I'm mostly thinking aloud. "He probably doesn't own a stereo or TV. He didn't even use a milking machine or generator for his dairy operation."

"Hard to figure." Glock shrugs. "Maybe he got it on sale somewhere or someone gave it to him. Uses it because it's strong."

"He has baling twine in the barn. Why not use that?"

"What are you getting at, Chief?"

I'm not sure how to express the thoughts running through my head without sounding prejudiced. But experience has taught me to listen to my instincts. Right now that little voice in my head is telling me this scene may not be what it looks like.

"I can't see an Amish man doing this," I say after a moment.

"The Amish are human, too," he says. "They have tempers. Limits. They snap."

He's right. It's rare, but the Amish have killed before. In 1993, Edward Gingerich murdered and then eviscerated his young wife. It's one of only a few documented cases on record.

"This doesn't add up," I say. "The level of violence. The handgun. The torture of the daughters. The speaker wire."

"Hard to swallow when it's the parent killing his kids."

Glock is one of the best cops I've ever known. He has loads of common sense, good instincts, and enough experience under his belt to know appearances can be deceiving. He's tough and loyal, sometimes to a fault. Last January, when we were investigating the Slaughterhouse Killer case, he risked his job to support me after I was fired by the town council. Above and beyond the obvious, one of the things I admire most about him is that he will give his honest opinion—even when he knows it's not what I want to hear.

"Are you telling me you think someone else came in here, shot them, and then made it look as if the father did it?" he asks.

"Sounds like a crazy theory when you put it that way."

Glock looks down at the body, but I feel the weight of his attention on me. "When I was a stationed in North Carolina, this crazy fucker cut up his kids and put them in a Crock-Pot with sweet potatoes. Later, when the shrink asked the guy why he did it, he told him he loved them too much to let them live."

"That doesn't make any sense."

He shrugs. "That's my point. You can't make sense of something that doesn't, no matter how hard you try."

I know he's right. Crimes like this baffle the mind. They break your heart. They'll tear you up inside if you let them. One of the old timers I worked with as a rookie once told me it's the cops who spend too much time trying to figure it out who end up going the way of Amos Plank.

"You don't want to get inside a mind like that," Glock says. "Talk about a scary fuckin' place."

The slamming of the kitchen door garners my attention. I look over to see the coroner, Dr. Ludwig Coblentz, standing in the kitchen, holding a suitcase-size medical bag. Wearing a cream-colored windbreaker over a flannel pajama top and tan Dockers, he looks like a cross between the Michelin Man and the Pillsbury Doughboy. But what he lacks in physical presence, he makes up for by being damn good at what he does. He's one of five doctors in Painters Mill and has been acting coroner for nearly eight years.

"Tell me this isn't as bad as what it sounded over the phone," he says.

"It's probably worse." I meet him in the kitchen and we shake hands. "Thanks for getting here so quickly."

He sets his medical case on the kitchen table. "How many?"

"Seven. The whole family."

"Good God." With the quick hands of a man who is as comfortable with his tools as he is in his own skin, he opens the leather case, works both hands into latex gloves, then slips a plastic, apron-like gown over his jacket and ties it in the back. Bending, he slides his Hush Puppy–clad feet into disposable shoe covers, pulls a small black vinyl case from the medical bag and looks at me over the tops of his glasses. "Show me the way."

"We've got three in here. Two in the yard. Two more in the barn." Motioning for the doc to follow, I enter the living room.

He heaves a sigh that sounds as old and tired as I feel. "I've been coroner for a while now, but I swear to God I'll never get used to seeing dead kids."

"The day you get used to that is the day you stop being human," I respond.

"Or find another line of work," Glock adds.

The doctor goes to the nearest victim, the teenaged boy, and kneels, setting the case on the floor next to him. "Some additional light would be helpful."

The work lights we set up earlier dispel much of the darkness, but they're not bright enough for the kind of work the doctor needs to do. Crossing to him, I shine my Maglite onto the victim.

The doc glances up at me, his eyes huge and troubled behind the thick lenses of his glasses. "Have you photographed the bodies?"

"We've got everything documented," Glock says. "You can move them if you need to."

Gently, the doc sets his hands on the boy's head and shifts it slightly. From where I stand, I see blood-matted blond hair. The doc's gloved fingers separate the hair revealing a neat, round hole the size of a pencil eraser a few inches above his nape. "This is the entry wound. This child was shot from behind."

"Any idea what caliber of bullet was used?" I ask.

"I can guess." He prods the scalp surrounding the hole. I see the pale flesh giving way beneath his fingers. Blood seeping from the hole, sucking back in when the pressure is released. "Judging from the size of the wound and the extent of skull fracturing, I'd say we're talking about a small caliber handgun. Close range."

"Can you be more specific than that, Doc?"

"Twenty-two caliber. Maybe a thirty-two."

"Nine millimeter?" I ask.

"Maybe. I can't say for certain yet." With the same gentleness with which he would handle a newborn baby, he turns the boy's head. Pink fluid leaks from the boy's left nostril. "Exit wound might help narrow it down."

My pulse kicks when I spot the hole in the wood floor. I look at Glock. "Get down in the basement, see if the slug went all the way through. I'll keep my beam on the hole. If the bullet went clean through, you'll be able to see the light."

"You got it."

I look down to see the doc once again turn the victim's head. The left side of the boy's face is purple with lividity. The doc presses two fingers into his cheek. "Livor mortis isn't fixed."

"What does that mean?"

"That means he's been expired at least two hours, but not longer than ten. Livor becomes fixed after ten hours." Once again he presses two fingers into the purple flesh of his cheek. "When I press here, the skin whitens, then refills. If he had been dead over ten hours, the livored area would remain stained."

"Can you narrow it down any more than that?"

"Body temp will tell us a lot." Turning, the doc digs into his tool bag and removes a pair of blunt-tipped shears. With the impersonal efficiency of the professional he is, he cuts away the boy's trousers and underwear. Seeing the boy's skinny, white body is unbearably sad. All I can think is that he should be alive. He should be laughing, teasing his younger brother, and annoying his older sisters.

"Kate?"

I jolt at the sound of the doctor's voice, and I realize he's handing me the clothes, waiting for me to bag them. Giving myself a mental shake, I go to my crime scene kit in the kitchen, dig out a large paper bag, snap it open. Back in the living room, I cross to the doc and hold open the bag while he drops the trousers inside. I jot the date, time and the name of the victim on the label.

"The body temperature drops between a degree and a degree and a half per hour." The doctor slides a specially designed high-tech thermometer into the boy's rectum. "This preliminary body temp will give you a ball-park idea of when he died. Once I get them to the morgue, I'll get a core reading from the liver, which is more accurate."

"Is it possible he lingered for a while after he was shot?"

"This child died instantly."

The timer on the thermometer beeps. He withdraws it and squints through his bifocals at the reading. "Ninety point six."

Quickly, I do the math. "That puts us between five and a half and eight hours ago."

"Correct."

I glance at my watch. "It's six-thirty A.M. now, so time of death was probably between ten last night and twelve-thirty this morning."

"That sounds about right."

"Can I borrow your scissors a sec?" I ask.

"Of course." He passes them to me.

I reach for the boy's wrist, cut through the speaker wire, and drop the wire into a second evidence bag. "Quite a bit of bruising at the wrist," I comment.

The doctor grimaces. "This poor boy struggled."

"I need to bag his hands so the CSU can check beneath his nails for DNA." When I glance down at the victim's hands, I see that the fingers are claw-like and rigid. "He's in rigor?" I ask.

"Not yet. Rigor usually starts with the face, the jaw, the neck."

"But his hands . . ."

"Cadaveric spasm more than likely. That happens when the victim experiences extreme agitation or tension in the moments before death."

I don't want to think about the horrors this boy endured before his death. I've been a victim of violent crime; I've seen my share of violence.

But I cannot imagine the terror and helplessness of being bound, watching every member of your family systematically shot and knowing you're next.

The doc moves to Amos Plank. I know it's an emotional response, but I feel inordinately repulsed by the elder Plank's body. Not because of the condition of his corpse, but because of what he may have done to his family. There's a part of me that feels as if the man doesn't deserve the reverence with which we handled the dead boy.

"Did you move him, Kate?"

I nod.

"Is he your shooter?"

"I don't know. Looks that way."

"Since we've some question as to whether or not this man is the perpetrator of these crimes and time is of the essence, I'll go ahead and get a core temp for you now. It's much more accurate this way and you'll be able to get to work on a time line." The doctor tugs up the man's shirt and exposes his abdomen.

Though entering middle age, Amos Plank is a lean man. I can see the outline of his ribs from where I stand. Minimal body hair. White skin that has seen little sun.

"You might want to note that there are no visible lacerations or bruises about the abdomen."

"Duly noted."

"I'm going to make a small incision." The doc places his hand flat against the abdomen, pulls the skin taut. Using a scalpel, he quickly makes the incision just below the lowest rib, about half an inch long. A line of blood appears as the skin opens, but the wound does not bleed. Next, he inserts the stem of a long digital meat thermometer, guiding it upward to just under the rib cage.

"Going to take a minute or so," he says. "I'll continue with the exam."

Setting his hands on the head of the corpse, he gently moves it from side to side. "Rigor has set in about the face and neck. Eyes are cloudy."

"Any idea when you might get to the autopsies?" I'm thinking about the two girls in the barn. I want to know how they died. If they were sexually assaulted.

"I'll juggle some appointments and begin immediately."

I'm watching the doctor examine the dead man's hands when a shadow on the corpse's wrist snags my attention. Grabbing my Maglite, I train the beam on the wrist. I almost can't believe my eyes. Just above the hand, a faint bruise encircles the wrist.

"Is that a bruise on his wrist?" I ask.

Doc Coblentz looks at me over the tops of his glasses, then his eyes follow the beam of my flashlight. His brows knit as he stares at the marks. "It certainly looks like it."

Before even realizing I'm going to move, I reach for the corpse's arm. I feel cold flesh through the thin latex of my glove. The stiffness of the joint associated with the early stages of rigor. In the stark light from my Maglite, I see clearly the circular pattern of the bruise.

"It's the same bruising pattern we found on the boy's wrists," I say.

Something pings in my head, like a piece of puzzle I couldn't make fit finally clicking into place. Realization trickles over me like ice water. Everything I thought I knew about this scene flies out the window. "He was bound," I murmur.

The doctor is already looking at the other wrist. From where I kneel, I can see the bruising there, too. The doc shoots me a grim look. "I don't believe we're dealing with a suicide here, Kate."

"The killer staged the scene," I whisper.

"That appears to be the case."

I think of the mother and baby lying dead in the yard, and a chill runs the length of my body hard enough to make me shudder. I think of the two girls in the barn, the evidence of torture, and all I can think is that there's a cold-blooded killer running loose in my town. A monster with a bloodlust for killing and an appetite that has spiraled out of control.

CHAPTER 4

Before this morning, I haven't smoked for nearly ten months. It's a stupid, self-destructive habit. But as I watch Doc Coblentz examine the tortured body of a dead teenaged girl, I wish for a cigarette with the fervor of a heroin junkie craving a fix.

I'm standing in the tack room with Glock and Skid. No one's talking. No one's looking at the bodies. I wonder if I look as demoralized as my fellow officers do.

Officer Roland "Pickles" Shumaker arrived on the scene a few minutes ago. Wearing his trademark trench coat and pointy-toed cowboy boots, he looks like he's just stepped off the set of some nuevo spaghetti western. He's seventy-four years old, acts like he's twenty-two, and doesn't look a day over eighty. He moves a bit more slowly than the rest of my team, has lost a good bit of his eyesight and most of his hearing. But he has nearly fifty years of law enforcement experience under his belt. In my book, that alone makes him more valuable than some wet-behind-the-ears rookie who doesn't know his ass from a hole in the ground.

"Looks like a goddamn massacre," Pickles says, settling into his grumpy-old-man persona as he enters the tack room.

He's right. The corpses are a macabre sight beneath the harsh glare of the work lights. This is the kind of scene that affects even the most hard-nosed of cops.

"We're not dealing with a murder-suicide." Looking from man to man, I tell them about the bruising on Amos Plank's wrists. "This is murder, straight up."

"Times seven," Skid mutters.

Pickles looks around the room, grimacing. "So the son of bitch who butchered these girls is still out there." It's a statement, not a question.

I can tell by everyone's expression that's where they want to be, on the street, hunting the killer. But we all know the investigation starts here, with the evidence. "I briefed the sheriff's office. They've stepped up patrols. T.J.'s been apprised; he's out there, too." I direct my attention to Glock, raising my voice to be heard above the drone of the generator. "Did you clear the outbuildings and silos?"

"Clear."

I look at Skid. "Did you search the creek area behind the barn?"

He shakes his head. "No one there."

"Tire tracks? Footprints?"

"If anyone was down there, he didn't leave us squat."

"We'll go over every inch of this place again once the sun comes up. No one does this kind of crime without leaving something behind."

Though the barn doors are open, the diesel exhaust from the generator is thick enough to choke a rhinoceros. No one's complaining. I think I can speak for everyone in the room when I say the smell of exhaust is preferable to the stench of blood.

"As soon as we finish here," I say, "we'll start canvassing and talking to neighbors. Hopefully, someone saw something."

"You going to call BCI?" asks Glock.

BCI is the Ohio Bureau of Criminal Apprehension and Identification out of Columbus, which is about a hundred miles west of here. It's a state agency run by the attorney general's office that offers a multitude of resources to local law enforcement, including a state-of-the-art lab, computer databases, crime scene technicians and field agents. The town council called the agency for assistance last year when a serial murderer stalked Painters Mill.

That's how I met field agent John Tomasetti. He was instrumental in helping me close the Slaughterhouse Murders investigation ten months ago. The case was a nightmare, especially for me because of my personal connection to the killer. Tomasetti got me through it. He's a good cop and an even better friend, and it's him I think of this morning.

"I'm going to request a CSU to help process the scene." I pull my cell phone from my pocket. "Maybe they'll be able to pick up hair or fibers."

The three cops nod in approval. But I know they're feeling territorial about this case. The atrocities committed against this Amish family have angered and outraged them. While they appreciate any help, they don't want some other agency encroaching on their turf.

"Chief Burkholder?"

I glance over to see Doc Coblentz standing next to one of the corpses. He looks grim and shaken, and I acknowledge that there is a small, selfish part of me that doesn't want to go over there. Some crimes are simply too terrible for the eyes to behold, the mind to comprehend. But the part of me that is a cop knows information is my most powerful tool.

Dropping my cell back in my pocket, I force my legs to take me to him. "What do you have?"

For a moment the doctor stares down at the floor, his expression troubled. And I realize with some surprise this veteran man of medicine is so upset by what he's seen that he can't speak.

"I've never seen anything like it," he says after a moment.

I'm aware of my team watching us from the doorway. It's an uncomfortable moment. I'm not very good at offering comfort. I'm not even very good at receiving it. I give the doc a minute, and then I ask the question that's been eating at me since I saw the bodies. "Do you know the cause of death?"

My question snaps him back. "I can't be positive until I get them on the table, but I have a theory." He glances toward Glock. "Have you photographed and documented everything?"

Glock gives a nod.

The doctor turns his attention back to me. "These two girls suffered long, horrific deaths, Katie. Look at this."

We move closer to the nearest victim, Mary Plank. She's about fifteen years old with the slender body of a girl on the brink of womanhood. Not yet an adult, not a child, but that special place in between. She probably still played like a kid. But her adult dreams were just forming in her head. She was pretty, with a kind face. It's unbearably difficult to look at her and think of how she must have been. Sweet. Innocent. Undamaged by life. I can't imagine the horrors these girls must have endured. I cannot fathom such brutality.

Gently, he places his hand against the girl's lower abdomen, between the pubis bone and the navel. With a long, cotton-tipped swab, he indicates the jagged mouth of a hideous wound. Something pink and watery peeking out. Using a wad of gauze, he wipes away some of the blood, and I discern the dark smudge of bruising around the wound.

"The clean lines here indicate the wound was probably made by a knife or some other very sharp instrument," the doc says.

"She was stabbed in the same area multiple times?" I ask.

"Not stabbed. I believe he opened her abdominal cavity."

"Why would he do that?"

"I can't imagine." He shakes his head. "Who knows what goes on inside the mind of a man capable of this kind of brutality."

"Can you tell me what killed her?"

"I can't be sure until I perform the autopsy, but judging from the amount of blood from this wound, it appears as if this is the fatal wound. She probably bled to death."

"She was alive when he did this?"

"Her heart was still beating. She may have been unconscious due to shock and blood loss. She could have been drugged, so I'll run a tox." He motions to her face. "She isn't gagged; believe me, she would have screamed."

I imagine I can hear those screams now. "Why?" is all I can manage.

"I don't know. Perhaps he was trying to retrieve a bullet," the doctor suggests.

"Maybe." But the theory doesn't ring true. It takes a special kind of cold-blooded to cut open a human body. "Seems like it would have been easier to dispose of the body."

He heaves the sigh of a heavily burdened man. "I don't know if it's significant, but this wound is very close to her uterus."

A shudder runs the length of my body. Unwanted images scroll through my brain. "I wonder if that's somehow symbolic."

"Could be."

"Or maybe he's a sadist and hates women."

The doc shrugs. "That's your area of expertise, not mine."

I motion toward the second victim. "What about the other girl?"

The doc moves to the second victim. Annie Plank. She was sixteen years old. Slightly heavier. Not as pretty as her sister. It breaks my heart to see these two young lives cut short.

With the same gentle deference he used with the sibling, the doc sets his gloved hand against her abdomen. The area has been wiped clean, and I spot the stab wounds immediately. These wounds are higher, just below her rib cage.

"She was stabbed. Three times, it looks like. I'm guessing, but I would venture to say at least two of those penetrated the stomach."

"Same weapon?"

"That would be my guess." He grimaces. "But I'm not convinced that's what killed her."

"What do you mean?"

Reaching up with a gloved hand, he gently rolls back an eyelid. It goes against every primal instinct I possess, but I force myself to look. The eyeball is milky and sticky-looking. The outside corner is bloodred. My perspective is not clinical, but one of outrage, sadness and disbelief that something this unspeakable could happen in my town, a place where people should be safe. I can feel my emotions knocking at the gate. My heart beating in my face. Sweat breaks out on the back of my neck, but I'm cold to the bone.

"The red area on the conjunctival surface is called petechial hemor- rhages," the doctor explains.

It's not the first time I've heard that term. "She was strangled?"

He shakes his head. "There are no visible ligature marks on her neck. No bruising." He indicates a thin white line just to the right of her mouth, across her nose and on her left cheek. "I'm guessing here, Kate, but I would say this is some type of adhesive."

"They taped her mouth?"

"And nose, evidently."

"They smothered her?"

"I can't say that definitively at this point, but asphyxiation would be my best guess."

"They tied her up. They stabbed her multiple times. And then smoth- ered her to death." The words are so twisted, so ugly, it hurts me to say them. All too easily, I can put myself in this young woman's place. I can imagine her terror and panic with a clarity that scares me. All I can think is, *How could somebody do this to another human being?* The part of my mind that clings to some semblance of innocence poses the question. An- other side of my brain that will never be innocent again knows the answer. There are monsters living among us. People who look no different than you and me. But they lack a fundamental component of the human spe- cies: a conscience.

"Did you get a temp, Doc?" I ask.

"I did." To prevent biohazard contamination of his notebook, he snaps off a glove and tugs the small pad from an inside pocket. "Ninety-four point six degrees."

I do the math. "These two girls were the last to die."

"An hour, maybe two, after he killed the people inside the house." He sighs. "It's possible the younger girl may have lingered a while, Kate. Particularly if the COD is exsanguination. She would have fallen uncon-scious." He shrugs.

I try to look at this through the eyes of a killer, but the perspective makes me feel dirty and guilty and decayed. "Why did he kill these two girls differently than the others?" I say, thinking aloud.

The doc arches a brow as if to say, *Don't ask me.*

Glock comes up beside me. "Maybe this guy's a sexual sadist. Came here for the girls, killed the rest of the family because they were potential witnesses or they were in the way."

I look at Doc Coblentz. "Were the girls raped?"

The doc nods. "There's some chafing visible, but the lighting is too bad for me to draw any kind of definitive conclusion. I really don't want to rule on that until I get them to the morgue."

I study the two dead girls. "There's a definite sexual element to this," I say. "But I think there's something else. Something obscure we're missing."

"Like what?" Glock asks.

"I'm not sure. There's something about way the bodies are displayed. The fact that they're nude. The torture aspect." I'm thinking aloud now. Brainstorming. Throwing out theories and ideas. "It's visual. Almost a theatrical element to it."

Glock is good at this and we play off of each other. "Was this pre-meditated?" he asks.

"If he stalked them, he would have known the rest of the family would be here," I say. "He would have known he'd have to kill them, too."

"Maybe his compulsion is so strong, collateral damage didn't matter."

Doc Coblentz cuts in. "This killer spent a good deal of time torturing these two young women." He tugs a fresh glove from his crime scene kit and works his fingers into it. "Look at this."

Glock and I follow him back to Mary Plank's body. Using a fresh swab, the doctor indicates a series of bright red abrasion-like marks on her buttocks, thighs and breasts. "Those are burns."

"From a cigarette?" My mind is already jumping ahead to the possibility of DNA on a butt.

"Propane torch."

"Sick motherfucker," Glock mutters.

Nodding grimly, the doc directs my attention to several stripe-like bruises about the buttocks and back. "I believe these bruises were caused by that small bat."

"He burned them. He beat them. Raped them." I feel that quivery sensation again, as if my stomach is slowly climbing into my throat. "And then he killed them."

For a moment the only sound comes from the *chug, chug, chug* of the generator.

Turning away from the girls, I address Glock. "Bag all of those tools and courier them to BCI. I want it there by the time the lab opens for business."

Glock is already reaching for the crime scene kit where the bags and labels are stored. "I'm on it."

"I'm going to make the call." I sigh, knowing that as bad as this day has been, it's probably going to get worse.

Pulling out my phone, I leave the tack room. Skid and Pickles are standing outside the door. Both still wear gloves and shoe covers. In an effort to preserve the scene and prevent the contamination of evidence, I've limited the number of people allowed in the barn and house to me, Glock, Skid, Pickles and Doc Coblentz. It will be up to us to deal with the dead.

"The doc is going to need some help getting those bodies down," I say.

The men aren't happy about the assignment; I recognize their green-around-the-gills expressions. But they're far too professional to complain.

"I want you fully geared, including hair caps. I want the victims' hands bagged."

Without waiting for a response, I walk briskly down the aisle. My boots thud with a little too much force against the packed dirt floor. I'm shaking by the time I reach the door. Once outside, I can breathe again, and I stand there, gulping air. After a moment I'm feeling calmer, and I notice that the eastern horizon is awash with color. Beyond, the leaves of the maple tree rattle in a cool breeze. In the driveway, three ambulances wait to transport the dead. All of these things remind me that I'm still alive, and that even in the face of death, life prevails.

I dial John Tomasetti's home number from memory. We've had an on-again, off-again relationship for about ten months now, but neither of us is very good at the relationship thing. Probably has to do with the amount of baggage we're toting around. Of course that didn't keep him from trying to get me into bed. It didn't keep me from succumbing when I probably shouldn't have.

To say we both have issues would be an understatement. Most of Tomasetti's stem from the murders of his wife and two children two and a half years ago in a horrific act of revenge by a career criminal. The parallels to this case don't elude me, and I realize that's why I've been putting off the call. He's a strong man, but even the strong have a breaking point.

But I need his help. His expertise. His instincts. His support. If I've learned anything in my years in law enforcement, it's that the living come first. We can always deal with the dead in our nightmares.

He answers on the third ring with a curt utterance of his last name. He's cranky upon waking. I wish I didn't know that about him.

"It's Kate."

A beat of silence ensues, and I wonder if he thinks the call is personal. I can practically feel his walls going up. Maybe he's afraid I'm lonely and drunk and calling him in the middle of the night to scream and rant, though I've never fallen to that particular low. "This is an official call," I clarify.

"What's up?"

"I've got a major crime scene here in Painters Mill. Seven vics. All DOA. No sign of the perpetrator. I need a CSU."

I hear rustling on the other end of the line, and I can't help but re-member what he looks like in bed. Boxer shorts. Tousled hair. Beard stubble thick enough to chafe my skin . . .

"Tell me about the vics," he says.

"Amish family. Five kids. Two teenaged girls were tortured."

"Sexual assault?"

"I don't know yet. Probably."

"Damn." More rustling. I can tell he's getting dressed. Stepping into creased trousers. Shrugging into a crisp shirt—an expensive one because John Tomasetti knows how to dress. He'll take his tie with him and put it on at the office. Stop at Stauf's for a cranberry muffin and double espresso. He likes his coffee strong.

"Do you know them?" he asks.

"No. They're from Lancaster. Moved here about a year ago."

"Premeditated?"

"Probably."

"What about motive?"

"I don't know. Looks . . . thought out. Killer spent some time with the two girls." I relay details of the torture aspect of the case.

"You have a suspect?"

"No."

The telephone line hisses, reminding me of the miles between us, both figuratively and literally.

"I'll get a CSU out there pronto to give you guys a hand with the scene." He pauses. "You want me to come down?"

I hesitate a moment too long. He knows what I'm thinking, and he snaps at me. "For God's sake, Kate. I can handle it."

"You don't have to come for this one, John. There were kids. A baby . . ."

"Let me get it cleared," he growls. "Give me a day or two to tie some things up."

"Thanks," I say. "See you then."

CHAPTER 5

The closest neighbor to the Planks is a pig farm owned by William Zook, who is also Amish. It's nearly nine A.M. when Glock and I pull into the driveway and park between the barn and house. About nine hours have passed since the Plank family was murdered, and I feel every tick of the clock like the jab of an ice pick. Having worked for two years as a detective in Columbus, I'm well aware that the first forty-eight hours are the most vital in terms of solving a crime. After that, the case goes cold and the chances of a good outcome decrease substantially. I don't plan on letting that happen.

The farmhouse is plain with badly weathered siding. The barn is octagonal with dirty white paint and tin shingles that have been peeled up by the wind. A tall silo with a rusty dome juts into a low, cloudy sky. A hundred years ago the farm had probably been a showplace. This morning, everything looks as old and tired as I feel.

In the side yard a dozen or more work shirts and trousers hang from a clothesline, flapping like flags in the morning breeze. To my right, pampas grass with spires that shoot ten feet into the air sways to and fro. Beyond, cornstalks rattle in a well-tended garden, and I know the woman of the house fills her days with pulling weeds and canning vegetables.

We exit the Explorer and start toward the front door. The smell of manure is overpowering. Most Amish farms are neat and well managed. The muck is scooped up several times a week and dumped into a manure pit, where it composts and is later used for fertilizer. Evidently, Zook doesn't exercise good manure management.

Next to me, Glock sighs. "I'll take you up on the mentholated jelly offer, now."

"Left it at the scene."

"Figures."

Having just left the Plank farmhouse, I can think of more disturbing smells than pig shit, but I don't comment.

We pass a small ramshackle barn surrounded by a rail fence and an ocean of oozing muck. Dozens of pink pig snouts poke out from between the rails, and I know they're watching us, hoping for a snack.

At the back door, I knock and concentrate on the trace of mentholated jelly that remains beneath my nose. The door opens to reveal a plump Amish woman wearing a brown dress, a white apron and traditional *kapp*. We stare at each other for several seconds before I recognize her. Twenty years ago, Alma Gerig and I went to school together. She's several years older than me, but our Amish school was so small, the older and younger children shared the same room.

She's gained thirty pounds since I last saw her. Her hair is more gray than red. It makes me wonder what my own life might have been like had I remained Amish. Though I see mistrust in her eyes, she offers a genuine smile. "Katie. *Guder mariye.*" Good morning.

"Hello, Alma." Giving her a passable smile, I flash my badge.

Her smile falters. *"Was der schinner is letz?"* What's wrong?

"I need to ask you and your husband some questions about something that occurred last night."

Stepping back, she opens the door wider. She's nervous now; I see it in the way her eyes flick away from mine. I don't believe it has anything to do with me personally or the murders. Mistrust between the Amish and the English police has been a problem in this town for as long as I can remember. My being formerly Amish has helped dispel some of the friction, but it hasn't eradicated it.

"Of course," Alma says. "Come in."

Glock and I enter a small living room. The plywood floor is covered with a blue and white braided rug that's tracked with dirt. Against the far wall, a walnut bench is draped with a worn quilt and a couple of throw pillows. I smell kerosene and frying scrapple and for an instant I'm reminded of my own childhood home. A bittersweet memory best left in the past.

"There was a problem at the Plank farm," I begin. "A shooting."

She presses her hand against her breast. "Was anyone hurt?"

"I'm afraid so." I don't elaborate. I want her husband there when I tell them about the murders. I don't believe the Zooks are involved. Still, I want to see their unrehearsed reactions when I tell them the news.

"Has something happened?"

I turn at the male voice and see William Zook approach from the kitchen. He's a tall, thin man with hunched shoulders and a salt-and-pepper beard badly in need of a trim. He wears a blue work shirt rolled up at the sleeves, a flat brimmed straw hat, trousers and suspenders. His eyes are sharp and suspicious when they land on me.

Showing him my badge, I get right to the point. "Mr. Zook, there was a shooting last night at the Plank farm. I'd like to ask you and your wife a few questions."

"A shooting accident?" His eyes narrow. "Was anyone hurt?"

Normally, I don't release the names of the deceased until I've notified the next of kin. Since the Planks are from Lancaster County, I'm still working on obtaining NOK contact information, which could take a few hours. With the clock ticking and a killer on the loose, I can't put my investigation on hold that long. If a member of the Zook family saw something, I need to know about it now.

"The entire family was murdered," I say.

"Ach!" William presses his hand to his chest.

Across the room, his wife gasps. "The children?"

I glance over at her and shake my head. "There were no survivors."

Quickly, I shift my attention back to William. His complexion has gone pale. He stares at me as if I've just plunged a knife into his chest. "Dead?" he whispers. "All of them?"

"I'm afraid so."

"Oh, dear Lord." Alma covers her mouth with both hands and looks at me over the tops of her fingers. "Who would do such an evil thing?"

"Did you see or hear anything strange last night?" I ask.

Both heads shake, but it is William who speaks. "The Plank house is over a mile away. Sometimes we do not see them for days at a time."

"When did you last see them?" Glock asks.

William shifts his attention to Glock, his brows knitting. "I saw Amos yesterday morning. I was repairing the fence, near the road. He was in the buggy and stopped to say hello."

"How did he seem?" I ask.

"Fine. We talked about the corn harvest. He wanted me to butcher a hog for him. I told him I would pick out a fat one for them."

"How did he seem to you? Normal? Nervous or upset?"

He shrugs. "He seemed the same as always."

Alma wrings her hands. "Who did this terrible thing?"

"We don't know." I turn my attention to her. "Were either of you close to the Planks?"

William answers. "We see them at worship."

"I quilted with Bonnie, Mary and Annie just last week," Alma puts in.

As a teenager, I spent many an evening cutting, pinning and sewing fabric. Quilting is the perfect activity for female bonding—and an even better forum for gossip. "Did Bonnie or either of the girls mention any problems? Family problems? Money problems?"

"They mentioned no such thing," Alma responds.

I look at William. He's standing so close I can see the crumbs from his breakfast toast in his beard. He smells of pig shit and hot lard. "Do you know if they had any enemies?" I ask. "Anyone who might have been un-happy or angry with them?"

"They were good neighbors." William shakes his head as if still reeling from news of their deaths. "A happy, generous family. I do not understand how this could happen."

"Has anyone made any threats against them?" Glock asks.

Alma looks upset. I can't tell if it's from the news of her neighbors' deaths or something else. "Everyone loved the Planks. They were very kind."

"What about the kids?" I press. "Did any of them ever get into trouble?"

Alma shakes her head. "The children were well behaved. Even Mary, who was going through her *rumspringa*."

Rumspringa is the "running around" period Amish teens go through when they turn sixteen or so. It's their time to experience the world without the social constraints of the Plain life. Usually, that entails some drinking and generally harmless misbehaving; nothing excessive. It's the period in which teens decide whether or not they want to be baptized. Most ultimately choose to join the church. I'm one of a small percentage who did not. But I had my reasons.

Footsteps on the stairs snag my attention. I look over to see two young boys wrestle down the steps. They notice Glock and me, and freeze, giving us dual deer-in-headlights looks.

"No roughhousing inside," William scolds.

His wife gives me a weak smile. "Our boys, Billy and Isaac."

"Do you mind if I ask them a couple of questions?" I know sometimes kids see things, know things parents do not.

For an instant, Alma looks alarmed, and I realize my being formerly Amish only goes so far when it comes to bridging gaps.

William calls the boys over and addresses them. "Billy. Isaac. Chief Burkholder would like to ask you a few questions."

I almost smile when both boys' eyes widen. "Just a couple of easy ones," I say in an attempt to put them at ease.

Both boys have thick blond hair blunt cut above their brows. Isaac is younger and looks at me as if I'm about to drag him off to prison for the rest of his life. Billy appears to be about fourteen or fifteen. But there's a childlike innocence in his expression that belies his age.

I offer my friendliest smile. "How old are you guys?"

"I'm eleven," Isaac says, his chest puffing out a little.

"That's pretty old." I smile, but my attempt at juvenile humor falls flat. I turn my attention to Billy. "How about you?"

"He's fifteen." Isaac answers for his brother.

"Did either of you happen to see anything strange over at the Plank farm the last few days?"

"What do you mean by strange?" Isaac asks.

I shrug, noticing the younger boy is much more articulate than his older brother. "Any English cars? Or maybe a buggy you didn't recognize? Strangers visiting? Anything like that?"

"No."

"Did you hear anything?" Glock asks. "Unusual sounds? Shouting? Crying?"

"No." Isaac looks toward his parents for direction. "Did something happen to the Planks?"

"I saw Mary's underwear!" Billy blurts the words, then slaps his hand over his mouth, his cheeks reddening.

The odd comment garners everyone's attention. Only then do I realize that while Billy is older than Isaac, his mentality is that of a much younger boy. I discern a slight speech impediment. He rounds his Rs and skipped pronunciation of the D altogether. The incidence of mental retardation is slightly higher among the Amish in comparison to the general population. There are several theories on the cause, the most prevalent being the small size of the gene pool. The majority of Amish do not marry outsiders; very few non-Amish join the Plain life. The gene pool has been closed for about twelve generations.

"When did you see her, Billy?" I ask.

"I dunno." When he looks up at me, I notice he suffers with strabismus, or crossed eyes. "One day. It was sunny. She was pretty."

"Did you see any strangers?" I ask.

"No strangers."

"What about cars or buggies? Did you hear any noises?"

"No." Biting his lower lip, he looks at his father. "Is Mary okay, *Datt*?"

I glance at William.

The Amish man grimaces, then sets his hand on the boy's shoulder. "Mary is in a good place, Billy. The whole family is."

CHAPTER 6

John Tomasetti arrived at BCI Headquarters at the Rhoades State Office Tower in downtown Columbus at just before nine A.M. He should have been thinking about his agenda for the day: the presentation he was supposed to give to a group of sheriffs that afternoon at the Marriott in Worthington, an interview at the Franklin County Correction Center down on Front Street with a suspect involved in the shooting death of a kindergarten teacher.

But Tomasetti's thoughts weren't on the day ahead of him as he stepped off the elevator on the fourteenth floor and headed toward his office. He'd been thinking about Chief of Police Kate Burkholder since her earlier call and a case that would take him back to Painters Mill. They'd kept in touch, but he hadn't seen her for almost two months. Things had been good between them—the friendship, the sex—but as was usually the case, distance had intervened. Or maybe things had been progressing a little too fast and with a little too much intensity. Kate was cautious, after all. That was one of many things he liked about her.

Tomasetti, on the other hand, had been dealing with other issues. Working through them. Trying to get his shit together. Or so he'd hoped. Regardless, he wanted to see her. He'd been looking for an excuse to drive down. They worked well together, and it sounded like she could use the help.

It bothered him that she'd hesitated to ask. Tomasetti knew what she was thinking. That he couldn't handle it. That walking into a case where a family with kids had been murdered would hit too close to home. Maybe she was right. Maybe this case would be like walking into his worst nightmare. Or maybe this was just one more hurdle on top of a hundred others he still needed to scale.

He was ruminating his options when he found Special Agent Supervisor Denny McNinch waiting outside his office door, pretending to look at the sleekly framed circa 1947 photograph of downtown Columbus perched on the wall like an old piece of siding.

"Morning." Denny shoved his hands into the pockets of his trousers and tried to look innocuous. "You got a minute?"

Tomasetti had been around long enough to know there was nothing even remotely harmless any time Denny showed up at your office before nine A.M. "Sure. Come in. Have a seat."

"In the conference room, John."

Uh-oh, he thought. The conference room was reserved for the big stuff. Hirings. Firings. Corporate-style powwows that entailed lots of forms in legalese, personnel files brimming with bureaucratic paper and, of course, the covering of managerial asses. It wasn't the first time he'd been summoned there.

Tomasetti made eye contact and smiled. "Do I need my lawyer?"

McNinch chuckled at the quip, but it was a humorless sound that conjured a deep sense of foreboding in Tomasetti's gut. "Not even your lawyer can help you this time, partner."

"Well, that's good to know."

They walked side by side down the hall, past cubicles where pretty administrative assistants stared at computer monitors and French-manicured nails pounded keyboards. He could feel their eyes on him, their collective curiosities pricking him like knives. Good fodder for lunchtime gossip.

Tomasetti didn't like the idea of walking into something unprepared. Since the Slaughterhouse Murders case ten months ago, he'd worked hard to clean up his act. He'd stopped taking the drugs his doctors had prescribed. He'd cut down on the drinking. He'd stopped thinking about putting his gun in his mouth and pulling the trigger. His work on the Slaughterhouse case had earned him a commendation and gone a long way toward restoring a reputation of which he'd once been proud.

But it had been more than just the case that had saved him from self-annihilation. He may not have survived if it hadn't been for Kate. Somehow, she'd managed to cut through the bullshit when no one else had been able to reach him. She made him want to be a cop again. Made him want to live. Made him want to be a man.

They reached the austere mahogany doors of conference room one. It was then that he knew this was no impromptu morning chat. He'd always known it was only a matter of time before his transgressions of the past caught up with him. When Denny shoved open the door, Tomasetti knew his day of reckoning had arrived.

Deputy Superintendent Jason Rummel stood at the glossy conference table, looking down at a smattering of papers spread out before him. He smiled when he saw Tomasetti. "Morning, John."

Too friendly, Tomasetti thought, and figured the meeting was going to be worse than he'd anticipated. "Morning."

Crossing to him, Rummel extended his hand and they shook. He was a short, wiry man with a pale complexion and a mustache that looked as if it had been fashioned by Adolf Hitler's barber. "We're glad you're here."

Tomasetti was vaguely aware of the vista of downtown Columbus through the window. The podium affixed with the seal of the great state of Ohio shoved into a corner. The flat-screen TV mounted on the wall. On the opposite side of the table, Human Resources Director Ruth Bogart had already set up shop. He recognized his thick and battered personnel file on the glossy surface in front of her. Next to his file were two pens, a legal pad, several ominous-looking forms and a Starbucks coffee mug smeared with lipstick.

Bogart wore a burgundy power suit with a hint of white lace at the neckline. She looked at him over the bifocals perched on her nose and smiled in a way that reminded him of a coral snake, right before it sank its fangs into you.

Rummel took a seat at the head of the table, reminding everyone he was the man in charge. Behind him, Denny closed the conference room door with an audible *click,* shutting them in. Tomasetti wondered if they were psyching him out. If the situation hadn't been so serious, he might have laughed at the absurdity of it. Back when he'd worked vice with the Cleveland Division of Police, he'd spent many an hour in interview rooms, psyching out perps. He didn't much like being on the receiving end.

Tomasetti sat across from Bogart. "Looks like the gang's all here."

She ignored him. Rummel cleared his throat. "You're a good agent, John. One of the best we have. I know we've had our differences over the last year or so, but I want you to know I have the utmost respect for you as a professional."

All Tomasetti could think was that the axe was about to fall. He could feel the hairs on the back of his neck prickling in anticipation of the blade. That's how Jason Rummel operated. Butter them up, then sink the knife in good and deep.

Knowing the value of playing the game, Tomasetti focused his gaze on the photo of the attorney general framed in gold leaf above Rummel's head. "I appreciate that," he said.

"I know that last case took a toll, John. Professionally. Personally." Rummel grimaced. "I know the timing on the whole thing was bad."

The words were a euphemism for the untimely murders of Tomasetti's wife and two young daughters two and a half years earlier. People used euphemisms when they didn't want to say the real thing. This time, because the reality of what happened was too terrible to say aloud. Tomasetti had no use for euphemisms, so he remained silent.

"I want you to know we take care of our agents here at BCI," Bogart added.

Tomasetti turned his attention to Denny McNinch and gave him a what-the-fuck-is-she-talking-about look. "You going to tell me what's going on here, or are you going to make me guess?"

Denny wiped his hands on his slacks. "It's that drug test thing a few months back, John. We tried to make it go away, but the suits want it dealt with. You know, policy."

Of course, he'd known. The big, bad failed drug test. Back when he'd been self-medicating, alternating between prescription drugs and booze. "That was ten months ago," he heard himself say.

"These things take time," Denny said. "There's a lot of bureaucracy involved and everyone seems to have a different opinion on how things should be handled."

Tomasetti smiled. Ten months ago, that same failed drug test hadn't kept them from sending him into the field in the hopes that he would screw up so they could fire him. "I think the official term is *politics*."

"No one's playing politics," Bogart said quickly.

"In light of your achievements, no one was in a hurry to rush to judgment," Rummel added. "We're not here to crucify you."

"That's a relief," Tomasetti said.

If any of them caught the sarcasm in his voice, they didn't show it.

Rummel looked at the human resources director and nodded.

Ruth Bogart looked down at the file in front of her. "We received a call from the superintendent, John. He wants the drug situation addressed. By the book. You know, to protect the interests of the agency. To protect you."

"You mean in case I go postal or something?"

Bogart shook her head. "That's not what I meant."

"Against any sort of liability that might crop up," Denny added.

"There were some meetings," she continued. "Jason went to bat for you, John. He put his own career on the line. They weren't listening."

I bet, Tomasetti thought. Rummel didn't put anything on the line for anyone, unless he had something to gain.

"Jason put in a good word," she continued. "Made some recommendations. He reminded them of the commendation, your years of service, both with BCI and the Cleveland Division of Police." She grimaced appropriately. "He reminded them about the ordeal you went through in Cleveland."

"I appreciate that." But he felt as if he were being tag-teamed by a pack of dogs. "So what's the verdict?"

Rummel looked appropriately grave. "The final resolution we arrived at is to place you on administrative leave."

"Temporarily, of course," Denny clarified. "You have a lot of friends here at BCI."

Tomasetti leaned back in the chair. "I guess it pays to have friends in high places." This time the sarcasm came through loud and clear.

Denny looked like his tie was too tight. "We figured you could use some time off. Get yourself back on track. Hell, get some things done around the house. Go fishing, for chrissake."

"We play it this way and you can come back with a clean slate. Pick up where you left off. Everyone wins." Rummel laughed. "Hell, I wish *I* could take some time off."

A laugh hovered in Tomasetti's throat, but he withheld it because he knew it would sound as bitter as it tasted. As far as he was concerned, BCI didn't give a good damn about him. They just wanted to sweep this dirty little incident under the rug where no one would trip over it.

"I guess that commendation only goes so far when it comes to politics," he said.

"This has nothing to do with politics," Rummel said.

Tomasetti let out a sigh. "How long?"

Bogart and Rummel exchanged glances. "As part of your leave package, you will be required to attend regular weekly sessions with a licensed psychiatrist contracted by this agency," she clarified. "And a drug test. Every week."

"You gotta pass it," McNinch added.

Tomasetti couldn't help it; he laughed. An inappropriate sound that echoed in the room like the growl of some wounded beast. "Oh, for chrissake."

"It's a condition of your continued employment," Rummel clarified.

That was the point when Tomasetti knew he was sunk. There would be no negotiation. No defending what he'd done. No undoing the past. No lying his way out of a reality he himself had created.

Of course, he tried anyway. "Those drugs were prescribed by the same doctors you're telling me to see now."

"Those drugs were prescribed by different doctors at different times," Bogart pointed out. "You abused that."

"Look, I don't think we need to get into ancient history." This from Rummel, the advocate, looking out for the well-being of one of his top agents. "That's not the purpose of this meeting. I mean it, John. This is an opportunity. Try to look at it that way. Make the best of a bad situation and move on from there."

All Tomasetti could think was that he'd been making progress. As far as he was concerned, work was the best therapy. Putting him on leave now was like yanking the rug out from under him just when he'd found his balance.

"What about my case load?" he asked, his voice sounding inordinately reasonable.

"Your open cases will be dispersed to other agents," Denny McNinch said.

Tomasetti didn't like to share. Not his cases. Not anything. He could feel the anger, the old bitterness rising into his throat. His heart bumping against his ribs, the blood squeezing through his veins with so much force he could feel it pulsing at his temples. "I guess the three of you have it all figured out."

Denny sighed. "I know this isn't ideal."

"Nobody likes this sort of thing," Bogart said.

"But we have your best interest as well as the interests of this agency in mind," Rummel added.

"Not to mention the best interest of your collective asses," Tomasetti put in.

Nobody had anything to say about that.

"Last time you guys had me in here, you were trying to squeeze me out the door," Tomasetti said. "You were willing to send me into the field to achieve that end."

Rummel grimaced, put on the face of a man owning up to a painful mistake. "Try to put yourself in my position, John. You went through a terrible ordeal. Nobody's blaming you, and you're not being punished for that. We've got a vested interest in your well-being. We want you well and back at work. But you've got to do this."

"I'm glad everyone has my best interest at heart," Tomasetti said, but the cynicism in his voice was unmistakable.

Rummel shot a pointed look at the personnel file in front of Bogart.

The human resources director opened the file and removed a sheet of paper and a form and slid both across the table to Tomasetti. "We'll need for you to sign the form. For the file, of course. The other sheet contains a list of doctors. You choose which doctor and call them at your convenience."

When Tomasetti made no move to pick up the papers, she added: "All of this will be kept in the strictest of confidence, John. You know that."

What he knew was that they had him backed into a corner. His reputation and career were on the line. As badly as he wanted to tell them to go to hell, he knew he couldn't. Not if he wanted to salvage what was left of his life.

He reached for the papers. The single sheet contained the names and contact information of six accredited psychiatrists located in the greater Columbus area printed neatly on BCI letterhead. The form was a human resource application for leave filled with legalese, already signed and approved by Jason Rummel.

"It's a good deal," Denny said.

Tomasetti picked up the pen.

Bogart leaned forward, put a red nail on the line at the bottom. "Sign right there," she said. "Press hard. It's in quadruplicate."

John Tomasetti signed his name on the dotted line.

CHAPTER 7

The October sun has burned through the clouds by the time Glock and I leave the Zook place. As I speed down the lane, I glance toward the Plank farm a mile to the north. The barn roof and the top of the grain silo are visible, but the hedge apple trees growing along the fence line block my view of the yard, house and outbuildings.

"Witness would have been nice," Glock says.

"Murder's never that easy."

He looks around. "We going back to the Plank place?"

"I thought we'd swing by David Troyer's farm first."

"Neighbor?"

"Bishop."

Glock arches a brow.

"Amish version of a priest."

"Gotcha." He pauses. "You think he might know something?"

"The Amish talk to their bishops. They confess. If there was something going on with the Planks—some kind of problem or crisis—there's a good chance he knows about it."

"Let's hope he's a good bishop."

"He is." I know this because he was my family's bishop. He was instrumental in placing me under the *bann* when I refused to confess my sins, but I never held it against him.

We find Troyer in the cornfield in front of his house, astride an antique corn thresher, driving his team of gray Percheron geldings. The thresher is an awkward-looking contraption that cuts and bundles cornstalks. A few yards behind the binder, the bishop's three grown sons stack the bundles into neat rows. Farther back, dozens of bundles of dry yellow cornstalks litter the field, and I know they've been at it since the wee hours of morning.

"They're trying to beat the rain," I say.

Glock looks up at the cloudless sky. "How do you know it's going to rain?"

"Checked the weather online this morning."

"For a second I thought you were going to reveal some ancient Amish secret for weather predicting."

We both grin. It's the first semblance of humor I've felt all morning, and it's a welcome diversion.

I park on the shoulder and we traverse the bar ditch. Standing at the fence, we watch the men work. Autumn harvest is a busy time for an Amish farmer. The days are long and the work is backbreaking. Though female chores most often take place inside the house—canning, cleaning, sewing and baking—I always managed to end up outside with my *datt*. I never told anyone, but I secretly enjoyed the sweat and dirt and physical labor. It was one of many ways I didn't fit in.

Spotting us, Bishop Troyer waves, letting us know he'll hand the reins over to one of his sons and stop to speak to us next time around.

"Is he bound by any kind of confidentiality?" Glock asks after a moment. "I mean like a priest and the confessional?"

I shake my head. "If he knows something, he'll talk."

It takes fifteen minutes for the team of horses to round the field. The second time around, Troyer hands the reins to his son and starts toward us.

Bishop Troyer is one of those people who always looks the same no matter how many years pass. He has a full head of thick gray hair, blunt cut above heavy brows and a full salt-and-pepper beard. He has the rounded belly of a well-fed man. As a kid, I remember asking my *datt* why his legs were so bowed. *Datt* replied that Bishop Troyer spent many hours as a young man training and riding horses. In hindsight, I think my *datt* was just trying to keep me off our old plow horse.

"Wei geth's alleweil?" How goes it today? Removing his flat-brimmed hat, the bishop wipes sweat from his forehead with a handkerchief.

"Ich bin Zimmlich gut," I respond.

He looks up at the sky. "We are trying to beat the storms."

"Looks like a good harvest."

"Best we've had in six years." His gaze slides to Glock and then back to me. His expression sobers. "Reuben Zimmerman came by an hour ago. He told me about the Plank family."

Word of a death spreads quickly in the Amish community. Word of murder travels even faster. Not for the sake of gossip, but because other families will drop everything and descend upon the injured or bereaved to help. In the case of the Planks, there's no one left to help. I tell the bishop what happened, leaving out as many of the details as I can.

He places his hand over his chest. I see the veins standing out on his temple. Sweat forming on his brow. For a moment I wonder if he's having a heart attack.

"Are you all right, Bishop Troyer?"

"It is the will of God." He shakes his head, blinking away sweat. *"Der Keenich muss mer erhehe."* One must exalt the King.

We spend the next ten minutes rehashing the same things Glock and I went over with the Zook family. The conversation shifts into new territory when I ask him if any of the Planks had come to him with a problem.

A shadow I can't quite read passes over his expression. *"Ja."* Wiping his face with the kerchief, he meets my gaze. "Bonnie approached me after worship with concerns about Mary."

"The younger of the two girls?"

The bishop nods, his brows knitting. "Bonnie did not want to speak to me with her husband present."

An uneasy *ping* sounds in my brain. The Amish are generally a patriarchal society. Secrets between a husband and wife are rare. What was Bonnie keeping from her husband? And what did that have to do with Mary?

"Do you know what she wanted to speak to you about?" I ask.

The bishop shakes his head. "We never got the chance to speak privately. I tried several times but Amos was always present." He shrugs. "I took the buggy to the house last week, but she said it was not a good time. I even met her at the shop in town where Mary worked part-time."

I didn't know Mary had an outside job. "Which shop?"

"The Carriage Stop."

One of Councilwoman Janine Fourman's shops. I make a mental note to swing by and speak to the manager. "Do you know why Bonnie wouldn't speak to you in front of her husband?"

"I do not know. Perhaps Amos is—was—a private man."

Or he was into something he didn't want anyone to know about. It's a powerful, uncomfortable thought. I know being suspicious of Amos is cynical, especially since he is among the dead. But as a cop, I know sometimes victims play an unintended role in their own deaths. I've seen more than one innocent person get in over his head. And I've seen them pay the consequences, too.

"So you have no idea why Bonnie wanted to speak to you about Mary?"

"No."

Beside me, Glock leans closer. "Did Bonnie or any of the Plank family seem upset lately?"

He considers the words and then nods. "Bonnie seemed upset sometimes, but she was a nervous woman."

"Did she ever seem afraid?"

He shakes his head. "I had planned to pay them another visit, but with the harvest . . ." He looks down at his boots.

The bishop and I have had our moments of disagreement over the years. He can be a hard, judgmental man. But he can also be kind and fair and generous. At this moment, looking into his eyes, I know he blames himself for not forcing the issue with Bonnie.

"What can you tell us about Mary?" I ask.

"I did not know the family well, Katie. They were new to the area. They kept to themselves more than most. Mary seemed like a kind, happy girl. Generous. Smart in school. She helped care for her younger siblings."

"Did she have a boyfriend?" I ask.

"I do not know."

"Do they have family in Lancaster?" Glock asks.

"I do not know." His face darkens, and I realize he feels guilty for his lack of knowledge. "Will you let me know if they left behind family in Lancaster County, Katie? Perhaps I can be of some comfort to them."

I touch his shoulder. "Of course."

As I drive away, I feel as if I know even less than when I started. Who were the Planks? Why did they leave Lancaster County? Why was Bonnie worried about her daughter?

The questions taunt me, but I have no answers. The one thing of which I'm fairly certain is that the Plank family left behind secrets. Where there is a secret, there will be a revelation.

I drop Glock at the Plank farm with instructions to assist the crime scene unit from BCI. The CSU will process the scene, dust for latent prints, collect blood evidence and footwear imprints, bag any hair and fibers and whatever else they can find. I know it's petty in light of the loss of life, but I find myself watching for John Tomasetti's Tahoe. I'm not sure if I'm relieved or disappointed when he doesn't show. In my current frame of mind, I'm probably better off not analyzing my feelings too closely.

On my way to the police station, I call Lois, my first shift dispatcher, and ask her to let all of my officers know there will be a briefing at the station in an hour so I can bring them up to speed on the case.

As I drive through downtown Painters Mill, life goes on as usual. I pass by the Carriage Stop Country Store where Mary Plank worked part time. I'm tempted to pull in, but I know the store isn't open for another twenty minutes, so I keep going. On the steps of the City Building, Mayor Auggie Brock and Councilman Norm Johnston are in the midst of some gesticulation-inducing exchange. Auggie spots me and waves; Norm pretends not to see me, which makes me sigh. His daughter was the victim of a serial killer last January. He didn't agree with the way I was investigating the case, and to this day he blames me for her death. One more demon riding my back, spurring and whipping, keeping all the others company.

Down the street, Tom Skanks, owner of the Butterhorn Bakery, squeegees the front display window with the verve of a New York City high-rise window washer. The elderly Farmer brothers sit in steel chairs on the sidewalk in front of the hardware store and argue over their morning chess game.

I should be comforted by the constancy of our existence. The routine of small town life. The prettiness of the town. The friendliness of the people I've sworn to protect and serve. Instead, I feel strangely indignant that life continues on with so little interruption when just down the road a family of seven has been wiped off the face of the earth.

The predator inside me has been roused. I look upon every man, woman and child with hard-edged suspicion. Maybe because I know the possibility exists that hidden somewhere behind all this normalcy, a monster roams.

The police station is housed in a century-old red brick building that had once been a dancehall. It's sweltering in the summer and cold as a meat locker in winter. But it's my second home; the people who work for me are my family. At this moment, I'm unduly thankful for them.

I enter to find both my day- and night-shift dispatchers at the window that faces the street. Lois Monroe is about fifty years old with pretty blue eyes and a disposition as prickly as her overprocessed hair. She might look like someone's mom, but I've seen her put more than one cocky young cop in his place. Mona Kurtz, on the other hand, is twenty-four going on sixteen with a head full of wild red ringlets and a personality that matches her hair to a T. Working on an associate's degree in criminology, she's totally enamored with all facets of law enforcement—and doesn't mind working third shift. Neither woman is perfect, but they keep the police station up and running.

Mona is kneeling at the window, braced, with her hands on the sill, straining to open it. Lois is using the heel of her practical shoe to tap on the seal, trying to break it loose.

"I'm afraid to ask what you're doing," I say as I pass the dispatch station. Both women turn at the sound of my voice.

"Oh, hey, Chief." Mona grins. "We're trying to get the window open."

"It's hot in here," Lois adds.

"She's having another hot flash."

Lois wipes her forehead. "If I don't get cooled off I'm going to have to call the fire department."

I steer clear of the hot flash comment. "You look like a couple of inmates trying to break out of jail." Reaching over the top of the desk, I grab messages from my slot. "Mona, did you hear back from Lancaster County?"

She crosses to me, and I try not to notice the black tights, red miniskirt and little black boots. "The sheriff's office checked the names over the phone and sent a couple of deputies to some of the Amish farms. I haven't heard back."

"Call them again. The Planks have got to have relatives somewhere." Notifying NOK is one of the most difficult aspects of my job. There's nothing I'd hate more than for someone to find out about a family member's death from the six o'clock news.

"Any media inquiries?" I ask.

"Steve Ressler," Mona replies. "Channel eighty-two in Columbus. Radio station in Wooster. The usual suspects."

Lois sighs. "I swear the gossips in this town are the best informed people in the world. Everyone's got everyone else on speed dial."

"Text messaging." Sliding behind her desk, Mona pulls the headset over her head. "It's faster."

"Our official response is 'no comment,'" I tell them.

Mona puts her hand over the mouthpiece of her headset. "What's your unofficial response?"

"We don't know shit."

She gives me a smile.

"I'll have a press release ready this afternoon." I turn my attention to Lois. "Glock'll get that window for you."

"If he can't get it open, I guess he can always shoot it." She gives the window a final whack, then gives me a sage look. "You guys have any idea who killed that poor family?"

"The devil himself, more than likely," I say and head toward my office.

An hour later, I'm sitting behind my desk thinking about murder. Ten months ago, I faced my first truly unfathomable case. The Slaughterhouse Killer investigation tested me to my limits, both professionally and personally. But while the case was a tough one, the fact that we were dealing with a serial murderer made him predictable to a degree. I knew his motive. His modus operandi. I knew he couldn't stop. And I knew that eventually his dark compulsion would lead him to make a mistake. The case nearly cost me my life, but in the end, I got him.

This case promises to be different. I don't have any parameters to guide me. No motive. No suspect. All I have to work with is a slaughtered family, a crime scene that has been stingy with evidence, and a jumble of unanswered questions.

"You look like you could use this."

I start at the sound of Glock's voice and look up to see him standing just inside my office, holding a brown paper bag from the diner. "If you're angling for a raise, you're on the right track," I say.

"Being married has taught me two things, Chief."

I smile. "Just two?"

He smiles back. "Understanding a woman begins with knowing what she wants even before she asks."

"Not bad." I take the bag from him. "What's the second thing?"

"When in doubt, bring food."

"You're a wise man, Glock."

"My wife thinks so." He takes one of two visitor chairs. "Some of the time, anyway."

I smell chili as I unpack the Styrofoam bowl, paper napkin and plastic spoon. The rest of my team shuffles in. Skid looks like he hasn't slept for two days. I know third shift has been hard on him. It was the only way I could think of to discipline him for mishandling a drunk-and-disorderly case a couple of months back. Pickles smells like cigarette smoke and looks as content as a sixth grader at recess as he drags in a chair. T.J. brings up the rear. He's my youngest officer and the only one of us who's had any decent sleep.

I address him first. "You up to speed on this?"

"Skid filled me in." He whistles. "Unbelievable."

I speak to all of them now. "On the chance the killer is an outsider, someone passing through town, I contacted the State Highway Patrol."

"You think that's the case?" Glock asks. "Or do you think he's local?"

"I don't know." I sigh, frustrated by the lack of leads. "We have to assume he's local for now."

Four heads bob nearly in unison.

I turn my attention to Glock. "CSU find anything?"

Glock scoots his chair closer. "Tomasetti sent two technicians. They were still working the scene when I left. Found a slew of latents. Some could be from the family. Blood evidence was done. Got a partial off the bloody print on the door." He looks down at his notes. "They found two slugs so far, including the one in the basement that went through the floor. Looks like the fucker who did it picked up his brass."

"Of course he did," I say dryly. "They able to get footwear impressions?"

"They were working on that. Tech thinks they'll get some decent impressions."

"Any latents on the instruments found in the barn?" I ask.

"Smears." Glock frowns. "No prints."

"That sucks," Skid says.

"Hair?" I ask, hopeful. "Fibers?"

"Both. They vacuumed the house and the tack room in the barn. Bagged everything and sent it via courier. Won't know anything until tomorrow at the earliest."

"Keep on the footwear thing. If we can figure out what kind of shoe and match it to someone in town . . ."

"You bet."

"Have the bodies been transported?" I ask.

"Paramedics were loading up when I left the scene. Doc Coblentz borrowed a resident from Cuyahoga County to assist with the autopsies. They're going to work through the night."

"That will speed things up." In the back of my mind, I wonder if Tomasetti will drive down. I wonder if I should have filed an official petition for assistance. "Were the techs able to give you a caliber from the slugs?"

"Not definitively," Glock says. "But it was a small caliber. Probably a twenty-two. Could be a thirty-two or nine millimeter. They're sending the Beretta to the lab for testing."

I address Glock. "They get a serial number?"

"Filed off," he says.

"That's interesting," says Skid.

"Yeah." I scan the faces of my team. "What else do we have in terms of evidence?"

"The instruments in the barn," T.J. begins.

"The speaker wire," Skid adds.

"Until the lab gets back to us," I tell Skid, "why don't you call around, see who sells speaker wire here in town?"

He nods.

"Anyone find any money?" I ask. "Valuables? Was anything grossly out of place or broken?"

The men shake their heads. "Aside from the bodies, there didn't seem to be a damn thing outta place," Pickles says. "Nothing looked as if it had been tossed."

I tell them about my conversation with Bishop Troyer. "Bonnie was evidently concerned about her daughter, but no one knows why."

"Might be a good idea to talk to her friends," Glock says.

"Can you follow up on that?" Get me a list? I ask. "I'm going to talk to the owner of the shop where she worked." I look at my team. "We need a motive."

"Murder for the sake of murder," Glock says. "It looks like whoever did it went in there to kill."

"And torture," Pickles adds. "Seems like that was a big part of it."

I nod. "I agree."

"What about robbery?" Skid looks around the room. "Maybe the murders were an afterthought. They went in for money or valuables, saw those two girls . . ." He shrugs. "Acted out some kind of twisted fantasy."

It's a stretch, but I've had too much experience with the utter senselessness of murder to dismiss it out of hand.

T.J. speaks up for the first time. "Do the Amish use banks?"

"Some do. Some don't." The perfect assignment for him comes to me. "See if the Planks had an account at Painters Mill Credit Union or First Third Bank and Trust. If the bean counters balk, get a warrant from Judge Seibenthaler."

"Will do."

I look at Pickles; I'm thinking about drugs now, a silent scourge that affects many small towns, no matter how postcard perfect the façade. Back in the 1980s, he worked undercover and singlehandedly busted one of the biggest meth labs in the state. Despite his age, he's always ready for action, the more the merrier, and if he gets to pull his sidearm, it's a bonus. "You still on top of our friendly neighborhood meth guys?"

"Some." Leaning back in his chair, he unwraps a toothpick and sticks it between his lips. "You think this is drug related?"

"Something ugly like this happens, and drugs come to mind." All eyes swing to me. "It's a desperate, money-driven business."

"Amish might be easy pickin's." Pickles chews on the toothpick. "Being pacifists and all."

He's right; generally speaking, the Amish renounce any kind of violence. "If some crackhead found out the Planks kept money at the house, they might think they could make off with some easy cash."

Glock pipes up. "How would anyone know the Planks kept cash on hand?"

All eyes turn to me, and I know they're wondering how the social crevasse that exists between the Amish and English might have been traversed. "Maybe one of the Planks mentioned keeping cash at the house while they were in town. Maybe the wrong person overheard and decided to rob them."

Skid looks doubtful. "You mean like 'My grandma keeps ten thousand dollars cash in her broom closet'?"

I shrug, knowing it's a stretch. But you never know when a stretch might become the real deal.

"Maybe it started out as a burglary," Glock says.

"Only the family was home and all of a sudden it's a robbery," T.J. adds. "Maybe they didn't want witnesses."

"That doesn't explain the torture aspect." I look from man to man. "If our perp went in for money or valuables, that level of violence just doesn't fit."

Glock weighs in with, "Or maybe the perp figured on robbery and didn't give a damn who got hurt. They do a home invasion, decide not to leave any witnesses. Maybe this killer is some kind of psychopath, high on God only knows what, and it turned into a fuckin' melee."

Pickles pulls the toothpick out of his mouth and uses it to make his point. "If the killer went into that house at night, surely he knew the family was home."

The direction our collective minds have gone makes me think of hate. Hatred of the Amish is unfathomable to most, but I know it is a cancer that is all too active. I wonder if hate could be part of this. Or all of it. "What about a hate crime?" I venture.

"Definite possibility," Glock says.

I meet his gaze. "Check into hate crimes against the Amish in Ohio,

Pennsylvania and Indiana in the last two years. I want names and addresses. That gets into federal territory, so the feds will have records."

"I'm on it."

I turn my attention to Pickles. "Who are the biggest dealers in the area?"

Pickles knows the answer off the top of his head. "Jack Hawley got popped two years ago with a key of coke. Did eighteen months at Terre Haute. Word is he's hanging with his old friends."

"These guys never learn," Glock mutters.

I jot the name on my pad. "Who else?"

"We know that goddamn Harry Oakes is selling meth. Got a network the size of New fuckin' York. But he's one paranoid son of a bitch. I can't see him doing this kind of thing."

"Who else?"

"The Krause brothers." Pickles gives a nod. "They're cooking shit out at their old man's farm. House is derelict, so they moved a trailer home out there. Lights are burning in those barns half the damn night."

"Where's the old man?"

"Sent him to an old folks home down in Millersburg."

"Huh." I think about that a moment, tap my pad with my thumb. "These names are a starting point. Let's go knock on some doors. Feel them out."

Glock sits up in his chair. "You want me to go with you?"

I shake my head. "I'll take Pickles."

The former Marine looks alarmed. "Those Krause boys've got guns out there, Chief."

I don't have anything against guns in general. I have faith in our constitution, and I believe a law-abiding citizen has the right to keep and bear arms. If I hadn't had access to a weapon seventeen years ago, I wouldn't be here today. Still, as a cop, I know that in the wrong hands a gun can become an instrument of death in a split second. "We're just going to rattle some cages," I say. "See what runs out."

"Chief, with all due respect . . ."

Pickles bristles at Glock's concern. "We can handle it."

I cut in before the situation escalates. "Pickles and I will take care."

He nods, but doesn't look happy about us going out alone.

I look at T.J. "I want you to canvass the area around the Plank farm." Gaining useful information via canvassing is a long shot since many of the Amish farms in the area are more than a mile apart. Many will not speak openly to the English police. But with nothing to go on and the clock ticking, it's worth the time and effort. "Ask about the family. Friends. Relatives. And see if anyone saw any strange vehicles or buggies in the area. Find out which homeowners keep firearms and what kind. Make a list."

"You got it."

Skid gives me a puzzled look. "What about me?"

"If I were you, I'd go home and get some sleep," I tell him. "We've got a long stretch ahead and it might be a while before you get another chance."

CHAPTER 8

Pickles and I hit the Krause place first. The farm sits on a dirt road four miles north of town. A decade earlier, Dirk Krause farmed soybeans, corn and tobacco. But as he got up in years and his capacity for physical labor dwindled, the farm fell to ruin. Instead of taking over the operation, his twin sons, Derek and Drew, let the fields go to shit. They sold the International Harvester tractor—for drug money more than likely—and leased the land to a neighbor. Talk around town is that the two sons, in their twenties now, work just enough to eke by. The brunt of their income is derived from selling crystal meth.

"You really think these losers had something to do with murdering that family?" Pickles asks as I turn the Explorer into the long gravel lane and start toward the house.

"Since we don't have squat as far as suspects, I thought talking to them might be a good starting point."

I park behind a rusty manure spreader surrounded by waist-high yellow grass. To my left, an ancient barn with weathered wood siding and a hail-damaged tin roof leans at a precarious angle. To my right, the house squats on a crumbling foundation like an old man in the throes of a cancerous death. Every window on the north side is broken. The back porch door dangles by a single hinge.

"Good to see they're keeping up the place." I slide out of the Explorer. The buzz of cicadas is deafening in the silence of the old farm.

"Place used to be nice," Pickles grumbles as he gets out. "Looks like a goddamn junkyard now."

"Except for that." I point.

In stark contrast, a brand new fourteen-by-sixty trailer home with a satellite dish and living room extension perches on an old concrete foundation. A bright red barbecue grill lies on its side outside the front door, ashes and chunks of charcoal spilling onto the grass. A few feet away, four metal chairs and a brand-new cooler form a semicircle. A white Ford F-150 gleams beneath the carport. I think of a pistol in the hands of a paranoid meth freak and find myself hoping neither man is crazy enough to shoot at a cop.

"Looks like someone's home," Pickles says.

"Let's do some rattling." I start for the trailer.

I've had a couple of run-ins with the Krause brothers in the three years I've been chief. I arrested Derek twice, once on a drunk and disorderly charge after a fight broke out at the Brass Rail Saloon. He got off with a fine and probation. The second time, however, he did time for assaulting a nineteen-year-old woman, beating her so severely she had to be hospitalized. I witnessed some of the assault and happily testified against him. I've kept my doors locked and my sidearm handy since he was released last spring.

I've never arrested Drew, but I know him by reputation. I pulled his sheet before leaving the station. He did time at Mansfield for possession of meth with intent to sell. No arrests since, but as far as I know he's just been lucky. I'm pretty sure both men are in the drug business up to their hairy armpits.

The curtains at the window move as I climb the steel stairs. Standing to one side—in case whoever's inside thinks I'm a space alien and decides to shoot me through the door—I knock on the storm door. My right hand rests on the .38 in my holster. I'm aware of Pickles behind me, his breathing slightly elevated. I can feel the adrenaline coming off both of us.

The door swings open, and I find myself looking at a chest the size of an SUV, DD cups and enough hair to make a fucking coat. I have to look up to meet his gaze.

"Derek Krause?" I recognize him, but I ask anyway.

"Who wants to know?"

His eyes are frighteningly bloodshot. His breath smells like week-old roadkill. The body odor that wafts up from beneath his armpits is strong enough to make my eyes water. "The police." I show him my badge.

"Oh, it's you." He looks past me at Pickles and smirks. "What'd you do? Raid the fuckin' old folks home?"

Pickles offers a harsh laugh. I don't take my eyes off of Krause. "I need to ask you some questions."

He looks down at me as if considering ramming his fist through my skull.

"Step outside," I say.

"You got some kind of warrant?"

"We just want to ask—"

"Then I ain't steppin' nowhere."

My teeth grind. Behind me, Pickles swears. I raise my hand slightly to silence him. "We just want to talk to you."

Derek tries to close the door. I ram my boot into the space. "Get out here and talk to us, or I'm going to come back with a warrant and tear this place apart."

"I didn't do nothin'."

"Nobody said you did."

He shoves open the door. I step back just in time to avoid getting hit in the face with it. "Down there." I point to the base of the trailer steps.

Sighing, he shoves past me. I glance at Pickles. He points covertly at his gun and raises his brows. *You want me to shoot him?* That makes me smile.

"What do you guys want with me?" Krause asks, shuffling down the steps.

I follow, hoping he's not in the mood to fight because he's huge. Two-fifty. Six-four. The last kind of guy I want to get into a scuffle with. "Where were you last night?" I begin.

"Here."

"Can anyone collaborate that?"

"My dog."

"Someone who can talk?" Pickles spits out his toothpick.

Derek sneers at him. "No."

I motion toward his vehicle. "Nice truck. Yours?"

He turns his attention to me. "It gets me around."

"Where do you work?"

"Farnhall."

Farnhall is a manufacturing firm in Millersburg that makes oil filters. "What do you do there?"

"I work on the line." Another sigh that reminds me of a bored teen-ager. "What's this all about?"

"Do you know the Plank family?"

"Never heard of no Planks."

"Where was your brother last night?"

"Dunno."

Now it's my turn to sigh. "Derek, come on. Work with me."

"Look, I ain't his fuckin' keeper, all right?"

"Was he home?"

"Yeah, he was here."

"What time?"

He lifts a big shoulder, lets it drop. "Eight. Nine o'clock."

"Which was it?"

"I don't know."

Pickles mutters a word that sounds like *dipshit*.

Krause looks over the top of my head at Pickles and snarls. "At least I'm not half senile like you, old man."

"That's enough," I snap. "Why aren't you at work today?"

"I'm sick, man. Got a stomachache."

"You don't look sick."

His massive shoulders lift, then drop. "Well, I am. Had the squirts all morning."

I raise my hands to shut him up. "Where's your brother now?"

Derek looks away. "Dunno."

"He's on probation, isn't he?" I know he is, but I pose the question, anyway.

His gaze goes wary. "I guess."

"Look, I can make this easy. Or we can do it hard. It's going to be a lot better for both of you if you cooperate. Now where is he?"

"He's at the bar, man. He's not s'posed to be, so cut him some slack, will you?"

"If he didn't do anything wrong, I don't have a beef with him."

"You cops always got a beef with us." Shaking his head, he puts his hands on his hips. "Can I go now?"

"Don't leave town."

"Fuckin' cops." Turning away, he slogs up the steps and disappears into the trailer.

I look at Pickles. "Nice young man."

Pickles grins. "You think he's scary, you should see his mama."

"Big lady, huh?"

"No, just hairier."

There is an underground society that runs beneath the Norman Rockwell–façade of most small towns, and Painters Mill is no exception. While regular folks are working at their jobs, paying their bills and raising their families, others are selling drugs, getting high and generally leading lives of crime.

In Painters Mill, the Brass Rail Saloon is the heart of that underground, and it's the first stop on my list after Pickles and I leave the Krause place. I'm surprised to see the parking lot half full. Then it strikes me that the Farnhall plant's first shift lets out at four o'clock. It's a quarter past, so the booze is just beginning to flow. Tongues will be loosened. Inhibitions will wane. Drugs will be snorted, swallowed, injected, bought and sold. We're right on time.

I park next to a vintage VW with a bumper sticker that reads: *If you don't like my driving call 1-800-EAT-SHIT.* In the back of my mind, I hear the clock ticking down those crucial first forty-eight hours. The passage of time taunts me. The Planks have been dead for over fourteen hours now and still I have nothing.

"So is Drew as big as his brother?" I ask Pickles as we get out of the Explorer.

"No, but he's a mean son of a bitch."

"Terrific."

"Smells better, though."

"Something to look forward to."

Ten yards from the entrance, I feel the bass rumble of rock music vibrating beneath my feet. I push open the door and we step inside. The place is as dark and dank as an underground cave. I look up, half expecting to see bats hanging from the ceiling. Cigarette smoke hovers like fog. On a lighted dance floor a dozen or so bodies undulate to some chainsaw rock music I don't recognize.

My eyes have barely adjusted when Pickles jabs a finger toward the bar. "Speak of the devil," he says.

I follow his point and spot Drew Krause. Pickles was right; he's not as big as his brother. Maybe six feet. One-eighty. He wears faded blue jeans and a navy T-shirt with the phrase *I didn't do it* emblazoned on the front. He looks like a normal guy, enjoying happy hour after a long day. But I learned a long time ago just how deceiving appearances can be. That's particularly true in the drug world.

Leaning against the bar as if he owns the place, he watches Pickles and me approach with the amusement of a parent watching a toddler take his first steps.

"Drew Krause?" I ask.

"Chief Burkholder." He turns his gaze to Pickles. "Officer Shumaker. What a pleasant surprise."

"I bet." I show him my badge.

"What'd I do now?"

"We'd like to talk to you."

Smiling disarmingly, he taps an index finger against the T-shirt. "Can't you guys read?"

I invade his space, letting him know we're serious. "We can do this here or I can embarrass you in front of all your buddies by cuffing you and hauling you down to the station."

"Well, to be honest, I'm not easily embarrassed."

I pull the cuffs from my belt. "Neither am I."

"Hey. Come on." Smiling, he raises his hands. "I'm just kidding around."

"Here's a newsflash for you, slick," Pickles says. "We're not amused."

"I'm getting that." Sobering, he looks from me to Pickles and back to me. "What can I do for you?"

"Where were you last night?" I begin.

He assesses me, a wily teenager poking fun at his clueless, overbearing parents. The bartender moves to within earshot, picking up a glass I know is already dry, and running his dingy towel over it.

"I was here," Drew replies.

"Can someone substantiate that?"

He looks at the bartender. "Hey, Jimmy. Where was I last night?"

The man behind the bar, rail thin and sporting a goatee that's going gray, concentrates on his glass. "You were here, running your mouth and your tab, as usual."

I give Jimmy a hard look, wishing I'd gotten Drew outside where we could be alone with him. Get him out of his element. Away from all his fair-weather friends. If he's the man with the drugs, there's no doubt his regulars would lie, cheat or steal to maintain a steady flow.

I glance at Pickles, lower my voice. "Go talk to the skinny shit behind the bar. I'll take Mr. I-didn't-do-it."

Reaching over a row of shot glasses lined up on the counter, Pickles snags the barkeep's shirt. "C'mere, slick."

I turn my attention back to Krause. "What time were you here?"

"Till closing."

"Were you alone?"

"Just me and about fifty of my closest friends." He makes a sweeping motion that encompasses everyone in the bar.

"Can anyone else vouch for you?" I pull out my notebook. "I want names."

His eyes narrow. "Usually I know why you guys are fuckin' with me. This time, I don't have a clue." He grins. "Whatever you're pissed about, I really *didn't* do it."

Grinding my teeth, I try not to think about the Plank family, their bodies slowly decomposing atop the stainless-steel gurneys at the morgue. "Names. Now."

He rattles off six names. Some I'm familiar with. Some I've never heard before. I plan to contact all of them. Drew had better hope they have good memories. "What time did you arrive?"

"Six or so."

"Did you leave at any time?"

"No, ma'am. I drank. Played some pool. Danced with a couple of chicks. That's it. I swear."

"Do you have a girlfriend?"

"I have a lot of girlfriends."

"Do you know Mary Plank?"

He stares at me, realization dawning. "I know I ain't got the greatest reputation in this town, but I ain't no killer. I didn't have nothing to do with those murders."

"How do you know about the murders?"

"Everyone's talking about it." He grimaces, but it looks rehearsed and insincere. "Look, I didn't have anything to do with that. I don't even know those people. Are you guys fuckin' desperate, or what?"

I get in his face. "That's right. We're desperate. We can make things desperate for you, too, since you're on parole. So if I were you, I'd get real serious about cooperating."

"Okay, okay." For the first time, he appears uncertain. "Look, I got off work around four. Went home to shower and change—"

"Where's home?"

"I live with my brother. On the farm."

"Then what?"

"I came here. Had a few drinks. Stayed until closing."

"Do you know any members of the Plank family?"

"I'm not trying to be a smart-ass or anything, but the Amish and I don't run in the same circles."

"Are any of your drug-dealing buddies whacked out enough to kill an entire family?"

He looks at me as if I've just asked him to chop off his little toe. I know the one thing he won't talk about are his druggie friends. Even among thieves, there is a code of honor. If that's what you want to call it, anyway.

"Look it, I got a job now. I'm legit."

I roll my eyes. "Everyone knows you and your brother are cooking meth at the farm."

"That's bullshit. A bunch of damn rumors from people who don't like us."

"Do yourself a favor and answer the question, Drew. Have you heard anything? Are any of your freaky friends desperate enough to do something like that?"

"I don't have any freaky friends. I'm outta the drug business. I learned my lesson." For the first time he looks rattled. Joe Cool losing his cool.

"You're full of shit." I jab my finger in his shoulder hard enough to send him back a step.

"Hey." He knows I'm daring him to make a move, but he doesn't take the bait. He's too smart to hit a cop.

"What about your brother?" I ask.

"He don't run with the dealers no more, either. I swear."

"Give me a name." I jab his shoulder with my finger again, harder this time. Vaguely, I'm aware people are staring at us. Happy hour revelers giving us a wide berth. "Give me one name."

"I don't know anyone." He takes another step back. "Not even the hard-core guys would do something like that. Seven people? And for what? Fifty bucks? No way."

He's right, but I'm not ready to let him off the hook. I have a particularly strong dislike for drug dealers. "Don't leave town, Drew."

"I didn't do anything wrong."

"Sooner or later, you will." I step closer and whisper. "When you do, I'll be waiting."

His face darkens. A tick quivers beneath his right cheekbone. In that instant, I catch a glimpse of the man beneath the I'm-just-a-farm-boy façade, and I know that if I didn't have a badge and a gun he'd wrap his fingers around my neck and kill me with his bare hands.

I smile at him. "See you around."

His cheek quivers; he doesn't smile back.

As I walk away, I hear him mutter something nasty about Amish cops behind my back. Pickles starts toward him, but I snag his jacket and keep him with me. "Let it go."

"I don't like that son of a bitch's mouth," he grumbles.

"Don't worry, Pickles. If either of the Krause boys had anything to do with this, they'll get what's coming to them even if I have to dish it out myself."

CHAPTER 9

Neither Painters Mill nor Millersburg have a morgue per se, so when an autopsy is required, bodies are transported to Pomerene Hospital in Millersburg, which has morgue facilities and now receives funding from two neighboring counties.

It's nearly six P.M. when I pull into the lot and park illegally in the emergency parking area. I'm hyperaware of the passage of time as I stride through the glass doors. The day is nearly gone and I've accomplished only a fraction of what I'd intended. I'd planned to speak to the manager at the tourist shop where Mary Plank worked, but I got tied up with other things and now it will have to wait until tomorrow.

A young African-American man waves at me from the information desk as I pass. I return the wave and head directly to the elevator that will take me to the basement. I've visited this part of the hospital more times than I want to recall in the last year. I keep hoping I'll get used to the sights and smells of death, but I don't think I ever will.

The elevator doors whisper open and I step into a hushed tiled hall. I pass a yellow and black biohazard sign and a plaque that reads: *Morgue Authorized Personnel.* At the end of the hall, I push open dual swinging doors and find myself in yet another hall. A middle-aged woman in a red power suit looks up from her computer when I enter. "Chief Burkholder?"

"Yes." I extend my hand and we shake.

"Doc Coblentz is expecting you."

The nameplate on her desk tells me her name is Carmen Anderson. "You must be his new assistant."

"I'm part of the new budget. Started last Tuesday."

I glance toward the door that will take me to the morgue foyer. "Hell of a way to start your first week."

"Doc says it's the first time he's had a full house since that semi hit that family out on the highway three years ago." She grimaces. "You guys know who did it yet?"

"We're working on it." I motion toward the door. "Is the tech still here?"

"Oh, yeah." She smiles. "Cute kid. He ought to be on soaps instead of hanging out with a bunch of dead people."

I feel a tad more upbeat as I go through the swinging doors. The autopsy room is straight ahead. To my right is a small alcove where the doc stores supplies, including biohazard protection. To my left, I see Doc Coblentz's glassed-in office. As usual, the mini-blinds are open. He's sitting at his desk. A young man wearing lavender scrubs sits in the visitor chair jotting notes on a chart. Both men look up as I cross to the office door.

Rising, Doc Coblentz extends his hand. "Chief Burkholder."

The technician stands. The receptionist is right; he's cute. And he looks young enough to be in high school. Or maybe I'm just getting older. "I'm Dr. Rohrbacher," he says.

"You look too young to be a doctor," I comment.

"I get that a lot." He offers a Whitestrip smile. "I always tell people I began my residency when I was fourteen."

"The real Doogie Howser." I smile back, but it feels stiff on my face. My mind has already strayed to the dead family in the next room and the chore ahead. "You guys have anything for me?"

"We've completed two of the autopsies." Rising, Doc Coblentz motions toward the hall. "You know the drill."

I go directly to the alcove and don the requisite disposable shoe covers, a blue gown, hair cap, and latex gloves. The men, gowned, gloved and capped, are waiting for me when I emerge.

"You'll have to excuse the mess," Doc Coblentz says as we move down the hall. "We finally got budget approved for fresh paint."

At the end of the hall, I notice the stepladder, drop cloth and institutional blue paint. "I like the blue better than the gray," I say.

"It's supposed to be a calming color." Coblentz pushes open the swinging doors.

I don't feel very calm as we enter the autopsy room. It's one place most cops go to great lengths to avoid. When I worked homicide in Columbus, I saw more than one veteran detective ralph his breakfast or break down and cry. Tough guys who would rather shoot themselves in the leg than display any kind of perceived weakness. My own response to death is visceral and more emotional than physical, especially when it comes to murder. I can only describe it as an intense feeling of outrage and a sense of indignation that burrows under my skin like some giant parasite. No matter how hard I try to keep those emotions at bay, they dog me day and night until the case is solved.

Ensconced in gray ceramic tile, the autopsy room is maintained at a cool sixty-two degrees. Though the ventilation and air-conditioning system is state of the art, the smells of formalin and decaying flesh are ever-present. Stark fluorescent light rains down on seven stainless-steel gurneys, all of which are occupied.

"We didn't have enough gurneys for all the bodies, so we had to borrow from another department," the doc comments as we enter.

Stainless-steel counters line three walls. I see white plastic buckets, trays filled with instruments I don't want to think about, and two deep sinks with tall, arcing faucets. A scale, similar to the kind you see at the grocery store for weighing produce, hangs above the counter to my left. It seems obscenely out of place here.

I'm not exactly sure why I do this to myself, this revisiting of the dead. There *is* some information a cop gleans from seeing a body up close and personal, but most truly useful information comes from the autopsy report. Still, I come here. I pay final homage. Maybe I do it because seeing the victims reminds me that there are real people behind every crime. I work for them now.

Two of the gurneys stand separate from the other five. I see a dark stain on the sheet cover, and I know those are the two autopsies that have been completed. "Which vics are finished?" I ask.

The technician looks at his clipboard. "Bonnie Plank. And Mary Plank."

"Did you get slugs?" I ask.

Rohrbacher nods. "Dug one out of the mother. It was pretty wrecked, but I sent it to the lab."

"You check for gunshot residue on the adult male?"

"We sent the clothing and skin surface residue to the lab. Should know something in a few days."

Doc Coblentz crosses to the nearest gurney and pulls down the sheet. Mary Plank's body looms into view. She's lying supine. A slender-limbed girl who had once been pretty. Her face is gray now. My gaze drifts to her mouth. It's slack and partially open, exposing straight, white teeth. Her left hand hangs limp over the side of the gurney.

I force my gaze to the rest of her body. The Y-incision is ghastly beneath the bright lights, the dark stitches running like tiny railroad tracks over pale flesh.

I move closer to the gurney. "Cause of death?"

"She bled to death." Using a long, cotton-tipped swab, Doc Coblenz indicates the wound on her lower abdomen. "Her uterus was removed."

Shock tears through me, like fabric being torn violently in half. "He cut it out?"

"Hacked is a better term. Cutting was extremely primitive. There was severe internal bleeding. She went into shock and ultimately expired from cardiac arrest."

"Why would he do that?"

Doc Coblentz looks at me over the tops of his glasses, and I sense he's about to fling something terrible my way. "Upon internal examination, we noticed what was left of the cervix was bluish in color, which is a sign of pregnancy, so we ran a few routine blood tests," he says. "This girl was pregnant."

"Pregnant?" Shock rattles through me, a punch that hits close to home and sinks in deep. Mary Plank was fifteen years old. She was Amish and unmarried. Premarital sex is rare among Amish teens, but it happens. They're human beings; they make mistakes. They keep secrets. I know this secret would have borne a terrible weight.

My own past sweeps unbidden through my mind, a rogue wave churning with murky silt and debris. I know intimately what it's like to be young and Amish and different. I remember the isolation and loneliness and the crushing weight of shame secrets can bring down on young shoulders. And I know that in the weeks before Mary's death, she would have suffered great emotional stress.

For a moment I'm so profoundly stricken, I can't speak. All I can think is poor, poor child.

"Kate?"

Giving myself a mental shake, I force my mind back to the matter at hand. I recall Bishop Troyer telling me that Bonnie Plank had wanted to speak to him about Mary. Had Bonnie known about her daughter's pregnancy? No one I spoke to remembered a boyfriend. Who fathered the child? Did Mary have a lover? Was she raped and never reported it? Even to her family or bishop?

"How far along was she?" I ask.

"Without the fetus, there's no way to tell."

"Did anyone find the missing uterus?"

"Not that I'm aware of." He looks at me over the tops of his glasses. "Once we realized she was pregnant, we took vaginal swabs, cervical swabs and did what's called a vaginal wash. On the outside chance she'd had *recent* sexual intercourse, Jason prepared a wet-mount slide."

"I don't know what that is," I say.

"The wet-mount slide revealed that she had live sperm in her vagina."

All I can think is that we now have DNA. "So she was raped and he didn't use a condom?"

"I don't think so. Most of these sperm were immobile. I would guess they were over forty-eight hours old."

Surprise lands another hard blow. "I didn't realize sperm could live that long."

"They can survive up to about seventy-two hours."

I blink at him, confused. "So she had sex or was raped well before the murders?"

"Correct."

I look from man to man. "Was she raped?"

Doc Coblentz shrugs. "There was no vaginal tearing or bruising of the pubis. Of course, that's not definitive proof it wasn't forcible rape. But there were no visible signs."

My gaze darts to Rohrbacher. "At least now we have DNA." I can't keep the optimism from my voice. This development could break the case wide open. "I'll have BCI check CODIS." CODIS is the acronym for the FBI's Combined DNA Index System. Beginning in 1994, DNA samples of offenders were taken and entered into a database. If the semen retrieved from Mary Plank's body is from an identified past offender, the FBI analyst may be able to match it with a name.

"How long will it take?" the doc asks.

"I'm not sure. A few days maybe. But if this guy's in the system, we'll have a name."

The possibility bolsters me. But I know if the DNA is not in the system we'll be back at square one. I look again at the girl's body. So young and with so many secrets. I wish I didn't know what that was like, but I do. And I feel a hell of a lot more than I should. I know what it's like to be part of a close-knit group, to desperately want to belong, only to be held apart by secrets.

"Any hair or fibers on any of the bodies?" I ask.

He nods. "Both. We sent everything to BCI."

If any of the hairs found are from the offender and include an intact root, we could have a second source of DNA. One more nail in the bastard's coffin. "What about Bonnie Plank?" I ask.

Rohrbacher replaces the sheet. Doc Coblentz shuffles to the second gurney. "She died from a single penetrating gunshot wound to the mid-back area. The bullet transected the lower cervical and upper thoracic spinal cord."

"She died instantly?"

"Correct." He pulls down the sheet. For a moment the only sound comes from the buzzing of the fluorescent lights and the hard thump of my heart. Bonnie Plank is a plump woman with ample body fat and breasts that sag to the left and right of her ribcage. The Y-incision has been stitched, but she hasn't yet been cleaned up. Her head is turned slightly to one side, and I see a blood smear on her neck. Several red droplets stain the sheet.

When I close my eyes, I can still see the image of her lying in the grass, clutching the baby. She'd been running away. They shot her in the back. *Who were you running from?*

"Any sign of sexual assault?" I ask.

"No."

At least she hadn't had to endure the final insult of a rape. "What about the baby, Doc?"

He grimaces. "The baby was killed by the same bullet that killed his mother. I won't have COD on the child until I complete the autopsy."

"Do you have anything preliminary on the adult male and two boys?"

"It appears all three suffered gunshot wounds to the head. They appear to be fatal wounds." He replaces the sheet, covering Bonnie Plank's body. "Dr. Rohrbacher and I are going to work through the night, Kate. We'll finish late tonight. I should have a full report late tomorrow."

"Thanks, Doc."

I'm ready to leave. The smell of death and the things I've seen and heard have torn down what little optimism I've been able to muster. But I have one more question that must be answered before I can go. "The killer made a half-hearted effort to make these killings look like a murder-suicide. Can you tell me definitively that Amos Plank's gunshot was not self-inflicted?"

He crosses to another gurney and lowers the sheet. Amos Plank's face is colorless. His lips are stretched taut over broken teeth. His tongue looks like a cut of meat that's been dropped into a blender.

Coblentz indicates the mouth area with the swab, then defers to his counterpart. "Dr. Rohrbacher?"

The young doctor looks at the body the way a bright student might look at some fascinating science project. "The bullet entered the skull through the mouth."

"That's consistent with suicide, isn't it?" I ask.

"That's correct," he concedes. "But the trajectory path of the bullet is not consistent with a self-inflicted wound." As if handling a piece of fragile porcelain, the doctor places his hands on either side of the head and turns it slightly so that the back of Amos Plank's head is visible. "The bullet exited here."

The exit wound is jagged and large and is located just a few inches above the neck. The flesh has begun to deteriorate, the edges turning red-brown. I can see white chips of bone inside the wound. "The bullet shattered the C1 vertebra as it left the body."

"Can you clarify that for me?"

"The trajectory is at a slightly downward angle. With a suicide, the trajectory is usually upward. The bullet would pass through either the parietal or occipital lobe and exit the rear of the skull. Autopsy will be more definitive, but I would say whoever shot this man was above him. This victim was probably kneeling, the shooter standing, therefore the bullet angled down, shattered the spinal cord at C1 and exited high on the neck."

"I concur." Doc Coblentz takes off his glasses. "Combined with the bruising on the wrists, we're going to rule the manner of death a homicide."

Though I had anticipated this, I'm still shocked by the images running through my mind. Amos Plank kneeling. A killer standing over him, holding a gun in the Amish man's mouth. An execution-style murder is unfathomable. But for someone to be cold enough to look into another human being's eyes and pull the trigger is pure, unadulterated evil.

CHAPTER 10

Dusk falls softly in October. The hard glare of the afternoon sun acquiesces to the cool hush of the night layer by layer. Darkness will not arrive peacefully tonight. Sitting at my computer in my cramped office at the station, I watch a bank of storm clouds to the west steal the final snatches of light from the horizon. Lightning flickers, outlining the silhouettes of massive thunderheads. I feel a storm of a different nature roiling inside me.

The Plank family has been dead for about eighteen hours. I should be relieved Mary Plank's autopsy uncovered evidence that could conceivably solve the case. Once DNA is extracted and CODIS comes back, we could have a name. I can't quiet the nagging voice in my head telling me it's not going to be that easy.

In order for CODIS to spit out a name, the perpetrator must already be in the system. He must have been arrested at some point in his lifetime. And the data must have been entered into the database, which doesn't always happen. What if he's got a previously clean record?

Of course the DNA and fibers will help me build a case, particularly if we make the arrest and it goes to trial. But if I've learned anything in my years of law enforcement, it's that nothing ever gets handed to you. We're a long way from making an arrest. I don't even have a suspect yet. That salient responsibility falls heavy on my shoulders tonight.

I spoke to the crime scene tech earlier and asked him to be on the lookout for Mary Plank's missing uterus. If there's a fetus inside, we might be able to extract paternal DNA. The tech said he would get a septic tank company out there tomorrow to check the lines and tank, in case it was flushed down the toilet. I'll have my own officers do a more thorough search of the grounds. But the small body part could be anywhere.

I should go home, eat a decent meal, and get some rest. The days and weeks ahead promise to be long and grueling. But I know I won't sleep tonight. Not when I have a dead family on my hands and a mass murderer running loose in my town.

Grabbing my jacket and keys, I leave my office. My newly hired second-shift dispatcher, a young woman who just had her twenty-first birthday, sits at the dispatch-switchboard station filing her nails. "Calling it a day, Chief?"

Jodie Metzger is blond and pretty and came with not one, but four glowing recommendations. Of course all of them were from men. I have a feeling those big baby blues had more to do with it than her typing speed or organizational skills. But I do my best to keep my preconceived notions in check. As long as she shows up on time, and does a good job with the phones and radio, I'm willing to give her a chance.

"I'm going to head out to the Plank farm," I tell her.

"All by yourself?" She gives me an I-wouldn't-be-caught-dead-out-there look. "Radio says we've got heavy weather on the way."

"Hopefully, I'll beat the storm."

"It's going to be kind of scary with no lights."

"I'll try not to scare anyone." Smiling, I yank open the door. "See you tomorrow."

Though the storm hasn't yet arrived, the wind has kicked up. Leaves skitter like crabs across the sidewalk as I cross to the Explorer. I can smell the rain and blowing dust now. I hope the storm holds off long enough for me to reach the farm.

I keep an eye on the sky as I head out of town. The first fat drops splat on the windshield as I turn into the lane of the Plank farm. The slow-moving-vehicle sign mounted on the rear of the buggy reflects my headlights as I park. I'm surprised to find the CSU van gone. I was hoping to speak to the techs before they called it a day. Hopefully, I'll have their report on my desk first thing in the morning.

Lightning splits the sky as I grab my Maglite and take the sidewalk to the back door. On the porch, crime scene tape flutters in the wind. The bloodstains are still there, but I know they'll soon be washed away by the rain. Ducking under the tape, I use the key and step inside.

The smell of death lingers. I shine my light around the kitchen. Smudges of gray-black soot from the fingerprint powder cover the countertops, the cabinets, the table and the sink. Several drawers stand partially open. Someone tracked mud onto a braided rug. I think of Bonnie Plank, and I wonder how many times she scolded her children for the same offense.

Outside, thunder rumbles with enough gusto to rattle the windows. Inside, the house is as still and silent as an underwater cave. I know this isn't the ideal time for a look around, after dark, when I can't see shit. But I know more about the Plank family now. Specifically, I know more about Mary. A young girl with a big secret and a host of problems that secret would have brought down on her life. That's when I realize her bedroom is the room I want to search again.

Standing in the darkened kitchen, I think about what might have happened the night of the murders. Had it been dark like this when the killer arrived? Had the Plank family already turned in for the night? Or had the house been lit with the glow of lantern light? Since most dairy operators rise as early as four A.M., they go to bed early.

"The Planks were in bed," I say aloud.

The mind of a killer is a dark, malignant place, viscous with a cancer of black thoughts and secret hungers most people can't imagine. A place most people don't want to conceive of because they'd never see the world in the same light. Getting inside a place like that is akin to climbing into a crypt and snuggling up with a decaying body. Still, I open that door and step inside. I conjure thoughts I hope will tell me who and why and how.

Lightning flashes, illuminating the kitchen for a split second. I shine my beam on the back door and wonder where the killer entered. There was no sign of forced entry. Did the Planks lock their doors? Or did someone let him in? Someone who knew him?

The killer enters through the unlocked back door. He's got a gun and a flashlight. He carries a coil of speaker wire in his pocket. He wears gloves. All of it shows intent, premeditation. He's scared, but driven— and excited. He knows what he wants, what he must do. He wishes for light, but compensates for the lack of it. Is he alone?

He moves through the kitchen and into the living room. His heart rate is up; he's breathing hard. Lots of adrenaline. Is he here to steal? Or is he here to kill?

He travels up the stairs, silent and slow. The first bedroom belongs to the parents. He rouses them from a deep sleep. He holds the gun on Mrs. Plank to keep Amos under control. He binds the Amish man's wrists first; he's the biggest threat. He binds Bonnie's hands next. The baby, little Amos, sleeps in his cradle beside the bed. Neither Bonnie nor Amos understands what the killer wants. They don't know he's going to kill them.

How does he keep them under control while he wakes and ties up the rest of the family? Does he threaten them with the gun? Does he have an accomplice? The questions come at me in a barrage, but I have no answers.

I slink back into the dark cavern of his mind, and I see him move to the next room. Ten-year-old David and fourteen-year-old Mark. He rouses them from sleep. The boys are confused and disoriented as he binds their hands behind their back. Amish children are taught to respect and obey adults. They wouldn't have put up a fight; they would have listened to him because the killer is an adult.

Sixteen-year-old Annie's room is next. Like the boys, she's frightened and disoriented. He binds her hands and moves on to Mary's room down the hall, rouses her from sleep. He's thinking about other things now. The girls. Pretty and young and innocent. Does their fear excite him? Does he see them as objects? Are they the reason he's here?

He herds all of them down the stairs. Does he carry the baby himself? No. The child is nothing but an annoying object to him. Does he leave the baby alone in the cradle? No. Bonnie died with the baby in her arms. The baby is *crying*. To shut it up, the killer unties Bonnie and lets her pick him up, carry him downstairs.

"Why did you come here?" I wonder aloud.

Did he plan to kill the entire family from the beginning? Some of them? Rape the girls? Did he wear a mask? Or did he kill them because they could identify him?

Downstairs. In the dark. A flashlight and a gun. Amos would sense what the killer had planned for the girls by now. He would be terrified, agitated, prepared to defend his family. But it's too late for that; his hands are bound. Amos tries to fight, so the killer forces the man to kneel, shoves the gun into his mouth and pulls the trigger. An explosion of blood. The violence begins. Horror. Death.

Panic fills the house now. Screaming. Bonnie goes to her husband. Touches him. She gets blood on her hands. The baby crying. The killer points the gun at the baby. *Shut him up!* Bonnie scoops him into her arms and runs, leaving the bloody handprint on the back door. Death chases her. A bullet in her back. She falls in the grass and mother and child die as one.

Three down. Four to go.

Screams echo throughout the house. The killer wants the girls now. Two more shots and the boys are gone. The girls scream and cry. They know what's next, only they don't. Why did he take them to the barn? He didn't. The girls break free. Run for their lives. Hands bound and barefooted, they can't outrun him. The screaming scares the killer. If someone hears them . . .

The killer follows them to the barn. Where are his tools? In his vehicle. The tools are evidence of premeditation. He came here not only to kill, but to rape and torture. Live out his darkest fantasies.

He catches them in the barn. Bound and terrified, the girls are easy to overpower. He chooses the tack room because there are no windows. No one will hear them scream.

The images running through my head offend me. Sweat breaks out on the back of my neck. It's a cop-out, but I can't think about the rest, and I climb out of that fetid place, back into my own mind.

I'm still shaking when I traverse the kitchen and enter the living room. Crepuscular light slants in from the two windows. I can make out the silhouette of a wooden bench. A low table where a solitary lantern sits cold and dark. I sweep my beam around the room. Three pools of blood mar the floor like dull black mats. My heart skips a beat when I sense movement to my left. I jerk my beam toward it, but it's only the curtains billowing in the wind. One of the technicians probably opened a window for fresh air.

I close and lock the window, then turn to face the room. I train my light on the pools of blood. I think of the dead children, and I know this house had once been full of light and chaos and life. Most Amish homes are welcoming, warm and loving; the family is a tightly knit unit. Of course, I didn't know the Planks. I don't know if their lives were happy or sad or someplace in between. The one thing I do know is that they didn't deserve to die.

Rain taps on the windows like impatient fingers as I take the stairs to the second level. I find myself thinking of Mary Plank as I walk down the narrow hall. So young and pretty. I think of her pregnancy. The fact that she had recently engaged in sexual relations. I wonder who she was seeing. I wonder if that relationship or her pregnancy had anything to do with the murder of her family. It wouldn't be the first time a reluctant father-to-be killed his pregnant girlfriend. The legal age of consent in Ohio is sixteen years old. Mary was fifteen. If her lover was an adult male, he could be charged with statutory rape. But is that motive enough to wipe out an entire family? No matter how hard I try, I can't get my mind around that.

And what about the torture aspect of the crime? In that moment, the realization that there's more to this than I'm seeing strikes a blow. A statutory rape charge isn't motive enough to wipe out an entire family. It doesn't explain the slaughter of two young women. I'm missing *something*. Something truly, stunningly evil. But what? It's like having a word you've been trying to remember all day on the tip of your tongue.

My mind rewinds, takes me back to the crime scene in the barn. I'm moving through the murk and into the tack room. I see the girls strung up like ghastly puppets. I see the tools the killer left behind. My mind's eye stops on the scuff marks left on the dusty floor. Everything inside me stops, focuses on those three small marks, and I know they are somehow meaningful. But how?

The possibilities niggle my brain as I take the hall to Mary's bedroom. It's a small space containing a single chest of drawers, a night table, and two narrow beds draped with intricate quilts. A plain dress and two *kapps* hang on wooden dowels mounted on the wall between the beds.

The chance of my finding anything useful tonight is slim. It's dark and the house has already been thoroughly searched. On the other hand, the parents' bedroom, kitchen and living room were the main focus of our earlier searches. No one had known about Mary Plank's pregnancy. I can't help but wonder: *How thoroughly was her room searched?*

Crossing to the window, I part the curtains and look out. The rain is coming down in earnest now. Water streams down the glass in a kaleidoscopic waterfall. The dormer window looks out over the tin roof of the front porch. Having been a mischievous teenager myself, I notice how easy it would be to sneak out the window. I check the lock, find it secure. When I shine my light on the sill, I'm shocked to see that the window is nailed shut. Had someone been coming to Mary's window? Or were the nails a father's effort to keep his daughter from venturing out? Whatever the case, the nails tell me the parents knew something was going on.

The generator has been removed from the scene, so I go back downstairs. I grab the battery-powered work light, lug it up the stairs to Mary's room and set it up on the chest of drawers. Donning latex gloves, I begin my search with the night table. In the top drawer, I find two Bibles, an ancient tome titled *Martyrs Mirror,* which is a record of persecutions suffered by European Anabaptists during the Reformation era. In the second drawer I find a hairbrush and comb. A *kapp* in need of mending. I smile when I see the mirror. Young Amish girls are no different than other girls when it comes to adolescent vanity. In some of the more conservative Amish homes, mirrors are forbidden. I wonder if Mary's parents knew about this one.

The night table nets nothing of interest so I move to the chest. I find boys' trousers with tears and holes that need mending. Underclothes. A baseball and well-used glove in the bottom drawer.

"Where did you keep your secrets?" I say aloud.

It's been a long time since I was a teenager. But I remember what it was like. The awkwardness. The longing for things I didn't understand, most of which I knew I could never have. Like Mary, I had secrets, and those secrets caused me untold agony. It's the loneliest feeling in the world to so desperately need the love and support of your family, and feel as if you don't deserve it.

I go to the bed. It's unmade, the covers turned down and rumpled. A faceless doll with blond curls lies facedown next to the pillow. I wonder if Mary tossed it aside when she was roused from bed by her killer. I pick up the doll and an overwhelming sadness engulfs me. Amish dolls are faceless because in the Bible, in Exodus and Deuteronomy, graven images are forbidden.

I set the doll against the pillow. Lifting one side of the mattress, I feel around, but find nothing. At the second bed, I do the same. Nothing hidden beneath the mattress. I'm probably wasting my time; frustration grinds inside me. Kneeling, I lift the quilt for a quick look beneath the bed. My beam reveals a lone sock surrounded by a dust bunny the size of my fist. I'm about to straighten when a flash of lightning brightens my view. In that instant of light, I notice one of the floorboards sticks up a scant quarter inch higher than the rest.

"What the hell?" Reaching beneath the bed, I pry at the oak plank with my fingers. Surprise ripples through me when it lifts easily. Using my shoulder, I shove the bed over a couple of feet. My pulse spikes when I see the hiding place—and the small book staring up at me. I should photograph it before moving it, but I don't have the camera with me, and I don't want to wait. I reach for the book.

It's a homemade journal, about six inches square and an inch thick.

The front and back covers are made of pink construction paper. Glued to the front cover is a slightly smaller swath of contrasting pink felt upon which the white lace cutout of a sheep is secured. Three holes have been punched along the left side. The paper is secured with pink ribbons tied into neat bows at each hole. The book is meticulously made by caring hands and with much attention to detail.

I open the journal. It's filled with lined notebook paper, the kind any kid would have at school, that's been painstakingly cut to fit inside. The words *Mary's Journal* are written in slanted cursive with blue ink. I turn the page and read.

May 19

I saw HIM today at the shop when Mamm *and I went to deliver the quilts. My heart was pounding so hard I thought I would faint. My legs were shaking so badly* Mamm *asked me if I was cold. I don't understand myself. He is not Amish. I should not be having these feelings. . . .*

May 24

He spoke to me today. Just to say hello, but my poor heart didn't know that. I could not look at him. Mamm *and I were delivering the second quilt (the green baby quilt I love). How I hated to see that quilt go. I felt as if I were giving away my own child! But I know some loving* mamm *will give it a good home, and it will be used to wrap a well-loved baby.*

May 29

I volunteered to stock candies this morning. Not for the money, but because if I work over six hours, I get a lunch break. I can go to the park, and I know he will be there. I feel terribly guilty for that. I know my feelings are wrong. Against the will of my parents. Maybe against God's will, too. But I wonder . . . how can something that feels so wonderful be bad?

I stare down at the words, aware of my heart drumming against my breastbone. Who is *he*? The father of her unborn child? Does she reveal anything about him at some later point in the journal? Realizing I need to take it with me and read it from cover to cover, I rise and scoot the bed back into place. I'm midway to the door when my cell phone trills.

"Chief, it's Glock."

"How's the canvassing going?"

"We finished half an hour ago. I wanted to let you know Dick Flatter and his wife remember seeing a truck they didn't recognize out on Township Road 16 last night."

Township Road 16 is a dirt track that runs along the north side of the Plank farm. "What kind of truck?"

"He couldn't recall. Said it was dark in color. Didn't know the make. He remembered it because he's pretty sure it doesn't belong to any of the neighbors."

"A make would have been nice."

"That would make our jobs way too easy." He pauses. "You want me to give BCI a call and ask for a list of dark pickup trucks registered in Holmes and Coshocton counties?"

"I'll call them."

"Anything new on your end?"

I tell him about the Mary Plank's pregnancy.

"That's a stunner. I mean, she was Amish and pretty young."

My own past flashes in the periphery of my mind, but I shove it aside. "Unusual, but not unheard of. Get this: she had live sperm inside her body."

"So we have DNA?"

"Going to take a few days. The BCI lab has to run it through CODIS. If our guy is a past offender, we'll have a name."

"If he doesn't have a record, we're fucked."

I look at the journal in my hand. "I was looking around out here and found a journal in the girl's room."

"A journal? Like a diary? Whose is it?"

"It's Mary's. She's at that age. You know, wants to write everything down."

"Never went through that stage."

"Might be a girl thing." I sigh. "I'm going to take it home and see if she names a boyfriend."

"The pregnancy kind of changes things, doesn't it? Guy doesn't want a kid, so he offs his girlfriend."

"I think there's more to it, Glock. Not enough motive there to slaughter an entire family. And it doesn't explain the torture."

"Some things just don't make sense no matter how you cut it. Maybe this guy's a psycho. Went berserk."

I consider asking him for his opinion on the scuff marks in the barn, but realize it's probably better to sleep on it and brainstorm in the morning when we're fresh. I sigh. "You heading home?"

"On my way there now."

"See you in the morning."

I disconnect and stand there for a moment, listening to the storm. I should be thinking about the case, but as I descend the stairs, it's John Tomasetti who dominates my thoughts. I should have let Glock call BCI. But I know why I didn't, and I'm not proud of my motivations.

By the time I reach the living room, I'm dialing his cell phone number. He picks up on the fourth ring, sounding distracted. "It's Kate." Pause. "Are you in the middle of something?"

"Nothing you can't drag me away from. How's the investigation coming along?"

I recap everything I learned from Doc Coblentz. "One of the neighbors recalls seeing a dark pickup near the Plank farm the night of the murders. I was wondering if you could do me a favor and get me the names of people in Holmes and Coshocton counties who own a dark pickup truck."

"Worth a shot. Make? Model? Year?"

"I don't know. I thought we'd start with blue and black."

"Well, that narrows it down."

I'm crossing the threshold into the kitchen when outside the window a flash of lightning turns night into day. Shock freezes me in place when I see the silhouette of a person standing outside the back door. Snapping the phone closed, I shine my light on the window. At first I think the BCI technician is returning from a late dinner break. But the instant my light hits the glass, the silhouette darts away.

Shoving the phone into my pocket, I lunge toward the door, yank it open. Thunder cracks like a gunshot as I step outside. Rain slashes down. I see the shadow of my Explorer. The silhouette of the buggy. Then out of the corner of my eye, I see movement to my right. I turn, catch a glimpse of a figure running across the yard.

"Stop!" I call out. "Police! Stop!"

The figure doesn't stop.

In the next instant, I'm bounding off the porch, sprinting toward him. Rain stings my face. Streaming bullets of water blind me as I run across the side yard. A flicker of lightning illuminates a white rail fence ahead and a cornfield beyond. I see the person go over the fence. In the back of my mind I wonder if the killer has returned to the scene. But why would he do that when my Explorer is parked in plain sight?

I grapple with my lapel mike as I sprint toward the fence. "This is 235! I'm 10-20 at the Plank farm! I've got a 10-88! 10-78!"

"Uh . . . roger that." The new dispatcher. A too long pause. "Um . . . who do I send?"

"Get on the goddamn radio and get someone out here now!" I shout.

"Ten-four."

I draw my .38. I'm running full out when something tangles at my feet. Wire, I realize, and then I'm falling. I reach out to break my fall, lose the grip on my gun. My hands plunge into mud. I land on my stomach hard enough to knock the breath from my lungs. I turn over, kick off the wire—a freaking tomato cage—and scramble to my feet. Scooping up my weapon, I lurch into a run.

My breaths come hard and fast as I scale the fence. I can hear the blood roaring in my ears. I shine the Maglite ahead, and see an ocean of corn. I burst into the first row. Mud sucks at my feet as I sprint to the next row. Husks slash at my face as I run down the row, pop into the next, continue on. I run blindly for several minutes, hoping to intercept my quarry. But he's nowhere in sight.

Finally, I stop, my lungs burning. "Damnit."

I nearly jump out of my skin when my cell phone beeps. I snatch it up with a cross utterance of my name.

"What the hell happened? I've been trying to call—"

Tomasetti. I close my eyes, try to steady my breathing. "Suspicious person at the crime scene," I pant.

"You alone?"

"Backup's on the way."

"Kate, goddamnit . . ."

"I'm okay." I'm out of breath. Too pissed to talk. "I've got to go."

He starts to say something else, but I disconnect. I tell myself it's because I'm standing in the middle of a cornfield soaked to the skin with an unknown subject in the area. But I'm honest enough to know that at least part of the reason I don't want to talk to him at this minute is because I need him. Such is the nature of our relationship. The thought of needing anyone scares the hell out of me.

Shining the Maglite in the direction from which I came, I see my muddy tracks being slowly eroded away by the pounding rain. A voice barks over my radio. "This is 289. I'm 10-76 the Plank farm, 10-77 five."

Glock, I realize and hit my mike. "Ten-fourteen heading west through the cornfield west of the house. See if you can intercept at Hogpath Road."

"Ten-four." The mike crackles. "You okay, Chief?"

"That's affirm."

By the time I reach the house, I'm dripping wet. The entire front of my uniform is covered with mud. Chunks fall off my boots as I cross to the Explorer. I'm cold and royally ticked off as I yank open the door and grab my rain slicker. I'm shrugging into it when headlights wash over me.

I look up to see T.J. emerge from his cruiser, Maglite in hand. He approaches me at a jog, his expression concerned. "Damn, Chief. You okay?"

"I'm fine." Quickly, I tell him about the journal and seeing the subject at the door. "I gave pursuit. I might have caught him, but I fell, lost him in the cornfield. Glock's going to try to intercept on Hogpath Road."

"Did you recognize him?"

"I didn't get a good look."

He pauses. "You think it was the killer?"

The experts say a large majority of killers return to the scene sooner or later. I've seen it happen myself a few times in the course of my career. This time, however, the scenario doesn't make sense. "My Explorer was parked in plain sight."

He shines the beam over my muddy uniform. "I've got a jacket in my cruiser. . . ."

The chirp of my radio interrupts. "Two-eight-nine." Glock's voice crackles. "I'm 10-23 Hogpath Road."

I hit my mike. "Any sign of the subject?"

"Negative."

"Damnit." The son of a bitch could have exited the cornfield at any point, gotten into a vehicle, and fled the scene. The rain will eradicate any tracks. "Take a look around. See what you can find." I sigh. "We'll come back at first light."

"Roger that."

Shaking my head, I brush at the mud on my jacket. "Damnit."

T.J. looks thoughtful. "You think the killer might've come back for the journal, Chief?"

"It crossed my mind." His expression becomes concerned, and I know he's thinking the same thing I am. "We need to keep the scene secure. I want a more thorough search of the house and outbuildings first thing in the morning."

T.J. nods. "Look, I came on duty later than everyone else. You want me to stick around?"

"That would be great. Thanks. Keep your radio handy, will you?"

"You bet." He looks around. "What are you going to do?"

"I'm going to go through the journal tonight and see if Mary Plank identifies a boyfriend."

He seems to consider that a moment. "You think the boyfriend killed the whole family?"

"I don't know. But he just became my number one suspect."

CHAPTER 11

"That sounded urgent. Is everything all right?"

John Tomasetti looked across the span of desktop at his newest nem-esis and resisted the urge to get up and walk out the door. "A case," he muttered. "Agency business."

Contemplating him, Dr. Warren Hunt leaned back in his sleek leather executive chair, the poster boy for patience and serenity, and nodded. "If you need to take care of business, there's an adjoining office you're free to use."

Tomasetti looked down at the cell phone in his hand and tried not to think about Kate. Or the fact that instead of sitting in this office humili-ating himself, he should be on his way to Painters Mill. "Let's just . . . get this over with."

The doctor smiled.

Tomasetti had never been a fan of doctors, but he hated shrinks with particular vehemence. He found all of their how-do-you-feel-about-that questions, their phony concern and not-so-covert glances at their watches obscenely disingenuous. Unfortunately, he didn't have a choice but to tol-erate Dr. Warren Hunt. The suits might call it progress, but John called it a crock of shit.

"Where were we?" the doctor asked.

Hunt was a nice enough guy. A little too preppy for someone his age; John guessed him to be in his mid-fifties. But he'd been through some tough times. He'd spent a year in Bosnia way back when. He'd been a cop in New Orleans during Katrina. But while those things held weight for Tomasetti, there was baggage, and then there was *fucking baggage*. He had the profound misfortune of possessing the latter.

"I think we were discussing my plethora of vices," Tomasetti replied.

Hunt gave a small smile, then looked down at the file in front of him. Tomasetti knew it contained records—damning personal information from past doctors—another proviso he didn't care for, but there wasn't a damn thing he could do about any of it. And so here he was.

"I see you've had some problems with alcohol," Hunt said. "Are you still drinking?"

Tomasetti looked across the gleaming span of rosewood, wondering how much of this would get back to his superiors. "I've cut back. A lot."

"You still running?"

"I'm up to a couple of miles." He hadn't run for a week, but then he didn't feel the need to confess.

"What about sleep?" Hunt asked. "You sleeping at night?"

"Better."

"Sleep disturbances? Nightmares?"

"Sometimes." For the last two and a half years—since the murders of his wife and two little girls—Tomasetti had been plagued by nightmares. More than one shrink had called them a by-product of post-traumatic stress disorder. They'd prescribed everything from Valium to antidepressants to antianxiety drugs to sleeping pills. The antidepressants seemed to do more harm than good, so John had stopped taking them almost immediately. The rest, however, he'd sucked down with the self-destructive glee of an addict.

Early on, the drugs had made his days bearable and the nights not quite so endless. He figured if he wasn't thinking about blowing his brains out, the meds were working. Things began to improve after the Slaughterhouse case—after he met Kate. He weaned himself off the drugs. Not cold turkey, but one pill at a time. At first, everything had been all right. He started running. Taking care of a body he'd abused for more than two years. Just when he thought he was going to make it, everything went to shit.

Tomasetti wanted his life back. He wanted his job back. He wanted to go to Painters Mill to see Kate, help her with the case. The phone call he'd received from her earlier drove that need into his brain like a six-inch spike. She wouldn't approve, but he worried about her. Too damn much if he wanted to be honest about it. But then he knew that bitch Fate had a habit of snatching away the things he cared about most.

His relationship with Kate was an anomaly; he'd never been a fan of female cops. Like their male counterparts, they could be a difficult lot. John figured he had enough problems just getting through the day without taking on a complicated woman. Not that he was looking. Not that she'd have him. Or so they both claimed.

She was one of the most interesting women he'd ever met. She was tough, capable and attractive as hell. This from a man who was not easily swayed by a pretty face. Evidently, he'd made an exception for her because she swayed him and then some.

In retrospect, Tomasetti knew that while it might have been the façade of tough that had initially drawn him to her, it was the barely discernible air of vulnerability that was the coup de grâce. Thrown together during a time of off-the-chart stress, and his fate had been sealed. Less than a week into the investigation, they'd ended up in bed. At first, it had been all about the sex. By the time he'd returned to Columbus, their relationship had turned into something else. Something he didn't necessarily want, but he'd come to learn life didn't give a damn about timing.

"So, you're still having nightmares," the doctor said. "How often? Once a week? Twice a week? More often?"

"A couple of times a week," John answered. "Not as intense."

"I wish you'd change your mind about the antidepressants."

"I think my brain has enough problems without adding to the mix."

"I know a few of the MAOI-class antidepressants have gotten some bad press in the last couple of years. But we could try one of the SSRIs.

There are several good ones on the market. The supervised use of an anti-depressant could be helpful in getting you back on track."

Tomasetti's life had been a train wreck for so long, he didn't think he'd ever be able to put the mangled pieces back together in a form that made sense. "Not going to happen, Doc."

"If you have a chemical imbalance—"

"We both know my being here has nothing to do with some goddamn chemical imbalance. It has to do with the people I care about getting slaughtered. How the hell do you equate that with a fucking chemical imbalance?"

"Stress hormones can affect serotonin levels."

"Or maybe I'm just pissed off because some piece of scum took my family away from me."

"Is that what you want to talk about today?"

"I don't want to talk about shit today. No offense."

"None taken."

"I think we both know the only reason I'm here is because I'm trying to salvage my job."

"Well, I'm glad you got that out in the open." Hunt gave him a passable smile. "How do you feel about being put on leave?"

"I'm pissed. I want to work. I *need* to work. My being here is a waste of taxpayer's money and a total waste of time. Mine and yours."

The doctor stared at him for a while, then said, "Look, John, I know you don't want to be here. I understand that. To be perfectly honest, you're not exactly the ideal patient."

"Now there's a revelation."

"The truth of the matter is you have some issues to deal with. Your not communicating with me isn't going to help. I can't do my job unless you talk to me. The sooner you're straight with me, the sooner you're out of here and back to work. We're not going to progress until that happens."

Tomasetti stared at him, aware that his heart was pounding. The words were a knot in his chest, being pulled inexorably tighter until he thought something inside him would rip apart. "I'm not getting any better," he said after a moment.

"Why do you think that is?"

"It's been two and a half years. I should be getting better. I'm not."

"Healing takes time."

"I'm getting worse."

The doctor's eyes sharpened, his expression taking on a knowing quality Tomasetti didn't like. "Are you talking about your trip to the emergency room?"

Tomasetti looked away, wishing he'd been able to salvage just one shred of privacy. He honestly didn't have much faith that this doctor could fix him, and he sure as hell didn't want to dredge up one of the most degrading experiences of his life.

"Why don't you tell me about that?" Hunt pressed.

Tomasetti shifted in the chair, caught himself fidgeting, and stilled. "I thought I was having a heart attack."

"But your heart is fine, isn't it?"

Tomasetti said nothing.

"What was the emergency room physician's diagnosis?" the doctor asked.

"He said I'd experienced an anxiety attack."

"Do you understand what that is?"

"I've read up on it."

"Why don't we talk about that?"

Sighing, Tomasetti looked out the window at the lights of the city beyond. Downtown Columbus was a bustling place this time of the evening. Happy hour was just heating up over at the Buckeye Pub on High Street. He could hear the traffic three stories down and wished he were out there. He wished he were anywhere but inside this office, inside his own skin, inside his own head.

"How much of this gets back to the suits at BCI?" he asked after a moment.

"Everything you and I talk about is confidential. You know that."

"You have to tell them *something*. How else do they know whether or not I show up?"

"I give them attendance reports."

"So how are they going to know when I'm fixed?"

A smile curved the doctor's mouth. "I'll include that in my final report."

"How will you know when we get there?"

"Let's just say we're not there yet." The doctor waited a beat. "John, tell me about the anxiety attacks."

Tomasetti thought about walking out. It wouldn't be the first time he'd walked out of a doctor's office. But he knew it would be counterproductive. The last thing he wanted was to sabotage his job. His relationship with Kate aside, it was all he had left.

He shrugged. "They're pretty much textbook. Pounding heart. Sweating. Chest so tight I can't take a breath."

"How do they make you feel?"

"Out of control." Tomasetti wiped his wet palms on his slacks, realized what he was doing and stopped. "Scared shitless."

"I can write you a prescription."

"I think I've had more than my share of pills."

Hunt frowned. "Let's go back to the nightmares for a second."

"What about them?"

"How do they make you feel?"

"They scare the fuck out of me."

"Why do they scare you?"

"Because someone I care about always gets hurt. Or worse."

"They die?"

"Sometimes."

"Are you there? Witnessing it?"

"Yeah."

"Do you try to help them?"

"I try. But I can't."

"Why not?"

"It's like I'm paralyzed or something."

"Are we talking about your family? Nancy? The girls?"

This was the part Tomasetti didn't want to talk about. If he said it aloud, he would have to acknowledge the possibility that it could really happen. "Not always."

"Who else is it you dream about, John? Who is it you can't help? Who can't you talk to me about?"

"Someone I care about."

"A partner? A cop? A personal relationship?"

"Personal."

"Okay. That's a starting point. Thank you." Hunt's eyes sharpened. "You know I have access to your personnel file, John. Because of the shooting you were involved in. I know about the case last January."

"Most of it was in the papers."

"I'm talking about the stuff that wasn't in the papers."

Tomasetti remained silent.

"Look, I used to be a cop. I know how close partners can get."

"She isn't my partner."

"But you were working with her. You were there for an extended period of time. You were under tremendous stress." Hunt looked down at his notes. "You got involved with the chief of police."

Since it was a statement as opposed to a question, Tomasetti figured it didn't require an answer. Not that he had one. Hell, he didn't know what was happening between him and Kate. Were they involved? It had been two months since he'd seen her. Did that equate to a relationship? Maybe it was all in his head because he spent so much time thinking of her. Dreaming of her. Things had progressed too quickly, and neither of them was prepared to deal with the consequences. That's what you got when you put together two people who were experts at sabotaging relationships.

"Is she the one you dream about?" the doctor pressed. "The one you can't help?"

"Sometimes."

"Do you want to talk about her?"

"I think we've talked enough for now." Rising, Tomasetti gathered his coat from the back of the chair.

"We've got twenty minutes left."

"Give it to the next guy."

"All right. Maybe we'll get into that next week."

Tomasetti left without responding.

June 5

I saw him at the park again. I sat on the bench by the gazebo and ate my lunch. He was taking pictures. I pretended not to watch, but I did. He has the most beautiful smile I've ever seen.

June 8

Mrs. Steinkruger snapped at me for daydreaming. I didn't deserve her words. I took an early lunch at the park. He was there and asked why I was crying. I told him, and he laughed. I felt like such a baby. I let him take my picture. The Ordnung *forbids it. Graven images and all that. But he said I was photogenic. That made me so happy I forgot all about Mrs. Steinkruger.*

June 12

I ate lunch at the park again. He was there and asked me if I wanted to take a ride in his car. I knew it was wrong, but I did it. Oh, it was such fun! But I was scared one of my Amish brethren would see me. I will never forget this day!

June 25

He took me to Miller's Pond. He snapped pictures while I ate my bologna sandwich. I love to watch him with his camera, so serious. We sat in his car and listened to music. Oh, how I love rock and roll!

June 27

He told me I was special. After lunch he removed my kapp. *I know it's wrong, but his fingers in my hair felt so lovely. He said I have pretty eyes. I want to tell* Mamm *and* Datt *that he is courting me, but I know they will not approve. I want him to be my* kal. *But he is an outsider. I'm afraid they'll make me quit my job and I won't be allowed to come into town anymore. For now, this is my secret.*

June 28

I thought of him all through worship. Mamm *asked me if I was ill. I laughed and told her no. But I miss him so much it hurts.*

June 30

I haven't seen him for two days. Mrs. Steinkruger asked me why I keep looking out the window. I wish she would be nicer to me.

July 6

I'm fifteen years old today! I rushed through my chores and got to work early. I ate my sandwich in the park, but he didn't come. I miss him. I was on my way back to the shop when he showed up in his car and asked me to get in. I should have said no, but I couldn't. He took me to Miller's Pond and gave me a gift! English clothes! Blue jeans and a pretty pink shirt. I love them!

July 7

It happened today. He kissed me. My first ever. I couldn't stop blushing. He thinks I'm a child, but I'm not. His mouth on mine was like poetry, soft and flowing and warm. Oh, I will never in a thousand years forget that kiss.

And so the saga of Mary Plank's life goes.

I lie in my bed, propped up with pillows, and listen to the rain against the window. I hold Mary Plank's journal in my right hand and a glass with two fingers of Absolut in my left. Reading the diary is like watching a train wreck in slow motion. I'm through the first month of her relationship with a man she hasn't yet named. A man who is not Amish. An older man who has no regard for her age or the problems that will arise if her parents or the Amish community find out about them.

Impatient with myself for feeling more than I should for this girl I've never met, I skim several pages, looking for a name or clue that will tell me his identity. I end up in mid-July.

July 15

I sneaked out of the house last night. I was so scared! I don't want to disappoint Mamm *and* Datt. *How I wish for their blessing! I know they would grow to love him as much as I do. He was waiting for me at the end of the lane. He took me to Miller's Pond, then we sat on the hood of his car and talked until the small hours of morning. I feel as if I've known him my entire life. I want to marry him!*

July 16

My feelings for him scare me even more than the sneaking out. On the days I don't see him, I'm sad. I know Mamm *and* Datt *have noticed. How can I tell them I love a man who is not Amish?*

July 17

I sneaked out and we went to a club in Columbus. I wore English clothes and drank alcohol. I know it is wrong, but I felt so sophisticated. He taught me how to dance! I didn't want to leave. It was the most exciting night of my life!

July 18

He met me at the park for lunch. We held hands and he kissed me. I know it's wrong, but I let him touch me. All the places a man touches a woman. I thought I would be embarrassed, but I wasn't. When I got back to the shop, I was afraid Mrs. Steinkruger would know what I'd been doing. All she did was yell at me for being late.

July 20

It happened today. I sneaked out and we went for a moonlight drive. He took me to Miller's Pond. Then we made love. It hurt, and there was blood. I had to wash my underclothes so Mamm would not find out. Sex before marriage is against the Ordnung. If I was found out, I would be expelled from the church. I would be let back in only after I confessed in front of everyone. I'm so confused. I feel guilty, but I love him. I pray for God to forgive me.

July 27

I haven't seen him for a week. I can't stop crying. I wait for him every day, but he never comes. Does he not understand how much this hurts me?

August 2

I sneaked out and he took me to a club in Columbus. We danced and danced. Later, he took me to the car and I lay with him again. I'm so confused!

August 7

I told him it was wrong for a man and woman to be together before their vows. He laughed when I told him I want to marry him. I was so angry I walked all the way back to the shop.

August 10

He apologized! He even brought me a gift, a necklace with a lavender stone. I will treasure it always. I wore it to the club and we danced. I drank wine, but this time it made me so dizzy I couldn't walk or speak. We went to the car and made love. I barely remember. Next time, no wine!

August 12

He loves me! I've been waiting for him to say the words as I could not say them first. He took me to a motel. Our lovemaking was the best ever. How I want to tell Mamm *and* Datt *about him!*

August 16

We went to the motel after the club. Even though I drank only water, I couldn't walk. I don't remember lying with him. (Maybe I am not getting enough sleep?)

August 21

Mamm *and* Datt *sat me down and talked to me. They're worried. I was so upset I was shaking. I want to tell them about my beau, but I know they won't approve. Maybe I could speak to Bishop Troyer. Maybe he would help them to have a more open mind. How can love be wrong?*

August 24

I sneaked out again. We drank beer and by the time we arrived at the club, my head was spinning. I tried to dance, but fell down. He teased me about my wild ways. I couldn't stop laughing. He had to carry me to the car. Still, it was wonderful to be in his arms. I hope God forgives me for my offenses!

August 28

He took me to a party in another town. The wine was strong, and when we arrived I could not walk or speak. He had to carry me inside. The party was strange. I remember bright lights and music. He made love to me. I think he took pictures. I was embarrassed, but he said they're only for him, for when he misses me. I don't want to do that again.

August 29

I didn't make it home until daylight. Mamm *and* Datt *know I sneaked out. Even though I'm on my* rumspringa, Datt *is angry.* Mamm *just looks at me with that hurt look in her eyes. They asked me who I was with. He told me not to tell, so I didn't. Lying to my parents hurts me. I feel guilty about the things I've done. But I love him so much.*

August 30

I was sick today. Nauseous and shaky. I don't know what's wrong. At the park, I told him I was sick and he bought me an ice cream cone. He's so thoughtful.

September 6

I met him at midnight at the end of the lane. I was so happy to see him. He gave me champagne. It tickled my nose. But it was too strong and I don't re-member much of the night. I think he took me to some warehouse? Not sure. I remember him undressing me and tucking me into the bed the way I do little Amos sometimes.

September 8

I refused to go with him when he came to my window. I'm angry about last night. He told me it was the English way and that I was just too immature to enjoy it. I'm not wise in the ways of the English, but it felt so wrong.

September 9

I missed my time of the month. I could be with child. What am I going to do? Is this God's way of punishing me for all the terrible things I've done? I'm so scared.

September 11

I'm sick today with vomiting. Mamm *won't let me go to work. I'm supposed to meet him tonight. How am I going to get away? I waited until midnight and went out the window. He was there, with a smile and a kiss. I love him so much. But, oh, how I wish he would stop hurting me.*

September 14

He took me to the warehouse again. I cried and told him I didn't want to go. I drank only water, but still felt as if I'd drunk a whole bottle of wine. I didn't want to get into bed with him. It is so wrong and I feel terribly guilty. I have to stop this. Why can't he just love me?

September 15

I woke up in the warehouse, sick and shaking. I told him I wanted to go home. He gave me water. But I think he put something in the water because after a few minutes I couldn't think straight. He made love to me and everything got confused again.

September 19

Mamm *and* Datt *are worried.* Mamm *cried and asked me to talk to Bishop Troyer, but* Datt *said no. They made me quit my job. I don't know how to tell them about the baby. Will they love it as much as I do?*

September 21

I was so ill I could not get out of bed. I couldn't do my chores. I don't know what's wrong. My brothers and sisters peeked in on me several times, but I can't speak to them. I pray my parents will forgive me. I pray for God to forgive me.

September 22

He came to my window! I shouldn't be, but I was so happy to see him. I sneaked out and we bought some wine. Then he took me to Miller's Pond. We watched the stars and he gave me my first wine lesson. The bottle was in a cute little wicker thingie and came all the way from Italy! He's so sophisticated. Later, we made love. I told him I want to marry him. I want to tell Mamm *and* Datt *about us. He got a little angry and told me they wouldn't understand. But I need their blessing, even if I am to leave the church. I'm so confused. I don't know what to do!*

September 24

I walked all the way to town and called him from the pay phone. He met me in the park, and I told him about the baby. He got really mad. I don't care. I love him. And I love our child. I told him I want to marry him and have his child. Forgive me, God, but I told him I would leave the Plain life to be his wife.

September 29

It's all my fault. My pregnancy. That my life is a mess. He's so angry with me. I think he hates me. I hoped the baby would make him love me. But everything is ruined. I pray to God for the wisdom to do the right thing.

October 2

I can't believe he came to my window. When I went downstairs he tried not to show it, but he was mad. He called me a stupid little whore. I know it was the wrong thing to do, but I went with him. I still love him. He drove too fast and it scared me so bad I started to cry. He took me to his house and gave me wine. Afterward, I couldn't move. I don't remember everything that happened next. All I recall are the bright lights, but I hurt down there the next day. I think he took pictures of me. I hate myself. If it wasn't for the baby, I might just step out in front of a car. Thank God for my baby. The child gives me strength.

October 4

He came for me, but I refused to go. He told me I was selfish. That everything is my fault. He says he loves me and our baby. But how can he when he treats me this way?

October 5

I was weak and went with him. We drove around for a long time and then we went to a fancy house in another town. He pretended not to be mad, but he was mean to me on the drive. He gave me wine. I dumped it without drinking it. I know why he drugs me now and I can't believe I've been so stupid.

October 8

I'm so ashamed of what I've become. What kind of mamm *will I be to my baby? I beg for God to forgive me. I'm going to end it. I'm going to tell* Mamm *and* Datt *everything. He met me at the end of the lane and took me to a house in town. I tried to tell him I didn't want to see him anymore, but he wouldn't listen. I pretended to drink the wine, but dumped it in the plant when he wasn't looking. When he went to the bedroom, I ran from the house. I was so scared, I didn't stop until I was out of town. I kept looking over my shoulder. Every time a car went by, I ran to the ditch and hid.*

October 11

I can't stop crying. I told Mamm *and* Datt. *I was so ashamed I wanted to die.* Mamm *cried.* Datt *couldn't look at me. We prayed and decided I would speak with Bishop Troyer. How can I confess my sins when they're so terrible?*

October 12

Who am I? What have I become? I hate myself. I hate him. I'm so ashamed I want to die.

October 13

I told Datt *the rest of it. All of it. And I think that broke his heart. It's the first time I've ever seen him cry. I feel so guilty and stupid. He's going to the English police. I begged him not to. If he does, everyone will know what I've done. I can't believe this is happening. Sometimes I wish I could just die.*

I finish reading Mary Plank's journal at four A.M. It's like watching a movie where you know some cataclysmic event is about to happen to some hapless character you've come to care about. A huge meteor spinning through space, drawing closer and closer to destination Earth.

It's indescribably sad for me to bear witness to a young Amish girl's descent into a world she is unequipped to handle. Maybe because I discern echoes of my own past in her words. My situation was different, but the parallels are glaringly there. We broke the rules and paid the price for it. The difference was that I didn't have a choice in what happened to me. Young Mary made the wrong choices over and over again.

In all those pages of teenaged angst, not once did she mention her lover's name. Not once did she reveal the kind of car he drives, the name of the club they frequented, the location of the houses they visited, or what he does for a living. At this point, I'm not even sure he had anything do with the murders. But I'm suspicious as hell. If Mary Plank fore-warned her lover of her father's plan to go to the police, he had a big mo-tive to do away with not only her, but her entire family.

I'm a firm believer that people are responsible for their actions. They are masters of their universe. There's no doubt Mary used poor judgment. Her only saving grace is that she was a kid. Raised Amish, she lacked the skills to deal with the world into which she let herself get dragged.

I'm betting the man she fell for was quite a bit older, much more expe-rienced, and knew exactly what he was doing: taking advantage of her innocence, her lack of sophistication, her naïveté. Not to mention her love for him. That alone makes him a bastard in my book. It makes me want to find him and tear him apart with my bare hands.

CHAPTER 12

The *clip-clop* of a hundred or more shod hooves fills the cold, late-morning air. Clouds of vapor spew from the flared nostrils of dozens of horses, frisky from the first cold front of the season.

I've spent the last two days in wait mode. Waiting is a big part of police work—the most difficult aspect as far as I'm concerned—and I'll never be good at it. I've walked the crime scene a dozen times now, talked to the same neighbors and asked the same questions a hundred different ways. But I always get the same answers: No one saw anything. Frustration has been my constant companion. I haven't slept much. Forget to eat half the time. And so I wait. For preliminary autopsy results. For various lab results. For fingerprints. For footwear imprint matching. Cartridge casings and bullet striation results. Hurry up and goddamn wait.

T.J. and I sit in my Explorer, the windows midway down, watching the somber procession. Black buggies, the sides of which are marked with chalk designating their order in the convoy, stretch as far as the eye can see. Some of the mourners come from as far away as Zanesville and Western Pennsylvania, and probably began their journey as early as two or three A.M.

Drizzle floats down from a glowering sky the color of charcoal. The smells of horses, wet grass and the tang of dry autumn leaves waft through the window. T.J. and I have been here since daybreak, when Bishop Troyer swung open the gate to the *graabhof,* or cemetery, and the gravediggers began their sad task.

I attended several Amish funerals growing up. The day before the ceremony, male friends and neighbors of the deceased build the unadorned, six-sided casket. Amish caskets are lined with fabric sewn by female friends and neighbors. Once the coroner releases the bodies, the dead are washed and dressed. Deceased males are usually garbed in white—pants, vest and shirt. The females are clothed in a white dress, apron and cape. Bonnie was probably dressed in the same clothes in which she was married.

"So you think the killer is going to show?"

I glance away from the procession and look at T.J. "I don't know. If he's Amish, he might."

T.J. nods. "English guy would probably stand out."

"A little." I spent most of the night re-reading Mary Plank's journal, and I can still feel the weight of her words pressing down on me this morning. I drank too much, but it's not the fuzzy ache behind my eyes that bothers me. I'd hoped the diary would offer some clue as to the identity of the man she was seeing, but she didn't name him. I looked for other details, too. His profession. Physical description. The make of his vehicle. The address of the places he took her. Was she being careful in case one of her parents found the journal? Or had he coached her, told her never to use his name even in her most private moments?

All that reading wasn't totally in vain because I determined two important things. I'm convinced Mary Plank's lover and the murders are related. And I know he's not Amish. With nothing else to go on, it's a starting point.

"You think the killer is Amish?" T.J. asks.

"No." He gives me a so-why-are-we-here look, so I tell him about the journal. "She was in love with the guy."

"Probably the source of the sperm, huh?"

"I think so."

T.J. considers that for a moment. "What about motive?"

"She was pregnant and barely fifteen years old. The age of consent in the state of Ohio is sixteen."

"So he could be facing statutory rape charges."

"Even more charges if he was drugging her and taking sexually oriented photos."

"Could be a pretty strong motive for murder." T.J. mulls that over. "But why kill the whole family?"

"She told her parents about this guy. She told them about the baby."

T.J. nods. "He murdered them to shut them up."

"If they threatened to go to the police, he knew he would be facing a multitude of serious charges. Rape. Maybe child molestation. Contributing to the delinquency of a minor. Possession of a controlled substance. If he published sexually oriented photos of her, child pornography." I shrug, disgusted by my own words. "He would have been facing years of hard time."

"Pretty powerful motive."

"It doesn't explain the torture aspect, what he did to those two girls in the barn."

"Hard to figure something like that." He turns thoughtful. "Probably removed the, uh . . . uterus to keep the police from getting their hands on paternal DNA."

"That makes sense in a sick sort of way. Maybe he included the sister to make the scene look like something else." I consider the level of cruelty and shake my head. "I can see this as a crime of passion. The guy snaps, kills his girlfriend, then guns down her family. I've seen it before. But this is so . . . brutal." My shoulder is getting damp from the drizzle, so I close my window. "We're missing something."

"Like what?"

"I don't know yet."

T.J. looks out the window at the stream of buggies turning into the gravel lot of the cemetery. "You think he's local?"

"If he doesn't live in Painters Mill, I'll bet he lives nearby."

"Right under our noses."

He goes on to say something else, but I'm no longer listening. My attention zeroes in on a silver Toyota parked on the shoulder fifty yards away. A dark-haired young man sporting a goatee and video camera gets out. Several buggies have stopped to make the turn into the cemetery lot. Mr. Camcorder had decided this might be a good time to get some Amish video for YouTube.

He's wrong.

While some of the more liberal-minded Amish will allow it, the majority do not like to be photographed. There are differing views as far as the origin of this aversion. Some believe it is the Bible's second commandment: *Thou shalt not make unto thyself a graven image.* Some of the old order believe if you have your photo taken or even a painting rendered, you'll die. Most Amish simply believe photographs are vain displays of pride, which goes against their basic values.

Grabbing my citation book, I shove open the door. T.J. calls out, but I barely hear him over the drum of my heart. My temper writhes beneath my skin as I start toward the tourist. I know full well anger has no place in police work. But the part of me that is Amish is outraged that some unthinking moron would try to capture such a private, heartbreaking moment for the sake of entertainment.

A second person gets out of the Toyota. A young woman with red hair and several facial piercings. Wearing cutoff shorts and a University of Michigan sweatshirt, she's sitting on the hood, watching the scene as if it were unfolding on the big screen.

I'm fifteen feet away when the man spots me. He lowers the camcorder and gives me an unctuous smile. "Hello, Off—"

I snatch the camcorder from his hand. It takes a good bit of control not to slam it onto the ground and stomp it, but I manage.

"What are you doing?" he demands.

"Hey!" The female slides off the car, her eyes flaring. "You can't do that."

I swing around, stick my finger in her face. "You take one step closer to me and you're going to jail."

She steps quickly back, as if realizing she's ventured too close to an animal that bites. "Fine. Whatever."

I turn back to the man. He glares at me. In a small corner of my mind, I find myself wishing he'd take his best shot so I could deck him.

"Give me back my camcorder," he says.

"You can pick it up when you pay your citation." I pull out the pad and start writing.

"*Citation?*" He gawks at me. "For what? Taking a photo? Ever heard of freedom of expression?"

"This is a no parking, no standing zone." I motion toward the sign. "Ever heard of that?"

This isn't the first time some photo-seeking tourist has stopped on this stretch of road to capture an Amish funeral on film. In light of several Amish-English skirmishes in the last few years, the town council petitioned the county to declare the shoulder within one hundred yards of the cemetery driveway a no parking or standing zone. With tourism being a large chunk of the local economy, the county obliged by putting up four signs.

"I didn't know," the man says. "I didn't see the sign!"

"Now you know." I slap the citation against his chest. "Have a nice day."

He throws his hands up in the air. "For chrissake!"

"This is a funeral. Show some respect." Stuffing the pad into an inside pocket, I start toward the Explorer, think better of it and turn to him. "And for your information, most Amish don't like having their picture taken. Next time, ask their permission before you snap."

By the time I reach the Explorer, the final buggy has pulled into the gravel driveway.

"I thought you were going to punch him," T.J. says.

"Too many witnesses."

He blinks.

I point at him and smile. "Gotcha."

T.J. smiles back. "So are we just going to surveil?"

I look through the windshield at the ocean of black-clad mourners. "I thought we'd make an appearance, see who's here."

We disembark simultaneously and head toward the graveyard, our boots crunching on the gravel. Beyond, a hundred or more plain headstones form neat rows in a meadow that had once been a soybean field. Dozens of black buggies are parked neatly along a lesser used dirt path. Nearer the graves, I see families. Young couples. The elderly. Children. Mothers with babies. All of them standing in the cold drizzle. The community came out in force for the Plank family. But then that is the Amish way.

Bishop Troyer reads a hymn in Pennsylvania Dutch as the pallbearers lower the coffins into the graves. When he finishes, heads are bowed, and I know the mourners are silently reciting the Lord's Prayer. I find the words coming back to me with surprising ease.

T.J. and I stand on the perimeter, two outsiders looking in. Like the Amish themselves, the scene is solemn and hushed. I'd like to discreetly record this for later review. Knowing how most Amish feel about graven images, I won't. Instead, I take in as many faces and details as I can. I'm not sure what I'm looking for; it's one of those things a cop feels. An instinct that tells me when something isn't right. A lone mourner. Someone making a scene. An argument. Unduly vigorous crying. Physical collapse. None of those things happen, but then I've learned not to expect the obvious.

The pallbearers are nearly finished filling the graves with dirt when I spot a slightly built young man striding toward me. I hadn't noticed him before, which is odd because he's the only other non-Amish person here besides T.J. and me.

"Chief Burkholder?" His gaze holds mine as he closes the distance between us, and I wonder how he knows my name. He's a scholarly looking man in his early twenties with slicked back hair and dark, square-rimmed glasses. He's well dressed in a charcoal custom suit with a matching tie I'm pretty sure didn't come from JC Penney. He looks out of place here among the black-clad Amish.

"What can I do for you?" I ask.

He sticks out his hand. "I'm Aaron Plank, Bonnie and Amos's oldest son."

CHAPTER 13

Half an hour later, I'm locked in my office with Glock and Aaron Plank. On the way to the station, I called Skid and had him run Plank through LEADS, which provides access to criminal history files. To my surprise, we got two hits. A DUI when he was eighteen years old. And an assault charge when he was twenty. Both times he pleaded no contest and paid his societal dues.

Plank sits across from me with his legs crossed. To the untrained eye, he might appear calm. But I'm a cop, and I don't miss the constant picking at a hangnail. The wiping of damp palms on wool-blend slacks. He's an unassuming young man. Attractive, with an earnest expression and honest eyes. But I know from experience never to make judgments based on appearances.

"I'm sorry about your family," I begin.

"I still can't believe they're gone. My sisters and brothers. Little Amos." Grimacing, he shakes his head. "Do the police have a suspect yet?"

"We're working on a few leads."

"I don't understand why someone would do that. So violent . . . My God." He looks away, the muscles in his jaws working.

"How did you find out?" I ask.

"Friend of mine heard it on the news, and called me."

"We looked for family. The sheriff of Lancaster County looked, but came back with nothing."

"I would have been hard to find."

"Why is that?"

He laughs, but it's a sad sound. "Well, as you can see I'm no longer Amish. The sheriff's deputies probably looked for Planks living in Lancaster County. He won't find any relatives there."

"No aunts? Uncles?"

"*Datt* had a brother. We had three cousins." He purses his lips. "They were killed in a buggy accident six years ago."

"That's a lot of tragedy to beset one family."

"It was horrible."

I let that settle for a moment. "When's the last time you saw your family?"

"I haven't seen them since the day I left for Philly over three years ago."

"No letters? Phone calls?"

"We never had a phone, so phone calls were out. I got one letter from Mary."

My interest surges. "What did she say in her letter?"

"Just the usual teenaged girl stuff. You know, who's courting whom. Who's getting married. Gossip." He smiles. "Amish style, of course."

"She ever mention a boyfriend?"

Aaron hesitates. "No."

I nod, but I'm wondering about the hesitation. "How long are you going to be in town?"

"I don't know. A few days."

Wanting as much information as I can get, I switch gears. "How long ago did you leave the Plain life?"

"Shortly after my *rumspringa*. I decided at that point not to be baptized."

"Any particular reason?"

His eyes flick away, then back. "That was about the time I realized I was gay."

Surprise ripples through me and at the same time my cop's suspicions jump. I know even before I ask that the news did not go over well with his parents. The Amish are generally tolerant. But that doesn't mean Aaron's being gay was met with approval. How bad had it been for Aaron?

His eyes dart to Glock and then back to me. "I'd been . . . confused about it for a long time. Since I was little, I think. I pretended I wasn't different. I hid what I was."

Religion pervades all aspects of Amish life. Most live their lives according to the *Ordnung*. The *Ordnung* is a sort of unwritten charter of basic Amish values that is passed down from generation to generation and varies from church district to church district. Over the passage of time, the rules evolve and, to some, they are open to interpretation. The more conservative Amish adhere strictly to the *Ordnung*. Some of the more liberal-minded live their lives a bit more loosely, going so far as to utilize electricity and drive cars. Having been born into a conservative family, I know how difficult life could be for someone in Aaron's shoes.

"How did they react when you told them you were gay?" I ask.

"They weren't pleased." Shrugging, he looks away. "They didn't understand. Thought I was perverted. Sick." He gives a rough laugh. "They wanted grandchildren."

"So your being gay caused problems between you and your parents?"

"To put it mildly." His gaze snaps back to mine, and he smiles sadly. "Chief Burkholder, I was not distraught enough to do something like this, if that's what you're getting at. All of this happened a long time ago, and I've long since come to terms. I still loved my parents. I just couldn't abide by their ways."

The familiarity of his words strikes a chord within me. I wish I didn't understand, but I do. All too well. I know what it's like to be Amish and not fit in. Though I haven't ruled him out as a suspect, my empathy is profound.

"Where were you the night of the murders?" I ask.

"Home."

"Where's that?"

"I rent a house. In Philly."

"Can someone substantiate that?"

"My partner, Rob Lane, was there part of the evening."

"What about the rest of the evening?"

"I was alone."

"What's Mr. Lane's contact info?"

Plank rattles off two phone numbers, and Glock scribbles them down.

"Tell me about your relationship with your parents," I say.

He shrugs. "Not much to tell, really. Once I told them I was gay, they sort of . . . shut down. At first they pretended everything was the same. They prayed for me."

"What was the catalyst for your telling them?"

"I met Rob. That's when I sort of figured out I wasn't going to change. When I began to question my parents' assertions that there was something wrong with me."

"How did you meet Rob?"

"He traveled to Lancaster County to write a book about the Amish. He was from Philly. I met him by accident. In town. I know this probably sounds hokey, but after a few minutes with him it was as if we'd known each other our entire lives. I let him photograph me. A lot of the other Amish wouldn't. I agreed to an interview and a few days later we . . . started a relationship."

"How long was he in Lancaster County?"

"Three weeks." He sighs. "They were the best three weeks of my life. We were discreet, but my parents couldn't handle seeing us together. They called it devilment."

"What happened?"

"They talked to the bishop. They forced me to talk to the bishop." He smirks. "I refused to confess. Needless to say it didn't go well."

"I talked to one of the bishops in Lancaster County. I specifically asked about relatives, but your name never came up."

"Well, there are several church districts and more than one bishop in the county. That's not to mention the rift in communication between the Amish and the English."

"Who was your bishop?"

"Edward Fisher."

I write down the name. "So what happened?"

"I was pretty much excommunicated."

"Were you upset?"

"You bet I was. I was seventeen years old. I hadn't even been baptized. Yet I would be cut off from my family and the rest of the community. No one would take meals with me." He gives a shrug. "I was sad because I knew no matter how hard my parents and the bishop tried, I couldn't go back."

"Must have been a tough transition."

"My parents and the Amish community made me feel . . . dirty. I had a lot of guilt."

"Were you angry?"

"I know what you're getting at. I'm not that way."

"You've got an assault conviction on your record."

His face reddens. "I guess you did your homework."

"I know about your juvie record, too."

"Oh, come on! I was a kid. I was confused and angry."

"Sometimes a confused and angry kid grows up to be a confused and angry adult."

"That's not the way it was."

"Look, Aaron, I'm not accusing you of anything. I'm just trying to get some answers. It would save both of us a lot of time if you just opened up and talked to me."

We fall silent a moment, and then I ask. "So what did you do as a juvenile?"

Shaking his head, he presses his fingers against his forehead. "I burned down a barn."

"Why?"

The muscles in his jaws clench. "Because my parents forbade me to see Rob."

I nod. "Was anyone hurt?"

"No."

"How old were you?"

"Seventeen."

"How did the cops get involved?" Having grown up Amish, I know many Amish parents would not contact the English police.

"A sheriff's deputy saw the smoke. Called the fire department." He sighs heavily. "We were trying to put it out when the fire trucks arrived, but it was a total loss. The sheriff's office showed up. In the end my father told them I'd done it."

"You must have been really angry."

"I was."

"You were arrested?"

He nods. "And charged. Arson."

"Went to court?"

"I pled no contest. Judge gave me two hundred hours of community service. Ordered me to help with the rebuilding, which came in the form of a barn raising a month later. Believe me, I paid for what I did."

"What about the assault?"

He flushed. "Look, it's not what you think. I'm not a violent person."

"You torched a barn. You slugged someone. What do you expect me to think?"

He settles himself. "I lost my temper. And, frankly, he had it coming."

"Who is 'he'?"

"Some guy at a bar. Some fucking . . . homophobe. He made a bunch of inappropriate comments."

"You touchy about your sexuality?"

"No, I'd just . . . had too much to drink."

I nod, but I'm not yet satisfied.

"Can I go now?" He stands abruptly, looks from me to Glock and back to me. "I just attended the funeral of seven of my family members. And you have the nerve to drag me in here and question me like I was some kind of criminal."

"I know this is tough," I tell him. "I know you just lost your family. But it's my job to get to the bottom of it. In order to do that I need to ask the hard questions."

"I didn't kill them."

"Nobody said you did." I take a breath, reel in impatience. "Sit down. Please."

"You're treating me like a suspect, for God's sake."

Aaron is not a suspect at this point, but I'm not inclined to tell him. I need to know all the family dynamics before I let him off the hook, especially the ones nobody wants to talk about. "You have motive. You have a record. A shaky alibi. What am I supposed to think?"

"I haven't seen my family for nearly four years!"

"That's a long time for anger to fester. Sometimes those emotions don't go away."

"Look, do I need a lawyer?"

"That's your prerogative."

"I didn't do anything wrong, but I'm not going to let you or anyone else railroad me."

I stare hard at him, trying to see inside his head, inside his heart. "Did you kill your family?"

"No!" His hand shakes when he scrubs it over his forehead, and he sinks back into the chair. "I loved them. All of them. I would never do anything to hurt them. Never."

"You believe him?" Glock asks a few minutes later.

"I don't think he did it." I'm sitting at my desk, watching Aaron Plank through the blinds as he gets into a newish Camry. "But I think he might be holding out."

Glock raises his brows. "You mean when you asked him about his sister having a boyfriend?"

I nod, relieved I'm not the only one who caught Plank's moment of hesitation. "I think he's lying about having been in contact with her."

"Why would he do that?"

"I don't know."

He nods. "Hard to tell when someone is lying."

"That's the thing about liars. There are good ones and there are mediocre ones. What separates the two is that the good ones convince themselves it's the truth. It's like the Big Lie theory, if you repeat a lie enough times, people will start to believe it."

"Adolf Hitler," Glock says.

I watch Aaron Plank pull away. "If someone convinces himself a lie is true, he's basically not lying."

I spend the next twenty minutes digging up everything I can find on Aaron Plank. Arrest record. Conviction record. Background check. But other than the juvenile record, the DUI and the assault, the information is unimpressive. He's a graphic artist, living in an established Philly neighborhood of renovated old homes where a high percentage of his neighbors are young gay professionals. Not exactly the profile of a mass murderer. But I know how difficult excommunication can be for a young Amish person. At the age of seventeen, Aaron basically had to reinvent himself and start over. Hatred can be a strong motivator. Did he hate his parents enough to murder his entire family?

It's hardly a viable theory. For one thing, I can't see him torturing his sisters or cutting the fetus from Mary Plank's body. In the short span of time I spent with Aaron, one thing I noticed is that he's got plenty of emotions, including guilt; he's not a sociopath. That's not to mention the other loose ends: Mary Plank's mysterious relationship, her pregnancy, and the sperm found inside her body. Of course, Aaron could have hired a paid killer. The torture could have been added for the sole purpose of misleading the police. But it's far from a perfect fit.

I also run checks on Aaron's partner, Rob Lane, but he comes back clean. I Google his name to find he's got two books to his credit. Zipping to Amazon, I enter his name and click on the title *Amish Country: A Place of Peace*. It's a lovely coffee table book chock-full of artsy black-and-white photographs, folk art, and literary musings. His tastes run to the avant-garde, but his talent is evident.

Locating the phone number Aaron gave me, I call Rob at his office. He's a well-spoken young man who just landed an editorial job with a well-known magazine. Despite my resistance, he charms me and then substantiates everything Aaron told me. He didn't sound scripted, but as I hang up, I wonder if the two men coordinated stories. It wouldn't be the first time someone covered for a lover.

Next, I call the Lancaster County sheriff's office and get transferred to a corporal by the name of Mel Rossi. I quickly identify myself and tell him about the case.

"I heard about the murders," he says. "Hell of a thing. You guys know who did it?"

"We're still working it." I pause. "I was wondering if you could have one of your deputies run out to Bishop Fisher's place so I could speak to him via cell phone."

"I can probably get someone out there today." Corporal Rossi has a strong New York accent. "Give me your contact info and I'll have someone call you."

I give him my cell phone number and disconnect. I wonder if the bishop will be able to shed any light on the Plank family. I wonder what he'll have to say about Aaron Plank.

I'm ruminating the possibilities when my phone trills. I look at the LCD display to see that the main switchboard is buzzing me. Absently, I hit Speaker. "Yeah?"

"Chief, you've got a visitor."

"Who is it?"

"Me."

The voice goes through me like a blade. I look up to see John Tomasetti standing at my office door. I shouldn't be surprised; I knew he was coming. A flurry of emotions whip through me anyway. Shock. Pleasure.

Uncertainty. All of which are followed by a thrill that feels like a thousand volts of electricity. For a moment I'm dumbstruck and can't think of anything to say. Then my brain is flooded with a jumble of words, none of which are appropriate.

I finally settle for, "What are you doing here?"

"I was in the neighborhood."

I can't tell if he's serious, and a nervous laugh escapes me. "You live a hundred miles away. You can't just be in the neighborhood."

He has the poker face of a card shark. I'm adept at reading people, but not Tomasetti. It's unsettling not knowing what he's thinking. He stares at me, unblinking, his expression as inscrutable as stone. "I thought you might like some help with the case."

Silence reigns for the span of a dozen heartbeats. Tomasetti looks away, shifts his weight from one foot to the other, and for a split second he looks as uncertain as I feel.

"In that case, have a seat." I punctuate the words with a smile, then look down at my notes.

He takes the chair across from me. "So, what have you got?"

Relieved that we share the familiar ground of police work, I recap everything I know about the case.

"Do you think it's possible this girl, Mary, embellished in the journal?" he asks.

"I don't think so." I fumble for the right words. "There was an earnestness to her writing. A naïveté that's hard to fake." I sigh. "She was in love with this guy."

"So the lover is a suspect."

"She was pregnant. A minor."

"Could be a motive. Who else?"

"There's Aaron Plank, but he's not really a viable suspect at this point." I glance at him over the top of my notes to find him staring at me intently. "That's not to say he didn't have issues with his parents. He was excommunicated when he was seventeen. That would have caused a lot of pain. Maybe even rage. Maybe he couldn't let go."

"Enough rage to shoot his brothers and torture his sisters?"

"That's my stumbling block. I can't see him doing that."

"Okay, what else do you have?"

"Home invasion–type robbery. Things go bad. The killings could have been an afterthought. Or it could be a hate crime."

"You're keeping all your options open."

"Nothing seems to be a good fit."

"Yeah, well, our jobs would be a lot easier if murder ever made sense." He picks up the journal from my desk. "She never names the lover?"

I shake my head. "Doesn't give us anything."

"Sounds like maybe he told her to keep her mouth shut."

"Probably. He was manipulating her. She certainly had cause not to tell her parents, especially after the way they reacted to Aaron's announcement that he was gay."

Tomasetti pages through the journal, then sets it back on my desk. "You develop any kind of profile on the boyfriend?"

"I think he's English. Older than Mary. Twenty-five to thirty-five years old. Charming. Manipulative. Dabbles in drugs. Maybe some amateur photography."

"Photography?"

"He took some photos of her."

He arches a brow. "You mean porn?"

"Maybe. I think he may have drugged her, too. She writes about it, but it's not real clear."

"You check the Internet for pics?"

"I haven't Googled 'Hot Amish Chicks,' if that's what you mean."

"That's exactly what I mean. People have all sorts of strange fetishes. Nuns. Feet. Whips and chains." He shrugs.

All I can think is that I should have already pursued that angle. I hit Speaker on my phone and dial T.J. He picks up on the first ring. "We think Mary Plank's boyfriend might have been taking pornographic photos of her. He may have been posting them online. I want you to go out there and see what you can find. You might start with some of the search engines. Check out some of the porn sites. You might also check to see if any of them have an Amish slant."

"Let me get this straight. You're asking me to surf Internet porn sites? Jeez, this has gotta be a first."

"Probably the last, too."

He sighs. "Okay, I'm on it."

I disconnect and look at John. He's got penetrating eyes. The kind that are hard to meet. Harder to hold. Impossible to read. I sense there's something going on with him. Some internal discord I can't put my finger on.

"Tell me about the brother," he says.

I give him the rundown on Aaron Plank. "He lives with his partner in Philly now."

"Bad blood between him and his parents?"

"He says no."

"With his entire family dead, what else is he going to say?"

"There is one person I can think of who might know something about family dynamics."

Tomasetti raises a brow.

"Their bishop back in Lancaster County," I say. "I'm waiting for a call back now."

"Worth a shot." He nods. "What else?"

"Glock's checking hate crimes."

"Hard to imagine someone hating the Amish."

"It happens. Unfortunately, a lot of it goes unreported."

"What kind of stuff are you talking about?"

I shrug. "Some people don't like the buggies because they're slow and hold up traffic. Or they think the Amish are stupid. They equate pacifism with cowardice." I shake my head. "I've seen buggies run off the road. People have thrown rocks at the horses to spook them. I've even heard of some teenagers throwing fireworks at the horses. A few don't like the religion."

"Or they just hate for the sake of hating."

He's staring at me again. That shouldn't bother me. I've been in this man's bed. He's held me. Kissed me. Made love to me. Yet here I am, uncomfortable and squirming beneath his gaze. Turning slightly in my chair, I look out the window, not sure what to say next or how to feel.

"How have you been, Kate?"

"Fine. Working a lot." My answer is a little too quick. I'm nervous about his being here, and he knows it. I turn back to him. It's been two months since I last saw him, but it seems like a lifetime. "How about you?"

"Saving the world." He smiles. "Living the good life."

I nod, not believing a word of it. "How long can you stay?"

"Till we close the case."

I want to ask him if he's up to the task, but I know the question will only piss him off. I admire and respect Tomasetti. Too damn much if I want to be honest about it. But he's been through hell in the last two and a half years. He's a troubled man with shadows so deep I haven't been able to penetrate them. He might say otherwise, but I'm not convinced he's up to working this case.

"I'm glad you're here," I say after a moment.

"I bet you tell all the agency guys that."

I smile.

A rapid knock sounds, then the door swings open. Glock steps in. His eyes widen when he sees Tomasetti. His gaze darts to mine. "Sorry, Chief, I didn't know you had a visitor."

"It's okay," I say, relieved for the interruption. "What do you have?"

Nodding at Tomasetti, he approaches, passes a sheet of paper to me. "Get a load of this."

I scan the paper. It's a ten-year-old police report from Arcanum, Ohio, a small town near the Indiana state line. Four men, all between the ages of nineteen and twenty-one, were arrested for severely beating an Amish man and cutting off his ear. The ear was never found, and therefore could not be reattached. One of the men, James Hackett Payne, later confessed to having eaten it. Each of the men was later convicted and sentenced to five to eight years in prison. My pulse kicks when I see that Payne, now twenty-nine, is living in Painters Mill.

"He did extra time on the hate crime designation," Glock says.

"I'll bet that improved his outlook on life." I pass the paper to John.

He scans the report and frowns. "It's a stretch going from felony assault to mass murder."

"Eight years in prison is a long time for anger to fester into rage," I say.

"What the hell kind of person eats a guy's fuckin' ear?" Glock asks no one in particular.

"Twisted son of a bitch," Tomasetti mutters.

"I don't get the hate thing," Glock says.

I shrug. "Some people see the Amish as easy targets." Both men's gazes swing to me. "They refer to the Amish as *clapes* for 'clay apes.' It's a derogatory term that somehow relates to farming. The incidents against them are known as *clape-ing.*"

Glock shakes his head. "I can't believe it happens enough for someone to coin a term for it."

I glance at him, knowing that as an African-American cop, he's experienced a few hate-related incidents himself.

"You got an address on this guy?" Tomasetti asks impatiently.

Glock grins. "You bet."

I rise. "Let's go talk to him."

"Going to wear my fuckin' earmuffs," Glock says.

CHAPTER 14

James Hackett Payne lives on the south side of Painters Mill in a three-story brick home that looks old enough to be historical. Surrounded by ancient maple and sycamore trees, the house sits on a large lot set back from a tree-lined street. A dilapidated privacy fence tangled with honeysuckle runs the perimeter of the backyard. I park curbside and we disembark.

"He live alone?" Tomasetti asks.

"To the best of my knowledge," Glock replies. "Inherited the house when his dad died last year."

"What's he do for a living?" I ask.

"He's on some kind of disability," Glock answers.

"Mental or physical?"

"Doesn't say."

"Terrific," Tomasetti mutters.

I start down the sidewalk toward the house. The place had once been grand, but years of neglect have turned it into a big, ugly eyesore. The front yard is a collage of tall grass matted with orange and red leaves. From where I stand, I see a detached garage at the rear. I take the concrete steps to the wraparound front porch and cross to the door. I press the doorbell, then open the storm door and knock.

"Creepy fuckin' place," Glock comments.

"Creepy fuckin' guy," Tomasetti adds.

A minute passes, but no one answers. "You guys hit the neighbors," I say. "I'm going to check the back."

Tomasetti and Glock exchange looks.

"For God's sake," I snap, "I'm just going to check the garage to see if there's a car inside."

Nodding, Glock cuts across the yard to the neighboring house. Tomasetti gives me a look I can't quite read, but heads in the opposite direction.

Leaves rustle at my feet as I cut through the grass toward the back of the house. I try to see in the window as I pass a small side porch, but the curtains are drawn. The place has the feel of a vacant house. No car parked out front. The leaves aren't raked. Yard is a mess. The curtains are drawn. I walk through the neighbor's yard along the privacy fence, which is too high for me to see over the top. Reaching the alley, I go left toward the garage.

The overhead door is closed, so I walk past it to the gate, push it open. The gate opens to the backyard. The first thing I notice is the knee-high grass and the cracked sidewalk that leads to the house. A broken clay pot lies on its side just off the porch. From where I stand, I can see a broken window that's been repaired with duct tape and a garbage bag.

"James Payne?" My adrenaline zings as I start toward the door on the east side of the garage. "This is the police. I need to talk to you."

The window is blacked out with some kind of paint. Someone went to extremes for privacy. That makes me nervous. From where I stand, I discern music coming from inside, a haunting tune from some nineties grunge band. I hit my mike. "There's someone in the garage out back. Come on around."

"On the way," comes Glock's voice.

Knowing Tomasetti and Glock are less than a minute away, I cross to the door and knock hard enough to hurt my knuckles. "Police! Open up!"

No one answers.

Annoyed, I try the knob. To my surprise, the door isn't locked so I push it open. The music becomes deafening. I feel the bass rumble all the way to my stomach. I don't know what to expect from Payne. But considering the violent nature of his past crime, I set my hand on my .38.

The smells of paint and burning candles assail me when I step inside. James Hackett Payne stands fifteen feet away with his back to me. It takes my shocked brain a second to realize he's naked, mainly because nearly every inch of his well-muscled body is covered with intricate tattoos.

For a terrible moment I think the red covering his hands is blood. Then I spot the massive painting before him and realize it's paint.

"James Hackett Payne?" I shout to be heard above the music.

He turns slowly, making no effort to cover his nudeness. I notice a dozen things about him simultaneously. He's got peculiar eyes that remind me of Charles Manson, only the color is blue and so light they're almost white. He's either bald or shaves his head and there's a tattoo of a wolf on his scalp. I wonder if he's some weird offshoot of a skinhead. I see spatters of paint on his chest. He's aroused; his member stands at half-staff and has a smear of red paint on it.

"Would you mind putting on your pants, sir? I need to talk to you."

He stares at me with an intensity that makes the hairs on my arms rise. He doesn't smile, but I see amusement in his eyes. "Of course."

He gestures toward a pair of sweatpants draped over the back of a chair. I nod and step back. I don't want this strange son of a bitch getting too close. I hit my lapel mike. "I'm 10-75."

Never taking his eyes from mine, he crosses to the chair. "Had I known you were coming I would have dressed."

"Had I known you were going to be naked, I would have called."

Glock and Tomasetti enter the garage. I glance over to see both men's eyes widen at the sight of Payne. They're seasoned cops; it takes a lot to shock them. I almost smile when I realize Payne has succeeded.

One side of his mouth pulls into a half grin as he jams his legs into the sweatpants. "My work arouses me," he says matter-of-factly. "I prefer to paint . . . uncovered. It puts me closer to my art."

I glance at the painting he'd been working on and another layer of shock goes through me. It's a stark painting with violent streaks of red, black and yellow. I discern the image of an Amish woman in the throes of childbirth. Two Amish males kneel between her knees, devouring a horribly deformed newborn.

I make eye contact with Payne. "We need to ask you a few questions."

He ties the drawstring waist. "Ask away."

Frowning, Tomasetti crosses to the stereo on the workbench and turns it off. Silence fills the studio. Payne glares at him. Tomasetti stares back, maintains his poker face.

"Where were you Monday night?" I ask.

"Here. Working."

"Can anyone substantiate that?"

He smirks. "God."

I tamp down a rise of annoyance. "Do you know any members of the Plank family?"

A slow smile creeps across his face. "No."

"You think something's funny?"

"I just figured out what this is about."

"What's that?"

"I guess I'm a suspect." He shrugs. "Am I?"

"You committed a hate crime against an Amish man ten years ago."

Another smile. "So that automatically makes me a suspect in a mass murder?"

For the first time Glock pipes up. "You ate your vic's ear, buddy. That's fuckin' off-the-chart strange."

Those weird eyes dart from me to Glock and back to me. "I paid my dues for that."

"So you know the Plank family?" I repeat. "Have you had any dealings with them?"

"I don't deal with the Amish." He lowers his voice. "Too much inbreeding. Half the kids are retards. All that bundling, I guess."

That's when I know that while this man might have paid his debt to society, the time he spent behind bars did nothing to cure the cancer of hatred that runs thick in his blood. Images of the Plank family flash in my mind. Mary's journal filled with so many hopes and so much pain. I think of the children, so innocent and with so much life ahead, and I want to tear into Payne with my bare hands.

"If you lie to me about anything we talk about today," I say, "I'm going to make you regret it."

Amusement rises in his eyes. "That's right. You're the Amish cop. How extraordinary. I'll bet you have a soft spot for them, don't you?"

I ignore the jab. "What kind of vehicle do you drive?"

He doesn't appear to hear the question. "I'll bet your family tree doesn't have many branches, either, does it?" An ugly emotion flashes in his eyes. "Did you leave the faith because you didn't want to marry a cousin? Or did they kick you out for being a dyke?"

I know better than to let a loser like Payne push my buttons. I'm well aware of the array of problems inappropriate conduct on my part can bring down on an investigation. But I'm also a human being and my tolerance has been stretched to the limit.

I lunge, ram the heels of both hands into his chest and shove him hard. Caught off guard, Payne reels backward, arms flailing. His foot catches on a rubber mat, and he goes down on his backside.

"Amish cunt." In a split second he's back on his feet. I hear Tomasetti and Glock move in, but they're not fast enough to stop me. I yank out my baton, snap it to its full length and swing. I aim at his left shoulder, but he ducks and the baton rakes a glancing blow across his back. Payne dances backward, snarling.

Two hands come down on my shoulders, fingers digging into my skin. "Kate, goddamnit."

I barely hear Tomasetti's voice over the wild beat of my heart. "Get off me!" Red crowds my vision, a rainbow of fury that spreads through me like a storm.

"Crazy bitch." Payne's lips peel back, revealing canine-like teeth.

I'm aware of Tomasetti dragging me backward. Payne starting toward me.

Glock steps between us, thrusts a finger at Payne. "Back off."

Payne glares at Glock. "She assaulted me! She can't do that! I'm a fuckin' law-abiding citizen!"

At the door, Tomasetti stops dragging me. But he doesn't release me. His fingers slide down to my biceps and he gives me a shake. "Pull yourself together," he growls.

I can hear myself breathing hard. In the back of my mind, I know I screwed up. I acted like some hotheaded rookie. I broke one of the cardinal rules of police work and hit a suspect without cause. The anger pulsing inside me doesn't give a damn.

Payne jams a finger at me. "You fuckin' cops are all the same. A bunch of fascist pigs. I ought to sue you."

Tomasetti sighs. "I didn't see her do anything wrong." He looks at Glock. "Did you?"

Glock shakes his head. "I saw Payne go after her."

Payne's face turns deep red. "I'm glad those Amish freaks are dead! Serves them right for being a bunch of hypocritical, incestuous bastards! How's that, bitch?"

My vision tunnels on Payne's face. I can almost feel my hands closing around his throat. My heart knocks so hard against my ribcage my chest hurts. I think of those dead kids, and I want to strangle him with my bare hands.

"Kate." Tomasetti's fingers squeeze my biceps. "Let it go."

I thrust a finger at Payne. "Don't leave town."

"Or what? What are you going to do about it? Hit me? Your days as a cop are numbered, bitch."

John pushes me toward the door. I dig in my heels, but he muscles me across the threshold and onto the sidewalk. "Cut it out," he snaps.

"Get your hands off me." I try to sound calm, but my voice shakes. "I mean it."

Glock pauses in the doorway, looks at Payne, and points at the painting. "That shit you call art sucks, man."

From inside, I hear Payne break into wild laughter.

* * *

No one speaks as John, Glock and I traverse the neighbor's yard. We reach the Explorer, and I yank my keys from my pocket.

"Can't take you anywhere, can we?" Tomasetti mutters.

"Can the lecture," I say tightly.

"What the hell were you thinking?"

I say nothing as I slide behind the wheel. The truth of the matter is I can't defend what I did. Payne baited me, and I hit on it like a bass on a lure.

Tomasetti glares at me. "You know better than to—"

"You didn't see those dead kids." I crank the key. "You didn't see those girls."

He slides into the passenger seat and slams the door. "You let him provoke you."

"That's hypocritical as hell coming from you."

"You played right into his hands. If he wants to push the issue, he can cause problems."

"Let him push." The tires squeal as I pull away from the curb. "In case you haven't figured it out yet, I push back."

Leaning back in the seat, Tomasetti groans, looks out the window.

From the rear seat, Glock clears his throat. "So what's your take on Payne?"

"He's worth looking at," Tomasetti says. "The torture aspect fits him better than the others."

I glance in the rearview mirror, catch Glock's gaze. "Dig up everything you can find on him. See if he's in CODIS. If not, get a warrant. I want a DNA sample from that son of a bitch."

"You think he knew the girl?" Glock asks.

Tomasetti shakes his head. "I don't think he'd have a relationship with an Amish female."

"Yeah," Glock agrees. "Too much hate."

"He could have raped her," I put in.

I feel John's eyes burning into me, but I don't look at him. I don't want him to see what I know shows on my face.

"Autopsy substantiate that?" Glock asks.

I shake my head. "Inconclusive."

I park in front of the police station and get out without speaking. I'm still angry, but now that anger is focused on myself. I feel like an idiot for taking a shot at Payne. I'm embarrassed because I did it in front of two people I respect. Two cops whose opinions matter to me.

I'm midway to the front door when Tomasetti breaks the silence. "I'd like to see the crime scene."

I know it's petty in light of everything that's happened, but I don't want to go back there. I'm feeling too battered, too vulnerable. I want to blame it on my confrontation with Payne, but I know the feelings zinging inside me have more to do with a dead Amish girl than an ex-con full of hate.

"Come with me," he says.

We stop on the sidewalk in front of the station. Glock's gaze goes from Tomasetti to me, and he clears his throat. "I'm going to get some queries going on Payne. See about that warrant."

"Thanks," I mutter and watch him disappear inside.

I turn my attention back to Tomasetti. He stares evenly at me. I stare back, determined not to look away despite my discomfort.

"You okay?" he asks.

"I'm always okay."

He looks away, studies the building behind me, then gives me a sage look. "It's not like you to go after a suspect like that."

"Nobody likes a bigot."

He frowns. "Or maybe I'm not the only one this case is hitting too close to home for."

I'm not sure if he's talking about Mary Plank in general, or the rape she and her sister may have endured before their deaths. The one thing I do know is that he's right; the case is hitting me in a place that's bruised and raw—and with a vehemence I'm not prepared for.

After a moment, I rub at the ache between my eyes and sigh. "We're not catching any breaks."

"We will." He pauses. "Do you have time to come with me to the crime scene?"

"There's one more person I need to talk to first," I reply. "It's on the way."

"I'll drive."

The Carriage Stop is a quaint gift shop located just off the traffic circle. I'm not big on shopping. In fact, I've only been in the store once and that was to buy a gift for Glock's wife, Lashonda, when she had her baby a few months back. The shop is a Painters Mill icon of sorts with a large selection of Amish quilts, birdhouses, mailboxes, flavored coffees and candles. It's owned by town councilwoman Janine Fourman and managed by her sister, Evelyn Steinkruger. My aversion to shopping aside, that affiliation alone is enough to keep me out.

"Mary Plank worked here part-time," I say as Tomasetti parks in front of the shop.

"I didn't know the Amish could take on outside jobs or associate with the English."

"It varies depending on the church district and how loosely the *Ordnung* is interpreted." I slide out of the Tahoe.

The bell on the door jingles merrily as we enter. The scents of candle wax, eucalyptus, coffee and a potpourri of essential oils—sweet basil, rosemary and sandalwood—titillate my olfactory nerves. To my left, old-fashioned wood shelves filled with every imaginable type of folk art line the entire wall. I see rustic wooden plaques upon which colorful hex symbols are painted. These are allegedly taken from old Amish barns. I smile at that because the Amish have never used hex signs to decorate their barns. Of course the tourists don't know that, and shop owners like Janine Fourman don't necessarily give a damn about cultural accuracy.

Ahead, several dozen Amish quilts bursting with color are draped over smooth wooden racks. To my right, an ancient spiral staircase sweeps upward to the second level where I see a small collection of books and dozens of handmade candles. In the center of the room, a snazzily dressed woman with coiffed gray hair stands behind an antique cash register.

"Hi, Chief Burkholder." She looks at me over the tops of tiny square bifocals. "May I help you?"

My boots thud against the wood plank floor as we cross to her. I flash my badge. "Evelyn, this is John Tomasetti with the Bureau of Criminal Identification and Investigation out of Columbus."

"You're here about that poor Plank girl." She shakes her head. "What an awful thing to happen."

"I understand Mary worked here part-time."

"Three days a week from ten to three. Such a pretty thing, and from such a nice family. I was shocked to my bones when I heard what happened to them."

"How well did you know Mary?"

"Not well, I'm afraid. She worked here about five months, but she was very quiet and kept to herself."

"How did you come to hire her?"

"Mary and her mother brought in quilts every so often. You know, to sell. They did lovely work. I mentioned once that I needed help with stocking the shelves. A few days later Mary's mother brought her back and she filled out an application." She lowers her voice. "I guess they needed to get permission from their pastor or something."

"What can you tell us about Mary?" Tomasetti asks.

"She was a good little worker. Pretty as a picture. Quiet, though. Always seemed to be watching you with those big eyes of hers."

"Had you noticed any unusual behavior on her part recently?"

"Not really. She did a lot of daydreaming. I'd walk by when she was supposed to be working and catch her staring off into space." She gives a small smile, as if we share a secret. "I actually had to reprimand her a few times, just to keep her on the ball. I hired her because the Amish have such a good work ethic. You know those religious types, they don't complain." She laughs. "But for an Amish girl, bless her heart, Mary was as lazy as a summer day."

That's when I realize Janine and her sister share more than blood. They also share a nasty streak that runs straight down the middle of their backs.

"Had you noticed anyone hanging around the shop?" Tomasetti asks. "Any customers talking to Mary? Males paying too much attention to her?"

"Well, all the males gave her a look when they came in. She really was a very pretty girl even though she didn't wear a shred of makeup and wore the same frumpy dress almost every day. But she never paid them any heed."

"Did you ever see her talking to anyone?" Tomasetti asks.

"Like I said, she was quiet. Didn't really talk to anyone."

"Do you have any other employees?" I ask.

"A couple of high school girls help out on the weekend. Otherwise, I'm it."

"Can you give me their names?" I ask.

She rattles off two names, and I jot them down.

"What about males?" Tomasetti asks. "Any males come into the shop on a regular basis?"

"You mean customers?" Steinkruger asks. "We get a few, but most of our shoppers are female."

"What about suppliers?" I ask. "Or have you had any work done on the place recently? Construction work, maybe?"

"Well, we have a coffee guy comes in once a week. Replenishes our coffees and creamers."

"Same guy every week?"

She nods. "Nice young man. Attractive. His name is Scott, I believe."

"Last name?"

"I don't know, but he's cute as a speckled pup."

I resist the urge to roll my eyes. "What's the name of the coffee service?"

"We use Tuscarawus Coffee Roasters. Fabulous coffee." She draws out the A so that the word sounds very northeastern. "Our customers love the Pennsylvania Dutch chocolate. Can't keep it in the store."

I write the name of the coffee service and the route man in my notebook.

Tomasetti asks the next question. "Did you ever see Mary with anyone? She go to lunch with anyone? Talk on the phone?"

Her brows knit and she slides her glasses onto her crown. "You know,

now that I'm thinking about it, I vaguely remember seeing Mary get into a car a couple of weeks ago. I thought it was odd, her being Amish and all. Those people have all those rules about fraternization."

My cop's radar goes on alert. "Did you recognize the driver?"

"We were busy that day. I just happened to look out the window. I didn't think anything of it because she was on her lunch break. I remember hoping she wasn't late coming back because we'd just gotten in a shipment of candy that needed to be priced and stocked."

"Do you recall what kind of vehicle it was?" I ask.

Her brows knit. "It was a nice car. Looked new. Shiny paint. Dark."

"Do you remember the color?"

"Black or blue." She puts her finger to her chin. "Maybe brown. Dark is all I recall."

"What about the make or model?"

"I'm so bad with those kinds of details. My husband worked at GM for thirty years. He thinks it's blasphemous that I don't know a Ford from a Toyota."

"That is blasphemous," Tomasetti mutters.

"I'm sorry. I only saw the car for a second."

"Do you know if the driver was male or female?" I ask.

She shakes her head. "I don't recall."

"Did you get the sense that Mary knew the driver?" I try.

"Well, I don't really know. But I can tell you she wasn't the kind of girl who would get in a stranger's car."

"This could be important, Mrs. Steinkruger. Do you remember any details at all about the vehicle or driver?"

She considers my question for a moment. "I remember thinking it was strange that she got in halfway down the block. She lowers her voice. "And she came back once smelling of cigarettes. I was going to tell her mother about it, but I forgot about it until now."

Tomasetti and I exchange looks. I can see that his cop's radar is beeping as loudly as mine.

"Did she have any English friends?" I ask.

"Not that I ever saw."

"Did she have a desk or locker here at the shop we could take a look at?" Tomasetti asks.

"We don't have anything like that here."

The bell on the door jangles. A group of golf shirt–clad, fifty-something tourists wander in.

"Thanks for your time," Tomasetti says and we head toward the door.

"Fruit didn't fall far from the tree in that family," I mutter beneath my breath.

He gives me an amused look. "Rotten fruit?"

"Putrid."

"Oh, Chief Burkholder?"

At the sound of Evelyn's voice, we stop and turn.

She speaks to us from her place behind the cash register. "I have Mary's final paycheck here. What should I do with it?"

"You might give it to her brother, Aaron," I say. "He may want to put it toward the cost of the caskets."

I'm thinking about Mary's diary as I get into the Tahoe. "The guy in the car could be our killer," I say. "In her journal, she mentioned meeting her boyfriend for lunch."

"Maybe we could get a couple of your officers to canvass the area."

"Okay."

"Not much to go on." Tomasetti starts the engine and pulls away from the curb. "I should probably read the journal. Can I get a copy of it?"

"I'll have Lois make you one."

"Might give me some insight. You know what they say. Two brains are better than one."

"That's a scary thought, Tomasetti."

CHAPTER 15

Tuscarawus Coffee Roasters is located in a small office complex on the north side of town. The barrel-tile roof and stucco façade cascading with English ivy lends it the ambience of an Italian villa. It shares space with two dentists, an insurance company, a photo studio and a high-end nail salon called Elegante.

We park in the only empty space and take the sidewalk to an arched entry. Beyond, I spot the sign for the coffee company.

"Nice digs," I say.

"Must sell a lot of coffee."

The door opens to a trendily decorated reception area with turquoise walls and mahogany colored molding. A black and silver sofa lines the wall to my right. The coffee table in front of it is piled high with *Coffee Lover Magazine*. To my left, an African-American woman sits behind an Art Deco–esque desk, tapping a sleek keyboard with long pink nails. A name plaque in front of her reads: *Director of First Impressions*.

"May I help you?" she asks.

I cross to the desk and show her my badge. "Do you have a route driver named Scott? He delivers to the Carriage Stop in Painters Mill."

"Oh. Wow. Cops." Her eyes dart from my badge, to Tomasetti and back to me. "Carriage Stop is part of Scott Barbereaux's route. Is he in some kind of trouble?"

"We just want to speak with him," Tomasetti says. "Is he in?"

She glances at the clock on her desk. "He usually gets in from his route at about this time. Hangs out in the warehouse, doing his paperwork. Let me page him for you." Using her pen, she presses a button on the switchboard. "Scott, please call 900."

Tomasetti gives me a look that tells me he's not in the mood to wait. "Where's the warehouse?"

"Well, um, I'm not really allowed to let you go back there."

His smile looks more like a snarl. "If your boss gives you a hard time, I'll arrest him for you."

A nervous giggle escapes her, and she points a pink nail at the door beyond. "Go through that door. Make a left. Take the door with the Exit sign. Loading dock is across the lot. Can't miss it."

The warehouse is a large metal building with two overhead doors that look out over loading bays. Four brown step vans, the sides of which are affixed with the Tuscarawus Coffee Roasters logo, are parked at the bays. We cross the small asphalt lot, reach the loading area and take concrete steps to the warehouse. A few feet away, a man in a brown uniform sits at a metal desk pecking at a computer. His name tag tells me he's the man we're looking for.

"Scott Barbereaux?" I hold out my badge.

He glances up from his work. His eyes widen when he spots my badge and uniform. Standing quickly, he puts up his hands as if to fend us off. "Look, if this is about that ticket in Wooster, I sent the money order in two weeks ago."

He's about six feet tall with broad shoulders and well-defined biceps. He wears the uniform a tad too tight, but it looks good on him—at least he thinks so. His face is tanned to a golden, healthy brown. Dark hair cut just above his shoulders has been artfully highlighted, giving an overall impression that he's spent the last six months on some topless beach in the south of France. I can practically smell the Bain de Soleil.

"This isn't about a ticket," I say.

"Really?" He relaxes, smiles, amused. "If it's not about the ticket then—" He falls silent, sobers as realization dawns. "Oh, shit. This is about the Amish girl at the store. Evelyn told me you cops were asking about me."

"That Evelyn is pretty fast on the dial, isn't she?" Tomasetti sidles around behind him and steals a look at the computer screen.

If this makes Barbereaux nervous, the man gives no indication. "That's just bizarre. An *Amish* family. Shit. You guys arrest anyone yet?"

"We're following up on a few things," I say vaguely.

"I just saw the girl last week. Friday. She was stocking preserves or something. Sweet kid. Quiet. Seemed to be a hard worker. Believe me, Evelyn gets her money's worth."

"Did you know her?" I ask.

"Mandy?"

"Mary," I correct. "Last name Plank."

"Just to say hello. I saw her at the store just about every time I delivered. Mostly on Fridays. They went through a lot of coffee. Evelyn offers it free to tourists, you know. I guess that's a good way to entice them, but . . ." As if realizing he'd drifted off topic he sighs. "I just can't believe someone could do something so frickin' bad to a helpless Amish family."

"Did you ever see Mary with anyone?" I ask.

"Not that I recall."

"Did you ever see her get into a vehicle?"

"I'm sorry. I never really noticed. My route's got a lot of stops, so I'm always rushed. God, now I wish I'd paid more attention." He runs his fingers through his hair, musses it to tousled perfection. "I mean, I've got nieces and nephews. I know you guys don't want to hear this, but I swear to God if someone ever hurt them, I'd go Dirty Harry on them."

"Did you ever speak to Mary?" Standing behind Barbereaux now, Tomasetti picks up a sheet of paper, skims it, sets it back down.

"I helped her lift some heavy stuff once. A case of jelly or jam or something. I think she was really shy."

"Did you ever meet any of her family members?" I ask.

He shakes his head. "I think I saw her mom once, but we didn't speak or anything."

Tomasetti makes his way around to the front of the desk. "Where were you Sunday night?"

"Shit. Me?" Barbereaux presses his hand to his chest. Mr. Innocent. "You don't think I had something to do with this, do you?"

"We're just collecting information," I add. "You know, to rule people out."

"Well, I was home all night. With my girlfriend, Glenda Patterson." He spells the last name. "We watched a movie. You can call her."

I jot down the name. "You two live together?"

"No, she's got her own place in Maple Crest."

Maple Crest is a new housing development that's gobbled up a good bit of farmland on the east side of town. "Anything else you can tell us about Mary that might help us?" I press.

"Not that I can think of."

"Did she ever seem upset?" I ask.

"Not really," he says. "She was always head down, working. Like I said, Evelyn kept her pretty busy."

"What kind of vehicle do you drive?" Tomasetti asks.

"Grand Am."

"What color?"

"Black." Barbereaux's eyes narrow. "Why?"

Tomasetti gives him a half smile. "We appreciate your time," he says and starts toward the door.

Barbereaux makes eye contact with me. "I hope you catch the asshole who did this," he says.

"We will," I say and fall in beside Tomasetti.

We're midway to the loading dock when I remember Evelyn Steinkruger's comment about Mary smelling like cigarette smoke, and I turn back toward Barbereaux. "Do you smoke?" I ask.

"Naw." He grins. "Those things'll kill you."

Back in the Tahoe, Tomasetti puts the vehicle in gear and pulls out of the parking lot.

"What do you think?" I ask.

"I think he looks like the fuckin' UPS guy."

That makes me laugh. My melancholic mood lifts just a little. It feels good, I realize, and I'm glad Tomasetti is here. "Where to?" I ask.

"Crime scene. I want to see the place before it gets dark."

Ten minutes later, we arrive at the Plank farm. Tomasetti pulls up behind the buggy and shuts down the engine. "Pretty place," he says. "Quiet."

"Isolated, too."

"Closest neighbor is what? About a mile away?"

I nod. "The Zooks. They didn't hear anything."

I get out and start toward the door. I'm in the process of unlocking it when Tomasetti steps onto the porch.

"CSU's all done?" he asks.

"Finished up late last night."

"Any idea who you chased into the cornfield?"

I shake my head. "Rain washed away any tire tread or footprints."

"You think it was the killer?"

I consider that for a moment. "I don't know. Why would he come back when my Explorer was parked in plain sight?"

"Unless you were his target."

"I don't think so. He was pretty quick to run. This guy was like a jack-rabbit. It was as if he was shocked to see me."

"Teenagers? The morbidly curious?"

"Maybe. I don't know."

We're standing in the kitchen. Around us, the house is so hushed I can hear the wind whispering around the eaves. The occasional creak of one-hundred-year-old wood. It has the empty feel of a vacant house now. Traces of the people who had once lived here are fading, and it strikes me that I don't want them to be forgotten.

"Bad scene." Tomasetti glances toward the living room where three pools of blood are marked with markers, then looks up at me. "CSU get anything useful?"

I give him the rundown of everything we've gathered so far. "We're waiting to hear from the lab on latents, footwear imprints, hair, fibers and DNA."

"I'll make some calls, see if I can light a fire."

"I appreciate that."

I cross to the window above the sink, look out at the field beyond. I should be thinking about the case, but even that is dwarfed by my keen awareness of Tomasetti.

"Kate."

I turn to see him standing a scant yard away, staring at me with those intense eyes. "Is this how it's going to be? We talk about the case? Make small talk?"

I want to pretend I don't know what he's talking about. Part of me wants to make him take that first perilous step into the quagmire of words neither of us is good at. "I'm just trying to get my footing here."

"Are you talking about the case or us?"

"Both, I guess." I give him a smile. "I think I'm better at the case stuff."

"Safer ground." But the hard lines of his face soften. "I wish you'd felt you could call me—"

"I did—"

"And ask me for help without worrying that I was going to lose it." He smiles. "All you have to do is ask. I'll be here."

"I didn't want to drag you into it." I motion toward the bloodstained floor. "Put you through this."

"I'm here because I want to be here." He looks around the kitchen, sighs, then turns his attention back to me. "I'm a cop, Kate. This is what I do. God knows it's not always easy. But that doesn't mean I'm going to turn tail and run every time there's a bloody crime involving a family."

"I know you can handle it," I say. "I didn't mean to imply otherwise.

But that doesn't mean a crime like this isn't going to bring back what happened to you. I don't like seeing you hurt, John. Maybe that's what I was trying to avoid."

"I appreciate that. But in all fairness, I think it's my call. Not yours."

"Duly noted." I soften the words with a smile. "If it's any consolation, I'm glad you're here."

We fall back into police mode. Our boots thud dully on the wood floor as we walk into the living room. The three pools of blood are dry now, brick-red and cracked around the edges. The smell is still discernible, but not as strong, and I realize the evidence of death is fading, giving way to the unstoppable force of life. It's a rule all of us must abide by. No matter what happens, life always goes on.

I take the steps to the second level, giving Tomasetti a few minutes alone to walk and assess the scene. I do a final sweep of the bedrooms, but I know there's nothing more to glean here. The rooms have been searched multiple times by multiple people. We've got everything we're going to get. It's not much, but we'll just have to make do.

Taking a final look at the empty hall, I go back downstairs. I'm anxious to talk to Tomasetti now, get his take on what might have happened, his theories, see if he has anything new to add that no one else has thought of.

I find him standing near the base of the stairs with his back to me. "What do you think?" I ask.

A quick glance over his shoulder and he walks away. Puzzled, I follow him. "At first we thought we were dealing with a murder-suicide, but—"

Tomasetti stops in the center of the living room, near where the bodies were found, and looks down at the bloody footprint. A current of worry goes through me when he sidesteps the dried blood and staggers left. I see his shoulders tighten. A sound that's part gasp, part sigh fills the silence.

Concerned, I take a step toward him. "John?"

Leaning forward, he puts his hands on his knees and sucks in huge mouthfuls of air, like a marathoner who has just finished a long-distance race.

Case forgotten, I cross to him. "John? What's going on? Are you all right?"

"Get the fuck away," he grinds out.

"What's wrong?"

No answer. He's trembling uncontrollably now. Every breath is a rasp.

"Are you sick?"

Keeping his back to me, he raises a hand as if to fend me off. "Give me . . ." He chokes out the words. ". . . goddamn minute."

Concern burgeons into alarm inside me. A dozen scenarios rush my brain. Is he sick? Having a heart attack? "John, talk to me," I try. "What's wrong? Are you in pain?"

His breaths rush between clenched teeth. I stand a few feet away, wondering what to do, how to help, growing increasingly worried. I can see the sheen of sweat on the side of his face. He's bent at the waist, his hands clenched into fists on his knees.

"Do you need an ambulance?" I ask.

"Give me . . . fucking minute," he says in a hoarse voice.

The urge to pull out my cell and dial 911 is strong, but I resist. If he needed an ambulance, he'd tell me. This is . . . something else.

I stand there, feeling helpless, my hand on my phone. I'm frightened and embarrassed for him. And I'm worried about his well-being. Slowly, his breathing regulates. The shaking subsides. A sigh escapes him as he straightens. Without a word, without looking at me, he turns away and walks into the kitchen.

Gathering my composure, I follow. He's at the sink, splashing water on his face. "What the hell was that?" I ask.

He yanks a towel out of a drawer and pats his face dry, looking at me over the tops of his fingers. "Had you worried, didn't I?"

"That's not funny," I snap. "You were in serious distress a moment ago. You need to tell me what's going on."

He looks away, takes a moment to toss the towel on the counter. "I didn't mean for you to see that."

"You scared me."

"Yeah, well, I scare myself sometimes." The lines on either side of his mouth deepen, and he sighs like an old man who bears the weight of the world on shoulders that have grown brittle and frail. "There was a time when I thought I could walk away from just about anything. I was one of those cops who could go directly from some bloody murder scene to lunch and not think twice about it. I was untouchable. Never had demons. Never felt too much. That was one of the reasons I was such a good cop. The job never got to me. I never let it." He pins me with a grim look. "All of that changed the night Nancy and the girls were murdered."

"That's understandable," I say. "But you dealt with it. You got help."

"I let a lot of doctors prescribe a lot of pills I was all too happy to take."

"But you've come a long way since then."

"Not far enough, evidently," he says dryly.

"I don't know what that means. And I don't know what it has to do with what just happened to you."

Tomasetti scrubs a hand over his face. "I'm having anxiety attacks, Kate. I've been to the emergency room." He takes a deep breath. "I'm seeing the company shrink. It's a condition of my continued employment with BCI."

The words hit me like hammer blows. My head is reeling. Knowing everything he's been through, I hurt for him. "How long have you been having the anxiety attacks?" I finally manage.

"A couple of months."

"Why didn't you tell me?"

"Not exactly the kind of thing a guy wants to discuss with his lover."

I think about that a moment, trying to ignore the knot in my gut. "What's the prognosis?"

"Going to keep me on the couch awhile."

"I'm sorry."

"Before you go all doe-eyed on me, you probably ought to hear the rest."

"Now, you're really making me nervous."

"Yeah, well, it's a pisser." He grimaces. "The deputy superintendent has no idea I'm here."

That isn't what I expected him to say. "What?"

"I'm on leave. It's mandatory."

"Because of the anxiety attacks?"

He sighs. "Because of ancient history."

"Maybe you ought to tell me everything." Despite my efforts, my voice is tight.

"A few weeks before the Slaughterhouse case, I didn't pass a drug test."

I'm still trying to absorb the part about the panic attacks. It's not easy. John Tomasetti is one of the strongest, most capable people I've ever known. To learn he's suffering with an anxiety disorder truly stuns me. "Is your job going to be okay?"

"The deputy superintendent says once I get a clean bill of health, I can go back, pick up where I left off." One side of his mouth curves, but his eyes remain sardonic. "I guess the good news is they haven't tried to put me back in the loony bin."

I'm one of the few who know that after the murders of his wife and kids, Tomasetti spent a few weeks in a psychiatric facility.

After a moment, he gives me a sage look. "The night you called me, the night you chased someone into the cornfield . . ." He lets the words trail, but I already know where he's going with it. "It scared the hell out of me."

"Is that why you're here? Because you're afraid something will happen to me?"

"That might be part of it."

I study the hard lines of his face, trying to see more than he will reveal. "You know nothing's going to happen to me, right?"

His smile is rigid and false. "We've been cops long enough to know you can't make those kinds of guarantees."

Before I can refute the statement, his cell phone trills, sounding inordinately loud in the silence of the house. Snatching it from his belt, he brushes past me and answers with a curt, "Tomasetti."

I watch as he pulls out a notebook and scribbles. "I got it. Fax the whole list to the station down here, will you? Thanks."

Shoving the phone back into his belt, he turns to me. "The dark pickup truck you asked about?"

I'm still thinking about everything he just told me. The rapid shifting of gears to another topic jars me. "You got something?"

"BCI broke it down by color and by county," he answers. "They're faxing it to Glock now."

"I thought you weren't official?"

He smiles. "I have friends in low places."

"How many vehicles?"

"Forty-two."

"How many black and blue?"

He glances down at his notes. "Six black and eleven blue."

I'm already pulling my phone from my belt, punching numbers. Glock picks up on the first ring. "You get the list?" I ask without preamble.

"Right here."

"Any of the owners have a record?"

"Working on that now." I hear computer keys clicking on the other end. "I got three. Colleen Sarkes. 2007 blue Toyota Tundra. DUI back in 2006. Another one last year."

"Males," I say.

"Robert Allen Kiser. Black 2009 F-250. Convicted domestic violence last year."

"Who else?"

"Todd Eugene Long. 2006 Black Chevy. Convicted on a burglary charge a year ago."

"Give me their addresses."

Click. Click. Click. "Kiser lives in town." He pauses. "Long lives in the Melody Trailer Park out on the highway."

The Melody Trailer Park is closest to me. "I'll take Long. Grab T.J. or Pickles and go talk to Kiser."

"I'm on it."

Shoving my phone back onto my belt I turn to Tomasetti. "I've got a name. Let's go."

He's already striding toward the door. "Saved by the bell."

The Melody Trailer Park is ten minutes from the Plank farm. The place has been around since before I was born, but its heyday has long since passed. Back in the seventies, it was the premier location for trailer homes and RVs. Young couples and retirees made the park a showplace for the up-and-coming. But time and circumstance have a way of eroding even the most en vogue of places, and the Melody Trailer Park was unable to escape its inevitable fall from grace.

Tomasetti turns the Tahoe onto a patchwork of crumbling asphalt pocked with potholes. A row of walnut trees runs parallel with a derelict privacy fence, separating the park from a wheat field to the south. Opposite, two dozen mobile homes line the street like wrecked cars waiting for the crusher. Most of the homes are streaked with rust and black grime that's run down from the roof. I see broken windows, flapping screens and one storm door hanging by a single hinge. Two mobile homes are missing the skirting that encircles the base to keep the plumbing from freezing in the wintertime.

Seeing this kind of poverty in my own backyard saddens me. My family and I were far from wealthy, but we weren't poor, either. My parents always provided food and shelter, and instilled a sense of security. My life wasn't ideal, but the problems I experienced had absolutely nothing to do with money.

"Dismal place," Tomasetti comments.

"Wouldn't want to live here when the temp dips below zero."

"What's the address?"

I glance down at my notebook. "Thirty-five Decker. I think it's the last street."

The final fringes of daylight fade as Tomasetti turns onto Decker. The lot numbers painted on the curb are faded, but we find number thirty-five at the end of the street. A handful of maple and sycamore trees surround a nicely kept mobile home, casting it into perpetual shadow. Fallen leaves the color of blood cover the yard and driveway. Some enterprising individual had built wooden steps and a deck off the front door. But time and the elements have bleached the wood to monochrome gray and eroded any semblance of prettiness. A black Chevy pickup with a big crease in the door is parked in the driveway.

"There's the truck," Tomasetti says.

I get out and head toward the front door. The steps creak as I ascend them, and I find myself hoping the wood holds. I knock and wait. In the driveway, Tomasetti peers into the truck windows. From where I stand, I see several beer cans in the truck bed. A toolbox. A length of nylon rope.

The door swings open, and I find myself facing a tall man with strawberry blond hair and a scruffy beard the color of peach fuzz. "Todd Long?" I ask.

His gaze flicks from me to Tomasetti, who's coming up the stairs. "Can I help you?"

I show him my badge. "We'd like to ask you a few questions."

He stares at my badge and his adam's apple spasms twice. "Uh . . . what about?"

"A crime that was committed a few days ago."

"I don't know anything about a crime."

Resisting the urge to roll my eyes, I sigh. "You don't even know what I'm going to ask you yet."

He stares at me, his eyes blinking.

"Can we come in?" I ask.

I can tell he doesn't want to let us in. But he can't seem to come up with a good excuse for refusing. Reluctantly, he steps back and opens the door. "Sure."

I step into the living room. The trailer is too cold for comfort and smells of cigarette smoke and burnt pizza. Todd Long is about six feet tall with a lean build and big, slender hands. His pale complexion and strawberry blond hair makes for a nice contrast with the navy Tommy Hilfiger T-shirt and faded jeans. His face is an interesting one with high cheekbones, a chiseled mouth that would put Marlon Brando to shame and eyes the color of a deep-water lake on a sunny day.

"What's this all about?" His eyes flick from me to Tomasetti. He seems nervous. I wonder what he's got to be nervous about.

"Someone reported seeing a truck like yours out by the Plank farm the night that family was killed," Tomasetti begins.

"What?" Long's face goes even paler. "Like mine? I wasn't there."

"You know about the murders?" I ask.

He turns slightly to face me, a deer being approached by wolves from different directions. "I heard about it on the news. That was some bad shit."

"Where were you Sunday night?" Giving us only half of his attention, Tomasetti strolls into the kitchen.

"I was at the Brass Rail." Fast answer with no hesitation.

"Can someone vouch for you?" I ask.

"Sure. I was with a buddy of mine."

"Who?" Tomasetti asks. "We need names."

"Friend of mine by the name of Jack Warner. The bartender might remember me, too."

I pull out my pad and jot down the name. "What time were you there?"

"I got there at about nine. Stayed till closing." His eyes flick from me to Tomasetti. "Look, I didn't know those people. Hell, I don't know *any* Amish folks. I sure as hell don't have any reason to hurt 'em."

In the kitchen, Tomasetti opens a couple of drawers, peeks inside. "Anyone borrow your truck recently?"

"No one borrows my truck." He watches Tomasetti open the refrigerator. He wants to tell him to stop snooping; I see it in his eyes. But he doesn't have the balls.

Tomasetti nails him with a hard stare. "I understand you're on probation."

Long blinks, runs slender fingers through tousled hair. "Yeah. I did something stupid a long time ago. Did my time."

"You know you can go back to prison for lying to the cops, don't you?"

"I don't have any reason to lie to you guys. I was at the bar all night. I swear. You can check."

Tomasetti shows his teeth. "We will."

"Any particular reason you're so nervous?" I ask.

Long swings around as if he's expecting me to attack him from behind. "Cops make me nervous."

"Why is that?" I ask.

"Because you guys charged in here like I did something wrong." Long's nervousness is giving way to indignation now. "I've kept my nose clean ever since I got out."

"Do you own a firearm?" I ask.

He blinks at me. "I'm on probation."

In my peripheral vision, Tomasetti rolls his eyes. "Is that a yes or no?"

"I sold my guns when I got busted. Needed the money to pay my lawyer."

"What kind of guns?"

"Deer rifle. Revolver that belonged to my grandfather."

I jot it in my notebook. "Who did you sell them to?"

"Pawnshop in Mansfield. I think I've still got receipts."

"Dig them out," I say. "We may need them."

"Okay."

"Do you work?" Tomasetti asks.

"I've been with the railroad for going on two years."

"What about a girlfriend?" I ask.

"What kind of question is that?"

"One you have to answer," Tomasetti snaps.

"No one regular."

A thought occurs to me, so I jump in with the next question. "Do you know a guy by the name of Scott Barbereaux?"

Long makes a show of thinking. "I don't know. Maybe I went to school with him."

"You need to be more definitive," I say.

He looks at me as if he's not sure what the word means. "I think I did go to school with him."

"Were you friends?" I ask.

Long shakes his head. "He was always sort of a jock. You know, played football and shit. I was . . . more of a hood, I guess."

Tomasetti stares hard at him. "You telling us the truth?"

Long can't hold his gaze, and fixes his eyes on the floor. "I don't have any reason to lie. I didn't do anything wrong."

"If I find out you told even one teeny weeny little lie," Tomasetti says conversationally, "I'll come back, and I'll make you regret it. Are you clear on that?"

I see sweat on Long's forehead and upper lip. His gaze meet's Tomasetti's then skitters away. "I got it."

CHAPTER 16

Tomasetti slides into the Tahoe and pulls onto the street. "That guy's sweating bullets."

"Interesting reaction for an innocent man."

"*Innocent* being a relative term."

"You think he's involved in this?" I ask.

"Hard to tell. The guy's a fuckin' squirrel." He glances my way. "What do you think?"

I find myself thinking of Mary Plank and the man she depicted in her journal. "I know perspectives vary—especially when it comes to a teenaged girl's heart—but I don't think Todd Long is the man she wrote about in her journal."

Tomasetti arches a brow. "Not exactly tall, dark and handsome."

"Not exactly."

"You know what they say about love being blind."

"Not *that* blind." For the first time I notice we're not heading toward the station. "Where are you going?"

"I need a drink."

The incident back at the Plank farm flashes in my mind, followed by a sharp snap of anger. "After what just happened at the farmhouse, you want a drink? Are you kidding me?"

He pulls into the parking lot of McNarie's Bar and parks next to a vintage Camaro. "Look, it's almost nine o'clock. You've been at it since when? The crack of dawn? Or maybe you didn't sleep at all last night."

The latter is closest to the truth, but I'm not going to admit it. Being with Tomasetti outside a work environment is dangerous business. Going with him for a drink promises to be downright catastrophic. "I need to get contact info on this Jack Warner guy, verify Long's alibi," I say.

"You can bet that jumpy son of a bitch broke his knuckles dialing his buddy the moment we walked out the door." Swinging open the door, he slides out.

Cursing beneath my breath, I stay seated. He crosses in front of the Tahoe and opens my door. "Come on. Let's get a bite to eat. We can talk about the case."

"That's not all we're going to talk about," I snap.

"You're not going to psychoanalyze me, are you?"

I shake my head. "You're a pain in the ass."

"I believe that's the nicest thing anyone's said to me all week."

McNarie's Bar is a dive in every sense, replete with red vinyl booths, scarred Formica tabletops, and air so polluted it's probably illegal in most states. But it also happens to be my favorite watering hole. The clientele are low key. The music doesn't rattle my brain. The burgers are decent. Mc-Narie, the bear-size barkeep and owner, is a good listener and a hell of a lot more discreet than most cops I know. After I closed the Slaughterhouse Murders case in January, I spent more than one evening shooting doubles in the corner booth. McNarie got me home safely every single time.

Tomasetti chooses a booth at the rear. Big Head Todd and the Monsters belt out their classic ballad "Bittersweet" as I slide in across from him. Trying not to fidget, I catch McNarie's eye and motion him our way.

"Nice," Tomasetti comments. "You know the bartender."

"Small town. Everyone knows everyone."

"Uh-huh."

The big man crosses to us and puts his hands on his hips. "Every time I see you two together I know there's some serious shit going down." He's got a full beard that hangs off his chin like a wool sock. Matching white brows ride low over red-rimmed eyes. "You know who did it yet?"

"We're working on a couple of angles," I reply.

"Bad medicine, killing a whole family like that." He shakes his head. "And Amish, too. Kids. Just can't see it."

"You hear anything, McNarie?"

"Not a goddamn thing. People are fuckin' scared, locking their doors." He glances back at the bar where a woman clad in denim waits for service. "You want the usual, Chief?"

I nod, embarrassed by the fact that I spend enough time in here to have a usual.

McNarie shifts a heavy-lidded gaze to John. "What about you?"

Tomasetti has the gall to look amused. "I'll have whatever she's having."

The barkeep hustles away. Tomasetti smiles at me. "The usual, huh? You're busted."

I look at him. Really look at him for the first time since he stepped into my office a few hours ago. I've known him for ten months now, and John Tomasetti has always been a little rough around the edges. But his face is more angular than usual. I know he's forty-two years old—eleven years older than me—but he looks even older. His eyes have seen a lot of things, and it shows in a way that has nothing to do with age. I see so much in his face, sometimes it's painful. Sometimes he's downright scary to look at.

To say that he has issues would be an understatement. I know about some of his demons. Most he won't talk about. Like the night a drug dealer by the name of Con Vespian tortured his wife and two little girls, then burned them alive. A lot of people wouldn't have survived that kind of loss. Tomasetti did; he still breathes and eats and walks and sleeps. But there's living, and then there's merely existing. I think Tomasetti falls into the latter group. I know he spends a great deal of time trying to claw his way out of some deep, dark hole.

He's one of those cops who skates a thin line. He drinks too much. A few months ago, he was mixing prescription drugs. It's a hazardous means of escape, especially for a cop. We both know the only reason he still has a job is because he's damn good at what he does. I wonder how long that will last.

"So how are you really doing?" I ask after a moment.

"Let's just say I'm a work in progress."

McNarie appears and sets two Killian's Irish Red beers and two shot glasses in front of us. Tomasetti gives me a knowing smile, and we down the shots first. The bite of vodka on my tongue makes me shudder.

"When are you going to come clean with your superiors at BCI?"

He glances at his watch. "I have a feeling they've probably figured it out by now."

"How are you going to handle that?"

"You mean how will it affect your case?"

"That's not what I meant." But we both know if we don't play our cards right, his unofficial status could become an issue.

He shrugs. "I'll lay low. Help you with the BCI end of things."

"All those friends in low places must come in handy."

"Kate, there's no law against my being here. I want to work. I need to work. I may not be official, but I can help."

The vodka begins to knead my brain with its magic fingers and my earlier annoyance fades to a vague and fuzzy restlessness. The kind I feel when I know I should be doing one thing and I'm off doing another. Like now.

Leaning back in the booth, he peels the label from the beer bottle. He's got great hands. Strong with long fingers, blunt-cut nails and calluses. I stop short of remembering the way those hands feel against my skin . . .

"I don't want you to risk your job because you're worried about me," I say.

He picks up the Killian's and sips. "I'm here because I want to be."

"To work."

One side of his mouth curves. "Right."

On the jukebox, "Bittersweet" gives way to Clapton's "Cocaine." I wonder if booze is Tomasetti's cocaine. I wonder if he's mine.

"I'm probably not very good at the whole being supportive thing," I say.

"You're better than you know." He smiles. "Better than my shrink."

I look at him over the top of my beer. "So how are we going to handle all this?"

He raises his beer and looks at me over the top. "I think we should just take it one day at a time and see what happens."

CHAPTER 17

Some cases are more complicated than others. It's not that the perpetrators are unduly cunning; most are as mindless as the crimes they commit. More often than not, it's the relationship dynamics of the cops involved that throw an investigation into turmoil. To my misfortune, the Plank case promises to become as complex as the DNA we're hoping will solve it. It's dredged up a part of my past I've been running away from for seventeen years. A past I knew I would eventually have to face.

I'm thinking about the choices I made as a fourteen-year-old girl, and the demons born of those choices, as Tomasetti and I head back to the police station. He hasn't spoken to me since we left the bar. The silence is uncomfortable, but I prefer it. I think he does, too. Or maybe the silence is safer than talking. God knows I'm no expert on men, but I'm pretty sure he wants to spend the night with me. I'm not sure I have the resolve to refuse if he presses.

It's almost ten P.M. when Tomasetti pulls the Tahoe into a visitor slot outside the police station and kills the engine. Hands on the steering wheel, he stares straight ahead. "Come with me to the motel."

Temptation tugs at me. He's a meticulous lover, and it would be so easy to lose myself in that for a few hours. I want to blame my indecision on the vodka. But the debate rioting inside me is a lot more complex than an alcohol-fuzzed brain. It scares me because I'm pretty sure what I'm feeling won't be appeased by an orgasm.

"I can't." I don't look at him, but I feel his eyes on me.

"I guess I'm still wondering if we're . . ."

"Maybe that's the problem. We haven't defined what we are."

"We have a relationship," he says.

I finally meet his gaze. "Based on what?"

"Mutual respect. Admiration." He smiles. "Really great sex."

"What about friendship?" I say. "Trust?"

"That, too."

In that instant I know if I don't get out of there, I'm not going to leave, so I reach for the door handle. "I have to go."

He grasps my arm. "Don't give up on us."

"I haven't." Opening the door, I slide out then bend to look at him. "See you tomorrow."

I'm one of those people who can get by on little sleep. Probably a good thing since I'm a functioning insomniac. Tonight, I don't know if it's the case or Tomasetti that has my brain tied into knots. Probably a little bit of both.

After leaving him at the station, I was too keyed up to go home, so I called Mona and got the lowdown on Jack Warner, Long's alibi. He owns Backwoods Construction Company, a small firm that specializes in designing and building log cabins. He's divorced. No minor children. No record—not so much as a speeding ticket. I don't have high hopes of gleaning any particularly helpful information. Still, the alibi needs to be verified, and since I can't sleep, I might as well work.

It's ten-thirty P.M. now, and I've been parked on the street outside Warner's house for half an hour. I knocked on the door when I first arrived, but there was no answer. Facing an empty bed at home and the temptation of Tomasetti back at the motel, I decided to wait for Warner.

He lives in a nifty little A-frame cabin with lots of glass and rustic detail. The house sits on about two acres; the trees are so thick I can barely see the porch light from the street. The lot backs up to Painters Creek—one of the most coveted areas in town—and is probably worth a small fortune.

As I study the property, I find myself thinking about Todd Long. The contrasts between Warner and Long are striking. Long is an ex-con who spends his days schlepping shit into railroad cars and his nights in a trailer. Warner, on the other hand, owns a construction business and lives in one of the nicest houses in town. What's the connection? Are they just bar buddies? Friends? Acquaintances?

I'm thinking about calling it a night when headlights wash over my car. A sleek black BMW convertible pulls into Warner's driveway. It doesn't elude me that Mary Plank had been seen getting into a dark-colored car. A moment later, the house lights blink on. Firing up the engine, I turn in and park.

As I start toward the front door, the forest around me comes alive with a cacophony of crickets and frogs from the creek. Somewhere nearby, an owl screeches. Moths and other flying insects circle the porch light. I ascend the wooden steps and knock. Warner answers almost immediately.

The first thought that strikes my brain is that he's a nice-looking man. I guess him to be about thirty years old with dark brown hair and eyes the color of espresso. He has the tanned skin of someone that spends a good bit of time in the sun. He's not exactly buff, but the size of his arms tells me he lifts weights. He wears a navy polo shirt with a designer emblem on the pocket. Jeans faded to perfection. Boat shoes with no socks.

"Jack Warner?" I hold up my badge.

He can't hide his surprise. "Yes?"

"I'm Chief of Police Kate Burkholder. I'd like to ask you some questions."

He looks past me as if expecting an armada of police cars, lights and sirens. "What's this about? Has something happened?"

"There's no problem, sir." I try to turn off some of my intensity. "I just need to verify some information."

"Whew." He puts a hand against his chest and laughs. "For a second there I thought maybe someone had been in an accident. My mom or sister." Another sigh. "I guess the late hour made me think this was some kind of emergency."

"I apologize for the late hour." I try a smile to put him at ease. "If you prefer, I can come back tomorrow."

"No, of course, not." Stepping back, he swings open the door. "I'm kind of a night bird, anyway. Come in."

I enter a large living room with textured stucco walls and tall ceilings bisected with rough-hewn beams as thick as a man's waist. A leather sofa and two cowhide chairs form a grouping adjacent to a massive river-rock hearth.

"Nice place," I say.

"Thanks. I designed it myself and had it built four years ago. Been working on it ever since."

Above the hearth, a striking black-and-white photo of a massive bear standing on a river bank with a big salmon in its mouth catches my eye. "You a photographer, too?"

"My nephew took that." He grins sheepishly. "Right before we started running."

I smile back.

He motions toward the sofa. "Have a seat."

I cross to the couch and sit, noticing the Mexican vases on the trunk-style coffee table. On the wall opposite me, I see a slab of rustic wood upon which a hex symbol is painted.

"Interesting piece of art," I comment.

He looks at the hex sign and smiles. "I tore down a barn for a guy down in Coshocton County a couple of months ago. The barn was almost two hundred years old. I asked him if I could cut out the hex symbols and keep them, and he agreed. I repainted them and sold them to one of the tourist shops in town. I liked them so much, I kept one for myself."

Something goes ping in my brain. "Which shop?"

"Carriage Stop right off the traffic circle."

"You go in there often?"

"You know, Christmas shopping. Birthdays." Moving a Navajo print pillow aside, he takes the chair across from me. "Would you like something to drink? Coffee?" He smiles. "A beer? I've got Little King's."

He's trying to charm me. Had the circumstances been different, he might have succeeded. Tonight, I'm too preoccupied with the case. "Can you tell me where you were Sunday night?"

"Sure." He leans forward, puts his elbows on his knees. "I left the office around six P.M. and stopped by the Brass Rail. Had a burger and a couple of beers. Played pool with some guys. I probably left around midnight or so."

"You always stay out so late on a work night?"

Another charming smile. "I'm not *that* old, Chief."

I don't smile back this time. "Were you alone?"

"I was with a couple of buddies."

"What are their names?"

His eyes narrow. "Well, I was with an old friend of mine by the name of Todd Long. Alex Miller from work was there, too." He cocks his head. "Do you mind if I ask why you're asking me about Sunday night?"

I pull out my notebook. "How long have you known Todd Long?"

"Oh, gosh, since grade school. I beat him up once when we were in sixth grade." He smiles. "We've been friends ever since."

"Good friends?"

"I've known him for a long time, but we're not real close." He shrugs. "We kind of drifted, especially after he got popped on that burglary charge. Different lives. You know." He pauses, gives me a sage look. "Is Todd in some kind of trouble?"

"I just wanted to verify his whereabouts."

Warner's eyes widen. "Wait a minute. That's the night . . ." Putting his hand to his chest, he falls back in the chair as if flabbergasted. "This doesn't have anything to do with that Amish family, does it? The family that was murdered? Jesus Christ, there's no way Todd had anything to do with that."

"I'm basically ruling people out at this point."

"That's a relief. For a moment there, I thought you were looking at Long."

"This is just routine." I tell him about the witness seeing a dark truck in the area. "We're checking the owners of every vehicle that matches that description."

"I gotcha." He whistles. "Pretty shocking crime."

"Did you know any of the Planks?" I ask.

"Never met them."

"What about Mary Plank?" I watch his eyes closely, but they reveal nothing.

"No, why do you ask?"

"She worked at Evelyn Steinkruger's shop."

"Ah." He grimaces appropriately. "Never met her. I'm sorry."

Rising, I start toward the door. "Thanks for your time."

"Hey, no problem. I hope you guys get him."

"Don't worry," I say. "We will."

Uncertainty dogs me as I walk back to the Explorer. I should feel better now that Long's alibi has been verified. But something about my visit with Warner vaguely disturbs me. Maybe because I can tie him to the shop where Mary worked. I know it's a small town and coincidences are more likely to occur. Still, it's enough for me to add him as a person of interest.

I've been racing against the clock for almost three days now, and all I have are dead ends leading to dead ends. A cycle that makes me feel like a hamster running on a wheel.

In the back of my mind I know there's no such thing as the perfect murder. Somewhere, someone left *something* behind. However small or seemingly inconsequential, it's my job to find it. I owe that to the Plank family. I owe it to this town and the people I've sworn to serve and protect. Most of all, I owe it to myself.

Seventeen years ago, I didn't get justice for a crime committed against me. But I'm a cop now. It's within my power to see this through, and get justice for another young Amish girl who can't do it herself.

* * *

The sun isn't quite above the horizon when I pull into my parking space at the station the next morning. Beside me, Mona's Ford Escort is covered with a diamond layer of frost. T.J.'s cruiser is parked farther down, and I know he's come in early to finish up his Internet assignment before he goes on patrol.

Mona sits at the switchboard-dispatch station with her feet on the desk, a lollipop in her mouth and a college text open in front of her. Her feet slide off the desk the instant she sees me walk in. "Hey, Chief."

"You look busy."

She grins. "It's been kinda quiet."

"That's the way we like it."

T.J. peeks at me over the top of his cubicle. "You got a sec?"

I enter his cube to see he has both his desktop and a laptop computer running. A printer I've never seen before hums from atop a two-drawer file cabinet, and I realize he brought it from home. "Find anything interesting?"

Looking uncomfortable, T.J. slides behind his computer. "I hit a few uh . . . porn sites last night and this morning. I'll tell you, there's some weird shit out there."

"Like murder weird or sex weird?"

"Both." He face reddens. "We're talking fetishes."

"Violence?"

"Foot fetishes, mostly."

"That *is* weird."

He taps a couple of keys on the desktop keyboard. "We have man on man. Woman on woman. Animal on woman." He looks at me. "You ever seen the size of a—"

"Just case stuff, T.J.," I cut in before he can finish.

"Oh. Right." Rolling his chair to the laptop, he types in a login and password. "I searched for anything Amish, and I was blown away by the number of porn Web sites into that sort of thing."

"To each their own," I mutter.

"I guess." He hands me a sheet of paper. "Here's a list of Web sites with IP addresses. I bought photo paper and printed some of the . . . uh . . . images. A lot of the female . . . uh . . . perpetrators don't match Mary Plank's description, but I went ahead and printed the ones that were even close. A lot of the . . . actors wear wigs and try to conceal their identity."

"Let's take a look."

"I found about a dozen." He hands me a manila folder with several eight-by-ten photos inside. "They're kind of shocking, Chief."

I take the folder and open it. He's right. The photos are not only shocking, but disturbing. Outrage rises inside me at the sight of a young woman clad in traditional Amish garb. Plain dress. Gauzy *kapp*. No makeup. She's Caucasian. Brown hair peeks out from beneath the *kapp*. The photo is relatively good quality, but her face is turned so that I can't make out her facial features. She may or may not be Amish; there's no way to tell, but it feels like sacrilege.

The woman and two men are on an antique-looking steel bed. I see rumpled white sheets. A windowless, white-walled room. Shadows raining down, giving the photo the stark ambience of an old film. The woman straddles a white male, who's lying on his back. He's in his late twenties or early thirties. Dark brown hair. Goatee. His head is angled so that I can't see his face. A second white male is grasping her hips and pumping into the woman from behind. Again, his face is turned. He's larger with a heavily muscled body. A weight lifter, probably. More body hair. Sideburns. No beard. No visible birthmarks.

I'm no prude, but this staggers me. I stare at the young woman's profile. Her head is thrown back as if in ecstasy. Her dress is open in the front and her tiny breasts are bared. I can't tell if it's Mary Plank. She has pretty skin and a girlish figure. She looks very young. So skinny I can see her ribs. But she still has the chubby hands of a child.

I try to take in the details with the unaffected eye of a cop, but I can feel the pound of outrage in my ears. The burn of embarrassment on my cheeks. A depth of sadness in my heart that surprises me.

"Is it her?" T.J.'s words snap me from my momentary fugue.

"Hard to tell."

"They kept their faces angled away from the camera the duration of the video."

"I can see why they don't want people recognizing them. This is pretty raw stuff." I glance at the folder in my hand. I don't want to look at the other photos, but I don't have a choice. "Get the domains and IP addresses to Tomasetti. Get BCI to run down the owners of the sites."

"Sure."

"In the interim, why don't you cruise out to whoisit.com and see if you can come up with contact information or names."

"Probably a long shot."

"We might get lucky."

I take the folder to my office so I can look at them in privacy. I'm midway there when the bell on the door jangles. I look over my shoulder to see Tomasetti enter, a cardboard tray filled with six biggie coffees in his hands. Glock brings up the rear holding a white paper bag. Despite my resolve to maintain an even keel, a small thrill that has absolutely nothing to do with coffee or doughnuts runs the length of me.

"Brain food," Glock comments.

Skid enters behind Glock. "Gotta have a brain for that, dude."

"Can't you guys ever bring anything even remotely healthy?" Mona usurps the bag from Glock and carries it to the coffee station. "Does an apple fritter count as a fruit serving?"

"We're cops," Skid says. "We eat doughnuts."

I feel Tomasetti's eyes on me as I head toward my office. I know dodging him is a stupid reaction. We're working together; more than likely, I'll be dealing with him every day until the case is closed. But just the sight of him shakes me up a little.

Sliding behind my desk, I open the folder and start flipping through the photos. All depict young women in various stages of undress and engaging in some form of sex. Oral. Anal. Threesomes. All wear Amish clothing. *Kapps.* Plain dresses. Practical shoes. But all semblance of plain or practical ends there. The photos are triple X and difficult as hell to look at.

I arrange the photos into two piles. T.J. did a good job, but none of the women's faces is fully visible. Of the twelve images, ten of them could be Mary Plank. All I can do at this point is give them to John and see if the BCI lab can magnify them and find some identifiable mark. A birthmark or scar I can connect to Mary Plank. There's a chance his technology people will be able to identify the owners of the Web sites. From there, they may be able to locate the person who submitted the image.

My brain is still working that over when I look up to see Tomasetti standing in the doorway to my office. "T.J. said you had some photos."

My eyes skitter away from his, but I force them back. "He got them off the Internet. Amish fetish stuff. A few could pass for Mary Plank." I shrug. "Can you have someone at BCI take a look at the domains and IP addresses? Maybe we can find the owner of the site or at the very least find out who posted the pics."

"We can try. The problem is that a lot of porn sites are based overseas where we have little or no control. Might take a while."

Sighing, I look down at the two piles of photos. "These are the most promising."

Taking the visitor chair across from me, Tomasetti reaches for the photos and begins flipping through them. I see his face darken. His brows knit. Frown lines appear on either side of his mouth. "Shit. Girls look young."

"They do." I reach for the case file, pull out one of the autopsy photos of Mary Plank and set it on the desktop between us for reference. "Can your lab enhance the photos? Maybe do some kind of comparison with the autopsy pic? If there's a birthmark or something, we might be able to make a positive ID."

"I'll get it couriered this morning." He focuses his attention on me. "You check out Long's alibi?"

"Warner panned out. Seems pretty solid. But get this: he sold some folk art to Evelyn Steinkruger at the Carriage Stop."

"So you can tie him to the shop." He thinks about that a moment. "Does he know the Plank girl?"

"Says no."

"What about the other truck owner?"

"Robert Allen Kiser." I glance down at my notes. "Glock talked to him. Kiser was at the Lion's Club meeting and reception that lasted until one A.M."

"Substantiated?"

"By about a dozen witnesses." I sigh. "After the reception, Kiser went home with his wife."

"What's Glock's take on him?"

"Said he seemed like a pretty solid guy."

"Everyone's a solid fuckin' guy."

I don't like the cynicism in his voice, but I feel that same sentiment growing inside me. I reach for the Speaker button and dial the switchboard.

"Mona, get me contact info and addresses for Glenda Patterson, will you?" Patterson is Scott Barbereaux's girlfriend. "Work and home."

"You got it, Chief."

I end the call and sigh. "You know a case is going to shit when you spend time checking the alibis of the alibis."

Across from me, Tomasetti is looking at the photos. His usual poker face has given way to raw disgust. "You ever work vice?" he asks.

I shake my head. "Went straight to homicide from patrol."

"It sounds weird, but I've always thought vice was somehow worse. A lot of nasty stuff. Prostitution. Drugs. Porn. Especially when there are kids involved." He shoves the photos into the file and closes it. "The thing about homicide is that the dead are dead. Gone. No more suffering. The living go on. They keep on suffering. Some keep on repeating the same tired cycle over and over again."

"The living always have hope," I reply.

He shakes his head. "Sometimes they don't."

My cell phone vibrates against my hip. I pull it out. My heart jigs when I see the sheriff's office of Lancaster County pop up on the caller ID.

"This is Deputy Phelps with Lancaster County. Corporal Rossi said I should give you a call when I located Bishop Fisher."

"You're there with him now?"

"Standing on his front porch, drinking a cup of coffee."

"Can you put him on the phone for me?"

"Sure can."

I put my hand over the phone and glance at Tomasetti. "I've got Aaron Plank's bishop on the line from Lancaster County."

"Nice work."

I smile and then Bishop Fisher comes on the line. I greet him in Pennsylvania Dutch, identify myself and then I ask him about the Plank family.

"It pained me greatly to hear about the passing of Amos and Bonnie Plank and their children." The bishop has the slow, thick accent characteristic to many Midwestern Amish. "But I know they believed in the divine order of things and the will of God."

"Did you know them well?"

"Yes. I conducted their wedding ceremony. I spoke to them many times over the years."

"Do you know why they left Lancaster County?"

For the first time, he pauses. "There were some problems a few years back with their son, Aaron. An *Englischer* was involved. Problems developed between Bonnie and Amos. Some members of the community could not condone Aaron's . . . relationship with this outsider, nor the way Amos and Bonnie handled it. In the end, Amos decided a fresh start in a new church district would be best, so he moved the family."

"What can you tell me about the problems?"

"Bonnie loved her son very much. She was a very tolerant woman. Willing to abide by almost anything to keep her son. Amos was not as tolerant. Neither was the community as a whole."

"So it caused a rift between them?"

"Between Bonnie and Amos as well as the Plank family and some of the community. Aaron was not repentant and refused to confess his sins. The *Ordnung* prohibited this relationship, particularly with an outsider."

"The community objected to a gay relationship?"

"There was a lot of talk." The old man's sigh is tired. *"Wer lauert an der Wand, Heert sie eegni Schand."* If you listen through the wall, you will hear others recite your faults.

It's not the first time I've heard the old adage. If the Amish as a whole have a fault, it is that at times they can be judgmental. "So the Planks left for a fresh start?"

"A fresh start in a new church district in Ohio."

"What can you tell me about Aaron's relationship with his family?"

"It was a stormy union. Troubled. Amos was a good father, a hard worker who provided well for his family. But he was not a patient man. Aaron was headstrong."

"Did they argue?"

"Often."

"Did either of them ever become violent?"

Another tired sigh. "There was a fight or two."

"Tell me about that."

"It happened about the time Aaron decided he would not be joining the church. Amos was upset and forbade Aaron to see the *Englischer*. One night, he caught the outsider in the barn with Aaron. I don't know what happened, but Amos lost his temper and went after the *Englischer* with his fists."

"And Aaron?"

"He picked up a pitchfork and used it against his *datt*."

There's no doubt in my mind why Aaron didn't mention that part of his juvenile record. "How badly was Amos hurt?"

"The wounds required surgery."

"Aaron was arrested?"

"The English police were called. He was arrested and taken to jail."

"But tried as a juvenile."

"I do not know the English laws, but I believe that was the case."

"Thank you for taking the time to speak with me, Bishop Fisher."

"I will say a prayer for the Plank family."

"I think they would like that very much."

"Gott segen eich." God bless you.

I disconnect to find Tomasetti staring intently at me. "Sounded like an interesting conversation."

"Aaron Plank attacked his father with a pitchfork when he was seventeen years old."

"Must have been pretty pissed off to do something like that."

"He didn't mention it when I talked to him."

"Maybe we ought to give him another chance to fess up."

"If he's still in town."

"Since there's only one motel, that ought to be pretty easy to figure out."

Grabbing my keys, I rise. "Damn, you're getting good at this cop stuff, Tomasetti."

"I was just trying to impress you."

"It's working."

CHAPTER 18

The Willowdell Motel is located on Highway 83 a few miles out of town. During the summer months, the place caters to tourists visiting Amish Country. During deer season, the motel caters to the dozens of hunters that flock to the area to bag that purported eight-point buck. The motel's one-size-suits-all décor doesn't differentiate between the two groups of clientele.

Tomasetti pulls the Tahoe into the gravel lot and we begin looking for Aaron Plank's Camry. "He might have gone back last night."

"He's still got the house to deal with," I point out. "He'll either need to hire a professional cleaner or do it himself. With so much blood, I'm betting he hires it out. At some point, he'll need to get the place appraised. If he wants to sell it, anyway."

"How much is a farm like that worth?"

"A hundred and sixty acres. Farmhouse. Barn. Outbuildings. It's a valuable piece of land. Traditionally, in an Amish family the eldest male child will inherit the farm when the parents pass."

"It's a stretch, but maybe he felt entitled. Kill the people who pissed you off and get a farm worth several hundred thousand dollars in the process. Maybe he decided to speed things up."

I shake my head. "I don't like Aaron Plank for this. James Payne, yes. But not Aaron."

"People have done worse for less." But I can tell by his lack of enthusiasm he's not buying it either.

We're midway through the lot; no sign of the Camry. "He's not here," I say.

Tomasetti stops outside the motel office. "Let's see if he checked out."

The heavy-set woman behind the counter tells us Plank checked out a couple of hours ago.

"He didn't happen to say where he was going, did he?" I ask.

"Sure didn't. But I can tell you he'd been drinking. I could smell it on his breath when he signed his receipt."

Back in the Tahoe, I'm feeling frustrated and tense. "Kind of early in the day for a nightcap."

"Especially if he's driving back to Philly." Tomasetti shrugs. "When in doubt, turn to alcohol."

I frown at him, then a thought strikes me. "Maybe he's at the farm."

"Tough place to stay if it hasn't been cleaned up."

"Maybe he decided to do it himself."

Glancing in the rearview mirror, Tomasetti hangs a U-turn. "Worth a shot."

Five minutes later we park next to the Plank buggy—right behind Aaron's Camry.

"Good hunch, Chief," Tomasetti says.

I glance toward the farmhouse. I see the kitchen curtains blowing outward, snapping in the stiff breeze. A nifty little gas generator sputters outside the window, the cord snaking inside. "Looks like he's airing the place out."

"Or cleaning up."

"Let's go find out."

We disembark and head toward the door. In the periphery of my consciousness, I'm aware of the birds singing all around. The crisp leaves rattling in the wind. A dozen or so cows hanging out in the paddock near the barn. Everything seems so benign. Except for the fact that a family of seven was wiped out in this very place just three days ago.

I ascend the steps and knock. Music floats through the open window. Classical guitar with a dash of Madrid. Several minutes pass. I'm in the process of raising my hand to knock again when the lock rattles.

Aaron Plank opens the door several inches and peers out at me. Even through that small space, my cop's eyes take in details. The first thing I notice about him is that he looks inordinately out of place in the big Amish kitchen wearing a paisley silk robe. His hair is mussed. His cheeks are flushed. His feet are bare.

"Can I help you?" No smile. No warmth. His voice tells me we've interrupted something he didn't want interrupted. The cop in me wants to know what that is.

"I'd like to ask you a few questions," I say.

Plank's eyes go from me to Tomasetti, who is standing slightly behind me. He makes no move to open the door. "This is kind of a bad time."

"I understand," I say. "But we only need a few minutes."

His gaze flicks sideways. "I'm kind of in the middle of something."

"So are we," Tomasetti cuts in. "A murder case. Now open the door and talk to us."

Aaron's mouth tightens into a thin, hard line. The door swings open as if by its own accord. Stepping back, he tugs at the belt of his robe. "I would have come down to the station."

"I'm afraid this won't wait." I step into the kitchen. The aromas of candle wax and coffee mingles with the fresh air gusting through the window. I see a high-tech coffeemaker on the counter. Dishes draining in the sink. A bottle of wine and two stemmed glasses sit on the counter. That's when I realize Aaron isn't alone, and I get a prickly sensation at the back of my neck. The kind you get when you know someone is watching and you don't know who or why. There were no other cars in the driveway, but I know he's got company.

"Who's here with you?"

Leave it to Tomasetti to cut to the chase. Listening, I cross to the living room. A dozen candles sit on the table, their tiny flames flickering in the breeze. Classical guitar streams from a cool little sound system on the floor.

"I don't believe we've met."

Both Tomasetti and I look up to see a dark-haired young man trotting down the stairs. He's got eyes the color of whiskey and just enough scruff of a beard to look en vogue. I know even before he introduces himself that the man is Aaron Plank's lover.

"I'm Rob Lane." Crossing to us, he extends his hand. "Nice to meet you. I just wish it were under different circumstances."

Tomasetti shakes the man's hand and introduces himself.

I step forward and do the same. "We spoke on the phone," I say.

"Of course." Rob's expression turns appropriately sober. "I couldn't believe it when Aaron told me what happened to his family, especially with their being Amish and in a town this size."

"You didn't mention you would be traveling to Painters Mill," I say.

"I hadn't planned to at the time." He grimaces. "But Aaron's been understandably upset. He asked me to fly out for the weekend."

I spot Aaron in the kitchen, pouring red wine into two glasses and start toward him. "Is there some place we can talk?" I ask him. "Alone?"

Frowning at me, he brushes past and hands Rob one of the glasses. "Anything you have to say, you can say in front of Rob."

I nod, wondering about the attitude change. Last time I talked to him, he was cooperative and forthright. Now, he's petulant. Why the turnaround? Is the grief over losing his family settling in? Did I come down on him too hard the last time we spoke? Or is there another reason for his abrupt turnaround?

"Why didn't you tell us you attacked your father with a pitchfork when you were seventeen?" I ask.

Aaron takes a swig of wine. "It's not the kind of thing you want to reveal to the cops when they're investigating the murders of your estranged family."

"Surely you knew we'd find out sooner or later."

He shrugs.

Tomasetti steps closer, crowding Aaron. "It's called lying by omission.

In case you missed that episode of *Law and Order,* Einstein, that's the kind of thing that usually makes the cops suspicious."

"I don't have anything to hide," Aaron says.

"You attacked your father and put him in the hospital," I say. "You didn't tell us. Now he's dead. It could appear as if you do have something to hide."

"I didn't kill my family. It's absurd of you to think so."

"Lying to the police doesn't exactly bolster our confidence in your ability to tell the truth," Tomasetti says.

Aaron glares at him, swigs more wine. "I'm not capable of that kind of violence."

"You stuck your old man with a pitchfork," Tomasetti mutters. "That's pretty violent."

"I had no reason to kill them."

"They condemned you for being different. They thought you were perverted. Maybe you wanted to pay them back for the hell they put you through when you were seventeen."

"All I wanted was to live my own life."

"They wouldn't let you do that, though, would they?" Tomasetti is goading him now.

"I forgave them a long time ago." Aaron's voice turns defensive.

"Did they forgive you?"

"I had no control over what they thought of me or my lifestyle," he says.

"This is a nice house, Aaron," I break in. "Are you going to keep it?"

"I haven't decided."

Tomasetti picks up an empty bottle of wine, makes a show of looking at the label, then sets it down. "Nice little love nest. Private. Roomy. Kind of ironic that the two of you are holed up in here now, drinking wine, hanging out, while the rest of your family is buried just down the road."

Rob steps forward. "You're out of line."

Tomasetti shows his teeth, but his eyes are focused on Aaron. "They put you through hell, Aaron. Especially your old man. He thought you were sick. Maybe this is your way of paying him back." He makes a sweeping motion with his hand. "Maybe you and lover boy are celebrating. Rubbing all that intolerance in their self-righteous faces."

"That's not how it is," Aaron retorts, his voice rising.

"Then tell us how it is."

Aaron divides his attention between Tomasetti and me. "I told you. I forgave them. I moved on."

"Is that why you're so upset?" Tomasetti asks.

"I was alone here! I needed . . . a friend. I called Rob."

"You haven't even cleaned up their blood yet, and here you are dancing and drinking wine and having veal parmesan for lunch. That's cold."

"W-we were going to hire a professional c-cleaner." Aaron stutters the words. "They can't come out until tomorrow."

"How much did you hate your father?" Tomasetti asks.

"I didn't hate him. He hated *me*. His *son*. He couldn't stand what I was." He turns his gaze to mine. Through the anger, his eyes plead for understanding, and for the first time I see the shimmer of tears. "I loved him. I loved all of them."

"Is that why you stabbed him with a pitchfork?" Tomasetti asks.

"I was a teenager. He was . . . ignorant. He didn't . . . *wouldn't* understand. I lost my temper!"

"I think you still have a temper," Tomasetti says. "I'll bet you'd like to stick a pitchfork in me right now, wouldn't you?"

Aaron hurls the wineglass to the floor, inches from Tomasetti's foot. Glass shatters, shards flying against the wood cabinets. Tomasetti doesn't even flinch.

"Hey." Rob steps between Tomasetti and Aaron, like a referee stopping a fight after a particularly devastating blow. "Come on, you guys. This has gone far enough."

"Going to go a lot farther if we get lied to again." Tomasetti jabs a finger at Aaron. "You listening?"

Aaron lunges at Tomasetti. I step forward, ready to intervene. But Rob catches Aaron by the arms, hauls him back. "This conversation is over," he snaps.

Tomasetti has the gall to look amused. "You might want to watch that temper of yours, Aaron. You don't want the cops thinking you're capable of violence."

"Fuck you!" Aaron screams the words.

"Enough." Before even realizing I'm going to move, I step closer, turn to face Aaron. "You need to calm down." Then to Tomasetti. "This isn't getting us anywhere."

Scowling, Tomasetti walks away. Bad cop. Time for me to move in. I turn back to Aaron. Something I see in this troubled young man's eyes touches me in a place I don't want to acknowledge. Maybe because Aaron Plank and I have more in common than he could ever know. Those parallels have been floating around in my subconscious since I learned of his excommunication.

"Come here." I motion toward the kitchen.

Feeling Tomasetti's and Rob Lane's eyes on me, I walk into the kitchen, aware that Aaron follows a few feet behind me. Once in the kitchen, I turn to face him. "You're not helping your cause."

He sneers. "You must be the good cop."

"You're not a suspect."

"Then why are you hassling me?" Crossing to the counter, he snags another wineglass and pours more merlot into it.

"Because you withheld information that might have been helpful." I return evenly. "What else aren't you telling us?"

He looks away, raises the glass to his lips, takes a too-big gulp of wine. "I heard you used to be Amish," he says. "Is that true?"

"I was. A long time ago."

"Then you know gossip is one of their favorite pastimes," he says. "You know they can be a bunch of judgmental pricks."

"Who are you protecting?" I ask point-blank.

"No one."

"Is it Mary? Was she into something she shouldn't have been? Are you trying to protect her reputation? Her memory? What?"

He looks down at the wineglass in his hand.

"Aaron, you need to talk to me. We're trying to find out who killed your family. If you know something, now is the time to open up."

After a moment, he raises his eyes to mine. "I know in the scope of things it doesn't seem important, Chief Burkholder, but I don't want anyone to know what I'm about to tell you, especially the Amish community. Mary cared about her reputation. It mattered to her. She wouldn't want them gossiping about her. About *Mamm* and *Datt*."

I give him the most honest answer I can. "I'll do my best to keep whatever you tell me out of the public eye."

His hand trembles when he sets down the glass. "I received a letter from Mary. About a month ago."

The revelation sends a jolt through me. "What did it say?"

"She wanted to leave the Amish lifestyle. She asked for my help."

"Why did she want to leave?"

"She said she didn't fit in, couldn't conform."

I know there's more. "Did she mention a boyfriend?"

He eyes me warily. "You know about him?"

"She kept a journal. I found it in her room. I've read it."

"A journal?" Emotion swells in his eyes. "Can I see it?"

"You can when I close this case. For now, it's evidence." I move closer to him. "What did she say about the boyfriend?"

"Just that he wasn't Amish, but she was crazy about him. *Really* crazy. Made it sound all romantic. You know, teenaged girl stuff. She wanted to marry him. Have his kids. Shit like that. She was sneaking out at night to be with him."

"Did she mention a name?"

"No."

I hold his gaze. "Do you still have the letter?"

"I tossed it." He looks away. "I didn't know it would be the last time I heard from her."

"What was the tone of the letter?" I ask.

"I swear to God she seemed fine. Just . . . confused. In love for the first time." His voice cracks on the last word. "I wish I'd dropped everything and driven down. I might've been able to do something." He closes his eyes, presses his fingers to his temples. "Mary always looked up to me. I was her big brother. She watched me leave the Amish way of life, and she wanted the same for herself." He sighs. "I had Rob to help me through it. She didn't have anyone. I wish I could have been there for her."

"Is there anything else you can tell me about the letter?" I ask. "Anything that worried you?"

He shakes his head. "God, I don't remember all the details. She kind of caught me up on family stuff. How fast little Amos was growing. She said everything was fine. I do recall that she talked a lot about the guy. She was definitely into him."

"Did she say anything that made you concerned for her safety?"

"No."

Disappointment digs into me. "Did you write her back? Call her?"

"I wrote her a letter." His face screws up. He brings his fist down on the counter. "I wish to *God* I'd had the courage to drive down."

"What did you say in your letter?"

He blows out a breath, composes himself. "I hooked her up with an Amish guy near Millersburg. He runs a sort of . . . underground railroad for young Amish men who want to leave the Plain life." He gives me a sage look. "That's one of the reasons I didn't tell you about this, Chief Burkholder. The man is Amish. He's married to an Amish woman and they have six children. If anyone finds out what he does, he'll be excommunicated."

For the first time, Aaron's reticence makes a certain amount of sense. "What's his name?"

"Ed Beachey."

I've never met Ed, but I know of him. "He owns a small cattle opera-tion down the road from Miller's Pond."

Aaron nods. "Ed gives these kids a place to stay. He gives them food. Counsels them. I told Mary to contact him."

"Did she?"

"I checked. Ed says she never did."

"You know I've got to verify all this with Ed," I say.

"No one knows he helps young men leave the Amish way of life. If it gets out, he's going to think I betrayed him."

"I'll let him know you didn't have a choice." I sigh, feeling deflated. "If you remember anything else that might be important, call me." I turn to leave. I'm midway to the living room when Aaron stops me.

"Chief Burkholder?"

I turn back to him.

"I just remembered something that might help." He looks more ani-mated as he crosses to me. "She mentioned something about meeting her guy out at Miller's Pond."

"She wrote about it. In the diary."

"Well, then you probably already know that one day when she was waiting for him, she carved their initials in a tree."

I stare at him, aware that my pulse is spiking. Initials won't solve the case, but they might help identify the boyfriend. "Do you know where the tree is? Near the water? The path? Parking area?"

He grimaces, shakes his head. "She didn't say. Just a tree. That's all I know."

I stare at him a moment longer. I'm still not sure if I like him, but one thing that's clear to me is that he loved his sister. "This would have been a lot easier if you'd just come clean from the start."

He closes his eyes briefly and in that instant I know he blames himself, at least in part, for his sister's death. Maybe for the deaths of his entire family.

"Nothing's going to bring them back," he says.

"No, but sometimes telling the truth helps you sleep at night."

*　*　*

It's been a long time since I've been to Miller's Pond, and I always forget how pretty it is. The dam is on the east side. Below the dam, a greenbelt thick with trees runs along Painters Creek. To the west is a cornfield. On the north side, a hay field is hip high with alfalfa. To the south, the yellow-green carpet of a soybean field stretches as far as the eye can see.

The pond itself is a good-size body of water. People swim here in the summer. They ice-skate in winter. Lovers park here at night. Teenagers drink and smoke dope. The area is secluded with no official parking area. The only thing that keeps the place from getting crowded is that you have to walk half a mile down a wooded path to get to the water.

Ed Beachey's place was on the way, so Tomasetti and I stopped by to ask him if Mary Plank had sought his help. The Amish man claimed she never contacted him. I believed him. I wanted to assure him his secret was safe with me, but I've learned the hard way not to make promises I might not be able to keep. Another dead end.

I told Tomasetti about my conversation with Aaron on the drive over. Neither of us is very optimistic about finding the tree with the initials. But with the case stalled and the clock ticking, he wasn't opposed to a quick look-see.

"Pretty heavily wooded area." He parks in front of the guardrail.

"I thought we could walk the path, see if anything pops out at us." I slide out of the SUV. It's so quiet I can hear the bees buzzing around the goldenrod and dandelions in the bar ditch.

Tomasetti gets out and slides on his sunglasses. "If you're thinking footwear impressions or tire treads, we're a month too late."

Our gazes meet over the hood of the vehicle. "I know it's a long shot, but if we can find the initials, it could help."

He nods, but I can tell he's not sold on the idea. "If we don't find the initials, at least we have a good supply of trees to bang our heads against."

"Pragmatist."

The Tahoe is parked in gravel. The asphalt ended about a quarter mile back. There's not much room for parking, but I can tell by the amount of trash on the ground that plenty of people come here. Where the weeds meet the gravel, broken glass shimmers like hot diamonds beneath the sun. I see dozens of tire tread imprints. Candy bar wrappers. A used condom. Most people are pretty good about picking up after themselves. But not the slobs. I've been standing in the sun for less than a minute and already I'm sweating beneath my uniform.

"Okay. So we've got a few thousand trees to check." He opens the Tahoe door, digs around for a moment, emerges with two Wal-Mart bags, passes one to me. "Here's your evidence bag."

"You're pretty resourceful, Tomasetti." I take the bag. "You a Boy Scout?"

"Got kicked out for smoking when I was nine."

"Figures." But I smile. "You wouldn't happen to have gloves, would you?"

He ducks back into the Tahoe and comes out with a handful of tissues. "These'll have to do."

"You BCI guys are high tech all the way." I take a couple of the tissues, tuck them into my back pocket.

Sighing, he works off his suit jacket and tosses it onto the front seat. He is wearing a light blue shirt beneath the jacket. The armpits and back are wet with sweat. He takes a moment to loosen his tie. I see chest hair peeking out of his collar and it reminds me he's got just the right amount of it.

"Anything else we should be looking for while we're here?" he asks.

I shake my head. "They came here several times. They drank wine, had sex."

"The boyfriend smoke?"

"She didn't mention it, but Evelyn Steinkruger said Mary came back to work once smelling of cigarettes."

"Even if we find a butt, chances are there won't be any DNA. Even if there was, it isn't against the law to smoke out here. Won't do us any good in terms of the case."

"Unless the DNA matches the DNA found inside her body."

"Good point." He rolls up his shirtsleeves. "Let's see if they left us anything to work with."

We begin in the gravel parking area. I walk the perimeter where flying insects swarm in hip-high weeds. It's late in the season so everything is yellow and dry and coated with a thin layer of gravel dust. Tomasetti walks the dirt track that leads back to the main road, checking the bigger trees along the way. I use one of the tissues to pick up a candy wrapper and place it in the Wal-Mart bag. All the while my brain chants the word *futile*.

It takes us fifteen minutes to scour the area. I've netted a handful of candy and gum wrappers, a plastic water bottle and a crushed Skoal can. Wiping a drop of sweat from my temple, I look around, trying to put myself in Mary's head. Ten feet away, Tomasetti looks the way I feel: hot and discouraged.

"She was breaking the rules by being here," I say. "She would have wanted privacy."

"He probably wouldn't want to be seen with her." He walks over to me. "Let's check the woods."

We head down the dirt path cut into the woods. The trees offer shade, but the mosquitoes have decided we're fair game. No one officially maintains the path; it stays open due to the amount of foot traffic. Once or twice a year, one of the local farmers cuts down any overgrown saplings or bushes with his tractor and Bush Hog.

As we trudge into the woods, I try to put myself in Mary's shoes. She was young, Amish and involved in an illicit love affair. Where did they walk? What did they touch? Did they leave anything behind?

"They drank a bottle of wine," I say after a few minutes. "He brought her lunch once. They watched the stars."

"Something concrete would be nice," Tomasetti grumbles.

"Initials would be a great start."

"A lot of damn trees."

"A lot of damn bugs."

Midway to the pond, I find a lone sock and toss it into my bag. Ahead of me, I hear Tomasetti slapping at mosquitoes and I smile. We don't speak as we work. The only sounds come from the chatter of sparrows, the high-pitched *whoit-whoit-whoit* of a cardinal and the occasional call of a bob-white quail. We don't pass anyone, and I realize Miller's Pond is quiet this time of day, this time of year. The kids are in school. Most adults are work-ing. Come four o'clock, the elementary age kids will invade the place like a swarm of ants. The high school kids will park their muscle cars in the gravel lot and spend the afternoon smoking cigarettes, stealing kisses and flirting. Later, Dad might walk down to toss in a line and hope for a bass. Where would have Mary and her illicit lover gone?

It takes us twenty minutes to cover the half-mile trail. I check every tree along the way, but the initials *M.P.* are nowhere to be found. The woods open to the dam. I netted a total of six items, none of which is promising. My brain keeps telling me to stop wasting time and get back to the station where we can work an angle that might actually pan out.

I'm sweating profusely as I take the steep bank to the pond. The body of water covers about two acres. A big cottonwood tree and two huge rocks mark the north end. A derelict dock sags on the south side. On the west side, the water is shallow and green with moss. Two long-dead stumps twenty feet from the water's edge act as lace-up benches in the wintertime. Beyond, the cornfield rattles in the breeze.

"You ever skinny-dip here as a kid, Chief?"

I glance over to see Tomasetti come up the dam. His face is damp with sweat. A mosquito bite stands out on his jaw. But he looks good when he's mussed. Details I shouldn't be noticing.

"Never skinny-dipped. Did plenty of ice-skating, though."

"Hot enough to swim today."

"Water will be cold. We had frost the other night." I smile. "Are you asking me to skinny-dip with you?"

He grins back. "Water looks kinda mossy."

"City slicker."

"We could forget about the water and get naked in that cornfield over there."

I laugh.

He smiles, but I can tell by the way he's looking at me he's not kidding. One nod from me, and he'd be all over me. The realization conjures a weird flutter in my chest.

He looks at the bag I tied to my belt loop. "Find anything?"

"Not really."

He holds up his Wal-Mart bag. "I found a SpongeBob Lego and a chewed-up dime."

Disappointment presses into me as we start back down the dam. The incline is steep and both Tomasetti and I skid part of the way. We enter the woods, and the mosquitoes descend on us like hyenas on prey. I'm going to need a shower by the time we get back. Of course, there won't be time for it.

We walk in silence. I'm only keeping half an eye on the path now, glancing occasionally at the larger trees we pass. I'm anxious to get back to the station. I want to run through the vehicle registrations a second time. I need to talk to Barbereaux's girlfriend to verify his alibi. I want a DNA sample from James Payne. Rob Lane, too.

I pick up the pace. The path curves and then straightens. The parking area comes into view twenty yards ahead. I see the hood of the Tahoe and dented steel of the guardrail. The telephone poles that run along the road. The trees open up and we step into bright sunlight. Heat slams down on me like a hot cast-iron skillet. I feel wilted and dirty as I head toward the Tahoe. I'm stepping over the guardrail when I notice the bottle propped against the shady side of a post.

I bend, pick it up using one of the tissues. The lower half of the bottle is basket covered. The label is crinkled, peeling and stained, nearly indecipherable. My brain pings when I see the word *Chianti*.

"I think I found something," I hear myself say.

Tomasetti comes up behind me, looks at the bottle. "If you're thirsty, I'm more than happy to take you to McNarie's."

"Mary and her lover drank a bottle of wine right here at Miller's Pond a few weeks ago. She mentioned it in her diary. I'll have to check, but I think she mentioned the wine was from Italy and said something about the bottle."

He looks skeptical. "Kind of a long shot."

"There's only one place in town that carries this kind of Chianti," I tell him. "Hire's Carry-Out, a little place out on Highway 83. I've got a date, in the diary. If they can identify the buyer, we might get a name."

"Worth a shot." But he doesn't look too excited. Maybe because it's not a crime to drink cheap Chianti here or anywhere else.

Still, it's worth a try. I drop the bottle into the bag, and we start toward the Tahoe. Without realizing it, we've picked up the pace. Two bloodhounds that have caught a scent, however faint.

Neither of us speaks again until we climb into the Tahoe. Tomasetti starts the engine, throws the vehicle into reverse. "So how do we get to Hire's from here?"

I call T.J. from the road and ask him to get Mary Plank's journal off my desk and skim through it for an entry that mentions wine. After several minutes, he finds it.

He reads, "'September 22. He came to my window! I shouldn't be, but I was so happy to see him. I sneaked out and we bought some wine. Then he took me to Miller's Pond. We watched the stars and he gave me my first wine lesson. The bottle was in a cute little wicker thingie and came all the way from Italy! He's so sophisticated. Later, we made love. I told him I want to marry him. I want to tell *Mamm* and *Datt* about us. He got a little angry and told me they wouldn't understand. But I need their blessing, even if I am to leave the church. I'm so confused. I don't know what to do!'

"Jeez." T.J. sighs. "Poor kid."

I tell him about the bottle. "Tomasetti and I are going to swing by Hire's Carry-Out."

"Anything I can do on my end, Chief?"

"Let's just hope they keep decent records."

CHAPTER 19

Hire's Carry-Out is located near the intersection of Highway 83 and Township Highway 62. The store carries staples like milk, bread, soda and cold cuts. But the brunt of their business is derived from the drive-through where they sell cold beer, wine and cigarettes. When the nearby speedway holds a race, the drive-through line has been known to back up traffic for a quarter mile.

I busted Art Hire a couple of years ago for selling a six pack of Little King's Cream Ale to a fifteen-year-old girl. He claimed she looked like an adult. Since he's old enough to know a size-C bra cup doesn't necessarily signify the legal drinking age, I threw the book at him. As I pull into the parking lot, I know it's probably optimistic to hope he doesn't hold a grudge.

The bell on the door jingles when we enter. The first thing I notice about the place is the smell. Old wood and dust with an underlying hint of freezer-burned meat. We make our way past shelves filled with bread and packaged pies. Art Hire sits behind a counter next to the drive-through window cash register. Above him, a baseball game blares from a small television mounted on the wall. He's smoking a brown cigarette that looks inordinately thin in relation to his bratwurst-size fingers.

He's a heavyset man with small, piggish eyes and full, feminine lips. He looks up from a copy of *Muscle Car* magazine as I make my way toward the counter and gives me a what-did-I-do-now look. Something tells me he hasn't forgotten about the selling-beer-to-a-minor incident.

"Mr. Hire, if you have a few minutes I'd like to ask you some questions," I begin.

His teeth are the color of ripe corn. "You'd think with seven murders on your hands, the police in this town would have better things to do than hassle law-abiding citizens."

Ignoring the jab, I pull the bottle from the bag and set it on the counter. "Is this from your store?"

He squints at the bottle. "How would I know?"

"Because you're the only place in town that sells this kind of Chianti."

Looking put out, he pulls a pair of readers from his shirt pocket, slides them onto his nose and leans forward to squint at the label. "Runs about five ninety-nine a bottle. Don't sell a whole lot. Most of our customers prefer plain old Bud."

"I need the customer's name."

"The only way we'll have that is if they paid with a check or credit card. If he paid with cash, you're shit out of luck."

"Can you pull the records?" I ask. "I believe I have the date it was purchased."

"Maybe." He lifts a beefy shoulder, lets it drop. "How far back?"

"September twenty-second."

His expression turns smug. "We only keep records for a month."

"What about security cameras?" Tomasetti asks.

"Can't afford cameras." He sneers at me. "Not with the cops in this town breaking my balls. That fine cost me five hundred bucks."

I try again. "What about credit-card receipts? Surely you keep transaction records longer than a month."

He returns his attention to the magazine, turns the page, ignoring us. "Nope. Sure don't. That would be against banking rules."

Annoyed, I look at Tomasetti and sigh. He gives me a small smile, then turns and walks down the narrow aisle toward the rear of the store. "Do you smell something?" he asks.

He's standing next to the walk-in freezer door. Only then do I realize what he's doing, and I withhold a grin. "As a matter of fact, I do. Smells like rotten food."

Hire sits up straighter. "What are you talking about? I just cleaned the freezer. There's nothing rotten anywhere in this store."

"You sure?" Tomasetti jabs a thumb at the freezer door. "Smells like you've got a dead cow in there."

"That isn't really a police matter," I say reasonably. "Maybe we ought to call the Health Department and let them handle it."

"Health Department?" Hire looks alarmed now. We have his full attention. "You have no cause to do that."

"They'll shut this place down in a New York minute," Tomasetti mutters.

I look at Hire. "That would be a shame. There's a race at the speedway this weekend. You'd lose a lot of business."

Hire raises his hands. "All right! I'll check to see if I have the damn name!"

Muttering beneath his breath, he stubs out his cigarette and slides off the stool. He glares at me, and then comes out from behind the counter. Without speaking, he heads toward the rear of the store. He's midway down the aisle when a buzzer sounds, signaling a customer at the drive-through. Hire stops and turns. "I gotta get that."

Tomasetti points at him. "I'll do it. You get the information Chief Burkholder needs."

"You don't know how to run the cash register."

"I'll figure it out."

Hire's face turns bright red. I see sweat on his forehead. He looks at me as if he wants to throttle me. "You cops aren't allowed to do stuff like this."

I don't like Tomasetti's tactics, especially since he's not here in an official capacity. But if it gets me the name, I'm willing to look the other way. "Just get us the name and we'll get out of your hair." I glance past him to see Tomasetti hand a carton of Virginia Slims cigarettes through the window.

"He's going to screw up my inventory," Hire whines.

"In that case, you'd better hurry."

Cursing, he takes me past a rattling refrigerated display case. Traversing the place is like walking through a camper jam-packed with enough food for a decade. At the rear of the store, he opens a narrow door. A pretty young woman with burgundy hair and big doe eyes sits behind a steel desk. She's drinking a Budweiser and smoking the same brand of cigarette as Hire. A plaque on the desk tells me her name is Cindy Hire, but I can't tell if she's his wife, daughter or sister.

"Can I help you?" She asks the question in a way that tells me the last thing she wants to do is help. That cooperative spirit must run in the family.

"I need the name of a customer who purchased a bottle of Chianti on September twenty-second," I say.

"We don't keep credit card info," she says. "It's against the rules."

I look at Hire. "Remember, the race this weekend."

Growling like a cross dog, Hire says to the woman, "It's in there. I haven't purged the records in a while. See if you can query by date. Get her the name and address of this customer."

For a second, Cindy looks like she wants to argue, then acquiesces. "I think the computer just keeps the number, expiration and name."

"All we need is the name," I tell her.

Putting the cigarette between her lips, squinting against the smoke, she begins pecking at the computer keys.

If my memory serves me, I'm pretty sure card processing rules mandate that merchants destroy or purge all credit-card information every so often due to the threat of data leaks and hackers. I find myself hoping Hire's computer system is in as much disarray as their store.

I watch as the computer screen turns blue, then data entry boxes appear. Squinting at the screen, Cindy types the date into one of the boxes.

"Got it." She hits Enter and waits. "Looks like the guy used a Visa. Card stolen, or what?"

Tomasetti peeks his head in. "Guy wants to know if you sell Cherry Berry ice cream."

"No."

He looks at me and raises his brows. "They get it?"

The woman gives a phlegmy cough. "I got it," she says. "Guy's name is Scott Barbereaux. Expiration date December next year."

Twenty minutes later, I'm sitting behind my desk, mentally sorting through my growing list of suspects. The newest addition is Scott Barbereaux. Of course, the bottle I found isn't incriminating in itself. All it does is place him at Miller's Pond near the date that Mary Plank was there with her mystery lover. It's a nebulous connection. But combined with the diary and his link to the shop where Mary worked, it's worth pursuing. I've been around long enough to know those kinds of coincidences don't happen without a reason.

But why would a man like Barbereaux risk everything to be with a fifteen-year-old Amish girl? He's good-looking, relatively successful and financially established. The kind of man who could have his choice of females. Why would he choose Mary Plank?

That makes me think about motive. If Barbereaux was involved in an illicit relationship with a minor female, he would have a lot to lose if the relationship ever became public, especially if she turned up pregnant or appeared in pornographic photos. If she'd told her parents and they threatened to take the information to the police, he would be facing time in prison. But is that enough motive to wipe out an entire family? And what about the torture aspect?

I remind myself that Barbereaux has an alibi. But lovers have been known to lie to protect the one they love. I decide Glenda Patterson is the next stop on my list. I also make a mental note to check Barbereaux's finances. A lot can be learned by the money people take in and spend.

I can't shake the feeling that I'm missing something important. It's there, floating around somewhere in my subconscious. But all I can see at the moment is white noise. My brain is tired and distracted. This case has reawakened some personal baggage I don't want to deal with. Maybe because I see too much of my own past in some of the choices Mary Plank made, and that's skewing my objectivity.

"What am I missing?" I say aloud.

This isn't the first case that's stumped me. Experience tells me when that happens to go back to the beginning. Look at the evidence again. Try to see it in a new light, regain an objective perspective. Pulling a fresh legal pad from my pencil drawer, I begin a stream-of-consciousness dump

DNA—semen inside Mary Plank's body. Where is the fetus? Get DNA sample from James Payne. Talk to Glenda Patterson. Does Scott Barbereaux have an alibi for September 22? Check his finances. T.J.—IP addresses. Dark pickup seen near the Plank farm on the night of the murders. Run through names of vehicle owners again. Evelyn Steinkruger—Mary got into car. Nice car. New. Blue or black. Barbereaux drives a black Grand Am. Canvass downtown area near shop. ID the driver. Check with the bank down the street—do they have an ATM camera? Mary went to the park often for lunch with her lover. Did anyone see them? Canvass park. Her lover liked to take photos. Important? Glock—check area photographers and photo studios. Skid—keep an eye on James Payne. How does he spend his spare time?

As I stare down at my notes, something prods at the back of my brain. Some thought or theory that hadn't yet congealed. I pull out the crime scene photos. I look at the bloody handprint on the jamb. The print in the living room. The instruments in the barn. Finally, I come to a single photograph of the three scuff marks on the dusty floor. I look at my notes and one line I'd written stands out like neon. *Her lover liked to take photos.* I stare at the photo, and I think: tripod.

"What's up?"

I glance up to see Tomasetti standing at the door to my office. "I think he may have photographed or filmed the murders."

"What?" He's already crossing to my desk. "How do you know?"

I show him the photo of the scuff marks. "No one could figure out what made these marks. Mary wrote in her diary that her lover was into photography. I think the marks are from a tripod."

Intensity tightens his features as he stares down at the photo. "Maybe that's why the girls were tortured."

"Jesus. A snuff film." The words feel like rancid grease pouring from my mouth. They make me sick to my stomach. I flip over the photo of the instruments. "He left these behind."

He stares at the photo, his expression unreadable. But his eyes are a little out of focus when he raises his gaze to mine, and I know this has brought back his own past, reminded him of the murders of his wife and children. My initial instinct is to reach out to him, but I don't. I know him well enough to realize that while he might need sympathy, it's the last thing he wants.

"I've got a contact down in Quantico," he says after a moment. "I'll give him a call, tell him to put his ear to the ground."

I nod.

He gives me a grim look. "The FBI has never been able to authenticate a snuff film, Kate. Never. They're an urban legend. A Hollywood invention."

"Maybe this is a first."

The muscles in his jaws flex. "I'll make the call."

The awful weight of this new possibility settles onto my shoulders with a crushing heaviness. I look down at my notes. "Did anything come back on Barbereaux?"

"One speeding ticket. Guy keeps his nose clean. Or else he's careful." He slides into the chair adjacent to my desk.

"I'm going to talk to Barbereaux's girlfriend to verify his alibi. Want to come?"

"Sure," he says.

I'm reaching for my keys when Lois appears at my door. "Chief?" She's wearing a gold pantsuit that clashes with her hair. "Evelyn Steinkruger is here to see you."

Tomasetti shoots me a look. "Busybody from the shop?"

"That's the one." I set down my keys. "Send her in."

A moment later, Evelyn Steinkruger walks into my office. She's wearing a red suit and matching pumps with heels so high my feet hurt just looking at them. Her eyes flick from me to Tomasetti and back to me, and I see a trace of curiosity in their depths. I almost smile when I realize she's wondering if it's all business between us.

"What can I do for you, Mrs. Steinkruger?" I begin.

She sets a quilted satchel the size of a small purse on my desk. "After you left, I remembered telling Mary she could keep her things on the bottom shelf in the storage room. I never thought about it again because she never carried sunglasses or a phone or iPod thingie like most girls do nowadays. I checked the shelf and found this."

I look down at the satchel. The workmanship is good, but it looks hand sewn, and I wonder if Mary made it herself. The fabric is pink with white and lavender flowers. Not an Amish print. She probably bought the material at a fabric store without her parents' knowledge and sewed it in the privacy of her bedroom. Though a purse isn't in any way against the *Ordnung,* I suspect whatever's inside it might be.

"There are a few things inside," Evelyn says. "Including some kind of computer plug-in thing. I thought it might be important."

My mind jumps at the mention of a flash drive.

"Did you touch or handle anything?" Tomasetti asks.

She shakes her head. "Just the satchel. I peeked inside, but as soon as I realized it was Mary's, I closed it and came straight here."

She waits a beat, her eyes flicking to the satchel. "Are you going to look inside?"

"I'll need to process it first," I say, ignoring Tomasetti's pointed look.

"Oh." She sighs, her disappointment clear that she won't be able to discuss her discovery with her friends over chai tea later. "I need to get back to the shop."

"We appreciate your bringing in the satchel," I say.

"In light of what happened to that poor family, I felt it was my duty."

She's midway to the door when I think of one more question I need to ask her. "Mrs. Steinkruger?"

She turns, raises a brow. "Yes?"

"Do you know Jack Warner?"

"I bought some folk art from him a while back."

I offer a smile. "Thanks. That's all for now."

Returning the smile, she turns and walks out.

"Interesting connection," Tomasetti says.

I nod. "I just don't know if it means anything."

"Everything means something."

I wait until the sound of her shoes fade and then I pick up the satchel. Tugging open the drawstrings, I upend the bag and dump its contents onto my desktop. I'm not expecting some earth-shattering revelation. But I find myself hoping the drive will give us something to work with.

A mirror, a tube of lip gloss, two crinkled dollar bills, a single dried flower, a quarter and a flash drive tumble onto my desktop. Ordinary items any young woman might have in her purse. Except the drive, and my cop's radar begins to wail.

"Flash drive might be interesting." Tomasetti states the obvious.

"What the hell is an Amish girl doing with a flash drive?" I wonder aloud. "The Planks didn't have a computer or electricity."

"And why would she leave it at the shop?"

"Good question."

"Let's take a quick look-see, then I'll courier everything to the lab," he tells me. "I'll call ahead, make sure it gets priority."

His unofficial status flicks through my mind, but I don't say anything. I'm too focused on the items laid out in front of me.

Quickly, I don a pair of latex gloves, thumb the lid off the drive and slide it into my computer. A couple of keystrokes and my virus protection software deems it safe. I go to the drive and pull up the first file.

"Could be photos," Tomasetti says.

"A face would be nice."

"That'd be way too easy. And not necessarily incriminating."

"Unless they're inappropriate. Even if we can't get him on murder, we might be able to get him on statutory rape or child pornography." I'm aware of Windows Media Player spooling up on my screen. Tomasetti watching my every move. I use the mouse and click the Play button. Images materialize. Music. The punch of shock freezes me in place when I recognize Mary Plank's face. "That's her."

Vaguely, I'm aware of Tomasetti coming around my desk to look at the screen. I can't take my eyes off the images playing out. I see Mary Plank clad in traditional Amish clothing. She's lying on a bed draped with a pink spread. I see a backdrop of cheap motel fare. Bad artwork. Mismatched lamps. Built-in night table. Chainsaw rock and roll.

We watch as a male enters the room. I can only see his back, but I take note of his appearance. White male. Late twenties. Light hair. Slight build. He's wearing blue jeans and an untucked navy shirt. On the bed, Mary raises her head and looks at him. Her eyes are unfocused. *Drugged,* I think, but the revulsion on her face is unmistakable, and a slow burn of outrage spreads through me because I know whatever is about to take place isn't consensual.

The male bends to her, kisses her hard on the mouth. She tries to twist away, but he pushes her back and begins to tear at her clothes. The sound of fabric ripping is drowned out by the blare of guitar and bass drum. Nausea seesaws in my gut when her pale flesh looms into view. I don't want to bear witness to what happens next. But I can't look away.

She still has the angular body of a pubescent. Gangly arms and skinny legs. Small breasts. Plain underclothes. She makes a halfhearted attempt to cover herself, but the man is relentless. Fisting her hair, he shoves her backward onto the bed and comes down between her legs. He shoves his jeans down to his knees. Then he's pumping into her. Her legs flying apart with every thrust. Child-like hands clutching the sheets. Tears streaming from heavy-lidded eyes. For a moment I'm afraid I'm going to throw up the coffee I just drank.

"Show us your face, you cowardly son of a bitch," Tomasetti growls.

But the man's face is angled away from the camera. All we can see is his profile.

"Do you recognize him?" Tomasetti asks.

Here I am—a cop—and the obvious question didn't even register. I'm too blown away by what he's doing to her. A fifteen-year-old kid. An innocent girl. An *Amish* girl. "No."

"We need a fuckin' ID. What about your guys?" Rising, Tomasetti starts toward the door. "This is a small town. Someone might recognize him."

I know it's a stupid reaction, but all I can think is that I don't want any of them to see her like this. I try hard to shake off the emotions curdling inside me. "Get Glock and T.J. in here."

Tomasetti disappears into the hall. Thankful I have a few minutes to regroup, I pause the video. I'm in the process of bagging the rest of the items when Glock, T.J. and Tomasetti enter.

I tell them about the flash drive. "It's tough to watch, but we're trying to identify the male."

"You think this is about the murders?" T.J. slides into a visitor chair.

I nod. "She's a minor. This is pretty hard-core stuff."

"There's a motive for you." Glock remains standing. "You think he's local?"

"Maybe." Tomasetti comes around my desk and stands next to me. "Play it."

Using my mouse, I click the Play button.

The four of us stare at the screen, frightened kids watching a terrifying horror flick. My initial shock transforms into rage as the images play out. I notice more details this time around. Mary Plank isn't just drugged; she's stoned out of her mind. Unable to move. Unable to protect herself. I see a total disconnect from reality in her eyes.

"Why would she keep something like this?" I wonder aloud.

"Why would she keep it at the shop of all places?" T.J. throws in. "Pretty public place."

"Maybe she was afraid someone would find it at the house," Tomasetti adds. "So she took a chance, kept it at the shop."

"Maybe she was going to take it to the police," Glock offers.

We stare at the screen. The man appears. The angle and lighting are better now. He's tall. Thin. Faded blue jeans. Strawberry blond hair. A weird flicker of recognition snaps through my brain.

"I've seen him before," I say.

Tomasetti jabs a finger at the monitor. "That's Long!"

Todd Long. The man we talked to just last night.

Rising, I grab my keys and jacket and address Glock. "I'm going to pick him up."

Glock and Tomasetti exchange a boys-club look that puts my teeth on edge. They think I'm going to go vigilante on Long. In some small corner of my mind, I acknowledge the possibility is there. Rage pulses inside me like a pressure cooker on the verge of blowing. I want to make him pay for drugging and raping a fifteen-year-old girl.

"I'll go with you," Tomasetti says.

I know he will stop me, but I'm too damn angry to appreciate it. The self-destructive side of me wants to tell him to stay out of it. But the part of me that is a cop realizes any misconduct on my part could jeopardize the case.

"Fine," I snarl.

"He might be at work," Glock says. "You want me to swing by there?"

"Take T.J. or Pickles with you." I look at Tomasetti, hoping the dark impulses jumping through my mind don't show on my face. "Let's go," I say and we head for the door.

CHAPTER 20

I break every speed limit in the book on the way to the Melody Trailer Park. Making a big arrest is always a thrill, particularly for a violent suspect that has been elusive. I can feel our collective adrenaline zinging around the inside of the cab. Beside me, Tomasetti grips the armrest. He looks excited—*too* excited considering his superiors have no idea he's here. It's a subject we should have dealt with already. I won't risk screwing up this case. I know from experience if some defense lawyer gets his claws on that kind of information, he'll use it to get his client off, guilt be damned.

The Explorer's tires screech when I make the turn into the trailer park. Pulling up to the curb two lots down from Long's place, I hit my mike. "This is 235. I'm 10-23."

Glock's voice crackles back. "I'm 10-23 at his place of work. Long didn't show up today."

"Get over here."

"Ten-seventy-seven five minutes."

I rack the mike. "Backup's on the way."

"Let's go." Tomasetti reaches for the door handle.

I grab his arm and stop him. "Are you armed?"

He glares at me. "What do you think?"

"I think you're only here to observe."

Temper flashes in his eyes. "Goddamnit, Kate."

"I mean it," I snap. "I want this done by the book."

"Fine." He shakes off my hand with a little too much force.

We disembark simultaneously. I can see Long's trailer from where I parked. The black pickup sits in the driveway. "Looks like he's home."

"I'll go around back," Tomasetti says.

Giving him a nod, I draw my .38 and ascend the wooden steps of the deck. Standing slightly to the side, I knock hard on the storm door. "Todd Long! Police! Open the door. We need to talk to you."

Out of the corner of my eye, I see Tomasetti disappear around the rear of the trailer. I hammer the door with my palm. "Police! Open up!"

A cop has got to be cautious when approaching a suspect's residence. Contrary to popular belief, the door doesn't have to be open for you to get shot. Depending on the weapon, a bullet can go right through a steel door. This particular door is made of wood and has a small diamond-shaped window just above eye level. Opening the storm door, staying to one side as much as possible, I set my toes on the threshold and put my eye to the glass.

The interior is dim. No lights. Curtains drawn. I see a living room with dark paneling. A kitchen with oak cabinets. Countertops littered with beer cans, newspapers and several days' worth of mail. A bottle of top-shelf whiskey sits on a glossy coffee table. Beyond, I see the outline of a flat-screen TV.

"Todd Long!" I shout. "Open the door now!" I'm about to pull away and wait for Glock to pile-drive the door when something snags my eye. Cupping my hands, I put my face to the glass. At first, I think the massive stain on the wall behind the sofa is food or drink. The kick of adrenaline in my gut tells some part of my brain it's not.

"Shit."

"No sign of anyone." Tomasetti takes the steps two at a time and stands next to me.

"I think that's blood on the wall," I say.

Grimacing, he puts his face to the window and looks inside. "I think you're right."

He's nearly a foot taller than me and has a better vantage.

"Any sign of a body?" I ask.

"Can't see much from this angle." He looks over at me. "Are you reasonably suspicious of foul play here?"

I jerk my head and try not to think of his unofficial status. "Do it."

He steps back, then lands a kick next to the lock.

Wood splinters and the door flies open. Before I can move, Tomasetti drops into a shooter's stance and thrusts himself inside. "Police! Put your hands up!"

My weapon leading the way, I follow him. Tomasetti goes right, toward the kitchen. I go left where the living room opens to a hall. I smell blood an instant before I see the body. On the other side of the room, Todd Long is sitting upright on the sofa, his arms and legs splayed. His head leans against the backrest. His face is angled up, toward the ceiling, as if he fell asleep while watching TV. From where I stand, I can see that the back of his head is missing. His hand grips a big .45 revolver.

"Aw, shit." Tomasetti's voice reaches me as if from a great distance.

"Looks like we're a little late," I hear myself say.

"Or maybe we timed this just right." I look at him and he shrugs. "Son of a bitch saved everyone a lot of time and trouble."

I don't agree with that; I have too many questions rolling around in my head. That's not to mention my need to see justice done for the Plank family. But my thoughts are too scrambled at the moment to rebuff his statement.

"I'm going to clear the rest of the trailer." Tomasetti heads down the narrow hall toward the bedrooms.

I can't take my eyes off the dead man. Sightless eyes stare at the ceiling. His mouth is open and filled with blood. I see powder burns on his lips. Broken front teeth. Blowback covers the wall behind him. I can make out tiny pieces of brain tissue, blood and small flecks of bone on the dark paneling.

Tomasetti emerges from the hall. "Clear." He glances at the body and for a second I'm afraid he's going to draw down and put another bullet in it. He motions toward the bottle of whiskey on the coffee table. "Looks like he got juiced up and took the easy way out."

Neither of us has any sympathy for a man who drugged and raped a fifteen-year-old girl. But I didn't want it to end like this. I feel as if someone yanked the rug out from under me. There's no sense of justice. No closure. Just a dead man, a dead family and a hundred questions that will never be answered.

Trying not to think about that too much, I hit my lapel mike. "I've got a 10-84 at three five Decker in the Melody Trailer Park. Can you 10-79?"

"Roger that," comes Lois's voice.

"Deceased is Todd Long. See if you can find contact info for NOK, will you?"

"Sure thing, Chief."

Movement at the door snags my attention. I glance over to see Glock enter, his eyes on the corpse. "Damn. Fucker bit it, huh?"

"Looks that way." But the scenario troubles me in some vague way I can't put my finger on. I thought this would feel better. Instead, it feels unfinished.

I look around the trailer. The place is messy. I don't relish the thought of an in-depth search; there's nothing I hate more than human filth mixed with a little biohazard. But I'm not going to be leaving any time soon.

For a moment, the three of us stand there, staring at Long's body. It's an anticlimactic moment; I'd been hoping for an arrest. I wanted to know what happened inside the Plank farmhouse on the night of the murders. I wanted to know why. I'm not proud of it, but a small part of me wanted to take my best shot at the bastard responsible.

"He didn't seem like the kind of guy to have an attack of conscience," I say to no one in particular.

"More than likely it was the thought of going to prison that did him in," Tomasetti replies.

"Going to save the taxpayers a bundle," Glock adds.

Sighing, I look at Todd Long's body and silently curse him. "Let's gear up and see what he left us."

* * *

In the sweltering heat of the day, Glock, Tomasetti and I thoroughly search drawers, cabinets, and any other conceivable hiding place. With painstaking care, we bag, label and box, preserving as much of the scene as possible. Our efforts pay off. By noon we've filled three large plastic storage bins with evidence, including photographs, half a dozen computer disks, two flash drives, several types of unidentified pills, a video camera, books on photography, pornographic magazines, clothing and a suicide note.

The note is hand-printed in pencil on a sheet of tablet paper. Holding up the bag, I stare at the childish lettering and say to Glock. "Long worked for the railroad. Can you run over to the office and get a sample of his handwriting so we have something to compare this to?"

"Sure." But he gives me a puzzled look. "You think he didn't write it?"

"I just want to cover all the bases."

Glock heads out the door. I'm aware of Tomasetti watching me as he places labeled and sealed bags into the last storage container. He doesn't say anything, but I know what he's thinking. I'm being too thorough, looking for things that aren't there. And no matter how much effort I put into this, the Plank family is still dead.

Doc Coblentz arrived on the scene half an hour earlier. Enough time to give me a preliminary assessment. "What do you think?" I ask.

The doc is wearing olive-green slacks. The back and armpits of his scrubs shirt are sweat-soaked. The doctor shakes his head. "I attended a seminar at Nationwide Children's in Columbus a couple of weeks ago. We toured the cancer center where most of the patients are pediatric. We're talking brain tumors. Lymphoma. Leukemia. Sick kids who'd give anything just to go outside and play." Motioning toward Long, he shakes his head. "I see something like this, and I wish there was some way this wasted life could be given to one of those children."

"I don't think life's that fair." That reality makes me sigh. I motion toward Long's body. "You think this was self-inflicted?"

"From all indications, he put the barrel in his mouth and pulled the trigger. Judging from the exit wound, the bullet angled slightly up, went through the cerebellum and exited the skull at the back of the head. Death would have occurred instantly. Of course, I'll perform an autopsy and tox screen. But my preliminary ruling is that this man killed himself."

The words make me feel deflated. Maybe because I wanted answers, and Long will never be able to give them to me.

Tomasetti comes up beside us. "I think we've got just about everything."

"Did Glock check beneath the trailer?" I ask, knowing it's a favorite hiding place for criminal-minded mobile-home dwellers.

He nods. "Pulled the skirting aside and crawled under. Nothing there."

I glance out the window. An ambulance idles in the driveway, waiting to transport the body to the morgue. I should be in a hurry to get out of there, where the smell of blood and death hang heavy. I should be anxious to review the evidence we've retrieved thus far so I can get the paperwork rolling and close the case. I should be anxious for life to get back to normal. For a reason I can't readily identify, I'm reluctant to leave. I feel if I walk out, I'll be closing the door on unfinished business.

Tomasetti picks up on my frame of mind. "Something bothering you?"

"I can't see Long killing himself like this."

"He's been to prison before. Maybe he didn't want to go back. Took the easy way out."

I sigh. "Damnit, I didn't want it to end this way."

"Could have been worse." He motions toward Long. "He could have run, gotten away."

I think of Mary Plank. The shattered hopes and dreams. So many lives cut short. And for what? Money? Sexual gratification? Cruelty for the sake of cruelty?

"I wanted to know why he killed that family," I tell him.

"Police work isn't always that neat." He gestures toward the storage containers. "I think the only answers we're going to get are in those boxes."

* * *

It's nearly dusk when Tomasetti and I arrive at the station, lugging the boxes of evidence from Long's place inside. The reception area smells like nail polish and Obsession perfume. Jodie, the new dispatcher, greets us with a *Cosmo* smile. She's wearing snug black slacks and a white body-hugging tunic. Too sexy for a police station. Just what I need. "Hey, guys," she says perkily.

T.J. and Glock stand upon hearing us enter and peer at us over the tops of their cubes. "Need a hand?" T.J. asks.

Glock lowers his voice. "This is your chance to show Jodie those biceps."

T.J. smacks the other man on the back of his head with a little too much force. "Shut up, shithead."

Their mood is jovial. I should be feeling the same now that one of the most violent cases in the history of Painters Mill has come to an end. I should be glad it's over. But I'm not, and I simply don't have the energy to pretend.

We carry the boxes to the storage-room-turned-command-center off the hall. Glock and T.J. shuffle out as I turn on my laptop and open the antivirus software. "I'm going to take a look at the drives."

"A lot of them." Tomasetti goes to the first box, digs around for a moment, then passes me a flash drive. I plug it into the laptop. While it's being scanned for viruses, I turn my attention to the suicide note and read it for the dozenth time, looking for some hidden clue that's just not there.

I can't take it anymore. I can't live with what I did. I loved Mary. She was sweet and beautiful and kind. But she told her parents about the kid. She was gonna tell everyone. And I went a little crazy. I'm so fucking sorry. Mom, you know I'm no killer. Don't feel guilty. I'm just so fucked up. The meth fucked up my head. I'm sorry you have to deal with this, but I'm not going back to prison. There's no other way. I love you, Blinky.

I shake my head, pissed by the lack any real answers. "Fucking coward."

I look at Tomasetti to find him watching me intently. "You okay?"

"I'm fine." I rub at the ache between my eyes. "I just hate the way this played out."

"Kate, look at this."

The tone of Tomasetti's voice jerks my attention back to him. I glance over to see him staring at my laptop screen, where he's already opened the first file. All thoughts fall by the wayside the instant my eyes hit the screen. The images come at me like knives. I see Mary Plank lying on an old-fashioned iron bed. A man wearing a full-head latex mask—some sort of grotesque jester—is on top of her, arms braced, his hips pumping. I see his neck muscles straining. Mary wears only her *kapp* and black ankle boots. Her eyes are unfocused, but the look of revulsion on her face is clear.

"Oh no." My voice is but a whisper. All I can think is, *I don't want to see this.*

"Looks like Long," Tomasetti says. "Same build."

The screen goes black. We stare for an instant, unspeaking. Tomasetti is in the process of reaching for the mouse when abruptly the screen jumps back to life. Same lighting. Same bed and sheets. Same bad feeling in the pit of my stomach. A man sits on the side of the bed. He wears the same jester mask, but this time I'm sure the man is Todd Long. My chest tightens when Mary Plank kneels between his knees, her head bobbing as she performs oral sex.

"She's been drugged." Tomasetti's words come to me as if I'm hearing them through cotton. "I'll bet the pills we found are some type of barbiturate. Or Rohypnol, maybe."

I want to respond, but feel as if there are two hands around my throat, squeezing my larynx, and I can't get any words out. I glance at the screen, and see yet another twisted scenario playing out in terrible black and white. I feel Tomasetti's gaze on me, but I don't look at him. I don't want him to see what I know is in my eyes.

This case isn't about me, but it hits home in ways I never expected, and with a force that leaves me gasping for breath. Tomasetti knows what happened to me seventeen years ago, but he doesn't know all of it. He doesn't know the deepest, darkest secret of all.

"Kate." He says my name gently, like a horse trainer trying to calm a frightened colt. "You don't have to watch this." He starts to close the laptop.

But I stop him. "Yes, I do." The words are little more than croaks, but I force them out. I can feel my emotions winding up. I know if I don't get a grip they're going to spiral out of control. My brain chants *Danger, danger, danger!* But I don't stop. "She was in love with him," I grind out. "She wanted to marry him. Have his child. Spend her life with him. She was willing to leave everything she'd ever known. And he did this to her."

The muscles in Tomasetti's jaw flex, and he looks away. "He got what was coming to him."

"That's not justice."

"Maybe not. But it's about as happy an ending as you're going to get with a case like this."

It's a hard, cynical view. But then John Tomasetti can be a hard, cynical man. At this moment, staring at the cruel realities playing out on that laptop, the world feels like a hard and cynical place.

I don't want to look at that awful screen, but my eyes are drawn to it. Another unspeakable scene stares back at me. I see the glazed eyes of an innocent girl. A young woman full of goodness and life. I see evil in its most insidious form. He raped her body, her mind, her heart. He committed upon her the ultimate betrayal.

I stand so abruptly, my chair nearly falls over backward. Tomasetti looks uneasily at me. "Kate . . ."

"Can you get this stuff to the lab?" I hear myself say.

"Sure . . ."

Before even realizing I'm going to move, I'm heading toward the door. I hear my breaths rushing out as I shove it open. It bangs against the wall, and then I'm running down the hall. I hear John say my name, but I don't stop. I see the dispatcher's concerned expression as I cross through the reception area. I'm aware of T.J. standing in his cube, staring at me. Glock calls out my name as I yank open the door. Then I'm outside. Only then do I realize I'm crying. Giant, wracking sobs that rip out of me with a force that makes my entire body shudder.

Relinquishing control of your emotions is the ultimate bad form for a female cop. Especially a female in a position of command. I need to get a grip. Suck it up and get the hell back in there. Start the paperwork that will close this godforsaken case once and for all.

But I'm in no condition to go back inside. I can't face my team. I'm too raw. Too far gone. Already over that precipice and tumbling down the mountain. I know Tomasetti will take care of any evidence that needs to be sent to the lab. The paperwork can wait until the morning. Climbing into my Explorer, I back blindly onto the street and head for the nearest haven I can find.

CHAPTER 21

I find refuge at McNarie's Bar. I didn't know where I was going until I turned into the gravel lot. It's the last place I ought to be. Not only am I the chief of police and still in uniform, but I'm in no frame of mind to be anywhere near alcohol. Or other living creatures. I suspect Tomasetti might be out looking for me, so I park in the rear lot, out of sight.

I'm not a self-destructive person. I learned that lesson at a relatively young age. But at some point during the drive from the police station to the bar, I stopped thinking. I stopped being reasonable. I stopped being so goddamn responsible. Sometimes none of those things make a damn bit of difference. Just look at the Planks.

It's seven P.M. when I walk in the front door. Happy hour has given way to the pool players and football-game watchers and the guys that just want to get out of the house for a little peace and quiet. It's another kind of peace I'm shooting for tonight.

I go directly to the small booth at the rear. The one in the corner where the tulip light is burned out and the only people who pass by are the ones heading into the alley for a snort or into the restroom because they've had too much to drink. I suspect McNarie keeps that corner dark on purpose.

An old Red Hot Chili Peppers song rattles from the jukebox as I settle in, facing the door. McNarie doesn't make me wait. He sets a bottle of

Absolut, a shot glass and a Killian's Irish Red on the table in front of me. "You need the glass or are you going to drink straight from the bottle?"

"Better go with the glass," I say. "Don't want to start any rumors about the chief of police seeking solace in a bottle." The fact that my state of mind is so obvious disturbs me.

I reach for my wallet, but McNarie stops me. "This one's on the house, Chief." He sets a pack of Marlboro Reds and a Bic next to the bottle.

"You don't have to—"

"I just heard you got the fucker responsible for killing that family. Nice work."

If only it were that simple. I thank him anyway, figuring I can make good with the tip.

He stares at me a moment, nods once. That's all. No questions. No morbid curiosity to sate. No phony concern. No lectures. McNarie is one of the reasons I come here. He lets me be. Tonight, I appreciate that more than he could know.

I break the seal before he even reaches the bar. By the time he picks up his towel and glass and resumes drying, I've already poured. The first shot goes down badly, makes me shudder, but then they always do. The second shot is easier. The third slides down my throat like liquid gold.

Brooding over a case is a counterproductive use of time for a cop. I should be feeling celebratory. A mass murderer is dead. A sort of primal justice has been served. I should be whooping it up with the guys. Slapping them on the back for putting in the hours and getting the job done. They should be here with me, toasting the death of a predator. Then I think of the Plank family and it hits me again that none of this can be undone.

Or maybe it's not the case at all that's bothering me. Maybe it's my own past that haunts me tonight. Maybe I've finally acknowledged all those jagged parallels between myself and Mary Plank. Parallels I didn't want to see. Things I thought were buried, but will never really die.

I'm midway through my first cigarette when I see Tomasetti come through the door. He looks out of place here with the words *big city cop* written all over him. He's got attitude and style with a little bit of bad-ass thrown in. Most cops dress like slobs. Suiting up is one of many things Tomasetti does well. The charcoal suit looks custom; the color plays nicely off the five-o'clock shadow. Pale blue shirt. Expensive tie. He holds his ground for a moment while his eyes adjust to the dim interior. His expression shifts when he spots me. I stare back, feeling busted, not sure if I'm pleased that he's here or annoyed because my zen of misery has been interrupted.

He makes his way to the booth and slides in across from me. I smoke, watching him, wishing I hadn't drank that third shot. An alcohol-fuzzed brain is a huge disadvantage when it comes to dealing with Tomasetti. He can be unpredictable and difficult, and I'm pretty sure I'm in no shape to deal with either.

"I guess it would be stupid for me to ask how you found me," I begin in way of greeting.

He catches McNarie's eye and gestures toward the shot glass. "I went by your house first."

"Not many places to hide out in this town."

"I guess the real question is why you're hiding."

I'm saved from having to answer when McNarie sets down a fresh shot glass, a second beer, and hustles back to the bar.

Tomasetti fills both shot glasses and downs his in a single gulp.

"I thought you'd stopped drinking," I say.

"I have, for the most part." He smiles down at his glass. "Just not tonight. But then this isn't about me, Kate."

Since I'm the last person I want to talk about, I say nothing.

Tomasetti doesn't give me respite. "Your guys are wondering what's up with you." He sets down the glass. "I guess I'm wondering the same thing."

"It was a tough case."

"It's over. You did a good job. The whole department did."

"The Planks are still dead. Those girls were still tortured."

"Kate." A thin layer of impatience laces his voice. "You've been a cop long enough to know that sometimes bad things happen to good people. It's out of your control. You gotta let go or it will drive you nuts."

Even though my brain warns me away from more alcohol, I pick up the shot glass and drink it down. "I'm too hammered to talk about it."

"Sometimes that's the best time to talk."

"Not for me."

He turns thoughtful. "Is it because they were Amish?"

I take a moment to study my glass, realizing I'm not sure how to answer. How can I put my emotions into words that will make sense to this man who sees the world in stark black and white? I'm not sure I want to open that Pandora's box because I don't know what will come flying out.

"You're probably the most levelheaded woman I've ever known," he says. "Getting caught up like this isn't like you."

I look at him over the top of my beer. "More your style, isn't it?"

He gives me a self-deprecating smile. "Why don't we save my analysis for next time?"

"I'm sorry. I shouldn't have said that."

"Don't apologize. Honesty is one of the things I like about you."

"I thought you liked my legs."

"That, too."

He gives me a half smile, and we sip our beers. The turmoil inside me eases. The silence becomes slightly more tolerable. Almost comfortable. He shatters it with his next question. "Is this about what happened to you seventeen years ago?"

My flinch is slight, but I know he saw it because his eyes sharpen. I can feel his gaze scratching at my shell, a predator trying to get to the soft meat inside.

"I don't know," I admit.

"There are some parallels."

I'm aware of my heart beating in my temples. The familiar clenching of my gut. It shocks me that even after all this time, talking about that day, about what happened—what I did—and the domino effect that followed, can shake me so profoundly. "Probably more than you know."

"Is that something I should be able to figure out?"

I stare at my beer. At the shot glasses. The tabletop. Anywhere but at him. I know it's stupid, but I feel if I look at him, he'll know.

He waits with a patience that makes me want to splash my beer in his face. I light a second cigarette, inhaling deeply, punishing my lungs, taking my time. I don't realize I'm going to say anything until I hear my own voice. "Two months after Daniel Lapp raped me, I found out I was pregnant."

My own words shock me. It's the first time I've spoken them aloud and they seem inordinately loud. I glance quickly around to make sure no one else heard, but the place is nearly deserted. The jukebox plays on. McNarie stands at the bar, watching the television, drying glasses with his dingy white towel. No one is looking my way. The earth didn't move.

Tomasetti isn't easily shocked, but I can tell by his expression this shocks him. He doesn't know what to say.

"I had an abortion," I say quickly. "I couldn't . . . have it. Didn't want it."

He scrubs a hand over his face. "Jesus, Kate."

"I never even considered having it. Not for one second. In the eyes of the Amish, that's considered murder."

"Not everyone sees it that way. Especially considering the circumstances."

"You're the only person I've ever told."

"A lot of weight to carry around all these years."

I smile at him. "You and I, we have strong shoulders, don't we?"

"Probably a good thing."

I look down at my bottle of beer. "When I read Mary Plank's journal, she became a real person to me. An Amish girl with a heart full of hopes and dreams. I was her once. All that hope. So many dreams. But I was lucky. I got my future. She deserved the chance to live her life. Long killed her twice. First he killed her innocence, then he took her life."

"This case brought it all back for you."

"I hadn't thought about my pregnancy or the abortion in years. I never let myself go there. Not even once." I'm alarmed when tears threaten. They are a female cop's worst enemy. One that can zap credibility faster than bad police work or sleeping around or both.

Because I can't look at Tomasetti, I put my face in my hands and sigh. "I know that in the scope of things, it's not important. It's over. Ancient history. The Planks are dead. Mary is dead. Long is dead."

"It's important." He slides his hand across the table.

For a moment I'm afraid he's going to take my hand. I'm relieved when he only runs his fingertips over my forearm. Too much kindness from him at this moment would crumple me.

"But life goes on," he says. "It's an unstoppable force. That was the hardest thing for me to accept when Nancy and the girls were killed. It's the living who are left to suffer. A hard truth, but that's the way it is."

"Tomasetti, you're not making me feel any better."

"What are friends for?"

I manage to give him a small smile. "You probably came here to get laid, and I blabbered all over you instead."

His laugh is deep and throaty. I like the sound of it, realize he doesn't do it often enough. And a flush spreads over me like warm oil. "Sounds like you've got me all figured out."

"Thanks for listening," I say after a moment.

"I'm glad you told me."

The bottle of Absolut sits half empty on the table between us. The jukebox has moved on to an old Neil Young rocker. I reach for the bottle and fill both shot glasses. There's more to say, but we both know enough has been said for tonight.

Tomasetti picks up his glass. "Are we going to get drunk?"

"I think so."

"You like to live dangerously, don't you?"

I raise my drink. "Another thing we have in common."

We slam back the vodka and set our glasses on the table with a little too much force. The alcohol runs like nitro through my blood now. I can feel it loosening my brain. A rusty faucet in my head breaking free, opening up.

"Do you think Long acted alone?" I ask after a moment.

He eyes me over the top of his beer. "Do you think there was someone else involved?"

"I don't know. There seems to be a lot of loose ends."

"What are you talking about specifically?"

I think about that for a moment. "How did one man subdue seven people? An entire family?"

"The Planks were Amish, Kate. They were pacifists. Maybe they didn't fight back."

"Sometimes the Amish do fight back. Instinct. Self-preservation." *I did.*

"There's no way they could have known what he had in mind. They probably thought he was going to rob them. Once he bound their hands, it was too late."

"How did he film and kill them at the same time?"

"Tripod. You saw the marks in the floor." His eyes narrow. "Are you going somewhere with this?"

"I don't think Long did the murders alone."

"We have no evidence to support an accomplice."

"What if Long didn't commit suicide?"

"How many shots have you had?"

"I'm serious. What if someone staged the scene to make it look like suicide?"

"And you're basing that premise on what?"

"Gut."

Tomasetti frowns. "Not very concrete."

"I think it's worth consideration."

"Maybe." He sighs. "Do you have someone in particular in mind?"

"James Payne. He's certainly capable."

"We don't have shit on him. No connection to Long."

"And what about Barbereaux? I'm playing devil's advocate here, but his name came up twice in the course of the investigation. We were able to connect him to Mary through the shop. And then there's the wine bottle."

"Pretty loose connections. And circumstantial, by the way."

"I think it warrants looking into."

"Kate, Painters Mill is a small town. People's lives intersect. Lots of young people hang out at Miller's Pond and drink."

"I don't think Long was smart enough to produce pornographic videos and sell them online."

"You don't have to be a rocket scientist to sell pictures of underage girls on the Internet. Any scum with a modem and an IQ over ten can do it. It's sort of a seller's market."

Even through the haze of alcohol, frustration climbs over me like a clingy little beast. "How do you feel about the snuff angle? Do you think it's viable?"

"I think it's a theory with nothing to back it up."

We sit there, thinking for a full minute, then I ask, "Did you get anything on the Web site owners?"

"We got as far as the Philippines. We're waiting for more info, but I'm not holding my breath. They're cooperating, but it could take a while."

I shake my head. "I can't see Todd Long walking into that farm house and killing seven people. That takes a certain kind cold-bloodedness. Long was a scumbag, a manipulator, a rapist, but he was a follower. I don't think he had that kind of bold in him."

I can tell by the hard set of his mouth, the way he's looking at me that Tomasetti doesn't buy into my theory. "Let's say you're onto something," he says. "How many people do you think were involved?"

"I think there was an accomplice." I consider that a moment. "If the semen isn't a match to Long, then we'll know there was at least one other person involved. Any word on the results yet?"

"Lab says four to six days. I tried to push them, but they're working under a backlog right now."

I don't want to wait that long, but of course I don't have a choice. "I don't believe Long is the man Mary wrote about in her journal."

Tomasetti pins me with a doubtful look. "What makes you think that?"

I flush, embarrassed because I'm tossing out some pretty radical theories when I've had too much to drink. "In the video, even though she's drugged, I see the revulsion on her face when she's with Long. But the man she wrote about in the journal . . . she was in love with him. There's a difference."

He peels at the label on the beer bottle. "I'll be honest with you, Kate. I think you're in this too deep. I think you're looking for things that aren't there. Do yourself a favor and close the case."

"The town council probably won't give me much choice. If the tourists don't come here, they'll go to Lancaster County."

"Ah, small-town politics." He shrugs. "If something changes, you can always reopen it."

He's right, but I say nothing. I'll close the case. Officially, anyway. But I'll keep looking. If I find out someone else was involved, I'm going to bring them to justice even if I have to mete it out myself.

I see Tomasetti struggling with something he wants to say, and I get an uneasy feeling in my stomach. "Are you going to let me drive you home?" he asks.

"I'm thinking about it."

"I've missed you."

For the first time, I'm thinking more about the man across from me than the case or my own woes. I don't know if it's the alcohol or the fact that we haven't been together for two months, but I want to spend the night with him. I want to forget about everything else for just a little while.

"I've missed you, too." I reach across the table and take his hand. "We're going to be okay."

"In that case," he says, "let's get the hell out of here."

CHAPTER 22

Tomasetti's gone when I wake. That surprises me because I'm a light sleeper. But having gone without any measurable sleep for the last few days, I was exhausted. Or maybe I just sleep better when he's beside me. The thought scares me a little bit.

He never says good-bye when he spends the night. The first couple of times it bothered me. Then I came to realize he doesn't linger because neither of us is very good at the morning-after thing. We're too cautious about revealing too much, laying too much of ourselves on the line, keeping all those dark secrets safe from a lover's prying eyes.

He always seems to leave a small piece of himself behind. I still feel his presence in my bed, in the house, on my body, in my mind. The echo of his voice. His rare laugh. The lingering scent of his aftershave. The softness of his mouth. The urgent touch of a lonely man. This imprint of him stays with me for days sometimes. At first it was disconcerting, but I've grown to like it. Already, I find myself wondering when I'll see him again.

Though it's only six A.M., I quickly shower and dress. Thoughts of the Plank family don't creep into my mind until I'm driving to the station. Even then, the hard edges are gone this morning. It's a step in the right direction.

I arrive at the station to find Mona's Escort parked in its usual spot. Skid's cruiser is parked next to it, and I know he's probably finishing up his reports before he calls it a day. Glock will arrive in an hour or so toting either bagels or doughnuts from the Butterhorn Bakery. Mona will complain about the calories. Lois, T.J. and Pickles will arrive and another typical day will begin. We'll talk about the murders and deal with the media. I'll call Auggie and officially close the case. My small department and I will go back to refereeing domestic quarrels, bar fights and corralling wayward livestock. Usually the normalcy, the routine of that would be a comfort to me. This morning, it makes me feel as if I've swept something smelly under the rug.

I walk in to find Mona sitting at her station, tapping her fingers to a Gin Blossoms tune that's cranked up a little too loud. "Hey, Chief. You're in early this morning."

"Couldn't sleep." I cross to the dispatch station, reach over and turn down the radio. "Any messages?"

"Media mostly. From yesterday afternoon. Wanting to know about the Long thing." She passes half a dozen pink messages to me. "Sorry about the radio. I didn't realize it was so late. I mean early." She grins. "Night shift flew by."

Since the messages are media-related, I hand them back to her. "Let them know I'll have a press release later this morning."

"Sure thing."

At the coffee station, I pour a cup and carry it to my office. While my computer boots, I go to the record storage box next to the file cabinet and carry it to my desk. *T. Long Suicide* is written in bold red marker on the side. The box contains only a fraction of what we found at the scene; most of it was sent to the BCI lab for processing. Still, I want to go through everything with a fine-tooth comb before closing the case.

Inside the box, I find the evidence log Mona put together. The preliminary report from Doc Coblentz. A manila folder contains a photo record of the scene. A plastic bag filled with pornographic photos of Mary Plank. In addition, there are two boxes of disks. All are copies; the originals were sent to the BCI lab. The first box is marked *Viewed*. These are the ones Glock, John and T.J. went through yesterday. The second box is marked *To Be Viewed*. These are the ones I need to look at this morning.

I set the box on my desk. Reviewing them is the last thing I want to do. I know the images that wait for me—rape and depravity—will negate whatever optimism Tomasetti left with me. But even though Long is dead and the case will soon be closed, all the evidence must still be examined.

Rising, I close my office door and slide the first disk into my computer. The drive whirs. I open Windows and click Play. The video opens to a sparsely furnished, windowless room. Stark white walls. A single bulb hangs down from the ceiling. A twin-size bed with an iron headboard and smaller footboard stands in the center of the room. Mary Plank is on the bed, lying on her side. She wears no makeup, but someone painted her mouth red. Her eyes are glazed. She wears a light blue dress, a white apron, gauzy *kapp* and ankle boots. I try to take in these details with the unaffected eye of a cop. But my chest tightens at the sight of her.

A man clad in blue jeans and wearing the jester mask enters stage right. *Bastard,* I think and I find myself glad Long stuck that gun in his mouth. He crosses to the mattress and kneels beside Mary. Leaning close, he whispers something in her ear. She smiles at him, then looks at the camera. "We're going to be playing a sexy game today," she says.

It's the first time I've heard her voice, and it shocks me. It's girlish and innocent with the slow inflection of the Amish. Smiling, she reaches for Long. He brushes his knuckles across her check, and I see a connection between them I hadn't noticed before. The music begins. An old Van Halen song, "Running with the Devil." As he undresses her, I focus on camera work, realize it's steady, probably being shot from a tripod.

I fast-forward through the disk, pausing only when something catches my attention. In terms of an accomplice, my efforts net zero. By the time the disk plays out, I'm shaking with outrage and disgust. I feel dirty and upset and unbearably guilty.

Popping out the disk, I mark it as *Read,* and place it with the other disks that have been viewed. I don't let myself think or feel as I slide the second disk into the drive. I steel myself against the black dread rising inside me. The voice inside my head telling me I can't do this. But I don't stop. I close the drive and click Play.

My pulse jumps when I recognize the Plank farmhouse. The living room. I see the two tall windows, the same lacy curtains. The lighting is bad, probably from some type of battery-powered light. The camera work is jerky, similar in style to *The Blair Witch Project,* telling me someone is manning the camera. I wonder if this video was shot the night of the murders. Or had Long been at the farmhouse before? And where are the Planks?

The screen goes black for an instant, blinks white, and then the kitchen looms into view. The camera work smoothes out, and I realize he must have set up a tripod. I can see the edge of the table from this angle. The back door. The cabinets and sink. It looks like unedited video. Long appears, adjusting the camera or maybe testing the lighting. He looks into the lens as if he doesn't realize the camera's turned on. He's got a serious look on his face. Is he angry? I wonder. Scared? Intent on killing? Is he about to fly into a rage?

The screen fades to black. The words *Death in an Amish Farmhouse* appear in red, Gothic-style lettering that reminds me of some high school horror film project. The screen goes scratchy. An instant later the image of Amos Plank lying on the floor flashes in stark black and white. I see a pool of shiny black blood. An open mouth and staring eyes . . . The image lasts for only an instant, but it's enough to make me queasy.

The camera pans back to the Plank kitchen. No movement. No people. That's when I realize I'm probably looking at unedited clips that were cut or not used. I think of the title and wonder if I'm seeing snippets of a snuff film. . . .

Staving off a rolling wave of revulsion, I stare at the screen, looking for clues. Doc Coblentz estimated the Planks had died between ten P.M. and midnight. It would have been dark. My eyes go to the back door, but the lighting inside reflects off the darkened window. I hit a couple of keys and zoom in. One hundred and ten percent. One hundred and twenty-five. I squint at the screen. The window is dark. It's nighttime.

That's when I notice the pale oval on the other side of the glass. At first I think it's a reflection. The person behind the camera. I hit the zoom again, taking it up to one hundred and fifty percent. The resolution goes grainy. But I'm almost certain someone is standing *outside* the back door, looking in. I can see the dark shadows of eyes. The line of a mouth.

"Who are you?" I whisper.

I hit Speaker and speed dial Tomasetti's cell. He answers on the first ring with his usual growl.

"Do you know someone at BCI who can magnify and improve video?" I ask without preamble.

"I'm still on the road. What's up?"

I tell him about the face in the window. "When I zoom, I lose resolution, so I'm not getting a clear image."

He sighs. "I'm about twenty minutes from the lab." He rattles off an e-mail address. "One of the technicians is a friend of mine. Send the file as an attachment. I'll swing by and we'll take a look at it."

An awkward pause ensues and I realize both of us are thinking about last night. We didn't get much sleep. Tomasetti breaks the moment and we fall back onto common ground. "You still think there was an accomplice?"

"I don't know."

"That would change a lot of things."

"It would mean there's a killer running loose in my town."

The line between us hisses. "I'll get back to you as soon as we have something."

"I'll be waiting."

They are two of the longest hours of my life. I'm nearly finished reviewing the disks when my phone jangles. I look at the display, but it's Lois, not Tomasetti. Snarling beneath my breath, I hit Speaker.

"Chief, Aaron Plank is here to see you."

Shock ripples through me. He's the last person I expected to see. "Send him in."

A moment later, Aaron walks into my office. He wears a corduroy blazer over khaki slacks and a nice pair of shoes. When he looks at me, his expression is sage and sad. "I heard about Todd Long," he says.

Curious as to why he's here, I motion toward the visitor chair adjacent to my desk. "Have a seat."

He takes the chair, wipes his palms on his slacks. "I'm heading back to Philly today. I wanted to talk to you before I left. To apologize, I guess."

"You don't sound too enthusiastic about that." But I give him a small smile.

"This has been tough."

"It was a tough case for all of us."

He fidgets, looking everywhere but at me, and wipes his hands again. Finally, he meets my gaze. "I just wanted you to know . . . I loved them. Despite what they thought of me, I loved my family. All of them. But Mary . . . she was special."

A lump rises in my throat, but I swallow, force it down. I don't know what to say. I barely know how to feel.

Aaron rises. Despite his youth, he looks like an old man this morning. Something in his eyes, in the way he moves. I realize this trip to Painters Mill has aged him in ways that have nothing to do with the passage of years.

He walks to the door, sets his hand on the knob, then turns to face me. "I'd like her journal when the police are finished with it."

I manage to give him a nod.

At that, he turns and walks out of my office.

I stare after him, trying not to acknowledge the ache burgeoning in my chest. I find myself wishing I'd thanked him for coming in. Wishing I'd said something to let him know I understood. Some things are just too damn hard.

My phone rings. I look down and see the BCI number on the display.

Mentally, I shift gears, slam the door on all those old emotions, and snatch up the phone. "What do you have?"

"The technician magnified the still." Tomasetti's voice is terse, tense. "He filled in the loss of resolution as best he could. I just e-mailed you the results."

Without setting down the phone, I open my e-mail software, hit Send-Receive. An e-mail from BCI with an attachment appears in my inbox. I open it and click on the attachment.

The tech did a good job of maintaining the integrity of the photo. While something with this level of touch-up would probably not be admissible in court, it's enough for me to recognize the face in the window.

"Oh my God," I hear myself say.

Shock sends me to my feet. I hang up without saying thank you. And then I'm running toward the door.

CHAPTER 23

I grab Glock on my way out. "We may have a witness," I say as I slide behind the wheel of the Explorer.

"You're kidding?" Incredulity laces his voice as he gets in beside me. "Why the hell didn't they come forward?"

"Because it's a kid."

"A kid? Damn. Who?"

"Billy Zook."

I see him running the name through his brain. "The Amish kid from the pig farm?"

"The Amish kid with a speech impediment and mental problems."

Glock chews on that a moment. "What was he doing at the Plank farm that time of night?"

"I don't know, but we're going to find out."

A few minutes later, I turn into the gravel lane of the Zook farm. A cloud of white dust chases me all the way to the house. I park next to a black buggy and swing open my door. Behind me, Glock mutters beneath his breath about the stench of pig shit. I'm so intent on my goal of speaking to Billy, I barely notice.

I knock hard on the front door and wait. The door opens halfway and Alma Zook appears. She's wearing a blue dress and black apron. I see food stains on the apron, bubbles of sweat on her forehead and upper lip. The smell of cooking tomatoes tells me she's canning.

Because I want her cooperation, I greet her in Pennsylvania Dutch. Her eyes flick from me to Glock and back to me. She knows I'm not here for chitchat and doesn't invite us in. The wariness in her gaze makes me wonder if she knows why I'm here.

"I need to talk to you about your son," I begin.

William Zook appears beside his wife. He's wearing muck boots, tracking shit on the floor, and I realize he must have rushed into the house through the back door when he saw us pull up. All I can think is: *They know why we're here.*

"We have already told you everything," William says.

"Then why didn't you tell me Billy was at the Plank farm the night of the murders?"

Alma gasps, sets her hand against her breast.

William opens his mouth, closes it without speaking. When he finally does, his lips tremble. "Why do you say these things about Billy?"

The Amish are generally honest to the extreme. But as with any group of individuals, they are not immune to human frailties. That is particularly true if they are protecting someone they love, especially a child.

I tell them about the video. "It's him. He was there. I need to speak with Billy. Right now."

William stares at me, looking stubborn and afraid, his jaw fixed. "He has the mind of a child."

"He might have seen the killer," I say. "He might be able to identify him."

Neither of them denies my accusation, but the door doesn't open.

"The evildoer is dead," William says. "I do not see how your speaking to Billy now will help."

"We think the killer had an accomplice." I look past him. Alma stands to one side, wringing her hands. "I need to speak with Billy. Please."

The Amish woman lowers her gaze, deferring to her husband.

"We have nothing more to say." William starts to close the door.

I thrust my foot into the jamb, stopping him. "I need your help."

"You are an outsider," he hisses. *"Dem Teufel und allen seinen Engeln ubergeben."* You were cast off from the church and committed to the devil and his angels . . .

It's a personal jab I should have expected, but even after all these years, the words make me feel somehow diminished. I remind myself William is only protecting his son. I don't want to force the issue, but I can't walk away.

"I'm not leaving," I say.

"He saw nothing," William says harshly.

"Have you talked to him about it?" Glock asks.

William doesn't answer. His expression turns stoic. I see him shutting down. I know neither parent is going to cooperate. The last thing I want to do is go back into town and get a warrant. While that will gain me access to Billy, it could take days to accomplish and would further strain relations between the Amish and my department.

I play my ace. "If the killer saw Billy, he could be in danger."

William pales all the way down to his beard. Next to him, Alma looks like she's going to be ill. I see their brains working this bit of information over, and I realize it's the first time they've considered the possibility.

"Please," I say. "I'll do my best not to upset him. I just need to know what he saw."

William opens the door and steps back. "Come inside."

Glock and I enter the living room. I see the same dirty rug. Plywood floors. Even from twenty feet away, I can feel the heat coming from the kitchen where pots rattle on the stove.

"Billy is a good boy." Alma stares at her hands as she wipes them against her apron. "But . . . *Er is weenich ad.*" He is a little off in the head.

I nod. "I understand."

William and Alma exchange a look that tells me I do not understand, and I get the feeling things are about to take a strange turn.

William runs his fingertips over his beard. "Billy is coming of age. In the last year or so, he expressed . . . interest in Mary Plank. He still speaks of her as if she is alive." His voice falters. "Just yesterday he asked me if he could take her to the singing after worship on Sunday."

A "singing" is an Amish social function for young people. Usually held after Sunday worship, teenagers sit around a table and sing and socialize.

William looks anywhere but at me. "His games are harmless, but they are not proper."

"What games?" Glock asks.

Alma's cheeks color. "He has become curious in the way that boys get. About the womenfolk, you know. Sometimes in the evening he will go off on his own. Last August, Mrs. Zimmerman down the road told me she caught Billy looking in her window." Another flush, darker this time. "Last weekend at worship, Bonnie Plank said she caught Billy looking in the window there at the farm. I talked to Billy. I told him the game was unfitting." She shrugs. "He was embarrassed and upset. I thought he understood. . . ."

"His games are against your English laws," William says.

"I don't care about the window peeping," I say. "I just want to talk to him about what he saw."

Alma glances at her husband. William jerks his head, turns away from the door. His boots thud dully against the floor as he crosses to the stairs. "Billy! Come down here please."

Giving me an uncomfortable smile, Alma sighs. "I asked Billy to confess to Bishop Troyer. The bishop urged us to keep Billy busy with chores. He said the extra work would help with the looking in. William has plenty of work and has done his best to keep him involved. The chicken coop. Feeding the hogs. Repairing the pens." She shrugs. "Billy prefers to be inside."

Footsteps on the stairs draw my attention. Billy notices Glock and me, and stops midway down. His gaze goes to his father. *"Datt?"*

His voice sounds small and scared. I see fear and guilt on the boy's face. He thinks he's in trouble. At that moment, I realize that while Billy Zook is mentally challenged, he's got the intellectual wherewithal to consider consequences.

"It is all right, Billy," William says. "You're not in trouble. Chief Burkholder just wants to ask you some questions."

The boy's eyes remain wary. He descends the remaining stairs with the caution of a deer approaching a river full of alligators. He's about my height, five feet six inches with the slumped shoulders typical to skinny teenaged boys. I notice he's got patches of acne at the base of both cheekbones. Stubble the color of a peach on his chin. He looks upset, so I do my best to put him at ease. "Hello, Billy."

He sidles up to his father and stares at his shoes.

I glance at William. He gives me a nod.

"Billy, I want to ask you a few questions about something that happened at the Plank house."

The boy doesn't move. He doesn't look at me or acknowledge my question.

"You're not in any trouble," I say. "I just want you to answer some questions for me. Do you understand?"

The boy looks up at his father. William Zook gives him a nod. *"Ich had nix dagege."* I don't object.

Billy makes eye contact with me and nods. *"Ja."*

"Your *mamm* was telling me you like to look in the windows of other people's houses sometimes. Is that true?"

His eyes skate away. Raising his hand, he nibbles on a fingernail, then gives a reluctant nod.

"Do you look in the windows of the Plank house sometimes?"

Billy looks at his mother. "Am I in trouble?"

"No, Billy," she says. "Just answer Chief Burkholder's questions."

"Billy?" Tilting my head slightly, I make eye contact with him. "Do you look in the Plank's windows?"

"Sometimes." He drops his head, puts his hands behind his back. "I like to see Mary. She's pretty."

"Did you look in the window Sunday night?"

He nods.

"Can you tell me what you saw?"

His eyes dart from his parents to me. His left knee begins to shake. He lifts his hand, tears at the ragged nail with his teeth. Tears fill his eyes.

"Did you see something that scared you?" Glock asks.

For the first time, the Amish boy looks at Glock. *"Ja."*

I lower my voice to sooth him. "Tell us what you saw, Billy."

"An *Englischer.*"

"What did he look like?"

"The devil." His voice trembles on the last word.

"Do you remember the color of his eyes? Or the color of his hair?"

"Strawberry man."

"Strawberry man?" My mind circles the term, trying to make sense of it. "What do you mean?"

"His hair was the color of a strawberry."

Disappointment edges into me. Todd Long had reddish-blond hair. "How many men did you see?"

Billy holds up two fingers.

My heart dips into a single, slow roll. All I can think is, *I was right; there is an accomplice!* It's a dark thought, but at this moment I want to get my hands on the second perp so badly I can already feel his hyoid bone giving way beneath my fingers.

"What did the second man look like?" I ask.

The boy struggles with the question, as if he can't put such a broad description into words. I try to narrow it down. "Was he a white man?" I ask. "Was his skin white like mine?" I motion toward Glock. "Or was it brown, like Officer Maddox?"

Billy grins shyly at Glock. "He had white skin."

Glock smiles back and gives him a thumbs-up, but Billy looks away.

"You're doing great, Billy," I say. "What color was his hair?"

His brows go together, as if he's faced with a difficult math equation. After a moment, he perks up. "His hair is like Sam's!" he blurts out.

"Sam?" I look at Alma.

"Sam is one of our horses," Alma explains. "He's brown."

Nodding, I turn my attention back to Billy. "Was the man big or small?"

Billy shakes his head. "I don't know."

"Do you remember what he was wearing?"

"Pants?"

I smile. "Do you remember what color they were?"

Another vigorous shake.

"What about his age? Was he old? Or young?"

"I dunno."

"What color were his eyes?" I ask. "Were they brown like Officer Maddox's? Green, like mine? Or blue, like your *datt*'s?"

His face screws up for a moment, then he shakes his head. "I dunno. I din look."

I'm no expert on interrogating children. Even less so a special child like Billy. But he's my only witness. In order to solve this case, I need the information locked inside his head. In the back of my mind, I've already decided to call Tomasetti and request a sketch artist.

I move on to the tougher stuff. "What did you see that night when you looked in the window?"

For the first time, Billy looks scared. He shakes his head from side to side, like a dog shaking water from its coat after a bath.

"Did you see Mary?" I ask.

"No."

"Who did you see?"

"The *Englischers*."

"What were they doing?"

The boy's brows knit. His mouth scrunches, a child faced with an unpleasant food. "Bad things."

"What did they do, Billy?"

"They made Mary's *mamm* cry."

I tamp down impatience. "How did they make her *mamm* cry? What did they do?"

"The Strawberry Man put Mr. Plank to sleep."

"Put him to sleep?"

"The way *datt* puts the hogs to sleep for sausage."

I look at William, but I know where this is going. With the exception of dairy cattle, the Amish butcher their livestock for meat.

The Amish man presses his fingertips against the bridge of his nose, then heaves a sigh.

"What do you do to the hogs, Mr. Zook?" Glock asks.

Zook shifts his attention to Glock. He looks shell-shocked. "I shoot them before I butcher them. It is more humane that way."

I return my attention to Billy. "What did you do after you saw them put Mr. Plank to sleep?"

"I don't like that part," the boy says. "So I ran home."

Something clicks in my mind, and I find myself thinking of the night I chased the yet unidentified intruder into the cornfield. "Did you go back the next day to check on Mary?"

The boy looks down at the floor, jerks his head. "She wasn't there."

"Who did you see?"

He draws a circle on the floor with the toe of his boot. "Are you gonna get mad?"

"No. I promise."

"I saw you."

"Poor kid saw it all." Glock and I are in my Explorer, heading back to the station.

"He's the one I chased into the cornfield that night." I sigh. "At least now we know there were two killers."

"Kid must've been scared to death," he says.

"I might feel better about this if I knew the second guy wasn't running around loose."

"We'll get him, Chief."

I wish I felt as optimistic. "The Strawberry Man is obviously Long."

"All we have on the second guy is brown hair. Not a lot to go on."

My disappointment is keen. I was hoping for a definitive ID on the accomplice. I rap my hand against the wheel as I pull into my usual spot at the station. "Damnit."

"What are we going to do?"

"Call in a favor."

Tomasetti isn't very optimistic, either. "Did the kid ID Long?"

"Yeah."

"And you want a sketch artist out there in the hope that he'll be able to give us a decent description of the second guy?"

"He's all we have. I think it's worth the time and effort." I'm sitting at my desk, looking out the window, trying not to feel discouraged. "Do you have someone you can send? Someone good with kids or experienced with the mentally retarded?"

"Do you want the bad news or the good news?"

"If it's not too much trouble, you can leave out the bad altogether."

"I wish that was an option." He sighs. "The suits caught wind of my involvement with this case."

"Just when you think things can't get any worse." Now it's my turn to sigh. "I'm sorry. I shouldn't be asking you for help."

"I offered."

"How bad is it?"

"The deputy superintendent is shitting bricks. He wants me in his office first thing in the morning."

"Doesn't sound good. You going to be okay?"

"I'm always okay."

"Tomasetti . . ."

He sighs heavily. "Look, Kate, I hate to say it, but my being involved in this could fuck it up for you."

I consider the repercussions of that a moment. "I'll go through official channels."

"Take too long. Look, I still have a friend or two left. Let me make some calls. When do you want the sketch artist?"

"Yesterday would be good." I look at the wall clock. It's nearly noon. "What about this afternoon?"

"Have to be late," he says. "Let me see who I've got."

"I owe you one, John."

He disconnects without saying good-bye. I know it's stupid to let that bother me, but it does. I feel guilty for asking for his help. "Thanks," I whisper.

CHAPTER 24

I burn half the day waiting for the sketch artist to arrive from Columbus. I get through two more of the disks we found at Long's residence. The content disturbs me so deeply, I can't continue; in the end they reveal nothing new anyway. By the time the sketch artist, Deborah Kim, walks into my office just after four P.M., I'm feeling snarlish and impatient.

"Thanks for coming." I try to muster a smile as I shake her hand. "I know it was short notice."

"Most police work is." She's fiftyish with a smooth, silver bob, a competent air and a sleek black pantsuit that makes me feel dowdy. "Tomasetti said it was important."

"I'll fill you in on the way."

On the drive to the Zook farm, I brief Deborah on the case and tell her about Billy. "He's got some degree of mental retardation."

She nods in a way that tells me she's done this before. "The key to a successful sketch in cases like this is to make the process as nonthreatening as possible. Encourage him to talk. Will his parents be there?"

I nod.

"Excellent. If we get stuck on something, they should be able to help."

By the time we get out at the Zook farm, it's nearly five o'clock. The

Amish generally eat dinner early, between four and five P.M., and I'm relieved we're not interrupting.

Alma invites us inside and ushers Deborah, myself, Billy and William to the kitchen table where we sit. Deborah removes a sketchpad, graphite and charcoal pencils, paper stumps, a chamois, and several erasers from her briefcase and sets them on the table in front of her. Next comes the FBI Facial Identification Catalog. I'm vaguely familiar with the book from my days in homicide. It contains pages of mug shots as well as every conceivable facial feature.

Alma pours coffee for the adults and a tall glass of milk for Billy, who proceeds to squirm in his chair like a worm on hot pavement. Deborah spends several minutes making small talk with him, asking about his parents, his school work, baseball and finally landing on a subject that appeals to him: his favorite pig.

"Her name is Sarah." Billy stops fidgeting. "She almost died when she was a piglet, so I bottle fed her." Grinning from ear to ear, he spreads his hands about six inches apart. "She was only this big."

"I'll bet she was cute," Deborah comments.

"*Datt* says she is the best pig we ever had."

Deborah gives him a warm smile. "What color is she?"

"Red with brown spots all over."

"You're very good at describing things."

He blushes, glances at his *Datt*. William Zook smiles at him as if to say, *Even though she's an outsider, it's all right to speak with her.*

"Do you like to draw pictures, Billy?"

He nods. "I am good at drawing pigs and horses."

"Do you like drawing faces?"

Uncertain, he looks at his father. "We are not supposed to make pictures of faces."

Deborah shoots a questioning look at me.

"Most Amish believe photographs and other images are vain displays of pride." I turn my attention to Billy. "But your *datt* spoke to Bishop Troyer and the bishop made an exception for this."

William nods again at his son.

"Would you like to help me draw a face?" Deborah asks.

Restrictions and rules momentarily forgotten, he nods enthusiastically. *"Ja."*

"Good! I could use your help." Casually, she opens the sketch pad and picks up a charcoal pencil. "I was wondering if you could help me draw a picture of the man you saw through the window at the Plank farm the other night."

A shadow passes over the boy's expression. He looks uneasily at her pad. "The bad man?"

"Yes, the one with hair like Sam's."

He nods, but his uncertainty is palpable.

Deborah opens the FIC catalog. From where I stand, I can see the rows of mug shots. "I thought we could start with the easy stuff. Like the shape of his face. Was it round? Square? Oval-shaped?"

Billy looks confused. "I have never seen anyone with a square face."

Chuckling, she slides the book across the table to Billy. He looks down at it where every conceivable face shape is outlined in black and white. Square. Oval. Round. The boy stares at it with the rapt fascination of a child.

"Which of these face shapes best fits the man you saw in the window?" Deborah asks.

"But he had hair and eyes!"

"We'll add those later," the sketch artist says patiently. "For now, let's find the shape of his face. Can you pick one out for me?"

Billy stares down at the drawings, his expression intent. After a moment, he puts his finger on one of the pictures. His nails are bitten down to the quick and dirty. "Like that, but he had eyes. He had a nose and a mouth, too."

"Okay. Let's add the eyes next."

The sketch progresses with excruciating slowness. Deborah is infinitely patient. Several times, Alma and William jump in to translate a term for Billy. The boy sometimes uses fruits and vegetables when he is referring to colors. "Like a peach" or "like corn right before harvest." Hair is "like a dog." Round is "ball."

Four hours and three cups of coffee into the process, it strikes me that despite Deborah's talent, the sketch is not going to happen. Billy is unsure about too many of the details and changes his mind more than a dozen times. Deborah spends much of her time reworking the sketch.

It's after nine P.M. when Deborah packs up her tools. I thank the Zooks for their time and help, and give Billy a five-dollar bill. I'm disheartened as I climb into the Explorer.

"I'm sorry I couldn't get a viable sketch for you," she says. "People see things in different ways. Billy isn't visually oriented, but I think he did his best."

"It was worth a shot." But all I can think is that I'm back to square one. "You must be exhausted. Would you like me to put you up at the motel for the night?"

"Thank you, but I'll drive back tonight." She grins. "Husband is expecting me."

I drop her at the station where her car is parked. Normally, I'd go inside and spend a few minutes chatting with Jodie. Tonight, my mood is so low, all I want to do is go home, dive into bed with my bottle of Absolut and pull the covers over my head. Of course, I can't.

I don't know if it's the cop in me, my empathy for Mary Plank, or some inflated sense of justice because of what happened to me when I was fourteen. But I cannot—will not—accept the possibility of someone getting away with these crimes. The thought is like a dentist drilling an exposed nerve.

On the way home, I brood over my lackluster inventory of suspects. With Long's posthumous confession, all I have left are James Payne, Aaron Plank and Scott Barbereaux. Of the three, I like Payne the best. He's got the three pillars of police work: motive, means and opportunity. Not to mention a heart full of hate. That puts him at the top of the list.

I think about Aaron Plank, try to consider all the angles, but no matter how I look at the big picture, I don't see him as a serious contender for murder, particularly with that level of violence.

My mind moves on to Barbereaux. He has an alibi, but that doesn't necessarily eliminate him as a suspect, mainly because I haven't yet verified it. Glancing at my watch, I realize that's something I might be able to get done yet tonight. Instead of making a left onto my street, I hang a U-turn and head east.

If you live in Painters Mill and you can afford it, the Maple Crest housing development is the epitome of location, location, location. The homes are spacious with large lots and lushly landscaped yards. A lighted waterfall cascading from a stone wall with the words *Maple Crest* etched into the rock greets me when I turn onto the smooth asphalt street.

Glenda Patterson lives in a stucco-and-brick ranch with high, arching windows and a giant maple tree that must have cost a small fortune to have planted. A sleek red Volvo sits in the driveway. The lights are on inside, so I pull in and park behind the car.

Patterson has her own interior design shop in Millersburg. She must be doing well, because a house like this one isn't cheap. I knock and try to ignore the little voice in the back of my head telling me this is yet another exercise in futility.

A moment later the porch light flicks on. I sense someone checking me out through the peephole, so I face forward and give her a moment to identify me. An instant later, the door swings open and I find myself facing a petite blonde with huge baby-blue eyes and a mouth a lot of women would give a year's salary to possess.

"Glenda Patterson?"

Those baby blues widen, and she cranes her head to look behind me. "Is everything okay?"

"Yes, ma'am. Everything's fine. I just need to ask you a few questions."

"About what?"

"A case I'm working on." I smile, trying to put her at ease. "I'm sorry about the late hour."

She relaxes marginally and gives me a nervous laugh. "I'm not used to seeing the police on my doorstep."

"I didn't mean to alarm you."

"It's okay." She steps aside. "Come in."

The house is warm and smells of eucalyptus and lemon oil. The living room is tastefully decorated with a minimalist style and bold colors that run to the avant-garde. Teal walls contrast nicely with a sleek, black leather sofa. Two matching turquoise chairs sit adjacent to a stainless-steel-and-glass coffee table. Pillows with metallic stitching draw the silver theme back to the sofa. It's an open concept home, and I can see the stainless-steel appliances and granite countertops of a state-of-the-art kitchen from where I stand.

"Nice place," I say.

"Thank you." She beams at the compliment. "This was my first big design project."

I nod approvingly. "You're good."

"Thanks." She flashes a professionally enhanced white smile. "I just opened my office six months ago."

"Business must be good."

"It is, after a bumpy start." She motions toward the sofa. "Would you like to sit? I was just about to have a glass of pinot noir. Would you like one?"

I pat my badge. "Better not, since I'm on duty."

"I understand." She crosses to the counter that separates the kitchen from the living room and pours wine into a stemmed glass.

"Do you live here alone?" I ask.

Nodding, she turns back to me and sips. "Just me and Curly."

"I take it Curly isn't a man."

She laughs. "He's an eighteen-year-old Siamese that's going senile. He's around here somewhere."

Since I'm not here to talk to the cat, I nod appropriately then get down to business. "I'm sure you've heard about the Plank family murders."

"I heard about it on the news, actually. I almost can't believe something so horrible could happen here in Painters Mill." Her brows go together. "Is that why you're here?"

I nod. "Where were you Sunday night?"

Her eyes widen. *"Me?"*

"Don't be alarmed," I say easily. "I'm just verifying some information."

"Oh, well . . ." She takes another sip. "I was here." Her eyes sharpen. "Is this about Scott?"

I ignore her question. "Were you alone?"

"I was with Scott Barbereaux," she says. "He's my boyfriend."

"What time did he arrive?"

"Gosh, I don't know." She bites her lip, thinking. "I made dinner for him—salmon, I believe—then we watched a movie. He probably got here about six-thirty or so."

"What time did he leave?"

"About seven-thirty the next morning."

"So he spent the night?"

"That's right."

"Did he leave at any time during the night?"

She gives me a distinctly feline smile. "No."

"How long have you two been dating?"

"About six months now."

"Do either of you date around?"

"We're exclusive."

"So you guys are pretty tight," I state.

"Yes, I would say we're tight."

"Has he ever cheated on you?"

Her expression cools to just below the freezing point. "Look, is he in some kind of trouble?"

"Not at all. I just need to clear up a few things."

"Well, your questions are kind of personal."

"I apologize for that." I pause. "Does he know a girl by the name of Mary Plank?"

"What?" She blinks at me. "The dead Amish girl? Are you serious?"

I nod to let her know I am. "Did he ever mention her?"

"I don't even think he knew the Plank family." She hesitates, an emotion I can't quite identify clouding her features. "Did he?"

It's an odd question coming from a woman who claimed just a moment ago that she and her lover were close, and I can't help but wonder if Scott Barbereaux is one of those men who has a difficult time with monogamy.

"I believe he may have had contact with her through the shop where she worked," I clarify.

Her eyes widen in a slightly different way, as if she's deciphered some hidden meaning behind my answer, and I realize despite her beauty, her obvious talent and her lovely home, Glenda Patterson is a jealous woman.

"Contact?" she repeats. "What do you mean? What kind of contact?"

"I believe he delivers coffee to the shop."

"Oh." She looks at me as if I've played a dirty trick on her and she fell for it hook, line and sinker. "These questions don't sound very routine, Chief Burkholder."

"I'm just establishing an alibi."

"Now you have it. He was with me. In bed. All night." She motions toward the door with her empty wineglass. "It's getting late."

"Thank you for your time." I start toward the door.

She trails me to the foyer. I open the door and step onto the porch. "Have a nice evening," I say.

Glenda Patterson slams the door behind me without responding.

My house is tucked away on a good-size lot on the edge of town. It's a small two-bedroom, one-bath ranch built back in the 1960s with hardwood floors and the original tile. A big maple tree stands like a sentry in the front yard. The backyard is shady with several black walnut trees. The grass needs mowing and the shutters could use a coat of paint. But this is my home, my refuge, and I'm unduly glad to be here tonight.

I park in the driveway and let myself in through the front door. The scents of candle wax, yesterday's garbage and the lingering memory of

Tomasetti greet me. Flipping on the light, I make my way to the bedroom and change into sweatpants and a T-shirt. I think about calling him as I make my way to the kitchen. But the thought makes me feel like a needy female, so I opt for my bottle of Absolut instead.

Like many cops I've known, I do some of my best thinking after I've had a few drinks. At least that's what I tell myself. Tonight, my mind is on the Plank family. On Mary. On the accomplice I now know exists. I can practically feel the son of a bitch slinking around town, smug in the knowledge that he got away with murder. The reality of that is like salt on a wound. I can't get past it. I won't because as surely as I'm standing here contemplating drinking myself into a stupor, I know someday he'll kill again.

Snagging a tumbler from the cupboard, I pull the bottle from the cabinet above the refrigerator and pour three fingers into the glass. I take the first heady drink as I walk back into the living room. The evidence box marked *T. Long Suicide* waits for me next to the door. The last thing I want to do is look at the remaining four disks. I don't have a choice.

I carry the box to my office. While my computer boots, I go back to the kitchen and retrieve the bottle of Absolut. I can't watch the disks without the crutch of alcohol. The warm swirl of it melts around my brain as I drop the first disk into the drive. Settling into the chair behind my desk, I click Play.

The images I've grown to hate fill the screen. I see humanity at its worst. Evil in its most vile form. A young woman's innocence shattered, her life stolen, her memory trampled upon. A culture raped for the sake of blood money. Still, I watch. I feel more than I should. And I hurt.

The first disk plays out. I slide the second into the drive and hit Play. Mary tries to cover her nudeness, but she's too uncoordinated from whatever drug was pumped into her. The man in the mask enters the screen. I see her revulsion, I feel that same terrible revulsion in my own heart. I watch as Long overpowers her. Then she's facedown with her hands and feet tied to the head and footboards.

I don't want to see what happens next. I don't want to know what he did to this young girl. I don't want to imagine the shame and self-hate she must have experienced afterward. I can only hope she was so drugged she didn't remember all of it.

Closing my eyes, I put my face in my hands. The gunshot snap of a strap against flesh jolts me. I look at my monitor over the tops of my fingers. Long whips her buttocks with some type of leather-covered bat. A riding crop, I realize. I flinch at the sound of the blows. They are not the fake strikes of some second-rate porn actor wannabe. Long hits her hard, putting some muscle into it. He's *hurting* her. Leaving welts that bloom quickly into bruises.

"Dear God," I whisper.

Briefly, I wonder why she didn't write about this in her diary. Then I realize if she'd been drugged, there's a possibility she didn't *remember*. I can only guess about the rest of it, but I suspect when she noticed the bruises on her body, she went into denial. Or maybe she was simply too ashamed and depressed to acknowledge just how awful and hopeless her life had become.

The next video is every bit as disturbing and offensive. It takes place in a nondescript room. A red-and-white comforter is spread out on a concrete floor. Once again Long wears the mask. His jeans are pushed down to his knees, and Mary Plank's plain dress is hiked up to her waist. They engage in intercourse, changing positions several times. When Long is finished, he rises, tugs up his jeans. Mary lies on the comforter, struggling to pull down her dress. Her heavy-lidded eyes stay on Long.

The mask toward the camera, he crosses to Mary. The camera pans in on her for a close-up. I see a hand on her upraised knee, pulling her legs apart. Something pings in my brain. I click Stop and freeze the frame. Long is standing on the far side of Mary. His hands are on his penis. Where did the other hand come from? Using the mouse, I back up a frame. Three more clicks and the hand comes back into view.

I set down my glass hard. I move the frames forward. *Click. Click. Click.* Long is standing on the other side of Mary. I click backward. The hand on Mary's knee looms into view. It's on the *near* side of Mary. The overall size of the hand, the wrinkling and size of the knuckles, and the blunt-cut nails tell me it's a male hand.

And it doesn't belong to Todd Long.

It's my first undisputable proof that there's an accomplice.

"I see you, you son of a bitch," I whisper.

I know it's possible Long cut footage or otherwise edited the disk, and it only *appears* that while he's standing on the far side of Mary, that hand is on her knee. I start clicking the mouse, trying to figure out how to enlarge the image. I can stumble through most computer programs, but by no means am I a whiz. The alcohol isn't helping. But I need a closer look at the hand to see if there are any identifying marks.

The computer isn't cooperating. I try a dozen ways to enlarge the image, but each time I lose too much resolution. I save the image to the hard drive and open it using different software. Finally, I succeed and almost immediately find what I'm looking for. Between the thumb and index finger, a scar the size of a dime stands out against tanned skin. I try to recall if Long had such a scar, but I don't remember seeing one.

Before I even realize why I'm reaching for the phone, I'm dialing Doc Coblentz's number. A sleepy-sounding woman answers on the sixth ring. A quick glance at my computer monitor tells me it's almost midnight.

Hoping I sound sober, I ask for the doctor.

"Please tell me you don't have another body," Doc Coblentz says without preamble.

"Just a question," I say quickly.

He grunts and I imagine him pushing himself to a sitting position. "By all means ask away," he snaps.

"I'm reviewing some of the disks we found at the Todd Long suicide."

The doc cuts in, perturbed. "And you're doing that this time of night because . . ."

Quickly, I tell him about the hand and the scar. "I was wondering if you recall a scar like that on Todd Long's right hand."

"I'll have to look at my report." He sighs, resigned to getting up. "Give me a minute to grab the file."

I hear shuffling on the other end of the line. The crackle of paper sounds and then the doc is back on the phone. "I've got a post mortem photo with a pretty good view of the right hand. There is no scar, Kate."

"Thanks, Doc. I owe you one."

"I'll settle for a good night's sleep." He hangs up.

I dial Tomasetti's number without setting down the phone. He answers on the fourth ring with a groggy snap of his name. It surprises me because he's usually awake at this hour.

"I'm sorry to wake you," I begin.

"I like it when you call me in the middle of the night." His voice is deep and low. "What's up?"

I tell him about the hand and scar.

"Are you sure Long didn't have a scar?"

"I just verified it with the coroner."

"I guess now all you have to do is find the man who belongs to the hand," he says.

"I could circulate the photo and ask for the public's help."

"If he catches wind of it, he might run. The guy's facing life in prison. Maybe the death penalty."

"Pretty strong motivation." I think about my options. "I could circulate the photo to area physicians."

"Hit or miss at best. Guys that age don't go to the doctor."

Silence fills the line between us. I can practically hear our thought processes, like static voices zinging between us. But it's the overtones of our more private thoughts that dominate.

"You go through all the disks?" he asks.

"Twice."

"How much vodka did that take?"

I glance at the bottle. "A lot."

"If I can get away, do you want me to come back down?"

"You have a meeting with the deputy superintendent, remember?"

"Won't be the first meeting I've missed."

"Tomasetti, I don't want you jeopardizing your career for this."

He sighs, a long, drawn-out sound that makes me wish he was here. "Or your case."

"I want you to come down." My voice quiets. "But for all the wrong reasons."

"You mean not necessarily for my cop skills?"

"That, too."

We fall silent, then Tomasetti asks. "Have you had any luck identifying the location where these videos were taped?"

"There's nothing distinguishable. I could probably send out a couple of guys to canvass some of the area motels, try to match up the décor. See if we can get a name that way."

"Probably didn't use a real name," he says. "One of the clerks might recognize Mary Plank from a photo. If they have security cameras, you'll have even more to go on. Might be worth a shot, Kate."

I like the way he says my name. I want to say more, but the words aren't there. I want to ask about the panic attacks. His job. I want to tell him I miss him. I want him to tell me he's going to be all right. Instead, I tell him about Billy Zook's inability to help us with the sketch.

"I talked to Deborah Kim when she got back." He sighs. "Composite would have been a nice break."

"Billy was the one I chased that night in the rain." Across from me, my computer screen blinks into screensaver mode.

"If he's a peeper, his being there makes sense."

"Had the killers seen him that night, they probably would have killed him, too."

"Right along with the others."

I think about Billy Zook and all the ways his involvement might have played out. All the ways a composite sketch would have helped. I feel like I'm on the verge of some discovery—some breakthrough—but my mind hasn't quite figured it out yet.

"What if Billy *had* identified the accomplice?" I ask.

"He didn't."

"Hypothetically speaking, what if he had?"

"Hypothetically speaking, we'd identify the son of a bitch and make the arrest."

"What if the killer knew there was a witness?"

"Kate, are you going somewhere with this?"

"I'm not sure." But my mind is spinning, taking me through some of the possibilities of what might have happened if Billy had been able to give us a decent composite. All the ways I could use the information to my advantage. "If Billy was a viable witness and the killer knew it, do you think it's conceivable that Billy could be in danger?"

"It's conceivable. Killers have been known to kill witnesses. But we're playing what-ifs." He pauses. "Should I be worried about something?"

"You'll be the first to know when I figure it out."

CHAPTER 25

At just before seven A.M., I'm in my office, sitting at my desk. For the last hour I've been trying to ward off a hangover headache with coffee, but I'm not having much luck. In the visitor chair across from my desk, Skid works on his shift report. Glock stands at the door, an apple fritter in one hand, a cup of coffee in the other. Pickles drifts in, smelling like cigarettes and English Leather and looking like death warmed over. He's not the morning type. Behind him, T.J. carries on a conversation on his cell. I can tell by the silly grin he's talking to his girlfriend.

"I know you guys want to know why you were summoned here so early." I glance at my watch. "Mayor Brock should be here any time."

"Speak of the devil," Glock mutters.

"That would be me." Mayor Auggie Brock appears at the door. He's a short, rotund man with hairy ears and overgrown eyebrows that remind me of an aging yorkie. He's snagged a powdered doughnut from the coffee station and bites into it with the relish of a starving man as he drops into the second visitor chair across from me. "I gave up my morning walk for this."

"Thanks for coming in so early, Auggie." I scan the faces in the room and take a moment to get my words in order. "While I was reviewing the disks from the Long and Plank cases last night, I discovered this."

Leaning across my desk, I pass out the photos I printed. "The hand you see in that still does not belong to Todd Long."

A ripple of surprise goes around the room. For the cops, it's a collective sound of sudden interest. For Auggie, it's the sound of a man who'll now have to deal with an unhappy town council. Nothing gets the bean counters more perturbed in a tourist town than a murderer on the loose.

Auggie looks like he's going to throw up. "Are you certain?"

"I'm certain enough to keep the investigation open."

He groans, a little boy whose balloon has just been burst by the neighborhood bully.

Glock speaks up from his place by the door. "Can we ID this guy using the scar?"

"We can try." I look at T.J. "I want you to take this photo to every doctor in town. Millersburg, too."

"I'm there."

I turn my attention to Glock. "I want you to talk to Scott Barbereaux. Tell him about the wine bottle we found. Ask him when he was at Miller's Pond. Find out who he was with. Verify it. Ask him about September twenty-second. Rattle his cage a little."

Glock nods. "My pleasure."

"Make sure you get a good look at his right hand," I add.

I look at the mayor. "Auggie, I was wondering if you could call an emergency town council meeting and let the members know about this. Tell them we're working around the clock and that I'll have a press release late this afternoon."

The mayor sighs. "Boy, it's going to hit the fan when they find out the case isn't as closed as they'd like it to be."

"Maybe you could remind them of what another murder would do to tourism."

"Good point." He gets to his feet. "Anything else, Kate?"

I shake my head, motion toward my team. "We're just going to go over some police stuff."

Grimacing, he nods and heads for the door.

I wait a beat, then give Glock a pointed look. "Close the door."

Arching a brow, he leans over and the latch clicks shut.

I scan the men's faces. "Let me preface by saying none of what I'm about to say leaves this room." Doughnuts, coffee and the earliness of the hour are forgotten. Their collective attention focuses on me. "We know the accomplice is still out there. As far as the investigation, we have two things going for us at this point. The scar. And the DNA from the semen we found inside Mary Plank. If the DNA belongs to Todd Long, we're back at square one. If it doesn't match Long, we may have our first big break. However . . ." I pause, let the word sink in. "If the accomplice isn't in the CODIS database, we'll be left high and dry."

"How long until DNA results come back?" Pickles asks.

"Tomasetti is pushing, but he can only do so much. The lab is back-logged. It's going to be a few more days." I grimace. "Too damn long. This killer is an animal. Savage enough to cut a fetus from a woman's body for the sole purpose of keeping us from doing a paternity test."

The men nod in unison.

"I think I figured out a way to smoke this bastard out of his hole," I say.

"How?" T.J. asks.

"We set a trap with bait he won't be able to resist."

He looks around as if wondering if he's the only one who's not following. "What bait?"

"Billy Zook."

A stir goes around the room. Not a stir of alarm. A stir of anticipation. The kind hunters feel in the moments before they embark on the pursuit of a dangerous animal.

"Does the killer know the Zook kid witnessed the murders?" Glock asks.

"Not yet. But if I release that information to the press, you can bet he'll be aware of it by the end of the day."

"The media's kind of a wild card, isn't it?" T.J. asks.

"Not if I feed them exactly what we want them to report."

"If we make it too easy and name the witness outright, the killer will smell a trap," Pickles says.

"I won't use names. But I'll mention the disk and the face in the window. I'm betting the killer kept a copy of that disk."

Skid nods. "First thing he's going to do is take a look at it."

"If we found the kid's face, he can find it," T.J. adds.

I nod. "It'll take some doing on his part. He'll need to review the disk, magnify the image. Identify and find the kid. But if we make it too easy, he'll know it's a trap."

Glock leans back in his chair. "How do you know the killer will be able to identify the kid? Hell, how do you know if he'll even read the newspaper?"

"It's not a perfect plan," I tell him. "But Painters Mill is a small town. Even with the kid being Amish, it's reasonable to think the killer will somehow learn about the witness. Once he does, he should be able to ID him."

"Lotta *ifs* in there, Chief," Skid says.

"I know," I reply. "But if you look at the killer's profile, I think he'll go for it. He's ruthless. He's smart. Cunning. Billy Zook can put him in prison for life. Maybe even get him lethal injection. This killer has already murdered seven people, including a toddler."

"Eight people if you include the baby Mary Plank was carrying," Pickles adds.

"Pretty solid motivation," Glock says.

T.J. raises his brows. "The killer could run."

"True. But I don't think he will. I believe he's established here. His life is here. He doesn't want to give it up. That's why he killed Mary Plank and her family." I shrug. "If you look at the situation through the eyes of a psychopath, it's a hell of a lot easier to eliminate a threat than it is to start over in another country."

Skid rakes his hand through his hair. "That's some cold shit."

"Have you run this by the Zooks?" Glock asks.

The thought makes me sigh. "It's going to be a hard sell."

T.J. looks from face to face. "But won't the boy be in danger?"

"No," I reply.

"How can you guarantee that?"

"Because he won't be anywhere in sight. I will."

Ten minutes later I'm on my way to the Zook farm. Glock offered to ride along, but I declined. The odds of my convincing this conservative Amish family to help are better if I do this alone. Even then, I have my work cut out for me. My Amish background will only go so far, particularly since I'm no longer a member of the church district. I'm an outsider encroaching on a society I turned my back on a long time ago.

The morning sun beats down from a severe blue sky as I head out of town. I pass an Amish man and a team of mules raking hay. I'm in such a hurry, I barely notice the scent of newly cut alfalfa. In that moment it strikes me there was a time when I had no concept of urgency. Life was slow and simple; my life path set on a course that would have been much the same as my mother's and grandmother's before me. All that changed the day I shot and killed Daniel Lapp.

I wave to the Amish man as I pass. I smile when he returns the wave. Turning into the gravel lane that will take me to the Zook farmhouse, I hope I'll be able to convince William and Alma to help me.

I park behind a black buggy. Midway to the house, I hear my name. I turn to find William and his youngest son walking toward me from the barn. Man and boy wear typical Amish work clothes—trousers with suspenders, blue work shirts and flat-brimmed straw hats. Their boots are covered with muck, and I realize they've been cleaning the hog pens and transferring manure to the pit.

William greets me in Pennsylvania Dutch. *"Guder Mariya."* Good morning.

I respond in kind. "I'm sorry to disturb your work."

"Isaac and I were just going in for the midday meal."

Under normal circumstances, anyone that visits an Amish home during a meal would be asked to join them. The Amish are generous with food, and the women prepare large portions. But because I have been excommunicated, he doesn't ask. I don't take it personally, but it doesn't bode well for what I'm about to propose. "Do you and Mrs. Zook have a few minutes to talk?" I glance at Isaac. "Privately?"

"There is much work to do."

"This won't take long."

He grunts an unenthusiastic reply without looking at me.

I fall in behind them. We enter the house through the back door. The kitchen is a large room and smells of frying food and cooking tomatoes. From where I stand, I can feel the heat coming off the stove. A rectangular table draped with a blue-and-white checkered cloth dominates the room. Alma stands at the stove with a spatula in her hand, turning something in a cast iron skillet. She looks at me when we enter, and offers a small smile. Canning jars rattle in boiling water, and I know she's probably been at the stove since the wee hours of morning. Though the windows are open, the room is uncomfortably hot and I break a sweat beneath my uniform shirt.

"Hello, Katie," Alma says.

Feeling out of place, I smile at her. "Hello, Alma."

The table is set for four people with plates, glasses filled with water, and napkins. William takes his place at the head of the table and growls, *"Sis unvergleichlich hees dohin."*

"Next month you'll be complaining about the cold." Alma sets a plate of fried ham, green beans, sliced tomatoes and a piece of bread slathered with apple butter in front of him.

"Wash your hands, Isaac," she says to her son. "And tell Billy to come down." She looks at me. "Katie, would you like to join us?"

William gives her a dark look.

Frowning, she puts her hands on her hips. *"Mer sot tem sei Eegne net verlosse; Gott verlosst die Seine nicht."* One should not abandon one's own; God does not abandon his own.

"She is under the *Meidung*," William growls.

"She is in our home."

I almost smile when William looks down at his food and concedes to his wife. Alma turns her attention to me. "I have fried ham with vegetables and bread. Would you like a plate?"

"I'm not hungry. But thank you." I look from Alma to William. "I'm here because I need your help."

William raises his head to look at me. "That is a first. The English police asking the Amish for help."

Isaac and Billy wrestle into the kitchen. William speaks sharply to them. "Sit at the table, boys. We will pray."

Eyeing me suspiciously, Billy and Isaac take the chairs to William's right. Alma sets a basket of bread in the center of the table and then takes her place to her husband's left. I stand near the kitchen doorway, perspiring in the sweltering heat, trying not to feel like an outsider as the family bows their heads and William recites the before meal prayer.

"*O Herr Gott, himmlischer Vater, Segne uns und Diese Diene Gaben, die wir von Deiner milden Gute Zu uns nehmen warden, Speise und tranke auch unsere Seelen zum ewigen Leben, und mach uns theilhaftig Deines himmllischen Tisches durch Jesus Christum. Amen.*"

Oh Lord God, heavenly Father, bless us and these thy gifts, which we shall accept from thy tender goodness. Give us food and drink also for our souls unto life eternal, and make us partakers of thy heavenly table through Jesus Christ. Amen.

Even after seventeen years, the words come back with a clarity that astonishes me. I recited that prayer a thousand times as a child. Memories fly at me out of the backwaters of my mind. My *datt*'s baritone voice. Sarah and Jonas and I trading food beneath the table. *Mamm* knowing what we were doing, but never busting us because she knew sometimes *Datt*'s punishments were too severe for the crime.

The memories scatter when William raises his head, grabs his fork and begins to eat. "What do you want from us?"

I didn't want to discuss police business with the children present, but I may not get another opportunity, so I plunge ahead. "It's about the Plank case. I need your help."

"I do not see how we can help," Alma says. "Billy did not see the man clearly—"

"The killer doesn't know that."

William and Alma look at me. Isaac stops eating and looks at me, a green bean sticking out the side of his mouth. Only Billy continues chewing, oblivious to the conversation. "I do not understand," William says after a moment.

"I want to set a trap. Make the killer believe Billy was a witness. To do that, I need access to your farm for a few days. So I can lure the killer here."

Alma opens her mouth to speak, but William beats her to it. "I will not allow you to put my family in danger."

"That is too dangerous for Billy," Alma says simultaneously.

I level a stare at them. "None of you will be in danger."

William sets down his fork. The look he gives me makes the hairs on my arms tingle. "We are Amish, not dumb farm animals."

"You know I don't think that," I snap.

William bristles. Glancing at his children, he motions toward the living room. "Isaac and Billy, go to your room."

Alma's gaze darts from me to her husband. "William . . ."

"Go!" He thrusts a hand toward the door.

Isaac snatches a piece of bread from the basket, and without a word, they flee the kitchen. William gives me an accusing stare. "I will not allow you to come into my home and frighten my children."

"William, if this wasn't important, I wouldn't be here. But I have a killer to catch. I have a responsibility to the people of this town to keep them safe."

"The killer is an *Englischer*," William growls. "This is not an Amish matter."

"The Plank family was Amish," I counter.

"I cannot help you." William resumes eating, using his fork and chewing with a little too much vigor.

"If I don't stop him, he'll kill again."

He chews harder, ignoring me.

Frustrated, I look at his wife. "If you'll just listen to what I have to say."

"I have heard enough." The Amish man stands abruptly. "Be ye not unequally yoked together with unbelievers; for what fellowship hath righteousness with unrighteousness? And what communion hath light with darkness?"

The passage is a doctrine that forbids an Amish person from doing business with outsiders. I heard it many times in my youth. I don't believe it now any more than I did then.

"Yes, we are two societies," I tell him. "Amish and English. But we are one town. And this killer doesn't differentiate between the two."

Without looking at me, William mutters something in Pennsylvania Dutch.

Alma puts her hands on her hips. "But what of the people who are in danger, William? If it is in our power to keep them safe, perhaps this is the path God would want us to take."

Her husband brings his hand down on the table hard enough to rattle silverware. "No!"

I'd known the plan would be a hard sell. The principle of separation from the outside world colors every aspect of an Amish person's reality. My own parents shared a similar view. In this case, I suspect that buried somewhere inside that philosophy, is also fear for his son.

Realizing there's nothing more I can say, I give William a final look. "The Amish are not the only children of God in this town. Think about that tonight when you're trying to sleep."

The level of emotion in my voice surprises me. Disgusted with them, with myself, I head for the door, yank it open, take the steps at a too fast pace to the sidewalk. I'm nearly to the Explorer when I hear my name. I turn to see William coming down the steps. Alma stands just inside the screen door, watching.

William reaches me and stops. For a long moment, neither of us speaks. Then he surprises me by saying, "I will talk to Bishop Troyer."

I don't know if that's good or bad because I have no idea if the bishop will give his blessing. I want to tell him keeping people safe is bigger than this clash of cultures. Because I so desperately need his cooperation, I hold my tongue. "Thank you."

"Gott segen eich," he says, then turns and walks away.

CHAPTER 26

I'm standing at the window in my office, thinking about John Tomasetti when the call comes. I hadn't expected to learn of William Zook's decision via telephone, but Bishop Troyer is one of the few Amish who has a phone and uses it. It's mainly for emergencies, like the time when Joe Yoder fell off the roof during a barn raising and broke his leg. But the bishop is also sort of an acting liaison between the Amish community and the English. When important calls need to be made, they are made to and from the bishop's home.

"This is William Zook."

"Hello, William." Anticipation makes my heart thud dully in my chest.

"Bishop Troyer has given his blessing. I will allow you to use the farm, but that is all."

My relief is so profound that for a moment, I fumble for words. "I appreciate that."

"I do not want Billy to be in danger, Chief Burkholder."

"None of you will be in danger," I say firmly. "Two of my officers will be taking you and your family to a safe house."

"I do not understand what that is."

"A house where you'll stay while we wait for the killer."

"No English house," he says.

I tamp down impatience while my brain scrambles for a solution. "Is there an Amish family you could stay with for a few days?"

He considers that for a moment. "Rachael and Joe Yoder. The storm blew down some of the pens and chicken coop. It will take Joe and me a few days to make repairs."

"All right. Two officers will be with you at all times."

William sighs. "So be it."

Half an hour later, Glock and I are in the shabby-chic warehouse offices of *The Advocate*, Painters Mill's weekly newspaper. Filled with the smells of paper and print ink, the publisher's office is a large room crammed full of artsy photos in stainless-steel frames, an antique desk and credenza, several tastefully battered leather chairs and dozens of stacks of newspapers that are taller than me.

Steve Ressler stands behind his desk, his hands on his hips, glancing at his watch every thirty seconds or so. He's a small, wiry man with red hair and a ruddy complexion that glows like a bad sunburn when he's frustrated or angry, which seems to be all the time. He's a hard-driving, type-A personality and always looks as if he's on the verge of having a stroke.

"I want you to run a special edition of *The Advocate*," I begin.

"A special edition? That's kind of expensive. Maybe I could just put something on the Web site. . . ."

"I need both," I tell him. "A story on the Web site as well as a special edition."

"Is there some news item I don't know about, Chief Burkholder?"

"I'm working on something now." I hand him the bogus press release. "Everything you need to know is there."

Ressler skims the paper, his red brows knitting. "This is pretty explosive."

"I'd appreciate it if you kept your source confidential," I say.

"Of course." Then Ressler sighs. "I hate to ask this question, Kate, but will I be compensated? Running a special edition is not cheap."

I give him a wry smile. "As chief of police, I've gotten pretty good at squeezing blood out of a stone."

"Excellent." His cheeks flush red with excitement. "When do you want me to run it?"

"This afternoon. In time for dinner."

"Gonna be tight." He glances at his watch, frowns. "That only gives me a few hours."

"Can you do it?"

"Yeah, but I'm going to have to hustle. I've got some ads and other stories I can use for fill." He's thinking aloud now. "I'm going to need to call in a few people. Ad girl. Layout guy. Typesetter. Circulation. Route people."

I look at my own watch. Almost one P.M. "How soon can you get it out?"

"Going to need at least four hours. That's pushing it."

"We need it out by five P.M. Grocery stores. Bars. Convenience stores. Doctor offices. All of your subscribers."

Heaving another sigh, Ressler looks at his watch. "Okay, okay."

"I don't have to tell you this is strictly confidential, do I, Steve?" I ask. "You can't tell anyone I was your source. Not your wife. Not even your dog."

"I don't have a dog," he snaps. "Who the hell has time for a damn dog?"

Glock and I hold back grins when we walk out.

Dusk at an Amish home is a special time. Sunlight slants through the windows, washing the rooms in golden light. Dust motes spiral and dance in the glowing shafts. Quiet falls and shadows lengthen. It is a time when the chores are done. The heat of the day is fading to cool comfort. Everyone's tired and looking forward to the evening meal, conversation, prayer and rest.

It's strange to walk the rooms of a farmhouse so much like the one I grew up in. Around me the house is so quiet I can hear the breeze hissing through the open windows, the tap of the curtain hem weights against the sills. The occasional creak of a century-old house settling. Sparrows chatter in the maple tree outside.

I'm standing in the kitchen and my memories are keeping me company. Some of those memories are good. There's laughter. A keen sense of belonging. The kind of security I felt knowing I was part of a family unit. But some of the memories are bad, too. I was introduced to violence in a pretty country kitchen much like this one. That single event forever changed my life and set me on a path I have not veered from to this day.

Despite the peacefulness of the house, an edginess creeps over me. The kind of dark anticipation you feel right before a storm. The thought that my plan won't work is a cloud that has shadowed me all afternoon.

I look down at the plain dress, apron, *kapp* and stockings folded neatly in my hands. I haven't worn traditional Amish clothing for about thirteen years, and it's disconcerting to contemplate wearing them now. It's the small, everyday things that take me back. Donning these clothes will be like stepping into a time machine and being thrust back to a time I'm not sure I want to revisit.

The special edition of *The Advocate* went out as scheduled two and a half hours ago. My copy was still warm from the presses when I swung by the diner and picked it up. Steve Ressler did a good job with the information I gave him.

> With the apparent suicide of murder suspect Todd Long, everyone believed the Plank case was solved. But in a shocking turn of events, The Advocate *learned from an anonymous source inside the Painters Mill Police Department that a new witness has materialized. This unidentified witness claims there was an accomplice.*
>
> *A call to Chief of Police Kate Burkholder netted a stern "no comment."* The Advocate *has since learned from a source inside the PD that an unidentified Amish boy witnessed the crimes and may be able to identify a second man responsible for the murders of the Plank family. In a videotape obtained from an anonymous source, the boy can be seen looking in a window, ostensibly at the Plank farmhouse on the night of the murders.*

When confronted, Chief Burkholder verified the information, but told The Advocate *that the Amish parents will not allow the boy to speak with the "English" police. "We believe the boy will eventually cooperate and identify an accomplice," she said yesterday. "Because of obvious safety issues, we're keeping his identity confidential."*

The Advocate *attempted to locate the Amish parents, but was unsuccessful.*

I called dispatch a few minutes ago and was told the phone lines were lit up like Christmas tree lights. The grapevine is abuzz with the news that a killer lurks somewhere in this peaceful little town. Alone at the Zook farmhouse, I don't believe the situation will stay peaceful for long.

In the main bathroom, I change into Alma's clothes. Most Amish do not use buttons or zippers, and I'd forgotten how tedious the pins are. Alma is larger than me, so I have room for the Kevlar vest. It's uncomfortable and hot, but I know better than to let myself get caught unprepared.

Since the Amish don't use mirrors, I have a difficult time with my hair and end up using a dozen bobby pins and tucking the loose strands beneath the *kapp* with my fingers. The feeling of déjà vu is overwhelming and strange as I walk back into the living room. I entered the bathroom as a cop; I walked out as the Amish woman I might have been.

Back in the kitchen, feeling conspicuous in the clothes, I pick up my radio. "Skid, are you in position?"

"That's affirm, Chief. Fuckin' stinks out here."

The apt description makes me smile. I positioned him in the barn where he has an unencumbered view of the house, the driveway as well as the back and side yards. "Might be more tolerable in the hayloft."

"Better vista, too. I'll head up there now."

"What about you, T.J.? Any movement?"

"Just me and the mosquitoes."

Since my Explorer is the only four-wheel-drive vehicle in the fleet, I put T.J. in it and sent him to a small parking area under the Painters

Creek Bridge. People go there to fish. It's relatively close to the farm, yet out of sight from the road. The only thing I don't like about the location is that he can't actually see the Zook house, which means we'll have to rely completely on our radios for communication. But if I call for backup, he'll be able to get here quickly.

"Keep your eyes open, guys."

"Roger that," comes Skid's voice.

"You think he's going to show?" T.J. asks.

"I'd hate to have to smell these damn pigs all week."

All of us know the livestock is the least of our problems. "Let's hope so."

I disconnect, and the silence presses down on me. Outside the kitchen window, birdsong is slowly giving way to the night sounds of crickets and frogs. An edgy energy runs like mercury through my veins. But impatience and a low-grade anxiety dog me. I've never been good at waiting, but I have a feeling I'll be doing plenty in the next few days. It's going to be hard because in the back of my mind, I know there's a high probability my plan will fail. The killer won't show.

That he'll kill again . . .

A glance at my watch tells me the newspaper has been in circulation for almost three hours now. I wonder if the killer has read the story. I wonder if he'll take the bait. If he'll review the video and identify the face in the window. If he'll come here to silence the only living witness . . .

It's not easy getting into the mind of a psychopath; they don't think the same way the rest of us do. I envision this going down any number of ways. The killer waits until nightfall. He's armed and wears a mask, does a quick and violent home invasion with plans to kill the boy in his bed. Another scenario is that the killer will use a stealthier plan. Wait until dark. Sneak in. Take the boy from his bed. And either kill him there or make it look like an accident. A fall from the loft in the barn would do the trick.

More than likely the killer will scope out the place first. Tonight, it's my goal to let him know the Zook family is home, totally unaware. They are vulnerable to attack. *Come get us. . . .*

Tomasetti has been on the periphery of my mind since he left. I'm not sure why I've put off calling him. Maybe because I know he's got enough on his plate at the moment. Or maybe a part of me fears he'll find fault with my plan, and I know that no matter what he says, I won't scrub it. Still, I want to talk to him. I want to hear his voice. I want him to make me laugh. The vehemence of those feelings scares me a little. One of many hazards of a relationship.

Pulling out my phone, I dial his number from memory. He answers with his usual growl of his last name.

"It's Kate."

"I knew you wouldn't be able to resist calling me much longer." His words are easy, but something in his voice puts me on alert. Some subtle note I can't quite identify.

"I wanted to fill you in on something I've got going on here," I begin.

"You catch a break?"

"Not exactly." I lay out the plan.

A charged pause ensues. "You've been busy."

"Things happened fast."

"You're at the Zook farmhouse alone?"

"Skid is in the barn. T.J. is parked out of sight by the bridge."

"What about your other guys?"

"Glock and Pickles are with the Zook family a few miles from here."

"Kate, that's not enough men."

That's when I realize he's been drinking. Tomasetti is good at pretending. Good at faking. Hell, he's an Academy Award–worthy actor half of the time. But I know him well. I know every nuance of his voice. I know how to read between the lines. I know he can be a prick when he's hurt or angry.

"Sheriff's office has stepped up patrols," I say. "It's all I've got."

"Why the hell didn't you call me? I could have helped."

"You're not exactly on active status."

"That never stopped you before."

"John, look, you've got a lot going on right now. And I've thought this thing through. We're organized. Prepared. I think we can handle it."

"You *think*?"

"I'm sure we can." But I fumble the words.

"Or maybe you didn't call me because you think I'm going to freak out at some inopportune moment and fuck things up for you."

"That's not true," I say evenly.

He cuts me off. "Better to wait until I'm a hundred miles away. A safe distance where I can't do any harm. Did you discuss my precarious state of mind with your team, Kate? Did they agree with your assessment?"

"I'm not going to justify that with a response."

"That's rich."

"I just wanted to let you know we might be getting a break soon. I wanted you to know what we were doing. How we were handling—"

"You wanted to let me know you can do this all by yourself."

The words sting. They make me feel like a selfish bitch. Like maybe this is more about me than catching a killer, and I've put my officers and myself in harm's way because I'm trying to prove something I don't have to prove. I defend my position anyway. "That's not true."

"Bullshit."

"You've been drinking."

"I'm sure you're shocked."

"Look, I just called to let you know what's going on."

"Waiting until now to call me was a goddamn bitchy thing to do."

"I can't talk to you when you're like this."

"I'm always like this. Wake the hell up."

Fury burns through me with such force my hands shake. "I'll let you know how it goes."

"Goddamn you, Kate. How the hell do you expect me to sleep tonight, knowing you're alone in that house?" he shouts.

"I'm not alone."

"You don't have enough backup. T.J.'s a rookie and Skid isn't exactly top notch. Do you think that's good police work? That's insane."

"They're good cops, and this is a good plan."

"Sometimes good doesn't matter! Don't you get that?" He's shouting at the top of his lungs now. "This guy comes calling in the middle of the night and gets by one of your guys, you're going to find yourself in big trouble."

"I'm armed. I'm wearing a vest—"

"Going to do you a hell of a lot of good if he takes a head shot!"

"John, you're overreacting."

"What the hell are you trying to prove, Kate?"

"I'm trying to catch the son of a bitch who killed seven people!"

"Or maybe you finally see a chance for retribution for what happened to you. Maybe you want to prove the Amish aren't easy victims. Maybe you're going to blow this guy's shit away the moment he walks in the door."

I almost can't believe what's coming from his mouth. "That's psycho bullshit, Tomasetti."

"I'm right and you know it! And now I've got to sit here and do nothing while you get yourself and maybe one of your guys fucking killed. Do you ever think of anyone besides yourself? Did it even cross your mind that I would worry? That maybe I wanted to be involved?"

"You're not part of this case!" I shout.

"And that's exactly the way you want it, isn't it?"

His words leave me reeling. The depth of his anger shocks me. Worse, it fills me with doubt. About the plan. About my motivations. About my abilities as a cop. "I don't need this."

"Evidently, you do."

"I have to go."

"Don't you fucking hang up on me!"

I snap my phone closed. His words ring in my head. For a full minute, I stand there, looking down at my phone, wondering what the hell just happened.

Turning off the phone, I drop it into my pocket and wander into the living room. Through the window, dusk wanes. Full darkness will be here soon. Several Jersey cows graze in the pasture. The long and narrow lane is empty. I can't see the road from the house, but I know Skid can see it from the hayloft. He'll let me know if anyone shows.

Still, the farm is large and there are a dozen places someone could approach and remain unseen. From the back pasture. They could slink along the greenbelt that runs along the creek. They could use the cornfield for cover. On the outside chance someone is watching, I decide to use the last of the daylight to make myself visible.

CHAPTER 27

The garden is a cornucopia of autumn vegetables and berries. Standing in the final remnants of daylight, I take in the perfect rows of corn, tomatoes, squash, cucumber and green peppers. The rear perimeter is a briar patch of blackberry bushes drooping with ripe berries. In the spring, I know strawberries abound, and it's a constant battle to keep the birds from stealing the fruit.

We had a similar garden when I was a girl growing up. I used to sneak into the garden and eat strawberries right off the plants, sometimes before they were even ripe. The season is long past now, but the blackberries are at the height of ripeness. I walk to the bushes. Being careful of the stickers, I pull off a couple of berries and pop them into my mouth.

Even as I enjoy the impromptu snack, I'm aware of the .38 in the pocket of my apron. The .22 mini-magnum strapped to my thigh. The knife in my ankle boot. I'm also keenly aware of my surroundings. It's so quiet, I would have no problem hearing a vehicle come up the driveway. But if the killer makes an appearance, I don't think he'll use the lane. He'll wait for full darkness, try for stealth. He'll probably enter the house via the back door, try to find the boy without waking the rest of the family and kill him in the most expeditious manner possible.

Determined to make the farm appear normal, I spend a few minutes picking weeds. I check the laundry left on the clothesline—at my request. Thoughts of Tomasetti try to pry their way into my brain as I stroll the yard, but I don't let them. I need to stay focused.

At dark, I go back into the house. I light the lantern on the kitchen table, filling the room with yellow light and the smell of lantern oil. I light a second lantern in the living room, then go upstairs and light another in the master bedroom. Just another ordinary night in the Zook home.

Back in the living room, I close the curtains and hit my lapel mike. "Skid, all clear in the barn?"

"Just me and these stinkin' pigs."

"T.J.?"

"Not a single car in the last half hour."

I sigh. "We may be here a while."

"What if they don't show, Chief?" T.J. asks.

I've been a cop long enough to know stings like this one rarely go as planned. There are so many variables it's hard to pinpoint where things might go awry. But the killer not showing is certainly high on the list.

"We don't have the manpower to stake this place out more than a few days," I say. "If he doesn't show tonight, I'll call BCI or the sheriff's office and request assistance."

"Good plan."

I end the call and sigh. In the kitchen, I find another lantern on the counter, light it, turn up the wick. I want it light in here. Crossing to the sink, I open the curtains. Lightning flickers above the trees to the north. A cool breeze wafts in, and I smell rain. The storm would be perfect cover for a home invasion. I go to the living room and pull open the curtains. I want him to see me. An Amish woman staying up late to mend trousers and socks or maybe work on a quilt. Her family is already in bed for the night. The doors are unlocked. They are the perfect victims.

"Come on, you son of a bitch," I whisper. "I'm waiting. Come on in and get me."

* * *

It had been about forty years since Tomasetti had a temper tantrum, but he felt one coming on now. He wanted to break something. Preferably, Kate Burkholder's pretty neck. Goddamn woman cop. What the hell was she thinking trying to pull off a dangerous sting with nothing more than a couple of cops to back her up?

But Tomasetti already knew the answer. He'd spelled it out for her over the phone. This wasn't about justice. It was about retribution. He ought to know. Two and a half years ago he'd killed a man in the name of revenge. Then he'd taken it a step further and framed a career criminal—a second man who'd been involved with the murders of John's family—for the crime. Tomasetti hadn't felt a goddamn thing but satisfaction.

Yes, John Tomasetti was a master on the subject of payback. He'd destroyed his career. Nearly finished off what was left of his life. All in the name of retribution under the guise of justice. What a goddamn joke.

He'd been pacing the house for an hour now, but it wasn't helping. The place was a dump. Empty. Like nobody lived there. That's how he felt inside. No one's home. No one who cared, anyway. The problem was, Tomasetti was beginning to care, and that was one place he didn't want to be.

He looked down at the tumbler in front of him and a wave of self-loathing swept through him. Picking up the glass, he hurled it into the sink as hard as he could. Glass shattered. Shards scattered like pieces of ice. He could smell the whiskey from where he stood. He could still taste the sour tang of it in his mouth. Feel the warm buzz of it running through his brain.

He shouldn't even consider driving down to Painters Mill in his current state. He'd been drinking, enough so that he shouldn't be driving. He shouldn't get anywhere near Kate. But it wasn't the fear of doing physical violence to her that gave him pause. Tomasetti didn't like where his head was when it came to her. He didn't want to care for her. He didn't want to care about anyone. He was just getting to the point where he could get through the day without thinking about Nancy and the girls. He could go the entire night without thinking about putting a bullet in his head. And now his feelings for Kate were jeopardizing all of it.

For the first time in a long time, Tomasetti's feelings for someone else were overriding his hatred for himself. But he knew the kinds of terrible things that could happen to the people he cared about. There was no way in hell he ever wanted to go through the horror of losing someone he cared for ever again. It was easier not to give a damn.

Kate hadn't left him a choice.

"Goddamn you, Kate."

Yanking open the refrigerator, he pulled out a bottle of water, uncapped it and drank it down without stopping. He wasn't drunk, but he wasn't exactly sober. He wasn't impaired, but that wouldn't keep him from getting a DUI if some trooper pulled him over, decided to give him a breath test. Tomasetti was over the limit in more ways than one.

Cursing, he snagged another bottle of water from the fridge, grabbed his keys off the counter and headed for the door.

It's three A.M., and the house is so quiet I can hear the oil sizzling on the lantern wicks. The wind hisses and sighs through the window above the sink. I sit at the kitchen table with two pair of trousers and an open sewing basket in front of me. I've made several passes in front of the windows, making myself visible. From all appearances I'm the only family member awake. I'm ready. I've been ready for half my life. Or so says Tomasetti.

I've tried hard to maintain my edge. But my focus has shifted to him a dozen times in the last few hours. I don't like the way we left things. I don't like the things we said to each other. There was too much emotion. Maybe even a little bit of truth. I'm not sure which is worse.

Rising, I carry a pair of trousers through the living room, passing close to the window, and walk into the bathroom. There, I sit on the side of the tub and hit my radio.

"You guys there?"

"If these sons of bitches don't show tonight, I swear to Christ I'm wearing a gas mask tomorrow," Skid says.

With the loneliness of the house pressing down on me, I'm unduly glad for his particular brand of humor. "T.J.?"

"Gonna storm, Chief. I've got the radio on and they've got warnings out."

"Keep your eyes open. They might try to use the rain as cover."

"Bring it on," Skid says.

"I'm going to douse the lights. But I'll be in the kitchen. Just so you know."

"Roger that, Chief."

Picking up the trousers, I leave the bathroom. The thunder is closer now, a low rumble that rattles the glass in the windows. The air is thick with humidity and the wet-earth smell of rain. I walk the house, turning down the wicks in each lantern as I pass. In the upstairs bedroom, I extinguish the last lantern when the first fat drops of rain hit the windows on the west side of the house.

I can feel the energy of the storm now. That sharp zing in the air, the anticipation of violence. I feel a similar anticipation running through my veins. Predator hunting predator. I'm ready for him.

The cloud cover obliterates any moonlight and the house is incredibly dark. I wish for a flashlight as I descend the stairs. But even blind and deaf, I feel as if my other senses are heightened. Even with the thunder and the drone of the rain, I would know if someone were in the house.

I'm reassured by the .38 in my pocket, the backup .22 sheathed at my thigh, the knife in my boot. I've branded the location of each weapon into my brain. When the time comes, reaching for the right one will be second nature, pure instinct, no hesitation. Pausing at the front door, I check the knob. Unlocked, the way I want it. I peek out the window. Lightning flickers, illuminating the white rail fence and the cherry tree beyond the porch. The rain is coming down in torrents. The branches of the trees sway in the wind, spindly fingers clawing at the night sky.

The rain will affect visibility. If someone were to approach the house on foot, Skid and T.J. may not see them. They wouldn't be able to alert me. But I'm not unduly alarmed. The killer is expecting an Amish family, not an armed cop.

Leaving the living room, I head toward the kitchen, keeping an eye on the windows. I've already decided that if someone were to enter the house, they'll probably do it via the kitchen door. It's the point of entry farthest from the bedrooms. Not visible from the road. And there's plenty of glass to break if needed. Tonight, that won't be necessary because I've left the door unlocked. . . .

I decide to spend the night there, at the table, where I have a decent view of both the rear and front doors. If I'm going to get ambushed, I want to see him coming.

I enter the kitchen. Cool, wet air brushes against my legs. The hairs at my nape prickle. Lightning flashes, illuminating the silhouette of a man, standing just inside the door. Adrenaline blasts through me. I reach for the .38. Hand in my pocket, fingers closing around the wood stock. Gun coming up. Finger on the trigger.

I've got you, fucker.

"Police!" My voice comes out as a scream. "Put your hands up now!"

Lightning flickers like a strobe. I catch a split-second glimpse of wet hair plastered to a pale face. Water dripping onto the floor. Recognition kicks my brain. Jack Warner, I realize and shock reverberates in my head.

He doesn't obey my command.

"Get them up!" I scream. "Now!"

I see something in his hand. Too dark to discern what it is. His hand rises. I fire twice in quick succession, center of mass. Thunder drowns out the sound of my gunfire. He stiffens, then drops to his knees.

Something clatters to the floor. Gun, I think. Keeping my weapon poised on the intruder, I kick it away. "Get facedown on the floor! Do it right fucking now!"

"You shot me."

His voice is startlingly boyish. I'm shaking violently, but my gun hand is steady. If he moves I have no compunction about finishing the job. "Don't move," I say as I reach for my radio.

"Drop the gun, bitch. Or I'll shoot you where you stand."

The voice comes from behind me. Shock is a knife slash across my back. *Two of them,* I think. For an instant, I consider spinning, taking a wild shot. But he's got me dead to rights. Lowering my weapon, I slowly turn. I see the silhouette of a man. The black outline of a sawed-off shotgun.

Lightning flashes.

Recognition staggers me. Scott Barbereaux levels the shotgun at my chest. I see deadly intent in his eyes, and I know as surely as the rain pounds down outside that he's going to kill me.

"Drop the gun, bitch."

Knowing I have a backup weapon, I offer the .38. butt first.

Barbereaux makes no move to take it. "Drop it and kick it to me."

Moving slowly, I do as he says, kicking it so that he has to come closer to retrieve it.

He directs his attention to his fallen comrade. "How bad are you hurt?"

"She got me twice," Warner chokes out. "I'm bleeding. I think it's bad."

"You're going to be okay. Hold tight."

In that moment, I realize I probably only have seconds to live. Terror sweeps through me. Vaguely, I wonder if I can hit my lapel mike without being noticed. Even if I can do that, I know that unless I can somehow keep Barbereaux and Warner talking, T.J. and Skid won't be able to get here in time to save me.

I look down at Warner. He's lying on the floor to my left, bent slightly, holding his abdomen with both hands. A slowly growing puddle of blood encircles his body like a black halo.

I turn my attention to Barbereaux. "I've got EMT training. Let me stop the bleeding."

Barbereaux hikes the shotgun. "Where's that fucking Amish kid?"

Only then do I realize he still believes Billy Zook can identify him. I try to think of a way I can use that to my advantage. A dozen lies fly at my brain. "I'll take you to him," I blurt out.

"You'll tell me where he is or I'll cut you down where you stand," he says between gritted teeth.

No matter what happens, the one thing I will not do is reveal the boy's whereabouts. "I'm a cop, Scott. If you kill me, they'll put a needle in your arm."

Behind me, I hear Warner whimper. "I need to get to the hospital."

I glance over at him. The puddle of blood has doubled in size. I can smell it now. That awful, metal-and-methane stench. "He's bleeding out. Let me help him."

His expression doesn't change. There's no sympathy for the dying man, no fear of discovery, just a deadly determination and all of it is focused on me. "You've got one more chance. Where's that fuckin' kid?"

"He's at a safe house, surrounded by a dozen cops—"

He moves so quickly, I don't see the blow coming. One moment I'm scrambling for a lie, trying to think my way out of this. The next I'm reeling sideways. For a crazy instant, I think he's shot me, then I realize he swung the shotgun, striking my left temple. I stumble, make a wild grab for the counter, careen into it hard enough to cave in the wood front, and go down hard.

The next thing I know, I'm on my back. Barbereaux straddles my chest, shoving the shotgun crossways against my throat. "Where's the kid!" he screams.

Around me the room spins crazily. Lightning is like a strobe on his face. The shotgun grinds hard against my windpipe and Adam's apple. I turn my head, try to raise my hands to push it away, but he's got them trapped with his knees.

"You better start talking!" he shouts.

I open my mouth, but the steel barrel is crushing my voice box. Cursing, he removes the shotgun.

I gulp air. "We set you up," I croak. "That kid didn't see anything. We knew you'd show." I cough. "Cops are outside."

"Well, aren't you a smart little bitch?" Cruelty and a barely controlled rage glints in his eyes. We stare at each other while the storm rages on. A few feet away, Jack Warner groans in agony. Then Barbereaux smiles. "If you're talking about that hayseed fuck in the barn, he's dead."

Skid. I stare at him, outrage billowing through me with such force my entire body trembles with it. *Not Skid. Not one of my own.* My brain chants the words like a mantra. And in that moment, I know I could kill this man with my bare hands if given the chance.

Somehow I muster the presence of mind to keep him talking. "It's over," I tell him. "We know about you and Mary Plank. She kept a diary." I barely hear my own voice above the roar of blood through my veins. "She wrote about you."

His eyes sharpen and for the first time I see uncertainty. He didn't know about the journal. I've got his full attention now, so I keep going. "We know what you did to her. We know everything."

"She was dumber than a box of rocks," he says. "Had the mentality of a ten-year-old."

"She was just a kid."

"She liked to fuck."

"She loved you."

His smile chills me. "If she'd named me in some book, we wouldn't be here, you lying bitch."

He slaps me open-handed in the face, then rises and walks over to Warner, taking the shotgun with him. I use that moment to take a quick physical inventory. My head throbs where he hit me with the stock. I think of the .22 mini-magnum strapped to my thigh, the knife in my boot, and I realize I still have a chance to get out of this alive. I push myself to a sitting position, then get to my feet. The room dips and spins, so I hold on to the counter for support.

A few feet away, Barbereaux bends and pulls Warner to his feet. Warner groans. "I need to go to the hospital."

"I'll get you there, buddy. Just hang tight. Let me figure out what to do with the bitch, and then we'll go."

The other man is too weak to stand, so Barbereaux yanks out a chair, muscles him into it, then turns to me, thrusts the shotgun at me. "What the hell am I going to do with you?"

He's going to kill me; I see intent in his eyes. It's just a matter of time.

The realization sends a shudder of terror through me. Holding his gaze, I ease my right hand down, feel the mini-magnum through the fabric of my skirt. I wonder if I can take aim and pull the trigger without having to draw the weapon out from under my skirt.

"You still have a chance to get away if you run now," I tell him.

"You know this isn't going to end nicely for you, don't you?"

"If you kill a cop, they won't ever stop looking for you. Ever."

"You're forgetting one thing." One side of his mouth curves. "They don't have my name."

"We have you on disk. It's only a matter of time before they tie you to it."

He smirks nastily. "I guess that's why you're here, dressed like that. Because of all that fuckin' evidence you've got."

"We've got the other disks, too. The ones we found at Long's place."

"Just when I was starting to think you're smart, you blow it by saying something stupid." He shakes his head, feigning pity. "There's nothing incriminating on any of those disks. Just that little bitch getting what she wanted. Who do you think planted them, for fuck sake?"

Now it's my turn to smile. "You screwed up. We've got you dead to rights on one of the disks." I need to buy some time, keep him talking, thinking.

Next to Barbereaux, Warner coughs up a spray of blood. "For God's sake . . . get me to the hospital. Fuckin' dying . . ."

Barbereaux steps quickly away from the other man, casts me an irritated look. "Bullshit, I went through every disk."

"You willing to stake your life on that?" I shrug, let the statement hang. When he says nothing, I add, "Technology is an amazing thing. You'd be surprised by the information those techies can pull off a disk these days. That scar on your hand?"

He glances quickly down, then back at me. The look he gives me is so utterly devoid of emotion that it's like looking into the eyes of a corpse. I sense he's going to raise the shotgun and kill me. The urge to appeal to his compassion is overwhelming, but I know it would be futile. He's a sociopath, incapable of feeling remorse. My heart pounds so loudly, I can no longer hear the storm. Keep him talking . . .

"How could you do that to those two girls?" I ask.

"It's a sick world out there. It was all about the money. The snuff flick went to the highest bidder." He says the words as if he's talking about negotiating the sale of a used car instead of the final minutes of life for two innocent girls. "Some people get off on the whole death thing."

His mouth twists into a terrible grin. "If we had more time, I'd like to get some vid of you in those clothes. A lot of men out there dig the Amish shit. I bet you've got a tight little snatch."

He's looking at me the way a wolf looks at a rabbit it's about to devour. In the back of my mind I wonder if T.J. saw them approach the house or if the rain obscured them. Staring at Barbereaux, I'm keenly aware of the .22 pressing against my thigh. The lapel mike of my radio just a second away. I know he'll gun me down before I can reach either.

I scramble for a way to keep him talking. "We know you killed Long, too."

"That motherfucker died of stupidity." Mild amusement drifts across his expression. "Lethal dose."

"There's still time for you to run."

"I don't think so." He raises the shotgun.

Terror paralyzes me. I can't breathe, can barely think. "If you kill me, they'll hunt you down. They won't stop until they find you."

"I'm not going to kill you." He glances at Warner and whispers, "He is."

I look at Warner. His face is the color of paste and slick with sweat. His glazed eyes find mine. "You're about to become another Todd Long," I tell him.

Warner opens his mouth to speak, but no words come.

Barbereaux's finger tightens on the trigger. *Out of time,* I think. Panic spreads through me like a wildfire burning hot and out of control. I launch myself at him. My palms hit the barrel hard, shove it up. The muzzle explodes. The concussion hits me in the face like a punch. Plaster rains down. Barbereaux steps back, brings down the muzzle, takes aim. All I can think is that I'm too far away to stop him.

As if in slow motion, I see the muzzle flash. Thunder explodes. The next thing I know I'm flying backward into space. My chest feels as if it's been caved in by an axe. I can't breathe. I can't see. A scream sounds in my head, and then the night rushes in and yanks me down into the abyss.

CHAPTER 28

Tomasetti hit one hundred miles per hour on Highway 62 just out of Brinkhaven. He knew it wouldn't look good if some local yokel stopped him. He wasn't in the best mental state, thanks to Kate. That wasn't to mention the booze he'd sucked down earlier. He wasn't sure what his blood alcohol level might be, but it was probably over the limit. He had his badge to back him up, but with some cops that only went so far.

The panic attack came out of nowhere. One moment he was putting the pedal to the metal, concentrating on his driving, on making time, on reaching Kate. The next moment, it was as if a giant hand reached into his chest and squeezed all the oxygen from his lungs. He couldn't breathe. His brain couldn't form a single coherent thought. The only thing he could discern was the grip of a fear so primal he honestly believed it might kill him.

Gasping for breath, Tomasetti backed off the accelerator. He gripped the steering wheel hard enough to make his knuckles ache. The Tahoe slowed. He tried to look for a rest area or exit, but there was nothing on this particular stretch of road, so he pulled into the bar ditch. The truck bumped over something, but Tomasetti was too far gone to discern what it was. He could hear himself gasping now. The sounds tearing from his throat reminded him of a wild animal in the throes of death. The hand squeezed his chest, twisted his lungs into knots. He couldn't draw a breath. His face went numb. Darkness encroached on his peripheral vision. He was going to pass out. Pain streaked up the center of his chest.

"Fuck," he choked out. "Fuck!"

Shoving open the door, Tomasetti stumbled from the truck. Vaguely, he was aware of insects flying in the headlights. The flicker of lightning on the horizon. Terror like he'd never felt before turning him inside out.

A few feet from the truck, he went to his knees. He couldn't believe the sounds coming from his mouth. Whimpers. Choking gasps. He fell forward, his hands plunging into wet grass. Mud squeezed between his fingers. Soaked into his slacks at his knees. Panic was like some small, clawed animal trapped inside him, tearing at his guts, trying to claw its way out for air.

Tomasetti didn't try to get up. It took every bit of effort he possessed to draw a breath. But his chest was too tight. Someone drawing a rope ever tighter, cutting off his oxygen.

His nose, lips and fingers tingled. He could hear his breaths rushing in and out, like a hacksaw cutting through wood. A hard knot of nausea rose in his gut. He opened his mouth, tried to suck in air. A string of drool hung from his lips. His stomach clenched. He tasted bile at the back of his throat. Gagging, he spit, threw up on the grass. Inhaled puke and gagged again. He didn't care.

Intellectually, Tomasetti knew what was happening. He knew this was a panic attack. He knew he wasn't going to die. That he should breathe deeply, count backward from one hundred, and tell himself it would only last for three minutes if he calmed himself down. None of that knowledge helped.

The next thing he knew his cheek was pressed against the cold, wet ground. He had mud in his hair. Dirt in his mouth. The rank aftertaste of vomit. He was lying on his stomach in the bar ditch in the middle of nowhere, in the middle of the fucking night. He'd blacked out. . . .

Cursing, Tomasetti slowly got to his feet. His nerves jittered beneath his skin. The muscles in his legs twitched. Fatigue was a black hole he was about to fall into. The fact that he'd survived gave him the strength to bend and pick up his keys.

He'd pulled over in a forested area south of Killbuck. The chorus of frogs and crickets was inordinately loud on the deserted stretch of road. At some point, it had begun to rain. Not a storm, but he could smell it coming. He could hear thunder, see the lightning above the treetops ahead.

Ten feet away, the Tahoe sat at a cockeyed angle in the bar ditch. It looked wrecked out, but it wasn't. Tomasetti hoped the damn thing wasn't stuck. He looked down at his clothes, wondering how he was going to explain the mud. He'd helped a motorist who had been stuck. He'd hit a deer and fallen when he'd gotten out to check the vehicle. On second thought, fuck it. He didn't have to explain. All he wanted was to get to Painters Mill. To Kate.

Opening the door, he slid behind the wheel and backed onto the pavement. The township road would take him to Clark, which was about twelve miles away. Painters Mill was another five. With a little luck, he'd be at the Zook farm in fifteen minutes.

I dream of death. Blackness is all around me. Inside me. Like hot tar that covers and burns and smothers. I fight for air, but I can't breathe.

Pain rattles me awake. My chest heaves, some primal instinct telling my body to get air into my oxygen-starved lungs. Every breath is an agony, and I choke out animal sounds. Confusion is a cotton ball inside my head, but I'm aware enough to know that my ribs are broken. Maybe my spine. Shit.

I open my eyes to darkness, but I can see the kitchen window. The occasional flash of lightning. I'm lying on the floor on my back with my arms above my head. I glance down at my chest. The sight of blood shocks me because I know it's mine. Black, wet stains on my dress, on my arms and legs. Drops and smears on the floor around me. I'm bleeding, but I don't know where it's coming from.

For several seconds I concentrate on breathing. My mind begins to clear. The memory of the shooting replays in my head like some bad movie. The kind where the idiot cop screws up and gets what he's got coming. Only this time that idiot cop is me. I'd expected one accomplice tonight, not two. A stupid mistake that would have killed me if I hadn't been wearing the vest. Of course the night isn't over.

I'm wheezing like an asthmatic. An involuntary groan grinds from my throat when I roll over and take a quick physical inventory of my injuries. Broken ribs. Maybe a collapsed lung. My shoulders and arms are bleeding. My face and neck sting, and I realize belatedly the wounds on my arms are from shotgun pellets. Not life-threatening, but I'm in a world of hurt. Worse, I'm in danger of Barbereaux returning to finish the job.

Where the hell is he?

Pain surges when I move my arms down to my sides. For several seconds, I can't draw a breath. A cry escapes me when I push myself to a sitting position. I grapple in my pocket for my lapel mike, but it's gone. My cell phone is gone. So is the .38. Lifting my dress, I glance at the leather holster at my thigh. Relief snaps through me when I see the .22. Whimpering with pain, I slide the weapon from its nest, pull back the hammer.

That's when it strikes me that Warner is gone. I glance over where I last saw him. A flicker of lightning reveals a puddle of blood and a single long smear, as if someone stepped in it and slid. That's when I hear voices coming from the living room twenty feet away.

"I need to get to the hospital. I'm in a bad way."

"Hang tight, partner. I know a doctor in Wooster. He owes me. He'll fix you up."

The shuffle of shoes tells me someone's coming my way. Grinding my teeth in pain, I quickly lay back down in the same position. But I keep my hand on the .22. It's a small revolver, but it's not so small that if they looked closely they wouldn't see it.

"Fuckin' bitch cop."

"She's dead," Warner croaks. "Let's go."

Something hard rams my shoulder, jarring my chest. An involuntary groan squeezes from my throat. I don't dare open my eyes. But he kicks me again, and I look up at him.

Barbereaux smiles down at me. "I bet you think you're real fuckin' smart, don't you?" He points my .38 at my face.

I've never felt so utterly helpless in my life. "Don't do this." I look at Warner. His face is ghastly white. Sweat coats his forehead. Blood covers the front of his shirt. He's holding his abdomen, listing, clutching the counter to remain standing. "He's going to kill you," I tell him.

"Shut up!" Barbereaux looks at Warner. "Don't listen to her." His eyes skate back to mine, his lips curling into a snarl. "I don't believe you about the trap. I'm only going to ask you this one time before I start putting holes in you, so listen good. You got that?"

I nod.

"Where's that fuckin' Amish kid?"

For a crazy instant I consider trying to get both of them with the .22. Empty the cylinder. Five shots. Hope for the best. My marksmanship skills are good, but I know my broken ribs will affect my speed. Wait for a better opportunity. Keep him talking.

"I wasn't lying." My voice comes out like a croak.

His mouth tightens into an ugly line. "Wrong answer." With the speed of a striking snake, he shifts the gun left. The explosion rocks my brain. The pain is like a wood chipper chewing up my left arm. I hear a scream that goes on and on, realize belatedly it's mine.

Whimpering, I look down. Blood gushes from my left forearm, a few inches below my elbow. The fabric of my dress is soaked. Pain and shock punch my brain, Mike Tyson in a murderous rage and taking care of business.

"Where's the fucking kid?" he screams.

"Safe house!" I choke out the lie with the vehemence of truth. It's all I can manage. The pain is overwhelming. Unbearable heat envelops my face. Dizziness crashes down on me. Nausea seesaws in my gut. *Don't pass out . . .*

"Where?" he says, calmer now.

Air rushes between my clenched teeth. Every breath rips me in two. I'm pretty sure the bullet broke my arm. I feel shock descending. But in that moment all I can think is that I still have the .22.

"You think I'm not serious about filling you full of holes, you bitch cop?" he says.

"Don't do it," I choke.

"How about if I show you just how fuckin' serious I am?"

Before I can respond, he shifts the gun. I brace. Reflex nearly causes me to bring up the .22, but I hold it steady in my right hand. If he breaks my right arm, I'm as good as dead.

Instead, he levels the weapon at Warner and fires. The bullet blows a hole the size of a dime in the other man's forehead. Warner's head snaps back. A surprised expression crosses his face. And then he drops like a rock.

Another layer of shock whips through me. I stare at the dead man, watch the blood spread into a pool on the floor.

Barbereaux turns to me, his eyes as dead as the man on the floor. "Looks like it's just me and you now." He levels the gun at my left thigh. "Broken femur's going to hurt. I suggest you start talking. Where's the kid?"

Adrenaline crashes through me. My arms and legs shake uncontrollably. I'm dizzy with pain and shock. But I know it's now or never. He's going to kill me and stage the scene so it looks like Warner and I exchanged gunfire, killing each other. Barbereaux's going to get away scot-free.

"At a farmhouse nearby," I say.

"Where?"

"Down the road. Five minutes. Left on Dog Leg Road." I give him a bogus address and then shift my gaze to the dead man. "He's still alive."

Barbereaux jerks his head left to look, and I make my move. Pain explodes in my chest as I level the .22 on him. He makes eye contact with me an instant before I fire.

Two shots. His body jolts. I see disbelief on his face. He brings up the gun. I fire the final three bullets. Two in the chest. One in the shoulder. No more ammo. My finger keeps jerking. The empty chamber clicks.

Click. Click. Click.

Barbereaux steps back. For an instant, time stands still. He stares at me. His mouth opens. I see blood on his teeth. More blood blooming on his shirt. He glances down at it. His knees buckle and hit the floor hard. Then he falls face down and doesn't move.

I struggle to my knees. The room tilts beneath me. Cradling my left arm, I crawl on my knees to Barbereaux. He lies perfectly still with his head to one side. He's alive; his eyes are on me. My .38 lies a few inches from his right hand. I know I'm screwing up the crime scene, but I don't care.

Picking up the .38, I level it at his forehead. "This is for what you did to Mary Plank, you son of a bitch." I feel nothing when I pull the trigger.

Only then do I realize I'm sobbing. Loud, wrenching cries that fill the house with the sound of pain. I need my radio to call for help. But I want my cell phone. I need Tomasetti.

Somehow I make it to my feet. I stumble around in the dark. In the light from the window, I glance down to see my left arm hanging uselessly at my side. Blood dripping off my fingertips. A steady roar of pain climbs all the way up to my shoulder. My hand is numb.

I find my cell phone and radio in the living room where Barbereaux must have set them. I hit the radio first. "Ten-thirty-three." My voice is little more than a whisper.

T.J.'s voice crackles, but I don't reply. Unconsciousness beckons, a big dark hole tugging me down. *Don't pass out,* a little voice inside my head warns. One more thing to do . . .

I hit the speed dial for Tomasetti. I hear his voice, but I'm not sure if it's in my head or if he's really there. "I got him." The weakness of my own voice surprises me. "I got the motherfucker."

"Kate, where are you?"

"Zook . . . farm."

"How bad are you hurt?"

"I'm not sure." My voice cracks. "Hurry. I need you . . ."

I need you . . .

Her words rang inside his head like the echo of a lover's scream. Tomasetti could tell by the sound of her voice she was injured. That she didn't know the extent of her injuries told him it was bad. The thought sent a bare-fisted punch of terror right through the center of him.

His hands shook so violently, he nearly dropped his cell as he dialed the Painters Mill PD. The night-shift operator picked up on the first ring. He quickly identified himself. "I need an ambulance out at the Zook farm. We've got an officer down out there."

Keys clicked. "En route." The line hissed for a second. "T.J. called a moment ago. He can't get Skid or Kate on their radios."

"Goddamnit." Tomasetti cranked the speedometer up to sixty as he sped through town. He blew the stoplight at Main and headed toward the Zook farm. "Get the sheriff's office out there, too."

"Roger that."

Snapping his phone closed, Tomasetti floored the accelerator, burying the speedometer along a straight stretch of highway, then dropped it down at the turn that would take him to Hogpath Road. The Tahoe skidded on the wet pavement as he hauled the wheel right. His headlights flashed over yellow corn to the left and the tall trees of a greenbelt beyond. Somehow he maintained control, pointed the Tahoe north, pushed the accelerator to the floor.

You're too late.

He tried to quiet the little voice inside his head. He remembered all too well that awful night in Cleveland. He'd arrived to find his house engulfed in flames, found his wife and little girls dead inside. It wasn't until after the autopsy days later that he'd learned they'd been tortured and burned alive.

You're too late.

"Shut up," he muttered. "Shut the fuck up!"

A person could bleed to death in a matter of minutes. The thought shook him so completely, he nearly ran off the road. He could feel the fear climbing over him, an ugly lumbering beast that tore him up from the inside out.

Too late. Too late . . .

The Tahoe fishtailed on the wet asphalt as he turned into the gravel lane of the Zook farm. The SUV kicked up stones and bounced over ruts. The farmhouse loomed into view. The place was pitch black. No vehicles. No lights on inside.

Where the hell was her backup?

Tomasetti drove over a sapling tree and through the grass, over the sidewalk. Ten feet from the back door, he hit the brakes hard, and the Tahoe's tires dug ruts into the soft ground, skidded to a halt.

Throwing open the door, he pulled his weapon and hit the ground running. He knew better than to enter the place alone. He knew he could be walking into a trap. He kicked in the door without knocking. "Police!" he shouted. "Police! Put your fucking hands up now!"

In the dim light slanting through the window, he saw three bodies. A lake-size puddle of blood. The black silhouette of a gun. His heart slammed hard against his ribs when a flicker of lightning revealed Kate. She was lying on her back, stone still. Her eyes were open and for a horrifying moment, he thought she was dead.

Too late. Too late.

The little voice taunted him. He stumbled toward her. Choking sobs squeezed from his throat. A scream of denial rang in his head.

She's not fucking dead! God wouldn't do that to me twice in one lifetime.

"Kate!" He dropped to his knees beside her. *"Kate!"*

Her eyes shifted to his. "Jesus Christ, Tomasetti, it took you long enough. A girl could bleed to death."

The relief came with such force that for a moment, he couldn't speak. He couldn't stop looking at her. Couldn't stop touching her. He could hear his breaths rushing in and out. His heart hammering in his ears.

Too many emotions knocking at his door. All he could think was that she was alive. He hadn't been too late.

"I ought to wring your neck," he growled after a moment.

"Now would be a prime opportunity," she whispered. "I'm in no condition to stop you."

"Ambulance is on the way." There was too much blood. Too much pain in her face. It worried him that she wasn't moving. "You shot?"

"Twice. Vest protected me, but he got me in the arm." Wincing, she tried to sit up. "I think they shot Skid. He was in the barn."

Tomasetti eased her back down. She felt weak. Cool to the touch. Where the hell was the ambulance? "We'll take care of him. Just be still for now, will you?"

She closed her eyes, and he felt her body relax. "Are they dead?"

He glanced at the other two bodies. The staring eyes and lack of color told him they were DOA. "Nice job, Chief."

"I'm going to ask for a raise," she whispered. "Hazard pay."

"Kate, you're bleeding. You need to stop talking. Okay?"

"You're a moody bastard, you know that?"

"That's what everyone says." But he smiled.

She smiled back. "Thanks for coming."

Fighting emotions he didn't want to feel, John Tomasetti bowed his head and thanked the God he had forsaken for the last two and a half years.

CHAPTER 29

The more things change, the more they stay the same. Or so I tell myself, anyway. I'm in the Explorer, idling down Main Street the way I have a thousand times before. Light rain patters the windshield, keeping time with a moody Everlast song about saving grace on the radio. To my right, two women in suits and heels stand outside the City Building, huddled against the rain, smoking cigarettes and making small talk. The aromas of warm yeast and cinnamon from the Butterhorn Bakery waft through my open window. I slow down as I pass the Carriage Stop Country Store on the traffic circle. In the display window, a dozen or more colorful Amish quilts hang, and for the hundredth time I find myself thinking of the Plank family.

Four days have passed since the night I shot Scott Barbereaux and Jack Warner at the Zook farmhouse. I want to think a sort of final justice was served that night. I want to believe I gave the sons of bitches what they had coming. But as is usually the case, things aren't always that cut and dried.

Because both perpetrators were killed at the scene, questions about what happened to the Planks will never be fully answered. What linked Scott Barbereaux, Jack Warner and Todd Long? The only connection I could find was that they went to high school together. I can tie Barbereaux and Warner to the Carriage Stop Country Store. But I'm left wondering: Is that where they met Mary? Did her natural beauty and innocence bring out some dark and primal hunger in them? Did they think her naïveté would make her an easy target? Did her being Amish make her easy to exploit? I'll probably never have definitive answers, but we did uncover evidence that helped fill in some of the blanks.

Several law enforcement agencies, including the Painters Mill PD, the sheriff's office, and BCI, conducted a search that produced dozens of disks, drives, computers, a laptop and hundreds of photographs. I've seen a lot in the nine years I've been a cop, but the outrages inflicted upon Mary Plank top all of it.

Because Glenda Patterson alibied Barbereaux, Glock and Pickles brought her to the station for questioning. Handcuffed and surrounded by cops, she spilled her guts. She claimed no knowledge of Barbereaux's involvement in the murders, going so far as to suggest he drugged her, left the house, and then sneaked back before she regained consciousness the next morning. We're still trying to decide whether to put her before a grand jury. She wouldn't be the first woman to lie to protect her lover.

Mary Plank's journal continues to haunt me. Throughout all of this, I worried I would never be able to prove beyond a shadow of doubt that Barbereaux was the man she wrote about. The man she loved. Just this morning, I learned that the DNA from the sperm found inside Mary's body was matched to DNA taken from Barbereaux. Evidently, he didn't know human sperm could live for up to three days.

Since the fetus and placenta were never found, there was no way to extract paternal DNA from the child Mary Plank was carrying, making it impossible to ascertain the identity of the father. But I know in my heart it was Barbereaux's.

T.J., Pickles and Mona spent two days in the woods surrounding Miller's Pond before finding the tree where Mary Plank carved her and her lover's initials. *M.P. loves S.B. forever.* Next to it, she'd carved a heart pierced with an arrow. While it didn't mean much in terms of evidence, it meant the world to me on a personal level. I had my proof.

I've spent the last couple of days piecing together a theory. I believe Scott Barbereaux delivered gourmet coffees to the shop where Mary worked. He also fancied himself an amateur photographer and did a few wedding and family reunion–type shoots at the store. I believe he met her there, charmed her, pursued her and seduced her. Unaccustomed to that kind of attention from an attractive male, Mary was swept off her feet. In the following weeks, he bought her gifts that seemed lavish to a naïve Amish girl. English clothes. Lingerie. Jewelry. He introduced her to music, sex and drugs. Once her judgment was skewed—either by her feelings for Barbereaux or the drugs—he began drugging her with dangerous barbiturates and sedatives, such as Rohypnol. At that point, he began photographing and videotaping her in pornographic situations, using his friends Todd Long and Jack Warner as actors.

There's no doubt in my mind that in some way, Mary loved Barbereaux. She wanted to marry him, have his child and lead a normal life. She was malleable; she wanted to please him. Her naïveté brought out something vicious in Barbereaux. He was a classic sociopath. He knew he could push her and he just kept on pushing. The power of that must have been heady. Toward the end—after he'd raped her body, mind and soul—it wasn't even a problem for him.

But what was the impetus for murdering the entire Plank family? I have a theory on that, too. After Mary confessed her sins to her parents—telling them about her relationship with Barbereaux, the drugs, the porn and the child she was carrying—her parents broke Amish protocol and decided to take the information to the English police. But they never got the chance to follow through. Somehow Barbereaux found out what they were going to do and decided to eliminate the entire family. But he didn't stop with just murder. They filmed the killings and sold the video on the black market as a sort of snuff film.

Mary Plank was not the first young woman the three men had exploited. Evidence discovered at Barbereaux's home proved there were others, ranging from fifteen to twenty-two years of age. We also discovered a bank account in the Cayman Islands. Records indicated Barbereaux was raking in a lot of foreign cash. In the last six years, he'd earned over five hundred thousand dollars from the sale of pornographic videos. Mixed in with the sex, were several snuff-like productions. The bulk of the money came from the Philippines, China, Nigeria and Ukraine. Since international borders were crossed, the feds stepped in. For the first time in the course of my career, I was glad to relinquish control of a case.

It wasn't until I'd arrived at the hospital that I learned Skid was still alive. During the storm, Barbereaux and Warner ambushed him in the barn. Skid's no rookie, but he didn't even have a chance to draw his revolver. They shot him in the back first. As in my case, the Kevlar vest protected him. But when the two men realized he wasn't dead, they shot him in the head.

Headshots are almost always fatal. In Skid's case, however, the bullet struck his forehead at an angle that caused the .25 caliber bullet to ricochet off his skull without penetrating the cranium. The impact knocked him unconscious. He sustained a concussion. The wound required seven stitches to repair. He's not complaining. Adhering to their usual bad cop humor, the guys are already giving him a hard time about the thickness of his skull. I've laughed about that a few times myself.

After three days in the hospital, I checked out against the advice of my doctor. Tomasetti was there to drive me home. On the way, I asked him to swing by Barbereaux's house. He balked, of course, but I guilted him into letting me have my way. By that time, Barbereaux's home had already been thoroughly searched by my team as well as BCI and the feds. I didn't care. It took me two hours, a double dose of Vicodin, and a physical confrontation with Tomasetti, but I tore the place apart. If it hadn't been for Tomasetti, I would have continued my mindless tirade until I collapsed. Despite my name-calling and cursing, he took me home.

Our relationship is complicated, but I'm thankful to have Tomasetti in my life. I'm thankful for this town. For the people I've surrounded myself with. I'm thankful for my job. It gives me purpose. It reminds me why God put me on this earth.

I'm not supposed to report back to work for a few more days. I'm not even supposed to be driving. I have four broken ribs and a broken ulna that required surgery and the insertion of a titanium pin to repair. But I've never been very good at following orders. I pull into my usual spot and kill the engine. I see Glock's cruiser parked curbside. Mona's Escort. As usual, Lois is early. Rain beads on her red Cadillac, and I know her husband spent half the weekend waxing it. Farther down, I see Pickles's old Corvette and T.J.'s brand-new Mustang. Taking a moment to gather myself, I head inside.

Lois and Mona stand at the dispatch station, bent over the switchboard, solving some new problem that's cropped up with our antiquated phone system. They look up when I walk inside. "Chief!" Mona's eyes widen as she takes in my cast and sling. My face still bears scabs from the pellets I took.

"It looks worse than it is," I begin.

Lois comes around the dispatch station. "I didn't think you were coming in for a couple more days."

"I'm not." I walk toward them. "Officially, anyway. I just wanted to check messages and make sure you guys aren't having too much fun."

Mona snorts. "Only fun thing around here is all the jokes about Skid's head."

"Emergency room doctor shaved the whole front," Lois adds. "Poor guy won't take off his cap." She looks at my cast and sobers. "How are you feeling?"

"Cast is a pain in the ass."

"Some graffiti might help that," comes a male voice from somewhere behind me.

I glance over to see Glock, T.J., Pickles and Skid emerge from their cubicles, staring at me as if I'm some mental patient that's escaped the psycho ward and wandered into the police station. Skid wears his Painters Mill PD cap. I see the edge of a bandage sticking out at his right temple. A black eye. Residual bruising on his right cheekbone. I withhold a smile . . . barely.

"You look pretty good for a guy who got shot in the noggin." My grin spreads despite my efforts. "How's the head?"

He grins back. "Pretty hard, evidently."

"All them rocks rolling around inside," Pickles growls.

"Fragmented the bullet so badly, BCI techs couldn't find all the pieces," Glock puts in. "That's a hard fuckin' head."

Everyone laughs, but I feel their collective attention on me. I wonder if I look as strung out as I feel. I wonder if they know Barbereaux was alive and defenseless when I took that last shot. I wonder if they know I flew into a rage at Barbereaux's house and that Tomasetti had to physically subdue me before he could drag me out. I wonder if it's obvious I've been hitting the painkillers just a little too hard.

"How's the arm?" Glock asks.

"Hurts like a son of a bitch."

Skid sends me a silly grin and moves his eyebrows up and down. "How 'bout those Kevlar vests, Chief?"

That makes me laugh, which is almost as bad as coughing because my ribs protest loudly. "Don't make me laugh," I say, touching my side gingerly.

Silence trickles over us, reminding me why I'm really here. "I just wanted to thank all of you for going above and beyond on the Plank case. It was a tough one." I sigh, surprised when my breath shudders. "You did a good job. We got them."

Pickles unwraps a toothpick and sticks it between his teeth. "McNarie says he's got a bottle of Absolut with your name on it when you're ready."

I smile, but for some reason his mention of McNarie's Bar only makes me think of Tomasetti. He returned to Columbus yesterday, and I haven't heard from him since. I wonder where he is this morning. I wonder what he's doing. I wonder if he's thinking about me. If he misses me as much as I miss him.

"You're looking kind of pale, Chief," T.J. says after a moment. "Do you want me to drive you home?"

"I'm heading that way now." I send him a smile, but it doesn't feel real. I'm aware of their stares, and I realize they're worried about me.

"See you guys in a couple of days." I start toward the door.

T.J. rushes forward and pushes it open for me. "Get some rest, Chief."

"I'll do that," I say and start toward the Explorer.

The *graabhof* is located on the township road west of Painters Mill. The last time I was here was for the Plank funerals. It was raining and crowded with mourners. I cited the tourist for illegal parking and met Aaron Plank for the first time. It seems like a lifetime ago.

Today, the graveyard is deserted and unbearably lonely. I park in the gravel driveway and shut down the engine. An arthritic-looking bois d'arc tree stands next to the gate like some ancient, battered sentry. Pain thuds dully in my arm as I open the door and get out. I know better than to mix Vicodin and vodka, but I lift the flask from my coat pocket anyway, and take a long pull of Absolut.

Drizzle floats down from a Teflon sky as I push open the gate and pass through. There have been several vandalism incidents here at the old cemetery, but the gate is never locked. I wonder if the Amish will ever learn.

A dozen rows of small headstones run in neat lines, parallel with the fence. The headstones are uniform in size. Some are older than others, faded by time and eroded by the elements; in an Amish cemetery, all the dead are equal. Most have a simple cross etched into their façades. Lower is the name of the deceased, their birth date and the date of their death. Some Amish bury their dead according to the order of death with little or no regard to family connections. In this cemetery, however, the dead are buried with their family members. In the case of the Planks, it wouldn't have mattered since they were all killed on the same night.

The graves are easy to find. Mounded and shiny from the rain, the freshly turned earth hasn't yet settled. The headstones are stark and white. Nothing gaudy for the Amish. They die as they have lived. Plainly.

I walk among the graves, reading each of the seven names. I never met any of the Plank family members, but I feel as if I know them. Envisioning them the way they might have been in life comes easily. Little Amos in the throes of his terrible twos, all giggles and temper tantrums. Ten-year-old David was a prankster, a sixty-two-pound package of mischief. Mark, fourteen years old and already taking on the responsibilities of a man. Annie, sixteen and full of dreams for a future with a husband and children. Lastly, I think of Mary. The lost one. The troubled one. *The one most like me.* The one I've identified with throughout this case. The one whose death touched me so deeply.

Reaching beneath my coat, I pull out the faceless doll I'd found on her bed the night I discovered her journal. I know it's going to get ruined, but it doesn't matter. I think Mary would want it here. Kneeling, I prop the doll against the gravestone. It's an incredibly sad sight. The faceless doll sitting against that smooth jut of concrete, getting wet. The doll that will never be hugged. Never be loved.

I know it's stupid, but that makes me think of the child I had once carried inside my body. I went years without thinking of what I did. I never second-guessed my decision, never regretted it. I sure as hell never let myself imagine what might have been. Today, for the first time in seventeen years, I do. It's a strange thought, but had I not opted to get an abortion after the rape, I would have a sixteen-year-old child.

Only then do I realize I'm crying. Open sobs that echo off the headstones and the bare branches of the bois d'arc tree. Rising, I pull the flask from my coat pocket and take another swig. The hiss of tires on wet pavement draws my attention. I look toward the gate to see Tomasetti's black Tahoe turn into the cemetery. I watch as he parks beside my Explorer and gets out.

All I can think is that I don't want him to see me like this. Quickly, I wipe my eyes, drop the flask into my pocket and watch him approach. He wears a charcoal-colored trench coat. London Fog. Beneath the coat, I see a crisp blue shirt and a gray paisley tie. Hermès. His strides are long and purposeful. His eyes are intent on me.

"For the chief of police, you're a damn hard woman to find." He reaches me and stops. "You didn't answer your cell."

"I'm off duty."

He nods, looks over at the graves. He grimaces upon seeing the doll, then he turns his attention back to me. "You okay?"

For a split second, I think I am. I'm going to make some snide remark about his city-slicker clothes and give him hell for disturbing me during a private moment. Or maybe I'll rub it in a little that my high-risk sting paid off. I'll make fun of Skid's partially shaved head. Brag about getting the sons of bitches responsible for the murders of this family. Instead, I put my face in my hands and burst into tears.

For a moment, the only sounds come from the patter of rain against the ground. The caw of a crow as it lifts from a twisted branch of the bois d'arc tree. And the sound of my sobs. Saying nothing, Tomasetti keeps his distance, waits me out.

"I'm sorry," I say after a moment. "I'm a mess."

"It's okay."

"No, it's not." I use my right sleeve to wipe my face. "I don't want you to see me like this."

"I've seen you naked."

Choking out a laugh, I raise my head and look at him. "Don't make me laugh."

"Sorry."

I blow out a sigh, try to settle myself. "I thought I'd feel better when this was over."

"Give yourself some time." He sighs. "You've been through a lot, Kate."

"I wanted to do more for them."

"You did your job. You gave them justice."

"I got justice for myself, too."

"You shot a murderer in the line of duty," he returns evenly.

"I shot him when he was down."

"He had a weapon. You didn't have a choice." Tomasetti's eyes sharpen on mine. "Guilt can do a number on you if you let it."

He's right, of course. The use of lethal force is a heavy burden for a cop to carry around. Even now, I feel the weight of it on my shoulders. But not in the way he thinks.

"I don't feel bad about killing Barbereaux," I say after a moment.

"Tell me you don't see his face when you close your eyes at night." He frowns. "Tell me that's not why you're hitting the booze."

"The only reason I feel bad is because pulling that trigger felt so damn good. What kind of person does that make me?"

"That makes you a cop that had to make a tough decision. That's all. No more. No less. End of story."

I can't hold his gaze, so I look out over the sea of headstones. "There were too goddamn many parallels, Tomasetti."

"I know."

"She was young and troubled and Amish. She was pregnant." I run my hands over my face, surprised because I'm crying again.

"She was naïve, Kate. You were never that naïve."

"I guess the moral of the story is you can't go back."

The rain is coming down in earnest now. His hair is wet. The shoulders of his coat are wet. I can feel water soaking through my own coat. "There's not enough good in this world," I say quietly.

"There's more good than bad. You just have to look for it. When you find it, you have to hang on tight."

He opens his arms, and I fall against him. His warmth and strength wrap around me like wings. Closing my eyes, I revel in the sensation of being held. "Have you found your good?" I whisper.

"Yes." He kisses the top of my head. "I've found it."

TURN THE PAGE FOR A SNEAK PEEK AT
LINDA CASTILLO'S NEW BOOK

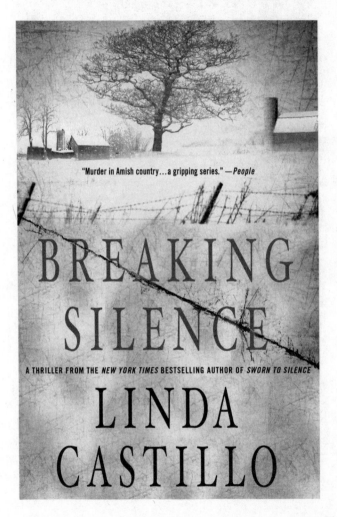

"Murder in Amish country...a gripping series." —*People*

BREAKING
SILENCE

A THRILLER FROM THE *NEW YORK TIMES* BESTSELLING AUTHOR OF *SWORN TO SILENCE*

LINDA
CASTILLO

AVAILABLE SUMMER 2011

Insomnia is an insidious thing: a silent and invisible malady that robs the afflicted not only of sleep but also peace of mind, sometimes for months on end. It dulls the intellect, demoralizes the spirit, and eventually leaves the affected open to a host of ailments, both physical and emotional.

I've never been a good sleeper, but in the last couple of months my occasional sleeplessness has degenerated into chronic insomnia. Sometimes, as I lie awake in bed watching the shadows dance on the window, I wonder how long a person can go without sleep and not suffer repercussions. I wonder how and when that ax will fall on me.

I'm staring at the glowing red numbers on my alarm clock when the phone on my night table jangles. I'm so surprised by the sudden blast, I jump, then quickly reassure myself it's Tomasetti calling to check on me. He's a friend, lover, and fellow insomniac, the latter being one of many things we have in common.

A quick glance at the display tells me the call isn't from John, but the station. Considering the fact that I'm the chief of police and it's 5:00 A.M., it doesn't bode well for whatever news awaits me on the other end. Still, I'm relieved to be called away from the dark cave of my own mind.

"Chief Burkholder, it's Mona. Sorry to wake you."

"No problem. What's up?"

"Got a nine one one from Bishop Troyers. One of the Slabaugh boys says he's got three people down in the manure pit out at the farm."

Alarm rattles through me. Born and raised Amish, I'm well aware of the dangers of a poorly managed manure pit. Methane gas. Ammonia. Drowning. The Slabaughs are Amish and run a hog operation just out of town. I can tell by the smell when I drive by their place that they don't utilize good manure management. "You call EMS?"

"They're on the way. So is Pickles."

"Victims still alive?"

"Far as I know."

"Call the hospital. Let them know we have multiple vics en route." I'm already out of bed, flipping on the light, fumbling around in the closet for my clothes. "I'll be there in ten minutes."

The Slabaugh farm is located on a dirt road a few miles out of town. Rain mixed with snow is coming down in earnest when I make the turn onto Township Road 2, so I jam my Explorer into four-wheel drive and hit the gas. Less than a hundred yards in, I find a Painters Mill PD cruiser stuck in the mud. I pull up beside it and stop.

The driver's side door swings open and Pickles, my most senior officer, slogs toward me through ankle-deep mud. Opening the passenger door, he climbs into my Explorer, bringing a few pounds of sludge with him. "County ought to pave that damn road," he grumbles as he slides in.

"EMTs make it?" I ask.

"Ain't seen 'em."

"This road is the only way in." The Explorer fishtails when I hit the gas; then the big tires grab, slinging mud into the wheel wells, and we bump toward the Slabaugh farm half a mile ahead. I'm well aware that the human brain can survive only about four minutes without oxygen before suffering permanent damage, so I drive too fast, narrowly avoiding the bar ditch a couple of times.

I'm afraid of what we'll find when we get there. Depending on how bad the ventilation is, gases emanating from a manure pit can be lethal. That's not to mention the ever-present risk of drowning, should someone fall in. Two years ago, a pig farmer by the name of Bud Lathy died when he went to the barn early one morning. It was cold, so the night before Bud had closed all the doors and windows. Without proper ventilation, the gases built up inside all night, suffocating several pigs. When he went out to feed the next morning, he fell unconscious within minutes and died of asphyxiation.

"Look out!"

My headlights wash over the small figure of a boy just in time to avoid hitting him. Adrenaline sweeps through me like an electrical shock. I stomp the brake and cut the wheel hard. The truck slides, missing the boy by inches, and comes to rest sideways in the road. "Shit."

Pickles and I throw open our doors and slosh through mud toward the boy. He's standing in the center of the road, looking lost and terrified. Despite the cold, he's not wearing a coat. I can tell by his flat-brimmed hat and suspenders that he's Amish. "Are you okay?" I ask him.

He's about twelve years old, crying hysterically, and soaked to the skin. "We need help! *Mamm* and *Datt* . . ." He points toward the long gravel lane behind him. "They fell in the pit!"

I don't wait for more information. Grasping a skinny arm, I usher him to the Explorer and muscle him into the backseat. Pickles and I slide in simultaneously; then I floor the gas and we start down the gravel lane.

I look at the boy in the rearview mirror. "Are they awake?"

"No!" he sobs. "They're sleeping! Hurry!"

A quarter mile in, the lane opens to a wide gravel area. The white clapboard house is to my right. The hog barn is straight ahead. I don't slow down until I'm within a few feet of the barn; then I brake hard. The wheels lock, cutting ruts in the winter-dead grass. Gears grind as I ram the shifter into park. I fling open the door. My boots hit the ground before the SUV comes to a complete stop. Grabbing my Maglite, I rush around to the rear of the vehicle, throw open the hatch, and snatch up a twenty-foot section of rope. A mix of rain and snow slashes at my face as I sprint toward the barn.

I shove the door open with both hands. "Police!" I shout. The ammonia and rotten-egg stench of wet manure staggers me, but I don't stop. I see lantern light ahead and rush toward it. Somewhere to my right I hear a young girl keening. A teenage boy and a younger boy stand just beyond the wood rails of a large pen, looking down. Shoving open the gate to the pen, I cross to them. "Where are they?"

They point, but I already know. The concrete floor is slightly angled so that the urine and feces from the pens drain into the six-foot square hole. The steel grate cover has been removed. I spot the snow shovel and hose on the ground a few feet away and realize someone had been cleaning the pens. I shine my flashlight into the hole. Six feet down, three people lie motionless in a pool of oozing black muck.

"How long have they been down there?" I snap.

The eldest male looks to be about seventeen years old. His terrified eyes find mine. "I don't know. Ten minutes." He says the words through chattering teeth. His face is the color of paste. He wears trousers with suspenders. The knees are wet with muck.

I shove my finger at him. "Open every door and window in this barn right now. Do you understand? Get some air in here."

"*Ja.*" Nodding, he sets off at a run.

I shine my light into the hole again. There are two male victims and one female. I can tell by their clothing that they're Amish. The two men are facedown. *Too late for them,* I think. The woman is faceup. Still alive, maybe. "We're coming down to get you!" I shout. "Can you hear me?"

None of the victims stirs.

"Hang on!" I hear movement behind me and turn, to see Pickles and the young boy approach. "Where the hell is that ambulance?" I snap.

Shaking his head, Pickles hits his mike.

I point at the boy. "Help your brothers open all the doors and windows. We need fresh air in here. If you can't get the windows open, break them. Go! Now!"

Nodding through his tears, he turns and runs.

Cursing, I glance down at the rope in my hands. The last thing I want to do is go into that pit; I've heard of more than one would-be rescuer unwittingly becoming a victim himself. But there's no way I can stand by and do nothing while a mother of four slowly asphyxiates.

That thought pounds my brain like fists. I look around for something with which to anchor the rope. Ten feet away, I spot the support beam. It's a huge six-by-six-inch length of hundred-year-old oak sunk in concrete. I wrap the rope around the beam, yank it tight. I'm in the process of looping the other end around my hips when Pickles walks up to me. "You're not going down there, are you?" he asks.

Ignoring the question, I walk to the pit and sit, my legs dangling over the side. "I need you to spot me."

Pickles looks alarmed. "Chief, with all due respect . . ."

"Get your gloves. Lower me down."

He looks at me as if he's just been told he'll be facing execution by firing squad. "You go into that pit without a respirator, and you'll be joining the other three."

"You got a better idea?" I snap.

"No, damn it." He doesn't make a move toward the rope. "Maybe we could loop the rope around them, drag them out one at a time."

"Goddamn it, Pickles. She's dying." I scoot closer to the edge.

He grabs my arm. "Kate, you ain't got no choice but to wait for the fire department."

I shake off his hand a little too roughly. But I know he's right. It would be worse than foolhardy for me to go down there. Some might even call it stupid. But I'm not always good at doing the smart thing, especially if someone's life is at stake. Or if there are kids involved. Urgency and indecision pummel me. I think of the children growing up without their parents and I want to scream with the injustice of it. In the last months, I've seen too many bad things happen to too many good people.

"Let's bring them up," I say after a moment.

Looking relieved, Pickles loosens the rope from around the beam, feeds me the slack. I get to my feet and step out of the loop. Standing at the edge of the pit, I widen the loop and toss it into the hole. Vaguely, I'm aware of the distant blare of a siren, but I don't pause. All I can think is that every second could mean the difference between life and death.

I guide the looped end of the rope toward the female victim. She's faceup, which tells me she probably hasn't drowned. If she hasn't succumbed to the gases, there's still a chance. . . .

She's closest to the near wall, almost directly below me, which means she'll be relatively easy to capture with the rope. Planting my feet solidly at the edge of the pit, I lean forward and extend my arm, trying to position the loop around the upper part of her body. A stiff cable would have been more suitable, but I don't have one handy and I don't want to waste time going back to my vehicle, so I've no choice but to work with what I've got.

After several tries, I'm able to drag the loop over the victim's arm. I jiggle the rope, work it up her arm all the way to her shoulder, then over her head, and draw it tight. It won't be a comfortable ride up, but I figure a few rope burns are a lot better than being dead.

"I've got her!" I shout. "Pull!"

Pickles glances around, spots the eldest boy a few feet away, and whistles to get his attention. "Give us a hand!"

The boy rushes over, grabs the rope, wrapping it several times around his bare fist. Hope is wild in his eyes. "Okay!"

In tandem, we begin to pull. The slack goes out of the rope. The woman's arm lifts out of the muck when the rope goes taut. Even though there are three of us, pulling 120 pounds out of thick muck is no easy task. Grunts and growls sound behind me as Pickles and the boy strain. Boots slide and scrape against wet concrete. I use my weight, leaning hard against the rope. I didn't think to put on my gloves, and the rope cuts painfully into my palms, but I put every ounce of strength I possess into the task.

With painful slowness, the woman's limp body inches out of the muck—first her head and shoulders, her torso and hips, and finally her legs and feet. I dig in with my boots, heaving against the rope. I'm too far from the pit now to see the victim, but I can hear her body scraping up the wall as we pull her upward.

When I see her arm and the top of her head at the rim, I glance back at Pickles. "Keep the rope taut."

His face is red with exertion, but he gives me a nod. I slide my hand along the rope until I reach the victim. Putting my hands beneath her shoulders, I give Pickles a nod. "Pull!"

I guide the victim onto the concrete. The first thing I notice is that her skin is cold to the touch. Her clothes are soaked with muck. Her lips are blue. I see tea-colored water in her mouth, so I drop to my knees and roll her onto her side. Voices and the shuffle of shoes sound behind me. I jolt when someone places a hand on my back. I look up, to see a uniformed firefighter and young EMT looking down at me. Both men carry resuscitation bags in their hands.

"We'll take it from here," the EMT says.

I look down at the victim. Filmy eyes stare back at me, and in that instant I know she's gone. The realization makes me want to slam my fist against the concrete. In the smoggy haze of my thoughts, I'm aware of the teenage boy coming up beside me, looking down at his mother. I hear the girl crying nearby. Another child falls to his knees, screaming for his *mamm*. That's when it hits me that these Amish kids are alone.

The next thing I know, someone—the firefighter—puts his hands beneath my arms and pulls me to my feet. I'm in the way, I realize. I feel shaky and cold, and I wonder if it's the gases from the pit that have rendered me useless or if it's the effects of my own impotent emotions.

The EMT kneels next to the woman, placing the mask over her face. I hear the whoosh of air as he compresses the bag, forcing oxygen into her lungs. A few feet away, two respirator-clad firefighters lower rescue equipment into the pit.

I look down at my hands. They're slick with a rancid mix of water, blood, manure, and mud. It's sticky on my skin, gritty between my fingers. I see rope burns on the insides of my knuckles and realize the blood is mine, but I don't feel the sting. At the moment, I don't even smell the manure. All I can do is stand there and watch the paramedics work frantically to resuscitate the motionless woman.

A few feet away, the four Amish children huddle, their eyes filled with hope that the *Englischers* and all their high-tech rescue equipment will save their *mamm* and *datt*. I see faith on their young faces, and my heart breaks, because I know faith often goes unrewarded.

"You look like you could use some air."

I turn, to see Officer Rupert "Glock" Maddox standing a few feet away, looking at me as if I'm a dog that's just been hit by a car—a badly injured dog that might bite if touched. I have no idea how he got here so quickly; he doesn't come on duty until 8:00 A.M. It doesn't matter; I'm just glad he's here.

"She's gone," I say.

"You did your best."

"Tell those kids that."

Grimacing, he crosses to me. "Let's get some air."

Glock isn't a touchy-feely kind of guy. I've worked with him for two and a half years now, and I can count on two fingers the number of intimate conversations we've had. It surprises me when he takes my arm.

"Goddamn it," I mutter.

"Yeah." It's all he says, but it's enough. He gets it. He gets me. It's enough.

He ushers me through the main part of the barn. It's not until I step outside that I realize I'm woozy. Though the barn doors and windows have been thrown open wide, there's not much of a cross breeze, and the air inside is polluted with an unpleasant mix of ammonia and stink. Not to mention all those nasty gases. I've been inside only for ten minutes or so, but I can already feel the effects. A headache taps at my forehead from inside my skull.

For a full minute, I do nothing but stand in the rain and snow and breathe in the clean, cold air. It feels good, like cool water on heated skin. After a minute or so, I look at Glock. "I'm okay."

"I know you are." Sighing, he shoots a glance in the direction of the barn. "Tough scene."

I think of the kids, and a lead weight of dread drops into my stomach. "Worst is yet to come."

"You want me to give you a hand with their statements?"

"I'd appreciate that."

"We going to do it here?"

I look around. We're standing twenty feet from the barn. Around us, emergency workers—paramedics and firefighters—move in and out of the big door. The strobe lights of a fire truck and two ambulances from Pomerene Hospital glare off the facade. To my right, the pretty white farmhouse looks cold and empty. The windows are dark, as if some internal light has been permanently extinguished.

"We'll do it in the house. The kids'll be more comfortable there. They'll need to eat something." I know it seems mundane, but even in the face of death, people need to eat. "I'll call Bishop Troyers to be here with them."

If Glock is surprised by my response, he doesn't show it. I don't have a maternal bone in my body, but I'm feeling protective of these kids. All children are innocent, but Amish youngsters possess a certain kind of innocence. They have farther to fall when that innocence is shattered. I was fourteen years old when fate introduced me to tragedy. I know what it feels like to be abruptly plunged into a world that is so far removed from the only one you've ever known.

I glance toward the barn and see Pickles and the four kids standing outside the big door. Firefighters and EMTs pass by them without notice. The last thing I want to do is question them about the horrors they witnessed, but as is the case with most of the curveballs life throws at us with indiscriminate glee, I don't have a choice.